The Last
Russian
Doll

The Last Russian Doll

KRISTEN LOESCH

BERKLEY
New York

BERKLEY
An imprint of Penguin Random House LLC

ISBN 9780593547984

Printed in the United States of America

Book design by Laura K. Corless

For my family

So few roads I traveled
So many mistakes I made

—SERGEY YESENIN

The Last Russian Doll

Prologue

In some faraway kingdom, in some long-ago land, there lived a young girl who looked just like her porcelain doll. The same rusty-gold hair. The same dark-wine eyes. The girl's own mother could hardly tell them apart. But they were never apart, for the girl always held the doll at her side, to keep it from the clutches of her many, many siblings.

The family lived in a dusky-pink house by the river, and in the evenings, the children liked to gather around the old stove and listen to their mother tell stories. Stories of kingdoms even farther away and lands even longer ago, when there had been kings and queens living in castles, stories of how those castles had been swept away into the midnight-black sea. The many, many siblings would drift away to sleep on these stories, and then the mother would take the girl and the doll into her lap and tell tales of the girl's father. He'd had the same rusty-gold hair, the same dark-wine eyes, in some other faraway kingdom, in some other long-ago land.

But one evening after supper, as the stove simmered and the samovar sang and the mother spoke and the children listened, there came the sound of footsteps outside the house. *Stomp-stomp-stomp.*

There came a knock on the dusky-pink door. *Rap-rap-rap.*

There came a man's voice, which had no color at all. *Open, open, open!*

The mother opened the door. Two men stood there, each carrying a rifle.

"You will come with us," said the men to the mother.

The mother hung her head so that her children could not see her cry. But the samovar ceased to sing and the stove ceased to simmer and the story stayed untold, and in the silence, the many, many siblings could hear their mother's tears fall to the ground. They ran to stop the men.

Stop, stop, stop!

Bang-bang-bang.

The siblings fell like their mother's tears. Their bodies lay as quiet and as still as the doll that the girl held.

"Is that another one?" said one of the men to the other, pointing to the girl, who had remained by the stove.

"Those are just dolls," said the other man to the first.

The men took the mother with them. Their footsteps began to fade. *Stomp-stomp-sto . . .* The mother's cries seemed far away and long ago. *No, no, no* ... The girl began to breathe again. *In, out, in.* She stood, with her doll beneath her arm, and she walked, across the blood-red floor, over her blood-red siblings, through the blood-red door, out of the blood-red house, all the way to the blood-red river. She forgot to wash her blood-red hands.

For fear of those men, the girl did not stay at the river, nor did she stay in that land. For fear of those men, through all her years, along all her journeys, she carried her doll. But she carried it too long, so long that she could not tell the two of them apart anymore either. So long that she could not be sure if she was the girl at all; if she was the one who was real.

PART

I

1

Rosie

The man I've come to see is nearly a century old. White haired and lean, with just a dash of his youthful film-star looks remaining, he sits alone onstage, drumming his fingers on his knees. His head is tilted back as he takes a hard look at the crowd, at the latecomers standing awkwardly in the aisles, their smiles sheepish. At the young couple who have brought their children, a toddler girl swinging her legs back and forth, and the older one, a boy, solemn faced and motionless. At me.

Usually when two strangers make eye contact across a crowded room, one or both will look away, but neither of us do.

Alexey Ivanov will be reading tonight from his memoir, the slim red-jacketed book sitting on a table next to his chair. I've read it so many times by now that I could mouth it along with him: *A hillside falls out of view, and voices, too, fall away. . . . We*

*are like castaways, adrift on a single piece of wreckage that is float-
ing to sea, leaving behind everything that linked us to humanity....*

Alexey stands up. "Thank you all for coming," he says, with
the knife-edge of an accent. "And so I begin."

The Last Bolshevik is an account of his time on Stalin's White
Sea Canal, told in short story form so that people don't forget to
breathe as they're reading it. Today Alexey has chosen the tale of
a work party's doomed expedition through a grim, wintry wilderness to build a road that no one would ever take. The holes that
the prisoners dug were for themselves. It would be their only
grave....

My hands feel clammy and heavy, and my toes begin to tingle
in my boots. The middle-aged man seated next to me pulls his
coat tighter around himself, while just up ahead, the young girl
has stopped swinging her legs and is as straight-backed as her
older brother.

In a lecture hall full of people, Alexey Ivanov has snuffed out
every sound.

He reaches the end of the story and closes the book. "I am
open to questions," he says.

There's a faint shuffling of feet. Somewhere in back, someone
coughs and a baby begins to fuss. A quick shushing by the mother
follows. Alexey is preparing to settle back into his chair when the
man next to me suddenly lifts a hand.

Alexey smiles broadly and gestures to the man. "Go on."

"My question is a wee bit personal," says my neighbor, in a
thick Scottish brogue. He shifts in his seat. "I hope you don't
mind...."

"Please."

"You dedicated this memoir to someone you only call *Kukolka*.

Is there any chance you will share with us who that is?" He doesn't say it, but somehow we all hear it: *Or who that was.*

The smile slides off Alexey Ivanov's face. Without it he no longer looks like the famous dissident writer, the celebrated historian. He's only an old man, stooping beneath the burden of over nine decades of life. He glances around the room once more, just as the baby, somewhere out there, lets out another startled cry.

Alexey's gaze lands on me again for half a second before moving on.

"Hers is a name I never speak aloud," he says. "And if I did, I would shout it."

* * *

I leave my row and head for the stage. The audience is filtering out, but Alexey is still shaking hands, chatting with the organizers. I've read all his writing, mostly while hunched over in a reading room in the Bodleian, and this is the effect of those musty hours, that pure silence: No matter how human the man might look, Alexey Ivanov has become almost a mythical figure to me. A legend. Someone right out of my mother's fairy tales.

"Hello there," he says, turning to me. He has a smile like a torchlight.

"I enjoyed your reading so much, Mr. Ivanov," I say, finding my voice. Maybe *enjoy* isn't the right word, but he nods. "Your story is inspirational."

I'd planned in advance to say this, but only after saying it do I realize how much I mean it.

"Thank you," he says.

"My name is Rosemary White. Rosie. I saw your advert in

Oxford. I'm a postgraduate there." I cough. "You're looking for a research assistant, for the summer?"

"I am," he says pleasantly. "Someone who can join me in Moscow."

I loosen my hold on my handbag. "I'd be interested to apply, if the position's still open."

"It most certainly is."

"I don't have much experience in your field, but I'm fluent in Russian and English—"

"I'll be in Oxford on Thursday," he says. "Why don't we meet up? I'd be happy to tell you more about it."

"I'm leaving tomorrow for Yorkshire. To visit my fiancé's grandmother. She lives alone." I'm not sure why I'm spewing information like this. "Would the weekend be alright?"

"Absolutely," he says. His voice is mild. All around us is nothing but people talking and bantering, a pleasing hum, but there is something in Alexey's eyes that suddenly makes me want to brace against a biting wind. Maybe the excerpt he just read out— the details of the White Sea, those barren roads, those long winters—is still too fresh in my mind. Maybe it's all people ever see, when they look at him.

*　*　*

It's past my mother's bedtime by the time I make it back to her apartment, but there's a sound coming from her room, a low moan.

I knock on her door. "Mum? You awake?"

Another half-smothered noise.

I push the door open. Mum's bedroom is filthy and gloomy and she matches it perfectly. Unwashed, unmoving, she is sitting up in bed, slouched against her pillows, the musky scent of vodka rolling off her in waves. I drop in on her at least once a month, stay with her a night or two here in London. I've been visiting more frequently of late, but if anything, she seems to recognize me less. Mum carried on drinking even after the doctors said her liver was bound to fail, was failing, had failed. She's drunk right now.

"I was at a talk," I say. "Have you been waiting up?"

Her jaundiced eyes dart around the room before finding me right in front of her.

"Well, good night, then." I set the pillboxes on her nightstand upright and wipe my hands on my slacks. "Do you want me to wake you in the morning?" I pause. "I'm going up first thing to York, remember?"

She sucks in her bony cheeks and starts to grasp at her sheets for support. She wants me to come closer. I seat myself gingerly at the foot of the bed.

"Raisa," she mumbles.

Raisa. My birth name. By now it feels more like a physical thing I left behind in Russia, along with my clothes, my books, everything else that made me *me.* My mother is the only one who uses it.

When she dies, she'll take it with her.

"Too many things to say." Her breaths are staggered.

I bite down on my first response. "You don't have to say anything, Mum."

"I know your plans."

"Plans? Are you talking about me and Richard?"

Her gaze locks on mine, but she can't maintain it. "You've been trying to get back to Moscow. For months now."

"It's not a secret. I didn't think you'd want to hear about it."

Mum tries to laugh, a gurgling noise. "I've overheard you on the telephone with the embassy. Why do they keep denying you? Is it because of what you study?"

"It's because of the hash you made of the paperwork when we moved here," I say, bristling. "I just want to go for nostalgia's sake. One last time, to see it. It's different now than when we left, Mum. With Gorbachev in power—"

"You're lying, Raisochka. You're going to search for that man."

She must be drunker than she's ever been, to mention *that man*. Fourteen years ago, as our rickety Aeroflot jet took off into a deep crimson skyline, London-bound, I dared to ask her about him. Mum only stared straight ahead. That was her answer: There wasn't any *that man*. I dreamt it. I might have dreamt all of it.

"If you go away now, I won't be here when you get back," she says.

"Mum, please. Don't talk like that. And if you would just let us—"

"You mean let *him*. Him with his proper money. Thinks he's better than me."

"Are you serious? Richard doesn't think—"

"The dolls." Her pupils dilate. "No one will ever find the dolls."

I open my mouth and snap it shut. The vodka's definitely talking now. Her bisque porcelain dolls are impossible *not* to find, no matter where you look. They resemble taxidermized babies, with their stiff hands, blanched faces, unblinking eyes. Luckily they're stored on a shelf in the living room, or they'd be witness to this very conversation. To my wavering.

After she's downed a few, Mum often sits and speaks to them.

"I'll look after them," I say wearily.

"Not those." Her voice shrinks to a whisper. "The other ones."

I should have known there'd be more. Probably spanking new, still in their boxes, maybe in the closet, under her bed. Watching from places I don't even know about.

"Just be careful. . . ." She's fading. "If you see . . ."

"Mum?" I say, but she's already asleep.

*   *   *

At half eight in the morning, Mum is still out. Her face is slimy with sweat, but she appears so relaxed, so restful, that she might well have died overnight. I touch her wrist for her pulse, faint as a stain, and then reach over to her nightstand to fix the pillboxes—she always knocks them over, groping for something to throw back—but the surface has been cleared. No boxes. No crumpled pound notes, no bottles.

All that lies there now is one of her porcelain dolls. Facedown.

I feel a burst of nerves as I turn it over. The doll has bland off-yellow hair. It wears a frilly hotel-maid frock, knee-highs, and block-heeled black shoes. I move my gaze to the face, to the gaping-wound eyes. The hair falls strangely around the cheeks. Loosely. And in half a second, I can see why.

The scalp is not attached to the body.

It's a fully separate piece. A circular, skin-colored skullcap to which the wig is glued. Wincing, I remove it, revealing the doll's hollow head. The doll is still smiling. In fact, now that it's partly beheaded, its smile looks even wider.

Mum has dismembered one of her precious porcelain prisoners, when I'm not even allowed to breathe near them.

I cast an uneasy glance inside the head.

Is there something *in* there? Behind the doll's eyes?

I reach in, blindly, feeling like I'm performing an autopsy. By touch alone, it's a key. I pull it out, hold it high, like maybe it'll tell me something. It doesn't. A tiny brass key, dulled by time. It wouldn't fit any door I know.

"Raisa?"

"Mum," I say, so startled I nearly drop the key.

She claws for me, and unwillingly I take her hand.

"I . . ." Something, possibly the bile from her liver, is so high in my mother's throat that it cuts off her voice. "Raisa . . ."

"What's this key for?" I try to pull away, but she's the one holding on to me now. My hand against hers feels sticky. The key is being branded into my palm. "Have you been hiding things inside a *doll's head*?"

"I'm sorry," she says, like that explains it.

Maybe it does. I'm sorry too, sorry that I'm the one who ended up here with her. That she wasn't able to leave *me* behind, because if she had, maybe she could have left *that man* behind too.

Everything that has ever gone unsaid hangs in the air between us, as thick as the smell of decay that emanates from the pried-off piece of cranium on her nightstand, and its original owner.

Or perhaps from what is left of my mother.

"I will help you, Raisa . . . to find *that man*."

"Mum, you're not making any—"

"This key is for my drawer in the *stenka*," she says in a single breath. She's using up all her air to get this out. "Ludmila is still there, living in our . . . in Moscow. You go, you look, you make your choice. You promise me?"

I can taste bile myself. I have no idea what she's asking me to do. "I promise."

"Open the window. . . ." Her eyes close to a sliver. "Too many shadows."

Mum's always on the verge of sleep while she talks to me, no matter what time of day it is. She just can't keep her eyes open.

The doll stares at me, wide-awake as ever.

"Mum, wait, can you . . ." I say, a plea, but my mother has stopped murmuring to herself. She lets go of my hand.

* * *

As the train pulls out of King's Cross, I rest my forehead against the glass. Richard is already in York. It'll be a decent drive out to where his grandmother lives, in a cottage that sits, or floats, in the nothingness of the northern moors. It is where Richard and I will marry in autumn. Mum has never been there, but she'd love how it looks rugged and angry one day, winsome and windswept the next. Like a landscape from her stories.

I've always hated her stories.

They're the single thing about her to become more vivid and not less, after a tipple. Strange little vignettes, fairy tales in miniature, often with a nightmarish tint. They all start with some version of her favorite line: *far away and long ago.* That line is not a coincidence. Most of my mother is far away and long ago.

* * *

As Charlotte shows us where the musicians will be set up and, with a slight huff, instructs us not to venture anywhere near her rose garden, a chilly gust of air whisks past. I shudder, and Richard's grandmother glances at me, her smile just as chilly.

"Does it not suit?" she asks.

"No, it's—it's beautiful."

Richard shrugs off his coat and puts it around my shoulders. We approach the house from the back. Charlotte's dog, some pesky, ankle-high breed, is yapping by the door, jumping up and down on all fours like a mechanical toy. The dog is usually to be found on his living room cushions, sniffing at a tray of treats. He is not the sort of dog that sneaks out on purpose. He isn't what most people would even call a dog.

"Have you slipped him some coffee?" I say wryly, to Richard. "Or some—"

Garlic?

The air is inexplicably laced with the smell of garlic, carrying farther than it otherwise might, in that brisk wind. It could just be *me*, having spent the week at my mother's, because Mum adds garlic to everything she consumes. Maybe even her drinks. As a teenager, I used to make snide comments: *Was there a garlic shortage or something when you were a kid?* And she'd laugh like I was being funny, and not like she was soused.

I was not being funny.

"Ro? You okay?" asks Richard.

"Is it the roses?" inquires Charlotte. "Their scent is peaking."

"I'm just cold, I think."

The dog is still howling and now sounds deranged.

"I don't know what could be the matter." Charlotte places a hand on the brooch pinned to her lapel. "Would you go around front, Richie? See if anything's amiss?"

I pull Richard's coat tighter around myself. The way the rat-dog is turned toward the back entrance, it's almost as if someone is standing there. As Richard walks off, the dog finally quiets down, appearing satisfied that the racket has gotten his message across.

The smell of garlic, meanwhile, has dissipated. Maybe it *was* the roses.

"I feel you're not quite yourself today, Rosie," remarks Charlotte. She makes a *tch* sound.

The sound is everything she thinks of me, rolled into a syllable. Another *tch* at me for not replying straightaway. I try to smile at her, but she doesn't try in return. What does she want, an apology for not being myself? Who is the Rosie who is herself? Rosie, whose name has not always been Rosie? There's often a glimmer in Charlotte that makes me wonder if she suspects something to be wrong with my story. But she's the one who retreated into this remote, rose-growing widowhood, far from friends and family, from her old married life. There's probably something wrong with hers.

"It's my mother. She's—she's unwell," I say.

"Forgive me. Richard did say. How terribly difficult for your family." Charlotte draws herself up. "Tell me, is your mother religious?"

"She has . . . certain views," I say. "She believes in the soul. In the afterlife."

Mum was once determined to make our whole family believe in it. She gave up on Papa pretty quickly, but she tried to wear me and Zoya down for years, evening after evening, sitting at our bedside, flattening her favorite nightgown over her knees as she leaned in close to us, spouting bits and bobs of morbid superstition about the human soul.

That nightgown is the only thing she wears, nowadays.

The dog has gone glacially silent.

"Nothing out front," reports Richard, strolling back toward us. "Shall we go in?"

Charlotte bends with impressive flexibility and scoops up her pet. His tail whacks like a metronome against her arm. Before I can follow, the aroma of garlic wafts by again, mixed with that of vodka now. A particular, potent combination, one that instantly brings all the dark underground walkways of Moscow to mind.

And Mum's bedroom.

My breakfast turns in my stomach, threatens to rise. I want to call out to Richard, who's up ahead, ask if he senses it too, but of course he doesn't. Because it's not there. Because this has been happening more and more lately.

I breathe through my mouth until I can't smell anything.

* * *

Mum's neighbor rings from London late in the evening. Mum has died. He brought in her shopping as usual and he could just tell, he says. I want to ask him to check again because Mum's been passing for dead for a few years now, but I don't. I crawl into bed and think about this ivy-slathered house and the moorland all around, wild and empty, extending in every direction, coming from nowhere, belonging to no one.

Moors. Moored. Unmoored.

Back in London, there is no funeral, no ceremony beyond the cremation. I take her ashes with me in a nondescript urn and I decline Richard's offer to stay behind. I'll only be an extra day.

I have to be in Oxford by the weekend.

I tidy up Mum's apartment, starting with the kitchen, with her grisly jars of home-pickled vegetables, not one of which I have ever seen her touch. I move to the living room next. The collective gaze of the porcelain dolls is on me as I pull plastic over the furniture, like they're waiting for me to turn my back.

I can't wait to sell them off. Ideally in parts, like a cheap car, so they stop leering at people.

In the bedroom, I try to avoid the sight of the bed. It almost feels like I'll still see Mum sitting there, glass-eyed as any doll, ghostlike in her nightgown. The bedsheets are still mussed. The smell of sick and sweat comes off them like radioactivity.

I throw open the windows to let the stale, liquor-soaked air out. To let Mum's soul out, by her own folklore.

The doll she mutilated is still on the nightstand. The scalp has been replaced, but unevenly. I pick it up, intending to put it aside so I can carry on sponging surfaces, but the chaff-colored wig doesn't look quite right to me. I didn't notice last time, in the paltry light, but several strands of hair along the hairline are matted with—

It *can't* be.

This can't be one of the ones she had back in— She didn't bring this with her from—?

I go back to the window, lean too far over, grip the sill. I need to get out of this apartment, just out, out, out, and never come back. I don't want to take anything in here with me. Not even the urn. What am I supposed to do with it, anyway? Put it in storage? On display? Should I have buried her instead, buried all the dolls with her?

Too late now.

I'll scatter her ashes. Mum wouldn't like it, of course. She'd want them scattered off the stage at the Bolshoi, if anywhere— over the musicians' heads, with bravas ringing out from every box. Mum was in the corps de ballet before getting married—before my sister and I came along, obliterating any chance she had of being promoted to principal—and she probably always hoped to die onstage, midplié. Zoya used to tease her as she practiced in the mornings. We'd fall over our own feet trying to go *en pointe* alongside her.

Katerina Ballerina.

I'm swaying with fatigue by late afternoon, and nearly miss my meeting with Mum's solicitor. He has a smart office and a sympathetic smile. He tells me she's left me the flat. It's mine now. That can't be right, I say, trying to argue with him. Richard and I have been paying rent on it. We send her a check every three months.

I have the mental image of checks being stashed away, pickled in jars.

Her solicitor feels sorry for me. I can hear it in his voice. He has a posh accent, like Richard's, the kind that can sand glass. He can show me the deed, he says. Katherine White, a property owner. For a second I think, *Ah, that's it. He's got the wrong person. My mother's name wasn't Katherine White. It was Yekaterina Simonova. Katerina Ballerina.*

* * *

Richard stands in the rain without a brolly, his college scarf around his neck, his hands stuck in his trouser pockets. I step off the coach and look askance at the dark sky, starched and flat over all of Oxford. A raindrop lands on my eyelashes. I used to wonder if Mum chose England because it is so colorless. Because she never wanted it to be able to compete with her old life.

He kisses me lightly on the mouth. "You're back so soon."

"I couldn't stand being there a second longer," I say, with a shiver. "I'll sort everything else out another time."

"You look cold. Should we stop in somewhere?"

Inside the dubious-looking eatery on the corner, I peel off my sour, wet layers. Richard lends me his scarf, which smells of him, of wood and ash and sherry.

"How are you feeling?" he asks, once the food comes.

"I'm fine. Honestly." I stab with my fork at a mushy mountain of peas. Richard's own mother died daintily over tea at Fortnum & Mason five years ago, the victim of a brain aneurysm. It's almost hard not to be jealous, when Mum deteriorated over the better part of a decade.

Sometimes it felt like she was going to live forever that way.

"Anything happening here?" I ask, my mouth half full.

"Nah. Dad rang yesterday, asked if you're done yet," he says. Richard's father seems to find it hugely amusing that I'm getting my doctorate. He's even asked why I bother. *You do know you won't need to work, Rosemary darling, after the wedding?*

I might not need the money. I always need to work.

"Dad's upset that Henry and Olivia split up," Richard continues, referring to his older brother and his brother's longtime, if not lifelong, girlfriend. "I neglected to mention that Henry's planning to quit his job and travel the Continent this summer."

"Right, about this summer." I swallow hard. "I might apply for a project in Moscow."

His eyebrows shoot up. "I know you were thinking of going out there, but—that's—that's unexpected. Have you talked to Windle?"

"She won't care. She might not even notice."

"The perfect supervisor." Richard chuckles. "But would you be home in time to get married?" he adds, half joking. He doesn't sound put off quite yet, but Richard is rarely put off. His sturdiness and his steadiness and his *sameness* are what endeared him to me in the first place. In Richard's world, people die neatly of invisible brain aneurysms. They do not self-destruct. In Richard's world, it is a shock when one's childhood sweetheart is not, in fact, the love of one's life.

"Don't be daft." The peas taste like bits of rubber in my mouth.

Did I already know Mum wouldn't be attending the wedding when we first set the date? Did I purposely put it just out of her reach, thinking that she'd only arrive late, her face cherry red, that she'd start snoring at the ceremony, arms and legs flung over other guests' chairs, her body draped over her own chair like a dishrag? That she'd still be in her nightgown?

"I'll need more time in Russia anyway," I add. "To let friends and family know about Mum." I can't think what people normally do when someone dies. But people normally have *other people*.

I shovel in more peas.

"Where's the position?" asks Richard. "There's a famous university in Moscow, isn't there, what's it called . . . ?"

"Lomonosov. It's just an idea."

Richard drops his gaze to his own platter of what might have been a shepherd's pie in a past life. I can tell he's turning this over in his head. Approaching it the way he does everything, including me the day we met: thoughtfully, confidently. Making it all look easy. He clears his throat. "I could join you."

"You've been so busy at work." The peas sit like lead in my stomach. "I don't know. Maybe I need to get away for a bit."

"That's all it is?"

"That's all it is." If Richard can just hold on for a few more months, then we never have to speak of my mother or Russia again. It'll be a silent addition to my wedding vows: *To have. To hold. To be Rosie and never Raisa, ever again.*

"But you could take time and space here, couldn't you?" Perhaps feeling guilty, he adds, "I know it was just you and your mum, the two of you, for so long. . . ."

The two of us. He's right. So why did it always feel like I lost my whole family over the course of one single night in Moscow? Like Mum's blood was spilled there too, all over our living room floor? Or at least her lifeblood, because she never practiced ballet again after we left Soviet Russia. *Defected,* people would say, but we didn't defect. We escaped. We *fled.*

* * *

The peal of bells from a nearby chapel tower is a lonely sound. Bells have rung in Oxford for centuries. That is how long my nights often seem.

Next to me, Richard stirs, but I don't move. I've been an insomniac for years, and it's the most awake I ever feel. My father would have understood. Papa would work late into the night, marking papers, doing exercises. Mum blamed the mathematician in him. *It's not good for numbers to run through a person's head,* she would say, *because there's no end to them.*

But if it's numbers keeping *me* up, they don't go very high: *one, two.*

The memory of those gunshots—

I feel a breath, right in my ear.

I sit up, jerkily, but there's nobody by the bed, nothing in the blackness. See what happens when you're up all night? When there's no boundary between light and dark?

My own breath sits hot in my mouth. *Think about something else, Ro, think!*

The only thing that comes to mind is Alexey Ivanov. He and I are meeting tomorrow and we'll have so much in common, won't we? *The Last Bolshevik* was published in Europe in the late 1970s and banned in Russia, forcing Alexey abroad for his own safety. But that era of political repression appears to be over. So much has changed in the USSR since 1985, under Mikhail Gorbachev, that Alexey's memoir was officially published in his homeland last year. He's being courted by the Soviet government and has even been offered citizenship again. . . .

This isn't helping.

I dare to exhale. It emerges like a pant.

Richard lifts his head from the pillow. He's used to this, seeing me too awake, owllike, at an indecent hour. "Your poor habits are contagious," he mumbles. "We may have to sleep in separate rooms after we marry."

"Isn't that tradition in families like yours?"

He gives a bleary laugh and kisses my shoulder, soft as down. His touch is always gentle, always generous, and slowly everything else recedes into the night.

Later, the bells are ringing again on the hour. I attempt to sleep with my face turned into the pillow. Richard won't be there, in Moscow. Only the night.

* * *

Alexey Ivanov's choice of café is cozy and low lit, catering mostly to university staff and students. The peaceful atmosphere fits him. He seems to do most things at leisure, sitting back in his chair, flicking at the label of his tea bag, looking out every so often toward the glass front of the café. Letting the conversation stall.

He's so relaxed that I start to feel harried. "I'd love to hear about your new project, Mr. Ivanov." I wrap my hands around my mug. "I know it's not my background, but I've been doing a lot of reading—"

"Why?" he asks.

"I'm sorry?"

"I looked you up. You're a first-year DPhil at the Mathematical Institute," he says. "In cryptography, I understand. Code breaking. This brings to my mind Bletchley Park. Very exciting. Why are you pivoting to Russian history?"

I was going to make something up outright, but I think he'd see through it. I have to hedge.

"I was born in Moscow." That part is true, but it feels like the lie. "My mother died recently, and it's made me reconsider a lot of things. I'd like to get to know my culture and heritage."

He gives me several seconds to elaborate, and when I don't, he simply nods. I imagine he's been surrounded all his life by people who didn't want to share the long history of their pasts. I almost want to ask him: *What is it like not only to share the past, but to broadcast* it? *To take a roomful of questions on it?*

"To be frank, I could use a bit of a different perspective," says Alexey. "The task at hand is unlike my usual work. I'm trying to find a woman I used to know. That's it. That's the project. We'll just have to see if I have enough time. Not free time," he adds, with a self-deprecating laugh. "Just time."

I look down into my tea, let the steam sting my eyelids. Mum's just died at age fifty-three. Papa died at forty-four.

Zoya died at fifteen.

Alexey takes hold of his tea bag's wilted label, lifts the bag out, then lets it slide back in.

"She went missing years ago," he continues. "I like to think she's ended up somewhere in the countryside. She loved the land. She used to say she could bask in it, bathe in it, drown in it. . . ." He sits back, as if he wants the line to reverberate. "Let's talk logistics. I'm prepared to take care of the paperwork and housing. You won't have to lift a finger in that regard."

That's what his advert alluded to, and exactly what I've been hoping to hear.

This is my chance. At long last.

"I'll be traveling a great deal when we get there," he goes on, "so you'd need to be capable of working on your own, but my real concern is that the work may bore you. Note-taking. Fact-checking. Cross-referencing. You may find it rather . . . busy."

"Not at all." I try to sound friendly, professional. Detached. "I'm really keen."

"I appreciate your enthusiasm, Rosie. Do continue to read, and grow your knowledge base. It's good for young people to be exposed to history. They just have to take care."

"Take care?" I repeat.

His blue eyes fix on me. "There is no enlightenment to be found in the past. No healing. No solace. Whatever we are looking for will not be there."

It rings out like the chapel bells, the way he says this. *Whatever we are looking for will not be there.*

Can a historian really believe that?

It doesn't matter. I know what I'm looking for; I've only been looking in the wrong places. Our first winter in England, in that seedy short-term flat, I remember Mum would stand every night by the window, looking through the curtains, one foot curled up like she might dance away. Lit candles on every surface, like she wanted the whole place to burn down. I'd be seated at the table, surrounded by schoolbooks, working furiously, thinking, always thinking, *If I can just make it to the end of this problem, if I can find this one solution, this one answer, everything will finally make sense.*

I can still smell that flat, the damp and the candles—

I can smell it right now.

Here. In this café.

If Alexey has noticed any shift in me, he doesn't comment on it. "She was mentioned the other night," he says, folding his arms over his tweedy jacket.

He's talking about the woman he hopes to find. I take a quick sip of my tea like everything is fine. Just fine. It's gone ice-cold.

"*Kukolka,*" he affirms.

Little doll.

The childish nickname is an unwelcome reminder of Mum's unholy collection, back in London. I take another sip, more of a gulp, trying to wash out the memory of those stiff strands of hair, tangled together by blood. No wonder she never let me touch them, not that I would have. And at least now I know the truth. Mum didn't just prefer those dolls to human company. She must have loved them, worshipped them. Of all the things we could have brought with us from Russia—and we weren't able to bring very much—she chose *them.*

* * *

After Alexey leaves, I linger in the café, observing the flow of customers. Through the glass I can see rain peppering the pavement, while the awning flaps in the wind, looking possessed. People burst in holding soggy newspapers, shaking themselves off like dogs. It rains constantly in Oxford. Nothing ever seems to dry, inside or out. But it's rarely enough to empty the streets.

The more the sky darkens outside, the brighter it feels in here. But it doesn't make anything clear.

Alexey's hired me; the job is mine. I should be ecstatic. Or at the very least, relieved. So why am I sitting here, petrified in place, watching a storm slowly gain momentum?

It feels neat. That's why.

Mum is dead, and now, suddenly, after months—years—of trying, I have a way back into Russia.

I don't believe in coincidences. I'm a mathematician, like Papa. I believe in patterns. In codes.

In keys.

I ferret the little brass key out of my bag, twist it round, between my fingers. Mum's drawer in the floor-to-ceiling *stenka* cabinet back home was always locked. I never questioned it. I thought she didn't want me and Zoya near her pretty ballet costumes.

What was beneath the costumes?

The Snow Was Porcelain and the Rain Was Glass

This is a collection for those who know that the first story can be understood only at the end, and that the final story is only the beginning.

You must now close your eyes to see what I am about to show you.

If you think your eyes are closed hard enough, then let me say: In a faraway kingdom, in a long-ago land, where the snow was porcelain and the rain was glass . . .

2

Valentin

Valentin can feel his lips going blue. The air is tinged with frost, making it painful to breathe, but he takes a deep breath anyway. It's a sizable group today and he hates to disappoint, especially when they're shivering so badly themselves, in the hostile wind blowing in from the river.

He gestures toward it, the lifeless Neva, as if he can see, across that expanse of glistening ice, the very future he has just taken pains to describe: a future in which everyone in his audience, the students in their blue caps and the workers with their tarred hats and unwashed heads, will partake equally. Yes, everyone! The elderly gentleman smoking and shaking his head, if he lives long enough; the fat droshky driver in his signature stole, who has stopped to listen only out of boredom; the young woman with the white shawl pulled over her hair and forehead, who stinks of money, so that even from here Valentin can smell it, even through the stench of the workers and the horse dung on the streets and the smoke from the factory pillars beyond . . .

As if sensing his gaze, she lifts her head. She does not smile. Nobody can, in temperatures like this.

Lulikov's wife.

It is unmistakably her. Most bourgeois wives have a tightly wound, overly curated sort of appearance. They all resemble one another. The beauty of Lulikov's wife, by contrast, is distinctive, perhaps even disturbing. The unhappy line of her mouth would be a mistake, the eyes another slip of the brush, but the rest of her could be painted onto the side of a lacquer box.

Valentin has never seen anyone appear so out of place. He wishes he could *unsee* her, because he is getting that strange sinking sensation, same as when he glances through the gates of the Winter Palace. It lives right in the pit of his stomach, that feeling—

That no matter how much he loathes the sight, he wants to keep looking.

"You will be no more, old Russia! Soon another world is born!" he shouts.

She is still watching him. What could have lured her out of her enclave of the city and into his? She ought to go home to her palace—Valentin knows it by sight, the one on the banks of the Fontanka—and bolt it shut before the people wake up and break down every door in the capital.

"And in this other world . . ." Valentin continues, but he forgets, briefly, what he means to say next. Against his own will, he recalls the first time he saw her, only a few weeks ago, when Lulikov brought her by the factory. She did not belong there either. It is possible that someone who looks like that does not belong anywhere. She was standing on the high platform that overlooks the main floor, poised as a statue, while Valentin was below. The opposite of how they are now. Through the spiral of smoke from his cigarette, their eyes somehow met, long enough for him to know what she was thinking.

Later he laughed about it, the poetry of it, with the others. Their owner's fancy new bride, undoubtedly of noble blood, flushed with that blood, lips parted, wanting *him*, Valentin Andreyev, the sailor's son, the orphan, the erstwhile pickpocket, the penniless worker.

Valentin Andreyev, the Bolshevik.

The smoke does not obscure anything today. He sees her too well, huddled in those furs, probably sable or ermine, her shawl falling from her face. She's a hothouse flower, is all she is. Eye-catching and ornamental. Pleasing but useless. Just another of Dmitry Lulikov's many knickknacks, because Lulikov—like all those in his class—is obsessed with things and appearances.

Valentin has no doubt the man gives his wife everything she could ever want. It's led to her wanting things she has no business wanting.

He feels the hushed beginnings of a headache. "There is a tide coming," he declares, staring right at her. "Everything that has lived until now on the surface will be dragged to the depths. Nothing, my friends, will be out of its reach."

* * *

In the evenings, at Viktoria's apartment—the only place that feels secure, safe from the Tsar's Okhrana nowadays—Valentin and his closest circle of friends debate what they would do if they ever kidnapped Dmitry Lulikov. Would they bully their owner into submission? Obtain promises of ten rubles an hour or an eight-hour workday? Would they dispose of him altogether?

The others have often said it would be easy to do it without anybody noticing, but to Valentin, that's the problem.

People *ought* to notice.

"What's that look of yours, then, Comrade Andreyev?" Viktoria teases from the table, as she ties a knot in her tawny hair.

Valentin smiles at her, absently, toying with his cigarette.

A factory owner is always the enemy of the proletariat. The more benevolent that owner, the more dangerous an enemy, because it makes the current system appear tenable. That's how it is with Dmitry Lulikov. He fancies himself a liberal, one of a new generation, who readily shells out for medical unions, for the workers' meeting spaces, even for a library. He constantly tours the factory, calls himself *hands-on*, maligns the other board members.

If they kidnap him, tie him to a chair in some dingy alleyway, how will people see what he is?

The Bolshevik fight does not take place with the enemy strapped down and nobody watching. The fight is public. For the world to see. If blood must be shed, it will be shed so that it spills broadly, so that it touches everyone's toes, so that everyone stands in it, so that all are complicit.

"Valya?" somebody says, addressing him, and he looks up. "Where are you?"

"Lulikov's wife was by the Liteyny today." Valentin lights his cigarette. "She stayed to watch me speak."

A guffaw, probably from Maksim, who got out of prison only last week.

"What was her name again?" asks Viktoria.

"I don't remember," says Valentin, but he does. *Antonina Niko-layevna,* was how Gochkin, their factory foreman, addressed her, placing undue stress on every syllable. Gochkin is the kind of sniveling low-level weasel who will rightly be among the first casualties of the revolution.

Antonina. It reminds Valentin of waves.

He's had affairs with wealthy women before. Most recently with the pretty widow Sitnikova, who consequently fed her husband's whole fortune into Bolshevik Party coffers. It's true that none of those women ever stood out in a crowd, as Lulikov's wife does, but it'll be even better fun this way. Valentin lets his mind wander back to the moment she pulled the shawl wholly from her head; she wore a lace band that held back her hair. He can picture her letting down that mass of hair in the mornings when she stands on her balcony, overlooking the flawless reflection of her palatial residence in the water of the Fontanka. He imagines her gaze sweeping over the city, over the back of every person toiling therein, every person bled dry by the system she represents.

"Go think about her somewhere else, Valya, you'll make us all blush," Maksim yells across the room to a murmur of laughter.

Valentin smirks at his friends, dashes out the cigarette. Sure, he desires her; there's no point denying that. But there is something he desires more. And so he will destroy her.

* * *

Lulikov's wife is not as predictable as the others. She is not at the Liteyny Bridge the next day, or the next, and he can't keep visiting the same spot every single day, speaking to the same clutch of pimply students and idle workers. He has only so many speeches. And little time.

And then, at last, there she is.

It is only by chance that he spots her, out on a stroll along Nevsky Prospekt. Many people consider Nevsky to be the artery of Piter, but it's only an ostentatious walkway for tourists. Nobody actually lives here; they come to escape their lives. Rich *and* poor.

She is peering through the windows of the newspaper offices, and Valentin kicks at clumps of snow on the parquet, waiting.

He stills his shoulders as she turns away, and sees him. He somehow overhears her intake of breath, above the chatter of passersby, the tinkle of sleigh bells, the whinnying of horses. He must be colder than he knew, for his voice has frozen in his throat.

"You're one of my husband's workers, aren't you?" She speaks first. "I remember you."

"And I remember you," he says, recovering himself.

"Are you hungry?" she asks, hesitantly. "I am on my way to the bakery, if you'd like something to eat. Of course there may not be fresh bread, with the shortages. . . ."

The *bakery*?

Valentin tries to parse this invitation, only to realize, a split second late, that she is offering him charity. Charity, to his face. She must be a philanthropist, one of those wealthy do-gooders who patrol the working neighborhoods looking for a cause to give meaning to their bloated, pampered, self-righteous existences. So that's what she was doing on her own in the Vyborg; that's how she came to be in one of his crowds.

She must *pity* him. He has never encountered that before.

Shame fills him instantly, more than bread ever could. Valentin wants to spit at her feet, right where she'll have to step, on her way home. Let her wipe him off her shiny fur boots if that's what she thinks he is good for.

Instead he smiles. "You're very kind," he says. "I accept."

* * *

A bell trills overhead as Valentin follows her into the bakery. It is a glittery, gleaming place, dominated by the mahogany countertop at the far end. Warily Valentin eyes the fat loaves of bread on display, sliced and still steaming. Beside the bread are trays of cakes and desserts, too many to count.

He can linger here by the entrance. He can resist going closer. But he can't keep his mouth from watering.

Is *this* what she considers a shortage?

The staggering inequality of it makes his fists curl in his damp gloves. In the factory barracks, whole families live off one bowl of cabbage soup a day, one spoonful of kasha. And here, only some minutes away, is bread so perfect it looks absurd. Inedible. Like a pastiche.

"Welcome back, Antonina Nikolayevna!" says the baker, rubbing large, doughy hands together. He does not look Valentin's way. "We've missed you!"

Antonina Nikolayevna again. That same slavish, slobbery way of pronouncing it. Valentin would not say it like that. He'd say it so she would hear it, really hear it, hear nothing else.

Lulikov's wife places her hands childishly against the counter. "The cream cakes," she says, "how many kopecks were they last week?"

"Oh," says the baker with regret, "but with inflation, you know . . ."

Inflation. What a joke this place is, this whole scene in front of him. Valentin has to look away to quell the urge to interrupt. If Antonina Nikolayevna knew anything about *inflation*, she might not be so easily dismayed, so quickly put off, but of course she doesn't know, and so she asks for a few slices of bread, and the baker begins to edge them off a tray.

"Or do you want something else?" she asks, turning to Valentin.

The baker mutters beneath his breath, and Valentin feels a mild stab of triumph. Lulikov's wife is either eccentric or insane, bringing riffraff off the street into a bakery with chandeliers overhead, but now he is here, he might as well enjoy it.

"That'll do for me," he says, like he shops here every day.

Outside, on the pavement, she hands him his portion. Half a slice of bread, nestled in crinkly white paper. Valentin wants so much to eat it. Every breath he takes feels buttered. But he'll take it to the barracks, divide it up for some of the kids. He wipes his mouth on the back of his hand, in case he's salivating, and stuffs the entire thing, paper and all, into his coat.

A light snowfall has begun, but the intoxicating scent of the bakery still hangs over them. It is dulling his senses. He struggles to think whether he ever stood like this, watching snowflakes moisten the sullen cobblestones, with the widow Sitnikova. Probably not. He didn't do much *standing* in her company.

"Thank you," says Valentin. "For the—bread." He pauses. "You listened to me speak the other morning, by the Liteyny. Does the cause interest you?"

"The cause?" she repeats, wide-eyed, as if she has never even heard the word.

No wonder *inflation* flummoxed her. The prettier they are, the more airheaded, empty as the puff pastries. He should have known. Valentin gives a low laugh, like it doesn't even matter, the cause, the silly cause! Oh, she *is* pretty, but there's no danger here. She's only a tool, a weapon, that he will wield in a war that is much bigger than either of the two of them.

"I'll be at the Liteyny again in a week's time," he says. "And the week after that. Always at six in the morning. If you are curious about the cause."

She only nods. They stand a moment longer, in silence, the snow falling quickly now, smoothing over the cracks in the pavement. In the whiteness she looks somehow like a figment of his imagination. Valentin has the strangest thought: that it would be better if she were. Better for her, of course. But also better for him.

3

Antonina

Tea is served in the Blue Salon at four in the afternoon, every day. Caravan tea, black and smoky, tasting like the inside of a cigar. That must be why Dmitry favors it. Tonya takes a cursory sip and turns a page of her book, trying to ignore her husband, who is seated at the escritoire, counting banknotes. *Ten, fifty, five hundred.* Everything in this house has a number.

Everything has a price.

"You want to come for a drive with me tomorrow, Tonyechka?" he asks.

She looks up, grudgingly. "Where?"

Dmitry has put his wallet away, and is fishing another cigar out of the sweet-smelling cedar box he stores them in. "I need to make a few stops."

Her tongue feels thick, twisted against her teeth. "The factory?"

"For example." A sigh, softened by a long puff. "There's an ongoing situation there that requires my attention. I have a few . . . rabble-rousers in my employ."

There is no reason that Dmitry should ever need to go in person to the factory, except that he likes to play the part. He is the workers' friend, as he explains it, more than he is their employer. He is no *better* than them. Only richer. But Tonya can't say all that, can she? "I'll come," she says instead. "I'll bring some baskets to the barracks."

"Wonderful idea. I do approve of your interest in philanthropy. Mama believes it will prevent you from becoming restless, here in the capital." He adds, abruptly now: "I'll be going away on Thursday, so you're aware. I won't be gone long."

Tonya manages a smile. Dmitry enjoys traveling afar in search of pieces to add to his beloved collection of rarities, treasures, beautiful objects. He sometimes leaves for weeks on end.

She has to be home by teatime.

Dmitry continues to work away at the cigar, evidently lost in thought. Against the watery hues of the blue wallpaper, his profile looks dashing, princely. Tonya has lived in this house long enough to know how the housemaids swoon over him: how different their master is from others of his station! He treats his inferiors with such respect, such benevolence! He is no hard-hearted despot, no devious tyrant, no cruel handler! They are right. He is none of those things.

Downstairs, at least.

* * *

You're unhappy here, Tonya," observes Anastasia Sergeyevna, when Tonya goes in to say good night to her mother-in-law.

Anastasia occupies the darkest of all the bedrooms in the house, because she gets aches behind her bad eye. The eye that does work is a bit too sharp.

"I'm . . . unaccustomed to city life," says Tonya, taking an uneasy seat on the divan opposite the bed.

"Mitya will have to take you back to our dacha in summer." Anastasia rustles her blankets. "But in the meantime, you look so *sad*. Do you need more routine? We should set aside a time for you to read to me daily. You do enjoy reading; Olenka tells me you are never without your volumes. And I, of course, no longer can."

The only light, the only life, comes from the fireplace, and Tonya cannot interpret the expression on Anastasia's face. She nods. "If you wish it."

"And what sorts of books do you like, child?"

"Short stories. Poetry. Pushkin has always been my favorite. My mother used to read him aloud to me," Tonya replies, bravely, but the dam that holds back all thoughts of home is breaking. She is awash in memories: of Mama by the fire, book in hand, eyes shining silver; Papa in the glass conservatory tending to his roses, the air steamy and sweet; the feel of the riverbank, the fatty soil squishing between Tonya's toes; happy laughter, languid evenings, a summer sun that dripped like honey. . . .

Unable to speak, feeling strangely swollen, she tucks in her skirts. Luckily Anastasia seems to have fallen asleep. The good eye has closed. The bad eye is not able to close. Its lid has frozen in place.

Tonya is already at the door, turning the handle, when she hears her name. She forces herself to look back at the heaping of pillows and deerskins upon the bed, the withered figure of Anastasia lost among them. The flames behind the grate lie low.

"What will make this house feel like home to you?" asks Anastasia. Her voice is not unkind. "What is it you lack?"

What she *lacks*?

What do her days consist of? Spending money on things she won't use, clothes she won't wear; daydreaming about someone she's barely spoken to; remembering his smile, his speech, the way his hair curls lightly at the neck, like he's just missed a cut; reading the same stories over and over, Turgenev's unrequited affections, Chekhov's starry skies and gooseberries, Pushkin's tragic true loves; drinking tea she pretends to like, with a husband she pretends to love.

It is a life of fancy and fantasy. If anything, she has too much.

Often, as Tonya wanders the city, as she sees the single aloof spire of the Admiralty catch the sunlight, or the seagulls swoop over the Neva, or the laundry on lines snapping in the wind as she walks through the endless yellow courtyards, alone, always alone, she feels like she is inside a music box. Spinning, spinning, slowing. Spinning, spinning, slowing.

"I lack for nothing," she says.

"Give it some thought." The good eye is pale, penetrating. "And if I can be of help, you must tell me."

* * *

Gochkin, the factory foreman, is deadly dull. He shows Tonya a table of machinery, tools, and gadgetry for which she has no name, while Dmitry greets some of his favorite workers. Her husband talks to them in the voice he might use for a pet, shakes hands, slaps shoulders, asks after babies.

Making vague apologies to Gochkin, Tonya steps outside, into the courtyard that leads to the barracks. The cobbles are slick with ice and grime, and she is not dressed for the outdoors; the cold pricks like pins. Nevertheless, as she draws close to the barracks, her furs begin to feel stifling. The jewelry on her wrists, neck, even in her hair, hangs heavy.

Dmitry likes pearls on her and imports them from abroad, the same way he *imported* her. Tonya might come from gentry, her father might be a prince, but her home village is so deep in the country it is hardly considered by the old St. Petersburg elite to be the *same* country.

To them, she is lowly country stock. Little better than a peasant.

There is a group of workers by the entrance to the barracks, young men talking, laughing among themselves. She hears him before she sees him, knows his voice by heart. Her pulse races. Everything else seems to slow, the wind, her thoughts, time itself. Should she turn back? But what if he sees her turn? Isn't this, secretly, why she came—to see him? Why, then, does she wish she had a rail to lean on, as she did the very first time, to keep her standing?

He has not noticed her yet. He is dark haired, bright eyed. Lean, but they all are. Handsome. So handsome that she feels itchy, like lice might have burrowed into her stockings.

"You have an audience, Andreyev," someone says, gesturing with a hand-rolled cigarette in Tonya's direction, and she reddens.

"He always has," remarks another.

He is the one they are calling Andreyev. He looks her way and his smile is charming, knowing, the same as it was when she invited him into the bakery. But she did right, didn't she? Isn't that what Dmitry's friends are constantly telling her to do: to extend charity; to elevate the sorry lives of the working classes? One such couple came to call at the house, just last weekend. They were horrified at what they'd witnessed in a workers' barracks, much like these, nearly foaming at the mouth as they described cockroaches clinging to plank beds, families jammed into spaces unfit for livestock, and the smell, oh, the *smell*!

The smell of someone like *him*. Of smog and soot. Of city streets. Of sweat.

They have looked too long at each other. He wipes something from his eye—dirt, or just the sight of her—and turns back to his friends. But to her surprise, he waves them away, and they disperse easily, disappearing into the crevices between the factory buildings. He is coming toward her, smiling still, seeming not to care that they are out in the open. That there is an invisible divide between people like him and people like her, a gulf, that nobody can cross.

Tonya feels shaky, shivery, as he approaches.

"I didn't think I would see you so soon," he says, tossing away his cigarette, crushing it into the muddy slush with his foot.

Years ago, Mama warned Tonya of feeling this way. Of wanting someone enough that your blood runs hot, until it bubbles. But this is worse than that, much worse. Tonya was far from the only one hanging on his every word, when he gave his speech by the Liteyny. Andreyev, whoever he is, is a performer, and it is easy to adore a performer. To forget that they perform for everyone.

Even worse yet, he *knows*. She cannot hide it, the blood-bubbling. He knows and he is mocking her for it.

"I'm bringing..." she says, faltering, showing him the basket.

He takes it without asking, or maybe she lets it go too easily.

"What's your name?" he adds, like it has finally occurred to him that they are strangers.

"Tonya," she blurts out, without thinking first. It is a faux pas. He is her husband's employee. She is the wife of the owner. And here she has just thrown at him her informal given name, a diminutive, as if they are equals! As if they could be friends! "That is—I mean—"

"Do you mean Antonina Nikolayevna?" The smile plays on his perfect mouth. "I'll see you Saturday, I hope. Antonina. On this side of the bridge, at six."

* * *

At teatime today there is a caller: the Countess Natalya Fyodorovna Burtsinova, heiress and socialite, mother and widow, Dmitry's closest friend. When she first arrived in Petrograd, last year, Tonya imagined that the Countess might become something of an older sister to her. A replacement for Nelly and Kirill, her own dearest friends back home.

By now she knows better.

Once the Countess has swept herself into the Blue Salon, Tonya rings for a tray. The two women regard each other until Tonya backs down, looks instead at the wallpaper, at the places where it snarls, where the ends do not quite meet. The Countess is a regular visitor, yet somehow she always catches Tonya by surprise.

"I'm afraid Anastasia Sergeyevna is indisposed," says Tonya, as politely as she can. "And Dmitry is not home."

"It's *you* I've come to speak to, darling," says Natalya. The older woman is self-assured, sly. She has the habit of rubbing the small silver Orthodox cross on her necklace. *Rub, rub, rub.* Today it matches her snakelike earrings. Natalya often accessorizes with silver, to offset—or to accentuate—the deep redness of her hair. Tonya used to think the Countess must paint her hair, for everything else about the woman appears deliberate, even the contours of her face, but the beetroot color is a family trait. Natalya's children are also flame haired.

Rub, rub, rub.

"Is it true that you set off every morning and walk the city alone?" asks Natalya.

"I enjoy the quiet."

"Well, it's not as quiet as it used to be. It's anarchy out there." Natalya taps her falcon-claw fingernails on the arm of her chair. "And perhaps you're unaware, being a country mouse, but when a young woman regularly ventures out on her own at odd hours, rumors tend to follow."

Tonya sighs as silently as possible. So *that's* what lies at the heart of Natalya's concern; the Countess is the kind of person who cares deeply about rumors and reputations. She is a high-society hostess, a popular invitee of the Imperial Court, known for dazzling salon parties, beloved or feared by all.

Natalya would have made a far better partner for Dmitry, who also cultivates his reputation like an exotic plant.

It could have happened. It came so close to happening.

Rumor has it like this: Years ago, Dmitry's family would summer at their dacha, which stood on the bank of a tiny northern lake called Tenevoe, far north of St. Petersburg. The only other property on their road belonged to Natalya's parents. The two families—one flush with new money, the other sitting on old—met and mixed. Natalya was the only child of parents whose affection was sparse. Her youthful infatuation with Dmitry might have passed—in time—if her parents had not panicked and married her off to the decrepit Burtsinov, far richer, twice married, with the face of a stoat and a personality to match.

Years later, it might have happened still, except that the Count managed to die just a month *after* Dmitry married Tonya.

Yes, there are rumors enough to float a barge, in this city.

"Dmitry knows I go for walks," says Tonya, succinctly. "He doesn't mind."

"He forgets that a wife is different from a servant or employee." *Rub, rub, rub.* "In any event, darling, I've only come to say that you'd do better to stay home from now on, what with the demagogues, the radicals, the demonstrators on the streets. And you yourself so inexperienced, so young, so provincial . . ."

The Countess is still speaking, but Tonya is no longer listening. The demagogues, the radicals. There *he* was, standing up there, speaking of freedom. Looking like freedom. *We will all live two lives, Comrades! One is finished, and the other is now!* His voice, his *voice*, and not just in front of a crowd, either. She thinks of the way he said her name, Antonina, the way it came off his tongue, his way.

*　*　*

Tonya awakens to find her fire has died. Unable to fall back asleep, she draws the curtains, opens the doors to the balcony. Her bedroom has a view of the Fontanka, which is frozen solid. She inhales. The air bristles in her lungs.

It is Saturday.

Still early enough, judging by the empty street below, to see *him*. Of course, it would be a long walk in the blistering cold, for nothing more than a few careless smiles, perhaps a word or two. On the way home she'll hate herself for it, although at least that self-hatred is always quite warming.

Or she could ring for breakfast, take it in bed. Olenka would tend another fire. There is nowhere to go, nowhere she has to be.

Is this freedom? Or her music box?

Can she tell the difference anymore?

For a moment, she hesitates, but only a moment. She dresses herself quickly—it's incomprehensible why it takes so very long when Olenka helps her—and tiptoes out of her own boudoir. The tiptoeing is mostly habit. Dmitry sleeps late, if he is even at home, and Anastasia rarely emerges from her room these days. The servants will not try to stop Tonya, though she can hear them, their conversations dim and chattery and echoed in the walls, like mice.

All the way through, along every corridor, Tonya keeps her shawled head bent. She goes out the grand foyer, shutting the bronzed doors gently behind her.

Outside, the wind bites at her face. Snow blankets the streets and is still falling, soft and sugary. No one is about but droshky drivers and a few lolling soldiers, but when the city wakes, it will spring to life in an instant. Her hands buried in her sable muff, Tonya hurries now to cross Nevsky at the Anichkov Bridge and continue up Liteyny.

It is close to a forty-minute walk to the Neva.

She reaches the bridge, glances up and down the empty embankment in bewilderment. There is an overturned sleigh at the mouth of the bridge, just the place for somebody like him to climb up, stand balanced upon the runners, start shouting about the frailty of the old Russia. But nobody is there.

What a fool she's been! He was only making fun, playing a trick; and she fell for it. She is still falling.

A rush of self-pity goes through her, from head to toe. She is about to retreat, when she remembers—*this side of the bridge,* he said.

His side. The Vyborg side.

Tonya removes her muff and wipes a layer of snow off her shawl. The chill seeps into her gloves. Bells begin to ring in the distance, high and haughty, while the wind swoops by, even higher.

Every night this week, before falling asleep, Tonya closed her eyes and toyed with thoughts of Andreyev, of him lying beside her in bed, murmuring, trailing his mouth across her skin. But in the morning, the idea always seems laughable. Her bed is full of drapey lace and silk sheets and crochet pillows. Her room is painfully crowded, with its wreath-patterned wallpaper, its eighteenth-century Italian landscapes, the rose-oil lamps burning at all hours, so that it always smells like a bath.

He does not fit anywhere in it.

Why cross the Neva? What does she hope to gain? Andreyev is a revolutionary; she knows this much. There is nothing awaiting her in the Vyborg but her own humiliation. Or else her ruin.

Better to keep hold of the fantasy, and let the rest of it go by.

Or—one last time?

Yes—one *last* time! One last speech. One last smile. And then never again.

As she walks, fortified by new resolve, she no longer even senses the cold. The bridge is longer than it looks, and she reaches the other side feeling mostly relief. The decision is made. But there is no one on the Vyborg end, either. The snow is shiny Christmas-ornament snow, unblemished by boot prints. She stops at the rail, leans against the cast-iron cladding.

She hears a sound, and turns.

He holds up a hand in greeting. He does not seem as he has throughout their other encounters. That young man was un-reachable, untouchable, invulnerable. This one is modest, his hands now in his pockets, like he was never addressing any crowd, never promising a thing.

Her stomach churns. "Did you not say this was where you would give your speech?"

"I did," he says, joining her at the rail.

"But there is nobody here."

His wool jacket is strewn with holes; the wind must sail right through. Flurries dust his hair, his shoulders, the look on his face. Yet she is the one trembling.

"There's you," he says. "Do you want me to shout, or will you come closer?"

How far will she go? How far has she already gone? They are right next to each other. Tonya moves closer anyway. She can't quite believe that he wants to be here, along this river, alone with her, wasting his time, his morning, like this. He belongs in the noise, in the fervor. In the fire.

And yet he *is* here.

"I told myself you wouldn't come." His voice is low, amused. "I thought the other day would be the last I'd ever see of you. Every time I see you, I think it will be the last day. But now I wonder"— he touches her shawl, tugs, and she is exposed to the frigid air—"if today is not the last day. If today is the first day."

"This speech sounds quite unlike your others," she says un-evenly.

"It is less rehearsed."

"I should go."

"If you want to go, then go."

"It's not possible for me to stay," she stammers. "You know I'm married, I'm— I've been mistaken. I'm sorry. You won't see me again."

He bends his head to hers. She realizes her own hands are reaching up to touch his face, to meet around his neck. It feels exactly as it does in her daydreams. Nobody has ever mentioned that. She almost wants to say so, but only to slow down this mo-ment, to bask, to bathe, to drown in it. He kisses the curve of her brow bone and it burns, worse than the cold.

4

Rosie

Deep within a birch forest, a road runs through like a scar. Along this road is a young traveler, but she is trapped behind a panel of glass. She can't reach out to touch the supple white trunks of the trees, all aglow in the afternoon sun. She can't feel the wind that breathes across the leaves, that slips between the branches. Instead she presses her face up to the glass and uses her finger to trace the shape of everything she sees.

It sounds like the opening of one of Mum's fairy tales.

But that traveler is only me, and the glass is only the tinted window of the black Mercedes that met me and Alexey at Sheremetyevo Airport.

"It won't be long now," says Alexey.

The birch forest fades as we approach Moscow proper. Decaying tenements and Stalinist architecture spring up on all sides while the traffic builds, slows to a trickle. Our driver, who's on loan to Alexey Ivanov from the government, curses as another car cuts him off.

"How are you doing back there?" asks Alexey, glancing over at me.

It is sweltering. My shoes have congealed around my feet. I'm light-headed from the flight, I haven't slept in almost a full day, and I'm ravenous. I wish I'd accepted his offer of a snack at the airport, even if all they had were shriveled sandwiches, reminiscent of the ones Mum used to make for me. She'd slap on the mayonnaise in between voracious swigs of vodka. *Thwack. Thwack-thwack.* Even now I can see the mayonnaise flying, hear the pickle slices screaming, taste the vodka in the bread.

"Just fine," I say.

Alexey leans over to the driver and says something he clearly doesn't intend for me to hear. I notice, still in a fog, as the driver changes course. Alexey's temporary new residence, granted so generously by the government, is supposed to be inside the B Ring.

But we are curving away from the city center. Driving westward.

Before I can make sense of this, we have reached the section of the Rublyovskoe Highway that zips together what look like large swaths of forest. This area is infamously riddled with the homes of Moscow's most powerful and influential people—and people who like to live behind high walls. As we turn off the highway, we start to see a few of those walls crop up.

Maybe Alexey wants to drop something off for a friend? Run an errand? See the sights?

Half an hour later, down a leafy, meandering lane, Alexey points out the window. A small dacha is coming into view, two stories high, made of red-painted wood. With its elaborate window detail, wraparound porch, and latticed balconies, it looks a lot like a gingerbread house.

"This is home," he says, as the Mercedes lurches to a stop.

Home?

He's already getting out. I unclip my seat belt, watching as Alexey heads up the porch stairs. He is slow and slim, but from a distance you can't tell how old he really is, and he somehow exudes an aura of absolute authority. Of power. Maybe that's what draws people to him, the way it's just spilling behind him as he walks, like a petrol leak.

He turns, gestures that he's going around back.

I step out of the car, blinking in the glare of sunlight. I test the ground beneath my feet. I am back in Moscow. Throughout our journey here, I'd hoped, feared, that I would return to my hometown and feel *different*. I would instantly reclaim the sense of continuity that comes naturally to most people, because they live their lives as a single thread. Winding and curling perhaps, but smooth and uninterrupted.

But I still have no such sense. For me, there is the thread that starts the day I was born in this city and stretches until one humid summer night in 1977. There is another that begins the moment Mum and I touched down at Heathrow and stretches until now. And I've never been able to tie the two together.

* * *

The driver has a sculpted, serious face. He says nothing. His close-cut hairstyle suggests time in the military or prison, places where people learn to say nothing. The silence is becoming unendurable. Beads of sweat pop up along my hairline and pool beneath my ponytail. If Alexey takes any longer, I might implode.

"My keys still work!" Alexey's voice, at last.

We loop around the porch, to a backyard terrace built for open-air meals. The table is covered in unwashed bowls and glasses, like Alexey might have been in the middle of dinner when he decided to defect. It's funny what gets left behind.

I look down at my bag, at my fingers around the handle, white from squeezing too hard.

Alexey fiddles with the locks and finally the door grinds open, into a small indoor dining area. The furniture looks faux antique, aged on purpose. The curtains are made of lace, and on every possible surface is an embroidered tablecloth. It feels like a set piece in a nineteenth-century Russian drama. *The Dacha*, starring me.

"You don't fancy it," notes Alexey, with his usual good humor. "I kept the style of the previous owner. I am not one to redecorate."

The driver peels off to collect more bags. I trail Alexey through the house until we reach the stairs.

"Your room is upstairs, last one on the right," Alexey says to me. "Go ahead and get settled in. Yes, I know, this isn't the Garden Ring, but I was thinking you'd need space to work, and this is the real Moscow summer experience, isn't it? A dacha, the forest, some peace and quiet? Eh? There's a motor bus stop down the road, and of course Lev will drive you anywhere you need to go...."

So he planned this. This isn't an impromptu stop.

We were never going to stay in the city.

The wooden beams above the stairwell are low, poorly placed.

The driver—Lev?—might have to go up on his hands and knees. Upstairs, the hallway is oddly dark. The wide windows I saw from the drive must be on the other side of the house, but it's a disorienting effect. I peek into the other rooms as I go by. Each one is furnished in the same style, with the same overabundance of embroidery.

Outside what is supposed to be my own, I hesitate.

The air smells strange. Dirty, asphalted.

One, two . . .

I jerk my hand away from the knob, but the door opens anyway.

There's somebody there. Standing by the bed.

It's not Alexey. It's not the driver. The smell is even stronger now, pulpy, like old books, and the figure is turning toward me. A woman, no, a girl, dressed to match this house, muted, slightly blurred, in lace—

It's me.

I grab for the door, pull it shut so hard the whole frame rattles. Turning, breathless, I see the driver coming down the hallway. He doesn't say anything, but he doesn't have to. I know what he's thinking. English girl on a lark in Moscow, going to pieces on the first day.

"Something wrong?" Alexey calls out from the stairs.

"Nope," I say, mostly a croak. I'm not sure he hears it.

Looking unimpressed, the driver hands me my suitcase. I take it. I push the door open again, shamed by his presence. It swings wide enough that he can probably see it all too: a child's room, with faintly floral décor, pale, pretty, no sharp edges. There's nobody by the bed. I'm just not getting enough sleep. I'm knackered. I'm hallucinating.

My first instinct is to telephone Richard, but Oxford is a couple hours behind Moscow. His workday is in full swing. And that's if this place even has a telephone. Or electricity—

Alexey appears on the landing, his smile one of concern. "I'd like to go out to dinner, Rosie, but you're welcome to stay behind and rest. I can bring something back for you—"

"No." I say it so quickly, he raises an eyebrow. "I'll come."

*   *   *

While the hostess makes an embarrassing fuss over us, I squint at the tapestry mounted behind the driver's chair. It is one of many that adorn the walls. Knights on horseback, buxom maidens, large predatory birds. Fiery scenes. Bold colors.

The hostess sashays away, drawing the driver's attention with her.

"Does she know who you are?" I ask Alexey.

"People assume we have money," he says. "We look foreign."

I've certainly never felt more foreign. My gaze wanders to a high pillar upon which a marble bust of a man's head has been placed. The faces of most people in here look just like the bust. Wan, male. Wealthy. Nobody else eats at a place like this. I turn to the raised platform not far from our table, where a floppy-haired youth sits on a stool with an acoustic guitar, crooning away. He sounds like a fur seal.

"Is he the son of the owner?" I ask.

Lev smirks.

"It's been years, but I used to play," muses Alexey. "I should ask for a turn."

He's having us on. He's going to steal the spotlight, right here in the middle of our meal? He's going to sing with a set of century-old lungs, strum with fingers that were once frostbitten to the bone? But before I'm able to protest, or just laugh, Alexey is already standing up. He winds between the tables, his head bowed, making his way to the platform. The guitarist pauses to hear what Alexey has to say, then scrambles off the stool, offering his instrument as penance, backing away, disappearing by instinct.

Alexey tries out a few chords, strums for a moment or two. The echo lasts longer than the notes. Already the restaurant is going quiet.

"The bright red ribbon in her hair, so distant and so fair, the memory is ageless. . . . I hear the song of another time ring forever in my mind, her lyrics written on its pages. . . ."

We are sitting in the same silence of that lecture hall in London last month. It seems to follow him everywhere he goes. I don't know how he does it.

"Why should I try to speak, when only she has the words? Can I find what I seek? Every answer is hers. Eyes so dark haunt my dreams, beauty depthless and pure . . . as a river that flows too far . . . beyond the reach of a restless heart. . . ."

His expression is casual, contemplative, but there's a distant note in his eyes. He isn't playing for this audience, or any audience. He's playing for someone else, across time and space, across memory itself.

But for whom? *Kukolka?*

"I've traveled far and years have flown. Never have I been alone, with her spirit here to guide me. . . . Sage and lily of the field to the seasons never yield, for I keep them safe beside me. . . . Can it be only fools who hope, desperate men repeating rote? Ancient promises that bind me . . ."

Lev makes a sound, breaks the spell. I whip my head around, oddly grateful for a distraction. The driver is fishing in his glass of water for the ice cubes, which he extracts and deposits in his serviette. He catches me looking and looks back, without any change in expression. He's attractive, dreamy even, but in a sort of hardened, unhappy way. The way of people who have seen and done things they don't talk about.

I give him a stretched-out smile. "I know we weren't properly introduced, but my name is—"

"I know your name."

"Right." I change tack: "So how long have you been a driver?"

"I'm not."

"I thought Alexey said—"

"He asked for someone for you." Lev amends this. "To help you."

"I don't understand. I'm—"

"You're his employee this summer, no?"

"Um—"

"Alexey Alexeyevich will be away a lot," he says, stringing together his longest sentence thus far. "He was worried about your security. A young girl. Alone in Moscow. With poor Russian."

"My Russian's not *poor*, it's *rusty*," I say defensively. "I'm a native speaker. I'm also twenty-four."

He shrugs.

"So you're my bodyguard? Is that what you do professionally?"

"No," he replies, stone-faced. "It is not."

He wants me to stop talking. Stop asking questions. I pin my gaze back on the tapestry. There's a prickle along my arms. This restaurant has air-conditioning *and* ice water. Two things I've never encountered in Moscow before.

I *want* to stop asking questions. I *want* not to have to sit here, drenched in a cold sweat, but I can't go back to England now. This is the only way to stop thinking about *that man* and how he killed Zoya and Papa in less than the time it took for me to run from the bedroom I shared with Zoya into the living room. How *that man* looked right at me, with his slate-gray eyes, and I believed that he was going to kill me too, but he didn't. He just left me standing there, in a widening pool of blood.

The tangy aroma of it filled the whole room, filled my lungs to capacity. I've never breathed it out.

* * *

After a late tea, I am in bed, lying rigid as a plank, already starting to have the slew of irrational thoughts that precedes a bout of insomnia: I'll never sleep again. I'll die from the lack of it. After I die, they won't be able to crack my lids shut for the funeral viewing, because my eyes are going to stay open like this for eternity.

I lean over to turn on the lamp. It doesn't work.

Needing air, I climb out of bed, twist the handle of the balcony door, and manage to squeeze through the few inches that the door permits. I'd forgotten that nights in Moscow are often warmer on the outside than the inside. The curtains flutter behind me, flatten against the door, but I don't feel any breeze.

The driver, Lev, is there, leaning against the rail, still dressed in his day clothes. This whole floor shares the same balcony; he must have the room next to mine. He strikes me as someone who's nocturnal by nature. He doesn't acknowledge me; we don't acknowledge each other. After a moment he dredges up a cigarette from somewhere within his jacket, cups his hands around it, exhales into the darkness.

Only it's not smoke that blooms in the air around me.

It's the briny scent of the Black Sea.

Every summer, when I was a child, my parents took us on holiday to the Black Sea at Sochi. Every trip began with Papa reminding us, eagerly, about the oxygen deficiency of the water. Almost nothing can live down there. But almost nothing decomposes, either. Buried treasure. Shipwrecks. Bodies.

No one survives but the dead.

In Sochi, Zoya and Mum would lounge on the beach until late afternoon, while my father would take me back to the hotel. Often, if they took long enough, Papa would write math problems for me to solve. Every year those problems got more difficult, but I didn't mind. It was magical, being alone with my adored father, with no sound at all except the wheezing fans and pencils scratching on paper.

There are the people who only see the surface, Papa said to me once. *And then there are the people who can see beneath. You know how beautiful it is when it's just snowed, back home?*

Yes, Papa, I said, to please him, even though I never thought snow was beautiful, at least not the gray sludge of a Moscow winter.

The snow is only a cover, Raisochka, he said. *It hides the dirt, the pavement, the rats, the rot. It hides the bodies, the gravestones, the history, all the things people must pretend do not exist, so that they can live. Every time you look at snow from now on, you remind yourself: There's something else there. Something I cannot see.*

But, Papa . . .

I'm going to show you something else now, he said. *It's a puzzle. A cipher. And you are going to break it. To go under . . .*

"Careful."

The memory splinters. The smell is gone.

What's *happening* to me?

"You almost went over," says Lev, unmoved. "You took pills or something?"

"No." I laugh. It feels empty. I have some sleeping pills, in fact. They're a last resort, but suddenly I'm thinking of everything else I've got stashed away in my handbag. Passport. Wallet. Loose coins. Scrunchie.

Mum's key, liberated from her doll.

This nightmare will be over soon. I know it.

"Good night," I say, and turn away before he can respond.

The Wedding Veil

In a faraway kingdom, in a long-ago land, a girl wore a wedding veil so thick that she wasn't able to see the man she was marrying. The wedding was pretty. There were feasts and songs and a crown was raised over her head. The couple were feted with bread and salt, and the girl's single plait was undone. Everything was coming undone. People she didn't know clucked about her, and she was taken everywhere, from the bathhouse to her bedroom and then to the church, but still she couldn't see what she had married.

Until it was too late.

5

Valentin

Valentin hasn't seen Tonya in two days. It feels like months. She is out of breath, smiling wide, clearly having run part of the way. Her white shawl hangs off her shoulders. They are alone in the *paradnaya*, the spacious downstairs foyer of Viktoria's apartment building. They were due upstairs forty minutes ago. The meal will have started without them.

He's startled to discover that he doesn't care.

"Sorry, I'm so sorry," she says. "I got lost. Shall we go up?"

"You're late enough that we don't have to. If you'd prefer not—"

"But I've dressed up to meet your friends," Tonya says sweetly. "If I were only going to meet you, I would have worn less, not more."

His throat closes on whatever he was going to say.

"Valentin Andreyev, the great Bolshevik orator, silenced at last," she says, sounding amused. He draws her close, in mock annoyance, presses a kiss against her lips. He does not intend for the kiss to turn deep, but it happens anyway, and when he pulls away, he still feels it, the shape of her mouth. A phantom-kiss. He has been experiencing her phantom-touches more and more lately. Her fingers interwoven with his, even after she lets go. Her hair brushing against his arm, even when she has left his bed. Phantom-knocks on his door, too, that he strains to hear.

They've been spending too much time together recently, perhaps. There are no longer weekdays and weekends. There are only Tonya-days and all the other days.

He follows her up the stairs. Her hand skims the wooden rail as if she thinks she might fall, and at the landing, she twists around, takes him by surprise.

"You've warned them, haven't you?" she asks. "About me?"

"Warned them," he muses. "Yes, about your appetite—"

"You know what I mean!"

"I do not. What is there to warn? Are you a spy for the Okhrana?"

"So you bring women here all the time, to socialize with your friends," says Tonya. "Is that it?"

"That is *exactly* it," he says.

"I suppose you have someone else lined up for tomorrow."

"Yes. Tatiana, I believe her name is. Or was it Maria?"

Tonya makes a face. "Aren't those the grand duchesses?"

Valentin laughs. "How would I know?"

"You should know your enemy, I would think," she says impertinently, and for one dizzying moment, he cannot remember that he has any enemy at all. Not the Tsar, not the monarchy, not the class system, not the big factory bosses, not her husband, not even her. If anything, at this moment, atop these stairs, about to face his friends, it feels like it is the two of them against the whole world.

It is such a stupefying thought that he can only stare.

"What's wrong?" she asks.

"No. Nothing." He coughs, nods toward the end of the hall. "Viktoria's is the very last door." The corridor is narrow, dangerously dark. Tonya slips her hand into his, and he leads the way, as though he knows exactly where he is going, as if he has ever been here before.

* * *

After dinner, Viktoria asks if anyone would like to read aloud to the others. It is a performative request, because the same friends always read. Not Valentin—he prefers to save his voice for the podium; but he likes to hear other people speak aloud to see where they lose him, on what words, what phrases, with what tone of voice. They always lose him eventually. It's impossible to pay attention to *Marxism and the National Question* for the tenth time.

To his shock, Tonya volunteers, and after she decides that not a single one of their books suits her, she *recites*.

She knows Pushkin from memory, and she should, for she has read the poet often enough. Sometimes, when she sleeps at Valentin's, she will even bring along her dog-eared, hardbound volume, and read aloud in bed, lying naked, flat on his mattress, while he smokes and wonders how anyone could believe in such romantic, watery nonsense.

His friends will not let him hear the end of it, after tonight.

"If you only knew," she begins. *"How terrible it is, to pine, to hunger for your love; to burn . . ."*

She is seated across the table from him, with all the others between them. Her hair falls loose from its pins, frames her face in the candlelight. *To hunger—* He feels suddenly sick, feverish, and he rises from his seat, nearly trips over the table leg. The others don't seem to notice; they are all watching her, and why shouldn't they when she looks like that, when she looks at *him* like that, and he goes into Viktoria's entryway but it isn't enough. His collar still feels tight; he still feels trapped.

In the hallway outside, in the darkness, his breath finally slows.

He gropes for a cigarette, lights it with a sigh. Maybe he *is* ill. Overworked. Overtired. He's become sloppy, irresponsible. Missed meetings, even demonstrations. The ones he does attend, he sleepwalks through, thinking only of—

"Valya?" Tonya is stepping into the hall. "There you are." She adds, softly now: "I think I should get back home."

"Of course," he says, recovering. "I can walk with you."

"I'll be alright. The night is so bright. You stay with your friends."

"Would you like to meet tomorrow?" he asks lightly, but his heart begins to pound hard again. Is this fear? Is it happiness? How can anyone know? "I don't have other plans." He *does* have other plans. He has pamphlets to write, speeches to draft, words to memorize. He has meetings to organize, votes to cast, a union to address. On top of all that, he has to work.

Tonya could earn his monthly wage by selling one earring. Her hands are like velvet, they have done so little work. He knows because he never stops feeling them.

Her despicable phantom-touch.

"No?" she teases. "Not with Tatiana?"

"No," he says, in the wrong tone of voice, "there's nobody else."

Her expression changes. "I know."

They stand still in the quiet hallway. There does not seem to be much else to say, or at least he can't think of anything. *Valentin Andreyev, the great Bolshevik orator, silenced at last,* she said. It was like she cursed him. She leans her head against him, and he knows she can feel his heartbeat, speeding, soaring, giving him away.

* * *

A dim knock, then a louder one. Valentin has barely put down his pen before there's another, more harried series of knocks. *Ladno, ladno,* he mutters to himself. The glass window of his basement room is foxed, difficult to see through, but summer light still leaks in, belies the hour. Four in the morning.

The famous White Nights of Piter.

Pavel was not supposed to come by until six. Viktoria's father is all but a father to Valentin, and he likes to show up on short notice and deliver long lectures, punctuated by cracks of his cane against the ground. Pavel's voice, too, is fatherly. Disapproving. Reduces Valentin to a child. That's why Pavel Katenin is a writer, and not an orator; the people cannot be roused to action, cannot be swayed to the revolutionary cause, by reminders of their own parents, of the past.

It's easier, in fact, to join the cause if you never had such things to begin with. If you have nothing to lose. If you were orphaned at age nine. If you began sleeping in a box by the wharf, stealing to survive. If Pavel was there one day, handing out political pamphlets and poetry to the sailors and street sellers, and took enough pity on you to feed you, clothe you, to get you a factory job, to introduce you to the underground.

Valentin has been avoiding Pavel.

He has something to lose.

Today's lecture will be in the vein of *You're neglecting your duties, boy. You're risking it all, and for what? What is the point of this? What is the plan?*

You're going to stop seeing her. Now.

Valentin tries to unclench his jaw as he reaches for the door.

But it isn't Pavel, standing there. It's *her*. Tonya. In the pale light, she looks tired, a bit purple beneath the eyes. She's from the south, of course, where night can be counted on year-round. She smiles expectantly, waiting to be let in. He ought not to let her in. She likes to arrive late when they have arranged a time and a place, and early if they haven't. As a result, their meetings have become spontaneous, unpredictable. Frustrating. She shows up randomly in his crowds, so that he can't think of what to say. She comes by the factory, with her godforsaken gift baskets, and he can't get any work done. Sometimes, some days, she fails to show up completely, and he is left to wait by the Liteyny Bridge, pacing, watching, wondering.

"You," he says.

"It is me, yes."

"I feel as though I've seen you somewhere before." He tries with all his strength not to return her smile. Fails. "Could it have been in a dream? Could it be that my life has been a pledge . . . to this moment of meeting you?"

"*Don't* make mockery of Alexander Pushkin," she says, feigning affront, "just because your speeches cannot compare with his poetry."

Once he waited for Tonya for hours. *Hours.* Valentin couldn't feel his extremities by the time he made it home. Then, upon reaching it, upon crossing his own threshold, into this very basement, he realized it didn't feel like home. Without any warning, he remembered what *home* once felt like: an even smaller room than this; his mother's brown eyes, the way they twinkled; his babushka's warm hands, closed over his own; even the cockroaches that clicked across the ceilings, even the dust along the floors.

His father standing in the doorway, bending low to greet him . . .

Valentin remembered the joy, the piercing, painful surge of it, of being loved. And as the memory drifted by, he felt more frightened than he ever had.

"Are you alright?" says Tonya, jarring him from his reminiscences. The morning cold shines in her cheeks, a pleasing contrast to her shawl. She wears that shawl *all* the time. It was probably hand-sewn by blind old ladies in Siberia. He often wants to rip it clean across; even now he feels the impulse in his hands, down to the fingertips.

But it's not the shawl he loathes.

It's that the shawl represents a rope. The one that binds her to her husband.

"Why shouldn't I be alright?" Valentin replies, rougher than he should.

"You have not let me in, for one."

He clears his throat. He pulls the door open. As the door closes behind her, Tonya begins to remove her gloves, her coat, her outer layers. She pulls the pins from her hair, lets loose the soft, quiet curls. During the day her hair is piled high on her head, in a severe, matronly style that resists his touch. It used to serve as a reminder of how far apart they were, of who they really were: Tonya, the princess, and he, only the usurper, peering through the palace gates, waiting for the day when he could burn it all down.

The time has come to burn it all down.

In the beginning, Valentin had bigger plans than simply draining Tonya's accounts. When the moment was right, he would expose their affair to the world. Lulikov has long been ripe for this kind of devastating public humiliation. The man's reputation is everything to him, and his response would no doubt be immediate, irrational, and crushing. The Mensheviks would have to come over to the side of the Bolshevik Committee. That moment is here; the Vyborg is already choked by strikes. Many unions have already risen up. Lulikov has his supporters in their ranks, but if the workers act as one, a factory takeover might even be possible.

So why can't Valentin go through with it? Why can't he act?

For months now he has grappled with his growing reluctance. Is it because Tonya herself might be punished for it? By her husband? By her peers? Because she might get hurt? Because she might not understand the sacrifices that people must make, to answer the call of the true revolution?

Watching as she pulls her fingers through a tangle of hair, right where it tumbles over her shoulders, he understands.

It's because he doesn't want this to end.

"Pavel will be here soon," he says hoarsely. His mouth feels dry, but of course this room is airless and grotty. Tonya never mentions it, but it must look like an animal cave to her, like a dungeon. This *has* to end. It was always going to end. In a way it ended before it even began, because what could someone like him possibly offer someone like her?

Home?

No, no, no. He runs his hands through his hair, but mostly to keep from touching her. He is light-headed with the urge to ask her to stay and meet Pavel. To meet the only family he has. The only family he ever believed he would need.

"Then shouldn't you hurry?" she says, an invitation, her chin tilted up, waiting for his kiss. But increasingly it is not just a kiss. Increasingly it has become a promise. *I want you as I have never wanted anyone. I want this as I have never wanted anything. I will come if you want me to come. I will stay if you ask me to stay.*

I am here whenever you need me.

"You have to go," he says. It takes him a second to know his own voice. It's his podium-voice. The one he uses for crowds. For strangers.

Her smile fades. "If I have come at a bad time . . ."

He can't look at her. He can't. He turns to the window. "I don't think we should meet anymore."

Silence.

"It's too dangerous for us both." His words, too, are podium-words. He's saying what he thinks he ought to say. Whatever might work. "The risk of discovery is too high."

"Since when have you cared about the risk?" she says, so low he can barely hear.

"I care about—" He stops himself in time. "I'm busy."

"Busy," she repeats.

"I've been neglecting my duties, because of this. Us." Now he sounds just like Pavel. He has to. It is a shield, and behind that shield, crouching, cowering, is the little boy in a box on the wharf, the one who believes, who *knows*, that if you have something to lose, somebody to lose, you will lose them. Home may have *felt* safe, but it was only a feeling, because look at you now, alone and half starved and stinking of fish heads! You cannot trust feelings. You cannot look back.

"I don't believe you," she says. "Tell me the real reason. Please. Did my husband say something to you?"

He shakes his head. Dmitry Lulikov's an idiot. It's right under the man's nose, but Lulikov doesn't seem able to conceive the possibility. It is no different to how the Tsar sees the crowds rioting for bread from his bedroom window, and believes they are cheering for him.

Gochkin often claims, lasciviously, that Lulikov no longer goes down to the docks, the neighborhoods where the girls have rouged cheeks, rag doll hair, rag doll limbs—at least they would after he was through with them. Not as much as he used to, anyway. *That's love, huh?* Gochkin will say, snorting with laughter.

It is love. Bourgeois love. The idea that people can possess one another, same as they do wealth and land and material goods.

The delusion.

Valentin has to get Tonya out of here, out of the cellar, out of his life, before he begs her never to leave. "There is no other reason," he says, turning back to her. It's hardly out of his mouth before he wants to take it back. Her face is open, hurt; she blinks too fast. She picks up something he had not seen her lay upon his desk; it is a book. He catches a glimpse of the spine: It's Blok. She has been partial to Blok's poetry lately.

How I am haunted by the sweet hope that you, someday, in a foreign land, that you will think secret thoughts of me. . . .

"If that's what you want," she says. Every word is stiff and cold.

"It's better this way," he says, but she is already going. She leaves the door half open in her wake. After a moment, he follows, goes up the steps to the courtyard, squints, but she's gone. He blinks up at the glowing sky. A lot of people enjoy the White Nights, find them festive. But Valentin feels exposed, in the never-ending light. Like there is nowhere to hide.

* * *

After several evenings on his own, Valentin decides to go to Viktoria's. He drums his fingers impatiently on his knees as she plays piano, her own fingers moving so fast he can't even see them, practicing the same chords, over and over. Viktoria's dedication to the cause is unremitting, but she's not her father. She is more practical, and less prone to lectures. She'll understand that there's a small tear in the fabric of Valentin's moral and political identity that he never even knew existed.

That through it, he is hemorrhaging out.

"It's been a while since you came over like this," she remarks, closing the lid. "Some people actually thought you might have been arrested."

"I've been preoccupied."

"With chasing Lulikov's wife around like a puppy?"

"Excuse me?" he says flatly.

Viktoria rolls her wrists, rubs them. "The other night, when the two of you were here for dinner . . ."

"What *about* that night?"

"The way you looked at her. No, not looked. The opposite of looking."

"I don't know what that means."

"You would be talking to other people, to the rest of us, making conversation, all as normal, but you were always aware of her. Always gauging your distance to her. And then, when she came up to you . . ."

Valentin stands up. "This isn't—"

"I've never seen you smile like that in all your life," she finishes.

"You haven't even known me all my life."

"Why are you so touchy? So you were smitten, so what? The Okhrana will not arrest you for that."

"Perhaps they should."

"I don't see what difference it all makes." Viktoria wrinkles her nose. "It's over, right? Papa said—"

"Yes, it's over." Now he wishes Viktoria would return to playing chords. Anything is better than the noise in his head. "I'll have nothing more to do with her."

Viktoria presses her lips together briefly. "Good."

"Good."

"No problem, then."

"*Sovsem net.*"

Viktoria eyes him for a moment, puts a hand over her mouth. The words are muffled: "I knew it. Oh, Valya! You became attached? To *her*?"

He can't reply. He can't say it. He doesn't even dare to think it. He did the right thing, ending their affair. He knows he did. And they will fade in time, these thoughts, these memories—

But thoughts and memories do not always fade.

If anything, they can grow sharper, can't they? Like that old family apartment. The smell of his mother's skirts as he trailed behind her. His father's voice, a hearty sound, like soup. His babushka's cured-leather hand. He had not thought of his family life for years before Tonya. He had no desire to recall it, any of it, especially not the way his parents stood by the window in the evenings, the way they laughed together, the way they looked at each other—

The way they did not look at each other.

The opposite of looking.

Something strange is happening. He feels it sprout in his chest like wings, feels it threaten to burst.

"You were just a plaything to her," Viktoria insists. "A toy. You know that, don't you? You have to forget about her! You have to! She'll be your downfall!"

He knows *that*. He believes it.

"Listen to me, Valya. Why don't you sleep here tonight? We can talk some more. . . ."

He often used to stay with Viktoria. It was always easy. Careless. Not as it's been with Tonya, the past few weeks in particular, like he can't get enough air.

In Tonya's presence, he suffocates to death, not only when her skirts are up and her stockings are laddered and her legs wrapped around him, but whenever she walks away from him, her head half turned to wave good-bye, half hidden by the shawl, and all he can think is, *Wait. Wait for me.*

"I don't think so," he says. "I think I have to go home."

6

Antonina

After the tea service is wheeled into the Blue Salon, Dmitry waves away the maid, does the pouring himself. He smiles at Tonya, a smile that blends in with the silver-blue wallpaper. She can't tell which way it is going. She doesn't want to. The tea is like syrup. Impossible to swallow, at least in sips.

She doesn't speak. She is too tight with misery.

Dmitry has been away from the capital for two weeks. He prattles on about factory matters, the *situation* that has required him to cut his trip short. Tonya already knows more about the *situation* than she ever wished to. The Bolshevik and Menshevik factions are at odds over whether to strike. The Mensheviks are older, many with families; they worry that the union cannot pay a living wage. The Bolsheviks are younger, hungrier. Louder.

"The trouble comes from the new Bolshevik Committee of the Vyborg," says Dmitry, but he does not sound too concerned.

"Their leader is one of mine, in fact. Andreyev. He's well-spoken. Good-looking. People flock to him without any understanding of his politics."

"Fascinating," says Tonya, holding her breath through the lie. It is anything but fascinating. Of course she was only one of a flock. They are all baby birds, in Valentin's crowds: necks craned, heads aloft, awaiting his scraps! Perhaps he made her feel special, but everything feels special if it happens in the backstreets. If it happens underground.

No more stolen moments. No more secrets. No more visits to that tragically small, dark basement. No more undressing in front of him, slowly, seeing his breath hitch, his fingers tremble as they bring the cigarette to his lips—

"Tonyechka, I almost forgot." Dmitry is setting down his glass. "I have a gift for you. You know how there is always one remote village in all Russia where they specialize in one craft, one artistry. . . ." With a quick laugh, he reaches behind his chair, produces a large box.

He is observing her too carefully as she takes the box, and she prepares her reaction. It's better rehearsed than Valentin's speeches, by now: *You've spent far too much money on me, dear husband! You shouldn't have! I am unworthy, undeserving, I am nothing compared to—*

Tonya's heart stops.

"Do you like it?" he asks, beaming.

It is a doll. A porcelain doll, like the ones in the toy emporiums, the size of a human infant. It wears a miniature version of one of her own gowns, itself another extravagant purchase by Dmitry: papery-white, silk-embroidered, with a thick velvet overdress. Bone-fitted so many times Tonya can feel it crushing her ribs just from looking down at this reproduction. But when was the last time he forced her to wear it? To the Mariinsky, in spring? It went missing at some point; Dmitry must have taken it with him for the doll maker's sake.

The doll's *kokoshnik*, however, is unlike any Tonya has seen before.

All she remembers of wearing such traditional headdresses is that they bear down so hard, you cannot look up enough to see the sky. This one is so tall that the doll's neck may snap. It could pass for a royal crown, there are so many gemstones, so many teardrop river-pearls woven into the thread, but it is made in the southern-country style of wool rather than damask.

The doll looks like a peasant-princess.

Like her.

A filmy material covers the forehead. Tonya lifts it off, tries to remove the *kokoshnik* without cracking the porcelain. The doll has *her* hair, yellow with a metal shine to it, nearly down to the waist.

In tongue-tied horror Tonya flicks the fine spider-leg lashes off the eyes.

The eyes are black.

Darker than hers by far. The doll maker must have received a description from Dmitry and not known where to stop.

It is like she is gazing down at her own shrunken corpse.

"It's stunning, isn't it?" says Dmitry proudly. "Though not as lovely as the original, of course."

Tonya mumbles some words of thanks, though she can't hear herself above the rushing in her ears. It is not lovely. It is repugnant. She never wants to see it again, but she'll see it when she looks in the mirror, won't she? The *original*. Dmitry is a collector, a curator. Tonya might be his crowning piece, but that is all she is.

* * *

Whenever Dmitry returns from afar, he always whisks himself off to the Astoria, as soon as possible. He can spend whole nights there, drinking with his friends. Usually Tonya would go see Valentin, but tonight her only companion is the doll. She moves it around her boudoir, from corner to corner, trying to find a place where it doesn't lock eyes with anyone who enters the room. The only consolation is that the doll's dress seems to have been cut out of the real gown, which means she will never have to squeeze into that particular monstrosity again.

Just have to squeeze past *this* one every time she crosses the boudoir—

"Antonina Nikolayevna?"

Tonya grabs for the doll as if it might answer for her. "What is it, Olenka?" she says, morosely, as the lady's maid bobs an off-balance curtsey.

"Forgive me for disturbing you, my lady," says Olenka, as dutiful as ever. "There's someone who's asking for you downstairs— that is, by the servants' door. He gives the name Valentin, and says he is a friend. I told him to come tomorrow, but he said . . ." She colors. "I mean, I can tell him to—"

"No need. He is an acquaintance." Tonya raises her chin. Her calm voice rings untrue, even to her. Why has he come? Is he not content with the damage done? What does he intend to do next, cause a scene? Humiliate her? Demand money? Every possibility is unthinkable. "I will come in a moment."

She remains in her boudoir just long enough to hear Olenka's footsteps disappear down the hall, and then, keeping her breaths long and steady, she follows. There will be a simple explanation. She probably forgot something in his apartment. He could have just left it there, by the entrance. But Valentin is trying to prove a point, obviously, about the balance of power between them; he knows that she will receive him, even at her own door. He is always trying to prove points. Always trying to make an argument. Always passionate, always afire. Always able to bring her to her knees, when she watches him take the podium—

Stop, stop, stop it!

She edges her way through the servants' kitchen, still bustling with maids putting away the dinner dishes, and out toward the rear entrance of the house, which leads into a barren inner courtyard. Visitors and guests never come through this way. It's for the help and for deliveries. It's quiet out here. Too quiet, if anything, for a conversation held at normal volume will resound throughout the house.

The evening light is low. She doesn't see anyone until she turns, and then, suddenly, he has rounded the corner. How *dare* he? How dare he come now, after the week she has endured, the longest they have gone without seeing each other since the start? She will act casual. Chilly if she can manage it. A flock—she must recall that word, if she feels herself weaken. She is only one of a *flock.*

"What do you want, Valentin Mikhailovich?" she asks hardily.

He grimaces. "What *is* that thing?"

"What . . . ?" She'd forgotten she was holding the doll. "It's just a doll. You have a lot of nerve, showing up like this. Do you mean to alert my whole household? Give my servants more to gossip about?"

He blanches.

She waits. She would cross her arms to keep him at bay, but the doll is in the way.

"I didn't— You are different than how I thought you would be," he says. "It was all different than what I expected. If we can meet somewhere else—where I can explain myself . . ."

"We have met all over this city, the past six months. You might have explained yourself then."

Valentin takes a half step toward her. "I have only come to tell you what I am—what I did—or didn't do—and to appeal to you. To ask you to forgive me." His jaw visibly tightens. "To ask you for another chance."

Another chance.

She has imagined this moment a thousand times over since their parting. That he would touch her hair, her face, exert no pressure, yet she would be drawn closer anyway; that he would make another speech, whisper it in the voice he uses only for her. They will not care if anyone sees; they will not stop if anyone speaks; *Heaven,* he will say, into her hair—

"No," she says harshly. "How can I trust you now? How can it be the same?"

"Antonina," he says, "please."

"No."

"I . . ." He appears in agony now. "I am in love with you."

"Don't speak to me of love. I know you don't believe in it. You laugh at Pushkin—"

"Forget Pushkin!" he says with force. "I will write poetry for you, if that's what it takes. I will write whole books of it. I will dedicate each one to you. A hundred years from now, people will read my words and be laughing themselves, that anyone could have ever felt as I feel for you!"

She smiles, coolly. "Oh, yes? You will make me famous?"

"If you wish to be famous."

"You may have to die in a duel, as Pushkin did."

A flame of hope burns in his eyes. "Duels are outlawed in Russia, Tonya."

"That will not matter, as you will be dead."

"You are right. It will not matter."

They regard each other. If she sends him away, he won't come back. Not because of pride, but principle.

It is only passion, Mama would say. *It passes as quick as it comes. One day your blood boils; the next day it simmers. The day after that, it stills.*

So why does it feel like the first day, only worse?

"You are very convincing," Tonya says, blithely, "but that has always been your talent. I can't be expected to make up my mind here and now. This talk of you dying in a duel has distracted me. It is much too tempting. I will have to . . ." She holds her head up high. "I will give it some thought. I'll come to you later if I decide to . . . Well, we shall have to see."

He lets out a long breath. Was he *afraid*? Valentin, who is not afraid of prison, of the Tsar's armies, of great heights, not even of cockroaches? Valentin, who hears nothing but the drumbeat of revolution, who sees nothing but the adoring crowd?

She knows without asking that he will wait. He will be at the cellar steps, no matter how long she takes.

"The doll is not invited," says Valentin, and Tonya laughs, in spite of herself, sees the relief in his face as he turns away.

* * *

The White Nights do not reach Anastasia's bedroom, which has begun to stink of death even with Anastasia still in it. When Tonya goes in to bid her mother-in-law good night, Anastasia Sergeyevna sits up higher in bed, welcoming, a bit wistful.

"Mitya told me about the doll. He means well, but he's terrible with gifts. Come, child," the old woman says warmly. "I have my own gift for you. A pretty handkerchief for a pretty little girl."

Tonya sits gingerly upon the bed. The sheets crackle. Anastasia holds up the handkerchief, one that is threaded with gold, beaded with pearl, and most remarkable for the raised, intricate design of blue flowers around the edges. Tonya takes it by a corner, with reverence.

"I was a young bride in this house, once," says Anastasia. "Not quite as young as— How old *are* you, child?"

"Eighteen on my next birthday," answers Tonya, still mesmerized. She weaves the handkerchief through her fingers. It is smooth as snakeskin.

"You remind me of myself. I was also too innocent."

Tonya looks up at her in surprise.

"You have seen only one side of your husband," says her mother-in-law quietly.

Tonya cannot answer.

"But I have seen all sides of my son." Anastasia smiles now, with the part of her mouth that still works. "Dmitry is like his father. He takes things crudely, by force. He has let you have your freedom—indeed, he will give anything if you ask him for it—but he will not let someone else have you." Anastasia's hand snakes out, grips Tonya harder than Tonya would have thought possible. "Whoever came to see you earlier this evening, I promise you, he isn't worth it."

So Olenka has tattled. But the servants will repeat, will invent, all manner of gossip. There is no way for Anastasia, for anyone, to separate the wheat from the chaff.

Tonya refuses to look her mother-in-law in either eye, good or bad. She wraps the handkerchief around her hand, once, twice. "I'm afraid I have an event tonight—at Nadya Kirova's house," she says. "A political . . . event. I don't have time to read to you."

"Of course. You have been most attentive to me, child. We will need a new book of poetry soon, won't we?" Anastasia's mouth lifts again. "And I've meant to say how glad I am to see you taking such an interest in politics of late. I myself sympathize with the people's cause, and I raised Mitya to do the same."

Tonya's face feels slick with sweat. "Good night, then."

"Good night." Anastasia reaches out, pats Tonya on the cheek. The touch of the old woman's hand is feathery, like the handkerchief. Anastasia is dissolving. Disappearing. "See? You are finding your place here already."

*　*　*

Valentin is at the bottom of the basement steps, against the wall. He is looking up, into that strange northern sky, and he does not see her right away. For someone who always seems in a rush, always moving, always thinking of better, brighter things, he has an astounding ability to remain still. Tonya watches him the way he watches the sky: in wonder.

Suddenly he turns, straightens.

Maybe all this happened by accident, last time.

This time she knows what she is doing.

She descends the stairs. Valentin does not speak and neither does she.

She turns her face up to his. His eyes search hers, for the briefest moment, before he pulls her to him. The first time he ever touched her, it was light enough that she thought she might be able to pretend it never happened later; there is none of that now. His hands are sliding beneath her dress, over her garter, and she gasps. He says something that she cannot understand; she tastes her own sweat, his, maybe blood, from biting down too hard. She cries out, buries her cry in his shoulder. It is over in minutes, maybe seconds. He does not release her for a long moment, thankfully, for her legs are wobbly, her whole body still seething.

"How long would you have waited for me?" she whispers.

She feels, rather than hears, his laugh. "At least another ten minutes."

"How lucky my timing is."

"And how lucky," he murmurs, "is mine."

Inside, they lie upon his mattress, talking so quietly she does not hear herself, half the time. She has not brought anything to read, and she will not read his texts for pleasure: Radishchev, Lenin, Chernyshevsky. *Whenever you do not have books,* Mama used to say, *you can tell the old stories. Fairy tales. Folktales. Not well-known literature; not written by the greats. Often not written at all.*

"Would you tell me one?" asks Valentin, putting out his cigarette.

"I don't remember them anymore."

Tonya took them for granted, back then. Surely Mama would always be there. Surely such stories do not end.

Maybe that is why she clings so hard to Pushkin. Pushkin is on paper, and it is all she has left.

"Make it up," he suggests.

"What? You can't just make it up."

"Of course, you're right," he says. "I forgot. Where do stories come from again? They show up on people's doorsteps? They're caught in fishnets? They're handed out by the Tsar himself at Christmas?"

"You're very irritating," she says, and Valentin smirks at her. "I can try, if you insist. But I am telling you now, I'm no good at it. I'm no orator. Nor are you, for that matter, a great listener! The way you tore out of the room at Viktoria's . . ."

"I couldn't stand it."

"Couldn't stand the sound of my voice?"

"Couldn't stand the way this feels like a dream," he says, "whenever I see you from any distance, Tonya. It is as if, in my heart, I still do not believe that someone like you . . ." Now he is almost inaudible. "But if all this is a dream, we could just remain like this, you and me. Right here. We don't have to wake up."

He sounds so young, perhaps even scared, that she cannot respond, much less with their usual banter.

Though she has spoken tirelessly of Otrada, of her parents, her friends, her upbringing, Valentin has not told her anything about his childhood. He has no interest in the past, his or anyone else's. All he ever says is that his life began the day he was adopted by the revolutionary writer Pavel Katenin. That he was reborn. That he has no family other than the Party, no purpose other than his politics.

But for once, in this moment, Tonya can see the little boy within. There was a time—there must have been a time—when Valentin Andreyev believed in something else.

"In a faraway kingdom," she says, softly, "in a long-ago land, a princess lived in a palace by the sea...."

7

Rosie

My first weekend back in Russia, and there's no coffee in the kitchen. I sink down into one of the softwood chairs at the table and breathe into my hands. There's no hot water in the shower, either, and no fly screens on the windows. The bug repellent I bought last minute in London feels like acid on my arms.

This place is disintegrating on every possible level. The plumbing, the house, the country—

"Ah, Rosie! How did you sleep?" asks Alexey, entering the kitchen. He bustles about, putting on a kettle, fitting a glass into a nickel-plated holder. As he goes, he hums to himself, the song he sang yesterday at the restaurant.

It's going to get stuck in my head, too. As if I need yet another thing to keep me up at night.

"How would you like me to get started?" I ask, as he places a cup in front of me.

Alexey takes his time to answer, swirls jam into his own tea. "You know what, we've only just arrived," he says, pleasantly. "Take a few days to reacquaint yourself with Moscow. Lev is at your disposal." More swirling. "I'm leaving tomorrow morning for Leningrad. There will be plenty for you to do once I'm back."

"Are you sure?" I can't keep the curiosity out of my voice. Isn't Alexey going to tell me who *Kukolka* really is? Or what he's doing to locate her? For someone whose entire life has been about describing the indescribable, about revealing the unimaginable, he's a bit *cagey*, isn't he?

Oh well. I reckon he's earned the right to be.

And I could definitely make good use of a few days.

I try the tea, which has the consistency of tree bark, and reach for the milk, but the milk's gone off. I've poured too much already, and the tea is covered with ropy white strands.

Nothing works in this bloody country.

Mum's key will probably break in the lock. I'll have to hire a carpenter to wrench apart the *stenka*, board by board. It'll bring down the whole wall. I'll spend the rest of this summer sifting through rubble, without even knowing what I'm looking for.

According to Alexey, what I'm looking for won't be there anyway.

I could scream from frustration, but instead I simmer in my seat, gripping my undrinkable cup of tea.

Alexey catches my eye and smiles. "It'll start to hurt," he says, "coming home. Because you meet your old self when you do. And the one has to kill the other."

* * *

My family's former apartment is on the other side of the city, toward the southeast, surrounded by belching chemical plants and industrial complexes. On my way home from school, I would often see people huddled by the outdoor pipes, for warmth. The Russia I grew up in has nothing in common with Alexey's cozy, Chekhovian dacha.

As we drive, I keep Mum's key in my hand. It tends to scald my skin, no matter which way I hold it.

"Take it easy," I say, as Lev changes gears relentlessly.

He grunts in reply. The tires squeal like they're being skinned. But even the cavernous potholes of Moscow's lesser-used suburban roads can't prevent my eyes from closing. This is the cruel reality of insomnia: I fall asleep everywhere I go, except to bed. Whatever keeps me awake is present only at night.

Whoever keeps me awake . . .

"Is this the one?"

I force my eyelids apart. The scene in front of me swims: an apartment building made of white concrete, with windows like pockmarks. I don't recall it being this white. Maybe they cleaned it.

Or maybe all I remember is red.

Lev begins to shoehorn the car into a parking space.

I shake the key out of my hand. It's left a toothy shape behind. Lev is already climbing out, pulling his dark hood over his head like he plans to burgle the building. My limbs feel like lead. I emerge carefully, glancing around the adjacent apartment complexes, all of them silent, stoic. Together, these buildings encircle a small courtyard, a sort of community park, featuring a dilapidated bench and a dead lawn that resembles a urine stain.

After several minutes, I'm able to face the first building again. Home.

It might look like an urban sanatorium, but it's the last real home I ever had.

"You know the code?" asks Lev.

"Code?" I echo, but he's right. I have my old house keys, but there appears to be an electronic number pad next to the front door, with doorbell buttons below it. Of all the possible improvements, upgrades, renovations, that the government could make to these state-owned behemoths—all of them peeling, crumbling, spewing dust, sweating asbestos—*this* is what they chose. To install keypad locks for security.

A decade and a half too late.

Of course Mum didn't leave me anything as practical as a key code. Or Ludmila's phone number. That would have made this much too easy. "I'll try the bells," I say, like it's no big deal, when in reality I want to tear this keypad clear off the wall. "Someone will let me in."

But nobody does. Midmorning on a weekend, and everyone's either watching television with the volume turned too high or out at the shops, bar the grouchy babushka on the fourth floor, who refuses to believe my story. The irony is that she was already living here back when my family lived here.

That's likely how she learned not to let strangers into the building.

No matter. A resident will exit or enter eventually and I'll slip in behind. To make my point, I seat myself on the curb. Lev sits down beside me.

"Thanks for the ride, but you don't have to do this with me," I say. "I know how to get back."

"Alexey Alexeyevich wouldn't want me to leave you alone here."

"This was my family's home for years. We did fine." Not really, but still . . . "Honestly, you can have the weekend off."

He lowers his hood, looks hard at me. "Okay," he says. "Boss."

Great. And now we are openly hostile.

We sit for ten minutes. Fifteen. Twenty. You don't get this kind of smoldering silence back in England. Someone would have broken it, mere seconds in. The weather. Football. Anything. Anything but this.

"I was born here," I say, cautiously. "In Moscow."

He nods to indicate he's heard me.

I let my bag drop between my feet. "Have you read any of Alexey's work?"

"The Last Bolshevik."

Ah, he speaks! "It's incredible, isn't it?"

"I didn't like it," says Lev.

"You didn't like . . . a memoir?"

"It is well written."

"I see," I say, trying not to lapse into sarcasm. "So it's the content that wasn't to your taste?"

"It is too careful. There is something missing." Lev's gaze flicks away from my face, like he's heard something by the door. "He left things out, things that didn't fit."

"But didn't he have to? For it to make sense to the rest of us?"

"You asked for my opinion."

This man has all the congeniality of that grouchy babushka. "Well, my mother didn't like it either," I say, a final attempt to keep our fledgling conversation afloat. "Someone gave her a copy once, and she actually burned it, cover to cover. By candle flame, of all things. I think she had this idea that he was making Russia look bad. She was always getting upset when people criticized the . . ."

I don't bother to finish. He doesn't care. He's being paid to sit here.

The silence resumes in full.

"I'll go," he says, after a moment.

"Sure. I'll get a taxi back."

"I mean I'll climb over. Let us in."

Climb?

I open my mouth to protest, but Lev is already up and walking toward one of the ground-floor apartments. He scales the side, swings his legs easily over the balcony rail, and disappears into the apartment, all in full view of the street. I stand up. I'm aware that my jaw has locked, in a gape, as he reappears, holding the front door open from the inside.

So he *is* a professional criminal.

It would explain a lot.

He lets me through. The door slams shut behind me. There's a small, airless space between the double doors, a chance to change my mind. I heave open the inner door, and it closes firmly, plunging us into darkness. A click, and there's a flood of harsh light from the long fluorescent tubes on the ceiling, illuminating the nasty, narrow stairwell, the shrieking graffiti on the walls, the driver's impassive face.

"It's on the eighth floor," I say, brushing past him. "Lift's over there."

The elevator is cramped and rattly. We have to stand much too close. I notice a scar on his neck, thin, white, and deep, disappearing into the hairline. He is no longer clean-shaven, but it only stands out more.

Who exactly has Alexey hired as my childminder?

When I look up, Lev is watching me.

"Combat knife," he says.

My own neck feels rosy. The lift creaks as it settles into place.

Outside, the hallway is the same bone-marrow shade it is in my memory. There are four separate flats on this floor, all of them behind double doors. I ring our old bell. I knock on the door, twice, three times, but there's no sound from within. My suspicion is that Ludmila never stays here, only uses it as a storage space. A common enough practice for landlords, and one that makes me feel a little less guilty for what I'm about to do.

My old house key fits seamlessly, even though I remember fighting with it as a kid. I often wondered if I had the wrong apartment. The wrong home. The wrong family.

At least like this, it feels less like we're breaking in.

That man didn't break in, in 1977. There was no sign of a forced entry, or any entry. The front door was still locked from the inside. All the windows were closed and intact. Nobody saw anyone going into or out of the building. Nothing from our flat went missing.

The only things *that man* took were their lives. Zoya's. Papa's.

An inexplicable, perfect locked-room murder, and the police were too in awe of it to solve it. They never recovered a weapon, never unearthed a motive, never even had a suspect. Civilian-on-civilian crime of this kind was so rare back then they probably convinced themselves it wasn't even possible. If someone shot you in the back of the head, and it wasn't the state, did it happen at all?

The authorities never believed that I saw anyone or witnessed anything. They claimed it took place before I even woke up. If only that were true.

Maybe then I wouldn't feel like it was my fault. Just because I didn't run fast enough into the living room. Just because I couldn't stop him.

Just because I survived.

* * *

Here it is, the square sally-port entryway, from which all the other rooms extend like claws. The doors are all closed, but I know what's behind them: Across from us are the bath and toilet; to the right, the kitchen-cum-dining room–cum–entertainment space, and my childhood bedroom; to the left, the living room, which doubled as my parents' bedroom.

I push open the living room door. The room is piled with books, newspapers, blankets, film reels, *Pravda*. A mound that could well be the sofa is backed up against the wall. Any chairs or tables have been swallowed by the mess. The floor is barely visible.

This is where it happened.

I press a fist against my mouth, turn deliberately to the *stenka*. It still looms over the whole room, but several of the glass panels are missing. The shelves that once housed my parents' belongings are empty. I should step forward, should get this over with, but instead I'm sinking, rapidly, into the quicksand of memory. Where's the key? The key, the key.

One-handed, I grope in my handbag. My fingers close around it, but the bag slips from my grasp. I can't let myself faint, not here. I can't lie flat on this floor and look up at the same ceiling that they did, as they died. I can't relive their deaths.

Or is that all I do?

"What's going on?" says Lev, his eyes narrowed at me.

"I'm a little ... dizzy. I can't ... Would you mind?" I show him the key, feebly. "It's for that drawer there. I can't."

He takes it without hesitation. Can he not sense it, whatever presence still lingers in this apartment? Ludmila must have. She's filled this place to the rafters, trying to push it out. I take a step back, away from the center of the room, feeling for the sofa.

Mamulya ...

Whose voice is that?

Mamulya ...

Is that *my* voice?

My voice from *when I was a child*?

I haven't thought of Mum as *Mamulya* in years. I don't even consider them to be the same person. *Mamulya* spoke in a gentle lilt. Mum sounded like whatever was destroying her liver was crawling up her trachea. *Mamulya* would pirouette in front of the mirror every morning, checking every angle. Mum had no angles anymore, in that shapeless nightgown that eventually became her second skin.

Mamulya died fourteen years ago. Mum died in June.

"It's open," says Lev. "Do you want what's inside?"

I will help you find that man, Mum said to me on what I now know was her deathbed.

I let myself wallow in a fantastical theory: Mum located the murderer herself, all those years ago. She hacked him to bits, pickled his parts in jars, and stored him in our *stenka*. That's the real reason we had to flee.

Lev is already reaching inside the cabinet for the contents. His expression is grim.

It's a half-foot-long doll.

I see it without understanding any of it: the golden mohair; the lacquered sheen of the porcelain; the brocaded dress; two dainty booted feet just poking out from underneath. The doll's hands are bare, stretched too far, as if they want to be held.

To be fair, she's been in there for fourteen years.

This is what Mum left for me to find? *This* is her idea of helping? Aren't there enough dolls in Russia? In the world?

"You want it or not?" asks Lev, standing, stretching, freeing his finger from the grotesque grasp of the doll's hair. He looks unnerved. Sure, he might have visible knife wounds and a penchant for breaking into buildings, but even he is no match for a child's plaything whose dead eyes never break contact.

The living room window is open, letting in a murmur of sound: the trebly chirp of summer crickets, the caterwaul of an animal, the stifled static of a neighbor's radio.

I don't have to take this doll with me. I can just put her back. We can both stay in the dark forever.

Mamulya . . .

The first book Mum ever read to me in the English translation was Tolstoy's *War and Peace.* She'd skip whole chapters, revisit her favorite lines again and again. Like General Kutuzov's advice to Prince Andrei—in what context, I don't remember: *There is nothing stronger than those two warriors, patience and time. They will do everything. . . .*

I'm done with patience and time. I have neither left.

"Yes," I say. "I want it."

* * *

Lev's driving style is quieter on the way home. Maybe he's afraid the doll might fall out of my bag.

It's evening by the time we arrive at the dacha. The air is warm, sultry. The growing spray of stars in the sky is reminiscent of the single time Mum took me to watch a Guy Fawkes celebration by the Thames. She was holding a bottle of something as pungent as insecticide; back then I didn't know what it was. She was smiling a lot. Too much. It hurt to look at her, so I looked up instead. The fireworks lasted some half an hour, and then they stopped, and when they did, it was like I was seeing darkness for the very first time.

So that's what's been here all along.

Now Mum's stopped.

What's been here all along?

Inside, I catch Lev on the stairs. "Wait," I say, with one hand on the banister. "Thanks. For your help at the apartment."

"It was nothing," he says, without looking back.

"I know Alexey has asked you to—look after me," I begin, "but I'll be alright. I know the city, and there's a lot of things I'd prefer to do on my own."

Now he looks. "How long have you been away from Moscow, *devushka?*"

"Devushka?" I say, taken aback. "I thought you knew my name."

"Do *you* know your name?"

"I— What?"

"He calls you Rosie. You call yourself Raisa."

So he heard me on the intercom with that old babushka. "That's none of your business—"

"My business," he says, "is to accompany you and keep you safe. No, I did not ask for this job. I would not ask for it. I was assigned. But I know how to do it, so let me do it. You can act as if you're alone, if you want." A low scoff. "But you seem to like to talk."

"It's been fourteen years," I say curtly. "To answer your question."

"Yes," he says, "it shows. *Devushka.*"

Wow.

I stay rooted in place long after he leaves, to make sure we don't run into each other in the hallway upstairs. Our conversation disintegrated too fast. I wanted to ask if he thought he could make it all the way up my family's apartment building, just by climbing the balconies.

The first thing I do, alone in my room, is pull apart the new doll. The *stenka*-doll.

The hard circle of scalp, with hair attached, comes off with a faint snap. A piece of paper pokes out of the doll's head, folded thinly enough that I can already see weblike writing. The only writing Mum ever did, as far as I witnessed, was of her own stories, back when she could reliably hold something that wasn't a bottle, but I don't want another fairy tale. I want facts. I want the truth.

I want *that man* to have a name.

I unfold the page.

It's no story. It's a map, browned and clearly torn from an atlas, covering most of Tula province, which lies south of Moscow. Among the quaint, quintessential names of Russian towns, someone has drawn a crude pinkie-nail-sized picture of a house and labeled it *Otrada.*

There is nothing else.

The White Glove

One day a princess found a tiny stain upon the littlest finger of the left hand of a pair of white gloves. She gave the glove to her maid, and instructed the maid to wash out the stain. The poor girl washed and washed for hours. The harder she worked, the bigger the stain grew. The maid grew desperate. At night, while everyone else in the palace slept, she found a bucket of paint, and she painted over the stain.

Now, again, the glove was white.

By morning it was dry. The maid brought the glove to show the princess. The princess looked carefully at the littlest finger of the left hand, and it seemed the stain was gone. Relieved, the maid took the left-hand glove upstairs to be put away with the right-hand glove. But as she passed by a window, she noticed that the fabric looked different, in sunlight, than it did indoors by the light of the oil lamps.

The stain had sunk into the thread. It had gone even deeper. It was spreading still.

8

Valentin

The weather is unusually mild today, but that doesn't explain why the whole city has poured out of the houses and offices and cafés and restaurants and schools and museums, and into the streets. Men, women, children, workers, shopkeepers, bankers, taxi drivers. Nothing explains it. There have been plenty of political demonstrations this year, but something is different today. Something that sings.

It goes to show that the power has always been in the hands of the people, only the people did not realize.

Valentin fights his way to the embankment, which swarms with protestors. They spill onto the ice of the Neva, which cracks and creaks beneath their weight. In his head, he amends the speech he will give later at Znamenskaya Square, ideally atop the statue of the Hippopotamus. If he ever makes it across the river.

People of Russia, the skin of our city is on fire, and soon the body will know. . . .

"Soldiers!" comes the shout, as a chunk of ice sails through the air with a shrill whistle. It lands a yard from his feet.

A mounted brigade of the Tsar's Cossacks has formed a half-moon by the bridge. Ice and stones and sticks are flying overhead. The Cossacks' horses are spitting froth, their ears pitched forward, their noses running. Shots ring out in the distance, which means police, or secret police. Not very secret anymore, of course. After today, after all this, there will be no more revolutionary underground. Valentin will no longer need an alias, code words, hollowed-out books, dark alleyways.

Everything can exist out in the open. Everything will be made equal.

He ducks away from the crowds, feeling damp hands sliding off him, rough clothing scraping against all sides. He has never seen the city like this, hungry and heaving. Awake. Alive. He wipes the sweat from his eyes, struggles to see. Whatever has infected the masses is infecting him too. On the podium, he would say that no one is better than anyone else, that the class system is a false construct. But on the podium he belongs to the Party.

Everywhere else, he belongs to her.

She is the single star around which all else revolves. If they were *equals*, he would have asked her to run away with him months ago. To live with him. To marry him. He has tried to ask, in his way, but there are some things you cannot use code words for.

We will all live two lives, Comrades! One life is over, and the other is now!

A red ribbon hooks into his shoulder, thrown from somewhere, curling sharply around his hand as he pulls it away. The noise all around is thunderous, but at the same time it is only a rumble. Valentin turns the ribbon over, and over again. The idea is mad. Pure madness. Tonya will laugh in his face. She often laughs in his face as it is. *Who knew that* you *would turn out to be the romantic, Valya?* But maybe he has always been the romantic. The dreamer. He is a revolutionary, after all.

Today the dream is coming true.

* * *

In the early morning the sound of machine guns echoes along the embankment. *Rat-a-tat-tat! Rat-a-tat-tat!* Valentin has not slept for two straight nights. His throat is scarred by shouting. In the past twenty-four hours, he has seen the stone eagles of the Romanovs pulled to the ground, smashed beyond recognition; he has seen the courthouses go up in smoke; he has witnessed policemen shot through the chest with their own firearms. He has watched the revolving doors of the Astoria spray blood like the light of a prism.

Tonya is there by the rail, facing the river, punctual for the first time in recent memory. She is clutching her precious shawl at the neck, for the wind is high enough today to whip it away. Her cheeks are sickly pale, and there are dark ponds beneath her eyes. Has she not slept either? Has the chaos of the revolution, outside her bedroom window, kept her awake?

"Tonya," he says, just loud enough. He is still hoarse, but he will spend whatever voice he has left on this. On her.

She gives him a sliver of a smile. Valentin wants to reassure her: There have been no attacks on the homes of the rich, but even if there are, people like her husband will flee out the back before anything happens to them. They'll barricade the doors with the servants, if that's what it comes to.

"*Lyubov' moya*," he says, coming close. She lets him take her by the hands. He feels it again, *rat-a-tat-tat*, but it is not volley fire. Her pulse is rapid in her wrists. "What's wrong?"

"I saw you, the first day of the protests," she says, "at Znamenskaya. On the platform, next to Alexander III . . ."

"Why didn't you come to me?"

"I couldn't reach you. There were too many people on the square." Her body goes rigid against his. "And the soldiers—I saw the fight. They could have killed you."

"I can't always stay up on the statues." He touches her chin, tilts it up. "Is that what troubles you?"

Tonya does not answer, only bunches her shawl tighter in her hand.

"Are you afraid something will happen to me?" he asks.

Again, nothing.

"Do you no longer wish for me to die in a duel, Tonya?"

She glances at him hotly, from beneath her lashes. "I don't want you to martyr yourself on Znamenskaya Square, that is all."

"So the only cause I am allowed to die for is you."

Another smoky-eyed glare. "Must you always be so flippant?"

"You will be pleased to hear," he says, "that I die a little each day when you go home to your husband."

"That's pithy," she snaps. "I suppose you wrote it down in advance."

"Is that how you think I spend my spare time?"

"I haven't any idea what you do in your spare time."

"Perhaps we should change that."

Her eyes widen. Part of him, most of him, wants to stop here, right where he always stops. At the precipice.

But now he has to fall.

Valentin knows full well that Dmitry Lulikov proposed marriage to her beneath a flowering fruit tree, in high spring, in the orchard outside her childhood home. Not at an ungodly hour along a half-frozen river as the city burned in all directions. No matter what he does, what he says, Valentin cannot make the moment feel like one of her poems. Her fairy tales. He cannot be her prince.

He wants to get on his knees, press his head into her hands, beg like he is a child.

"The police districts have surrendered," he says instead. "All that's left is for Nicholas to abdicate the throne."

"Do they not say his brother will take his place?"

"I mean that it is time to take a side."

"How simple you make that sound."

"The choice is simple," he says evenly. "I love you and wish to be with you. If you don't feel the same—"

"Then what?" It is a challenge. "Then we shouldn't meet anymore?"

"Then we shouldn't meet anymore." To say it aloud feels worse than getting his stomach kicked in by Tsarist soldiers. He says it even stronger: "We won't."

"And if I choose you? What will I do if you lose interest in me? My husband will not have me back. I have no friends in this city. No *comrades.*"

"Do you think I will lose interest?"

She looks surprised.

"Do you think that I will lose interest in you, Antonina?"

In the distance, the machine guns still fire. *Rat-a-tat-tat! Rat-a-tat-tat!* It is the music of revolution. Petrograd is collapsing around them. The wind still blows, stronger now. She pulls a strand of hair from her mouth. He longs so badly to lower his head, to cover her mouth with his, to have an answer that way, but she needs to say it. He needs to hear her.

"I know I have nothing to offer you," he says quietly, "but everything I ever do have, will be yours. And I promise not to die on Znamenskaya Square. I will not go near Znamenskaya Square."

A brush of a laugh, on her lips.

"Go home and pack a case," he says, though he can hardly speak, through the surge of hope in his chest, "and I will meet you at our bridge. At eight o'clock."

She breathes out, soft and slow.

Please—please—

"Alright," she says. "I will come."

"You will come."

"Eight o'clock."

They both fall silent as he slips the scrap of red ribbon out of his pocket. Valentin takes her hands, turns them. His own are shaking. He needs to go home, get some sleep.

When he wakes, his other life will begin.

He ties the ribbon around her wrist.

Once, years and years ago, on the last night he ever spent in his aunt's home, before Valentin ran away to live on the wharf, as his aunt's blows rained down on his head, he tucked his body into the smallest shape possible and he let himself believe that his dead parents were coming to save him. That they were crossing all of Russia in a horse-pulled troika, that they would sweep him into their arms. But of course they were not coming. Nobody came.

It was the last time he ever let himself believe.

Until now.

She pulls her shawl over her face. Before he realizes it, she is already walking away. She turns to wave at him and he waves back, his insides churning. He sees, in the street beyond, a serene line of the Tsar's Cossacks on horseback. Their lances gleam in the sunlight and their horses' tails dance in the wind.

9

Antonina

It is teatime, even in the midst of a revolution, and the Countess Burtsinova has come again to call. Today she has brought along her daughter. Akulina is nine years old, skinny, mopey, often scratching at a fingernail, hiding behind her shock of red hair.

This is the very worst moment the Countess could have chosen.

Tonya receives them in the Blue Salon. She sits perched on the edge of her chair, doing her best to play hostess. But there is a layer of gunpowder hanging over the city so thick that she can taste it in her mouth, even in here, and she nibbles queasily at a slice of linseed cake, the only pastry they have left. She can't banish the taste.

It is ten past four.

"Do I bore you, darling?" The Countess Burtsinova is looking at her with one eyebrow raised, like a fishhook.

"I apologize, Natalya Fyodorovna. The situation in the city is distracting me."

"Of course. Soldiers! Guns! Angry mobs! Didn't we see it all on our way here, Lina?"

Akulina gives something of a nod.

"Tell me, Tonya darling, that you have ceased to take those daily walks of yours, at least."

Tonya has to proceed with caution here, as she would on the weary spring ice of the Fontanka, for Natalya is too much a stranger to be trusted, and too close an acquaintance to be rebuffed. She swallows her nausea. "I have seen no reason to give them up."

"Please, Tonya, enough." Natalya makes a sound, a resigned laugh. "You have been seen with Valentin Andreyev. The Bolshevik."

Tonya licks her lips. "He is a friend. I admire him."

"*Admire*. What a word for it."

Natalya knows. There is no use denying it further, and this moment of truth is somehow delicious. But still something twists in Tonya's gut.

She is pregnant.

She has thrown up onto her bedsheets several times this week. Twice just last night. She has missed her monthly bleeding. She knows all the early signs, remembers how Mama used to cherish them—Mama, who had so many stops and starts, tiny sorrowful bundles that had to be whisked away by the midwives at midnight. Tonya's baby already seems to have such a slender chance of survival, with such family history—

Can she keep the pregnancy healthy in a basement?

Can she give birth on that filthy mattress?

Will Valentin hear her screams over the roar of the crowd?

"I don't deny that I see the appeal," says Natalya, ever sly.

"Your Bolshevik has a reputation for climbing atop more than statues, you know. He knows what he's doing. Many of his past— let us call them admirers, as well—have donated nicely to his cause."

"Thank you, you've opened my eyes," says Tonya stoutly. "Shall I ask him for my Fabergé eggs back?"

Natalya draws back as if she's been slapped. "Andreyev doesn't care about you, Tonya! Some men, they're in love with something greater, something more perfect, than any one person could be—"

"Is that what you tell yourself, Natalya Fyodorovna?"

"What *is* this vile new streak in you?" demands Natalya. "And do you know what it will do to Dmitry to hear you have been cavorting around town with—with one of his *workers*! With a *Bolshevik*! I can't even bear the thought of how hurt he will feel. He must not find out, Tonya. I, personally, will swear to him that any rumors he hears are untrue. It will all blow over in time, and in return, you will never see Valentin Andreyev again. Fair is fair."

A sharp silence descends. Tonya's hand on the plate is unsteady. The cake is sawdust in her mouth. She does not avert her eyes from the Countess.

Natalya smiles. It splits at the edges. "I assume it is settled, then."

Tonya has long known that Valentin does not do anything in the half-light. He believes in absolutes; it is what separates his Party from the other revolutionaries, the Mensheviks, the Socialist-Revolutionaries, the Anarchists. There will be no compromises. It will be all, or nothing.

This life, or him.

This palace, or that cellar.

Royalty, or revolution.

* * *

In the bathtub, Tonya hugs her legs to her chest and sighs.

There is no doubt that Valentin thrills her. That he has only to look her way, and her heart races; her body seems to ripple. Sometimes it is like being burned at the stake. But Mama would say that that is no good thing. The shouting on the streets today could turn to normal conversation tomorrow; the squalor of his basement may not feel as romantic when she has nowhere else to go. The very politics that seem to sustain him can just as easily break him. If it all comes to nothing, he will grow disillusioned and embittered. They will turn on each other.

Will she regret giving up so much to be with him? Will he despise her for regretting?

She knows what kind of father Dmitry would make. He would buy the most expensive pram in the city, would order bonnets from Paris, handcrafted wooden toys from Germany, baby bath soap from England. She knows, because he treats *her* in this way, as if she is a statuette, one that he must take down from its shelf and brush off daily. At teatime.

But he could also drop her at any moment. Crack her open.

The water is turning lukewarm, just as Olenka appears in the doorway, holding a jug. Olenka coughs, comes forward. Olenka comes from a village outside Petrograd and sends her money home. The maid used to work in the textile mills, and the other servants say there is enough fluff in her lungs to make a full set of bedding. One day many years ago, as the story goes, Dmitry's mother happened to be visiting Olenka's workplace on a charitable mission. The hour was lonely enough for the girl's weepy cough to be discerned over the sound of grinding machinery. The kindhearted Anastasia *saved* Olenka, installed her as a servant in this very house.

That is what the Lulikovs do. They save people.

No. They collect people.

"Olenka," says Tonya, "have you seen my handkerchief anywhere? I'm going out tonight. I would like to take it with me."

"Which one, Antonina Nikolayevna?"

"The one from Anastasia Sergeyevna. The blue beaded one."

"I'm sorry," the lady's maid demurs. "Do you want me to look for it?"

There is no time. It is already nearly six. "It's alright." Did she drop it in the street? Leave it somewhere? Did one of the servants steal it? Its loss is small, but somehow foreboding, and despite the comforts of the bath, to which Olenka has just added new, warmer water, Tonya feels cramped and cold.

* * *

When Tonya goes to say good-bye to Anastasia, the room seems even darker than normal, the curtains shut, the fire long doused. They have made this place an early grave. The Lulikov matriarch is propped up against her pillows, her eyes going to glass. She sounds as consumptive as Olenka, every breath a labor.

She speaks before Tonya reaches the bedside.

"Oh, child." Her lips barely move. "What have you done?"

The words bounce around the room, leave Tonya feeling seasick.

"When Mitya first wrote to me from Tula, I begged him to leave you where he found you. Feral in the countryside." Anastasia's good eye blinks hard. "I warned him that he would spend the rest of his life defending a face like yours. And I warned you, too. To keep yours down."

Tonya has forgotten how quiet it can be when nobody speaks, when one cannot hear the gunfire from outside.

"It's over," says Anastasia.

Everything appears to be spinning, sparking around them. "Over?" Tonya's cheekbones twinge. She should not have eaten the linseed cake. With Valentin she is unlikely to have such problems. There will be no linseed cake. "Has Natalya Fyodorovna told him?"

"On the contrary. The Countess Burtsinova believes ignorance to be bliss. But I refuse to let you make a fool of my son. A laughingstock of my family."

"I must . . . I must go," says Tonya dimly. "I am going."

Anastasia's eyes appear to part company, the good one blazing at Tonya, the bad one shrinking away. "Tonya, what's the matter with you? Tonya?"

A violent throb in her temple, and then Tonya's field of vision begins to furl inward. The world is shedding light. Mama used to faint, too, in pregnancy. Made it look peaceful, even pretty. Papa always knew right before it was about to happen, and would rush over and catch her. That is what is left when your blood no longer bubbles, maybe. Just someone who knows without asking.

* * *

Tonya watches from the bed as the doctor rearranges the items in his vinyl-lined bag. Hollow tubes. A stethoscope. What appear to be devices of torture. Dmitry sits at the edge of the bed, his hand placed protectively on her ankle.

"What time is it?" she asks, woozily.

"Just past seven," he answers.

"If the maid is to be trusted," says the doctor, "you may expect the baby to arrive in summer. Pregnancy is a delicate time," he adds, with a tut. "Your wife is much too thin, Dmitry Dmitryevich. I advise her to remain abed as much as possible."

Dmitry takes Tonya's hand, kisses it flat. His mouth on her skin is cold.

"What has happened?" she says, struggling to speak.

"You fainted, and Olenka revealed that you have not— That is, there is reason to think you are with child. Rest for now, Tonyechka," he says, distantly. "I'll have someone bring up your supper."

The doctor says to Dmitry that he will look in on Anastasia before he departs. He is as slow-moving as tar. Tonya waits until the doors click shut behind the two men. Alone at last. She gets out of bed. Black spots flicker around her eyes, but she is able to stay upright. Her slippers slap against the floor.

There is no time to pack. She will have to go as she is.

She wraps her shawl around her head. She pauses to listen, and then she moves the door handle. Again, and then once more. The shawl begins to feel tight. She braces her body against the frame and pulls, then pushes. If she were more familiar with curses, the kind that Dmitry uses when he reads the papers or the kind that Valentin speaks right into her ear, she would try them now.

Instead she sinks to the floor and puts her head between her knees.

The door is locked.

* * *

Tonya sleeps fitfully. Each time she wakes, she tries the door, to no avail, and she is again close to fainting, beset by floaty spots, so she returns to bed, turns on her side, and cries.

When she is fully conscious again, it is already morning.

A headache licks at her as she sits up, looks around. Everything appears the same as it was last night, except that the custom-made porcelain doll, the one with eyes like a jackdaw's, has been moved from the boudoir here into her bedroom. It has been placed in a chair directly across from the bed.

She laughs, a tinny noise to her own ears. Dmitry likes to keep his collections together: his porcelains on display in one room, his Gzhel ceramics in another. As if they are galleries; as if the house is a museum.

In *this* room, he will keep his dolls.

Tonya has no tears left by the time Olenka enters with a tray and a newspaper. She looks blankly at the headlines. Tsar Nicholas II has just abdicated the throne. The three-hundred-year dynasty of the Romanovs is ended. The people of Russia have been set free. Olenka curtseys, coughs, and goes out again, locking Tonya in.

10

Rosie

I compose a letter to Richard that is full of deft little touches. I explain how our resident cockroaches frolic in the cocaine-like powder that is meant to kill them. How the electrical-voltage meltdowns are more reliable than the current. How the supermarket meat runs like it was just sluiced off the animal; how the cashier uses an abacus to calculate my total. I can imagine Richard reading this, smiling, enjoying the glimpse into daily life in Russia. But it is a superficial, touristy view. I could send a blank postcard of Red Square. It would have the same effect.

But what should I write instead?

I might be losing my mind. Or else I'm being haunted.

Or both.

I read and reread my words. I gnaw on my pen until the cap falls off.

Lev comes into the kitchen, enthusiastically greeting me, as ever, with a nod.

As soon as Alexey gets back from Leningrad, we'll be rethinking this little arrangement. In addition to acting like a surly shadow, Lev is too noticeable, too striking. I'm sure he knows it, too. It must be why he always wears a black jacket over a gray hoodie, with the hood pulled up. In July.

It won't be possible for me to blend into crowds when he splits them down the middle.

I turn the paper over. I give him my brightest smile. "Are you up for a longer drive today?"

*　*　*

I awaken to a soupy wind in my face, the open car windows letting in a puzzling mix of aromas: pine trees and wildflowers, wood tar and petrol. I must have fallen asleep on the motorway, because we already seem to be crossing the precise spot where city and country meet. This is Tula province, which I've always associated with country Russia: rolling hills and lakesides, troikas and teahouses, silver bells and painted windowsills. Tula is home to Yasnaya Polyana, erstwhile residence of Tolstoy, Mum's favorite writer.

But this is not Mum's fairy-tale universe.

The rural roads are unpaved, unmaintained, and as we drive on, the undergrowth thickens, darkens the landscape. A few elderly people sit on stumps, right there along the lanes, staring hard at nothing.

The silence was definitely less awkward when I was asleep. Lev hasn't even asked for directions. He maneuvers the Mercedes with disregard, one arm dangling out the window as he smokes. With every turn, the car shrieks in protest. It might not last the summer.

After miles of little but wilderness, a small log cabin material-izes between the trees. The unpainted door hangs off its hinges. Planks of wood are missing from the frame and porch rails. A noisy family of sparrows occupies the roof, and something dashes by, a blur of brown. More cabins emerge, degraded into shacks. A tableau of decay.

The village—Popovka, according to the map—has clearly been abandoned. These places often die off as the young people move to cities. We follow the single central road that cuts between the cabins, and Lev slows as I scrutinize them for any sign of human habitation.

A movement from one of the porches catches my eye.

It's a rocking chair.

It's rocking on its own. There's nobody in it. Back and forth, to and fro.

I edge away from my window, just as an old man appears in the doorway. He cradles something in his arms, stiff and straight, the way you would hold someone else's baby. His face is sallow; he might be younger than Alexey, but he has aged worse.

"Let's stop," I say. "He might be able to help."

The Mercedes shudders and dies. I smooth down my sum-mery frock, which sticks to the backs of my legs as I step out of the car. I haven't dressed for trekking through bramble. The mush-rooms beneath my feet make a crunching noise as I go closer, and now the object in the man's grasp takes shape. It's only a crum-pled piece of cloth.

Nature is reclaiming all of this, the land, the village, the vil-lager, but it will never have that rag.

"Good day." I stumble over the greeting. "We've come from

Moscow, looking for a house that's supposed to be not far from here. Called Otrada?"

The old man's eyes are dusty with cataracts. "I know Otrada," he says, shifting the rag-ball to his other arm. "Come, come inside."

I follow him before I can think too hard about it, with Lev close behind.

The interior of the cabin is cramped and dismal. One corner overflows with Orthodox icons and candle stubs; pushed against another is a thatch-covered bag of dirt that I suspect to be a bed. Beside the long, silent stove stand a slanted table and a pyramid of food jars, not unlike Mum's own collection. Their contents appear monstrous, the white sweet onions like human eyeballs, the gherkins like fetuses.

There are no chairs, only a wooden bench at the table. Our host indicates we should sit, and so we sit. The bench is also slanted. I unfold the doll-head map and show him the smudge of a drawing.

"Where did you get this map?" the old man asks me.

Lev sighs.

"It was my mother's," I say, ignoring him. "She left it in our apartment."

"There is nobody at Otrada anymore."

"Could you tell me the way?"

"There is no way." His voice sharpens. "Not in, not out."

Between the old man's obstinance, Lev's sulky presence, and the wet, earthy smell of the cabin, my patience is starting to thin. I look around for anything that might help. There's some old correspondence on the table: *Dear Kirill Vladimirovich* . . . I glance out the window, impatiently, toward the car.

And then I smell something else.

Charcoal.

The image of a house begins to fill my mind. No, not a house, only ruins, in the grip of greedy vines, in the middle of a desolate field, a few weeds and wildflowers sprouting through. On all sides looms a white birch forest, the trees stripped of bark, like people stripped of . . .

Until this moment, the mysterious smells never evoked anything but my own memories. They never took me beyond the borders of my own life.

This is different. I've never been to this place.

I turn to the old man. My mouth feels funny. "Was there a fire?"

His pupils grow large in my direction. It doesn't help him see me.

"Please, Kirill Vladimirovich. My name is Raisa," I say wildly. I can feel Lev's gaze burning holes into me, but I don't care. "My mother has sent me here, to find Otrada. So that I can understand what happened to my family—"

"Take this," the old man commands, holding out the ball. The rag is so ratty, so disgusting, that it can't shake itself loose. He says, louder now: "Take it. *Take it!*"

I take it. I'll *eat* it, if it means he'll help me.

He opens his mouth and I think he's going to ask for it back, but instead, he *sings*. He sings a line from that famous wartime ditty "The Blue Kerchief," and then he sings another, another. Somewhere in there, beneath the leathery skin and the cataracts and the anguish of dementia, is someone who desperately wants to do more than sing. I can almost hear that person screaming from within.

As he warbles on, the only thing I can think with any certainty is that the cloth he has just handed me is not blue. It is in that no-man's-land of color. Too long faded.

He's too long faded.

"Thank you for your hospitality," I say, folding the map back up. "We'll get out of your way."

The old man spits and crosses himself. "You have to go on foot," he says, almost a hiss. "Find the creek, and follow it down to the lake. On the other side, through the birch . . ."

A short pause. "And then?"

"And then . . ." His face has gone as gray as the rag. His eyes roll back in his head. Then he stops. A smile appears on those crusty lips, so vacant it is almost sinister. Whatever chance I just had is gone. He has withdrawn to the refuge he has found for himself in his mind.

* * *

The sky has turned a resplendent, radiant purple, heralding the romantic stretch of evening before the light will wane and turn this village into a graveyard. I thought the house would be impossible to find, but it sits squarely at the end of what may have been a carriage path, on the opposite side of the lake from the village, just as the old man described. An hour's hike, one way. We'll have to turn around now if we don't want to bivouac out here.

But the house is no longer a house.

Just those blackened walls, choked by creepers, in a forlorn field.

I was right. I wish I'd been wrong. It's one thing to remember things that have happened to me, even if by force; but this is a more insidious violation. Like somebody grabbed hold of my mind not to pull out something old, but to shove in something new.

Lev is checking his watch.

"Just a minute. I want a better look," I say.

"It's not easy to drive these roads in the dark."

"Maybe try something lower than fifth gear?"

He glowers at me. I step past him, go closer, and the walls get taller, taller, until I am treading on the vines, knotted and gnarled, thick as rope. This near to the house, there are no wild-flowers. The ground has been scorched clean.

So why is there a smear of color?

I know what it is even before I've pulled it free of the creeper limbs. Their grasp is strong enough that it's like trying to shake off a person. *This* doll, long exposed to the elements, looks much older than the one in the *stenka*. Its hair is limp, slicked down around the cheeks. The face is girlish, gruesome, marred by what look like animal bite marks.

"Of all the things to survive a fire," Lev mutters, coming up behind me.

"It didn't." I wrap the hair around the head, as not to lose the skullcap by accident. "It's perfect. Not burned at all. Someone left it here *after* the house was destroyed."

Was it Mum? Leaving dolls everywhere she went, like sacrificial offerings?

"But why . . . ?" He doesn't bother to specify. There's no one question that can encompass all of this.

I turn to him to say that we can leave, but Lev seems transfixed by the remains of the house, now that we are right on its threshold. Otrada must have been immense, in its time, but now that I have what I came for, I don't want to explore further. I already know what's left, after everything else burns down. Charred remains. A lifeless shell. Emptiness at the heart of it all, but just enough still standing, to look normal from afar.

* * *

*T*ick, tock, tick, tock, says the clock on my bedroom wall. I've switched off the lights, but I can't make the mental images go dark: that husk of a house, the grasping vines, the naked birch. I pull my blanket higher. I am tempted to pull it right over my head.

A sound, a whisper, shatters the silence like glass.

One, two . . .

I stay stock-still in bed. Like an animal playing dead. *It's the wind in the trees. It's Lev, still awake himself, outside on the balcony. It's Alexey, back from Leningrad. It's . . . it's—*

It's in the room with me.

I squeeze my eyes shut. With my eyes still closed, I try to turn on the bedside lamp. It's not working. Again. It works during the day. I know it does. I'll try again. I reach out, stretching for the switch.

Somebody else's hand is on it.

I hear screaming, so loud it hurts my head. A shrieking, a primal sound, and it's me. It's coming from me.

"Hey!" Lev is there. The overhead light is instantly on. He sits down on my bed and grips my shoulders, hard, but I'm still screaming, and finally he shouts over me: *"Hey!"*

All I can do is point, helplessly, to the lamp. Lev finds the switch. It turns on, emits its usual pasty light.

"Blyad'," he says, leaning back. There's a cussword I haven't heard in a while. I'd laugh if I could breathe deep enough, after all that screaming. "What happened?"

"There's somebody— There was . . ." How am I going to make the case to Alexey now, that I don't need a bodyguard? I'll be lucky if he doesn't hire even more. Lev is saying that he'll have a look around, but he doesn't think there's anyone here. He sounds pretty sure. Maybe he patrols the hallways at night. Maybe no one sleeps in this house.

Nothing sleeps—

"I just— I have an overactive imagination." I'm not convincing myself, let alone him. "It actually feels sometimes . . . like I'm being haunted." *Shut up, Ro, shut up!* I can't shut up. It's the middle of the night. I am in my pajamas, in a room designed to make anyone feel about five years old, and I'm seeing monsters in the dark.

"Haunted?" he repeats. "You knew someone who died?"

"My family." It's out of my mouth before I realize.

His eyes are solemn, like a fox's. "Bad deaths?"

"They were killed. They . . . I'm here in Moscow to find out who killed them." I can feel the valve finally releasing, the pressure lifting. I slump against my pillow, eyeball the ceiling, press my palms together until I can't sense whatever it is I just touched. I always thought it was because of Mum that I could never say any of this aloud. But in fact, it's that I'm afraid of it, in England. I don't want it to contaminate my future.

Here in Moscow, I've already lost everything. In a way, it's liberating. Who cares what I say? What I do? What happens to me? Haven't I already lived my worst nightmare?

"Are you a detective?"

"I'm a PhD student," I say croakily. "I study codes. Encryption."

"Convenient for solving mysteries."

Was that sarcasm? "I'm not so sure. All I do know is that I'll never give up. There's an answer, and I'll keep going until I have it. However long it takes." I'm now regretting this moment of weakness. "Anyway, I didn't mean to disturb you. I'm sorry."

"Nichego."

We sit for a moment in the usual hideous silence before he makes a move toward the door.

"Good thing Alexey's in Leningrad, huh?" I say, for some reason not wanting to end on *nichego*. Nothing.

"Alexey Alexeyevich is in Moscow."

I sit up straighter. "What do you mean?"

A shrug. "He stays at the apartment the government gave him. On Vorovsky."

An apartment—? On Embassy Row? Did I mishear him say Leningrad? Alexey must want his privacy; I can understand that. But the idea of this eerie storybook house, tucked away in a forest, left to its fate, of an owner who visits only by day, is unsettling.

He's tucked me away too, hasn't he?

Get a grip, Rosie!

I leave the lights on after Lev departs. I'll leave them on all night, every night, from now on. Alexey can afford the bill. Alexey, who secretly spends his nights elsewhere. I still can't wrap my head around it, any of it. I may not have read History, but I know something is off about my role. You don't hire an assistant and then give her a week's holiday first thing. My note-taking on the list of books he prepared for me, meanwhile, just feels like faff. Alexey *lived* through all the things in those books. Does he really need my help understanding them?

What does it mean?

It means my head aches, and I can't sleep anyway, so I get out of bed. Whatever Alexey is up to, it's a secondary problem. I slide the latest doll out of my bag, the Otrada-doll. I unwrap her hair. My pulse barely ticks as I prize off the head circle. Maybe if I'd known how easily they come apart, the dolls never would have scared me to begin with.

Alright, Mum, what's next? Where will you take me?

The Great
and Terrible Monster

In a faraway kingdom, in a long-ago land, the townspeople were afraid of a monster said to live in the sewers. They whispered to themselves of his hunger, his cruelty, how his teeth were like needles and his eyes as yellow as yolks, how his fingers were sausages, his fingernails meat hooks.

One day the monster burst out of the gutters and began his rampage. He seized and slaughtered. He was worse than the people had feared, because he did not look the way they had feared. He looked like one of them. He did not have meat-hook fingernails or needles for teeth. When the king's soldiers came to defend the city, they did not know whom to kill. So the monster was free to do as he wished, and everything that the townspeople had ever prophesized came true.

That was when a woman who lived in the town murdered her husband.

She stabbed him with a knife and threw him over a bridge and into a river. Her husband's body disappeared into the water, and she thought of how, at any other time, she wouldn't have been able to get away with it. But now, even if he did resurface downriver, he would do so alongside a hundred other blubbery corpses. Dukes and duchesses, schoolmarms and ship merchants, cheese makers and undertakers.

He would be one more body that no one would notice.

11

Valentin

The morning light breaks over the city he loves, turns all the rooftops golden. Valentin's eyes sting as if he spent the night buried in sand. He glances up and down the river, but he is seeing double, likely from sleeplessness.

Double of everything and everyone. And none of Tonya.

The corniced mansions along the Fontanka shimmer like a mirage. Only the street sweepers are out at this hour, and they look at Valentin as if he is litter, as if they might brush him away too. He trudges on, until at last he sees it, *her* house, pink granite, proud looking. It was built not too long ago, apparently, replacing an original structure. The bourgeois do prefer things to be new. It is a way of possessing them more completely.

There is only one balcony, curving around the central window on the second floor. Behind it, a tremor of movement, and Valentin turns away, pulls up his collar. He'll go around back as always, to the separate, sordid entrance, for people without calling cards.

He knocks at the back door. His hands are cracked, bleeding from cold. He wipes at the blood, futilely.

A maidservant answers. She has a frown that looks permanent and deep lines etched into her forehead, disappearing into her white cap. "Delivery?" she says.

"I have a message for Antonina Nikolayevna," Valentin says, roughly. "Will she see me?"

"My mistress is not well," she says, with a sniff. "Who are you?"

"Valentin Andreyev."

"Wait here."

He turns the corner, lights a cigarette, tries not to panic. There *was* an unusual sheen to her face yesterday. He hates that he needs it to be true: She was not well, so she could not come. He will stop by the bookstalls on the way home, look for something she might like. He will read to her every night, instead of the other way round, until she is well again—

"Is anybody there?"

Valentin ducks back into the yard. A different maid steps past the threshold, this one in a plain black gown and no cap, her hands behind her back. It's the one he spoke to the last time he was here. People like her will be hardest to liberate, when the real revolution comes. They have been in servitude so long they won't know how to stand, even when there's no one holding them down.

"Sir," she says in her froggy voice, "Antonina Nikolayevna does not wish to see you again."

"You remember me, don't you?" he says urgently.

"I have been told to inform you, sir—"

"Told by whom?"

The girl produces whatever she had been fumbling with behind her back. Not just her hands, but a piece of paper torn from personal stationery, with Tonya's initials embossed in the corner. The paper reads:

> *I loved you, and perhaps the love in my soul has not entirely diminished*
> > *But let it not trouble you any longer. . . .*

Valentin looks from the lines to the frayed-looking maidservant and back again. Tonya has recited this famous poem to him many times; it is in her most beloved volume. As he stares at the sheet of paper, he recalls how sweet her lips looked as she spoke the words, how he heard none of them. He never paid attention to the poetry itself. He felt lovesick enough on his own, without any help from Pushkin.

All he ever saw was Tonya.

This is what he missed.

> *I have loved you so sincerely, so softly,*
> > *May God grant that another loves you as I have.*

The maid coughs. "She requires that you do not return, sir."

Valentin stumbles back to the street, to the embankment. He tears up the sheet of paper, lets the pieces go over the rail, into the river, which is still only ice; every piece is carried away by the wind. He makes it as far as he can away from the house, picking up whatever he can find off the ground, snow, sticks, a broken umbrella, throws it all, viciously, over the rail into the river. It is still only ice. It is all only ice.

* * *

A girl like that wants what she can't have. They told him so. He has no one to blame but himself.

He couldn't have honestly thought she would live in a basement.

He convinced himself, yesterday, of something impossible, because the impossible was already occurring. The promise and glory of revolution, the red flags waving amidst the plumes of smoke; all of it blinded him.

Never again. He will never make this mistake again.

The cold slinks around him like a serpent. Valentin can't bear to go home. He could go to Viktoria's, but he'll save that kind of mistake for later. He cannot unclench his fists, and the streets are full of people to fight, but he's liable to kill someone or let them kill him. If he goes to work, if he sees Dmitry Lulikov's sneering face, he will pummel it into pieces. Nor does he wish to hear talk of a potential strike. The time to strike, even to negotiate, has passed. It is time for an uprising. He will lead it himself.

Let Tonya see the blood-red banners of the Bolsheviks hang from every window across Piter. Let it remind her of the ribbon he once tied around her wrist.

But before he does all that, he will go to Pavel's. Pavel will smack his cane against the ground, deliver a harsh talking-to: *Better that it happened now, at this tender age, so you'll have got it out of your system.*

She was a disease, boy, but you'll be stronger for having sur-vived it.

Yes, Valentin had another family once; yes, he used to be somebody else; yes, with Tonya, he was that somebody again.

He doesn't know *why* it felt like that, with her. He doesn't know how. But Valentin does know this: He may never be rid of the past, but nor can she, or anyone, bring it back. Tonya, in the end, is nothing more than any other petty bourgeois. She will have to pay. They will all have to pay.

12

Antonina

The servants have stripped Tonya's bedroom bare. Her furniture is removed, her shelves, her vases, even the rose-oil lamps. The only things left are a chamber pot and the doll. The doors to the balcony are now locked too. Olenka brings meals on a tray, but Tonya eats so little and vomits so often that even if she did make it out to the balcony, the wind might carry her off.

Dmitry still takes daily tea with her, only now the tea service is rolled into her bedroom. The doll sits there in the chair between them, with its gutted gaze. Tonya has never been so desperate for teatime to last. The tea has less taste than water, but she drinks whole cups of it. She listens to Dmitry's reports of the outside world: A Provisional Government rules Russia now, though it contains many of the same ministers and officials as the old Imperial regime. The Tsar and his family have been banished to the Alexander Palace at Tsarskoye Selo.

"How it must feel," she says through her teeth, "to be imprisoned in one's own home."

"It's the doctor's advice, Tonyechka."

"Can I not go out onto the balcony? I need the air, the sunlight—"

"It's almost summer. It'll never be dark at all then."

"I won't jump," she persists, "if that's what you fear."

Dmitry looks to the doll as if for guidance, but then the doll has become a more recognizable version of Tonya than she herself is. Its face is not sticky and sour; its hair has not grown matted as wool. And unlike her, it never resists him. He moves it around as he pleases. He should have married the doll.

"My mother has been asking for you," he says, a tad irritably. "I suppose we could find a time for you to see her."

"I can read to her," says Tonya, seizing on this. "Every day, as I used to!"

"You mustn't stray too far from the bed. You are carrying my baby, Tonya."

His baby. It would be his, not theirs. He can't even *think* otherwise, because everything else *is* his. Even if Nicholas II is no longer in power, there are many more in this city who have not given up their thrones. Perhaps there will have to be yet another revolution before the people can truly have anything of their own. Even their babies.

"After the baby comes, you should go up to the dacha," Dmitry continues, "get away from the city for a while. You liked it there last summer, didn't you?"

"Why not just send me to Tsarskoye Selo?"

He looks at her sternly. "Don't speak to me like that. I am your husband."

"*Husband?* You are my jailer!"

"Hold your tongue, Tonyechka, or I will cut it off."

In one of the other rooms, Dmitry keeps a vast collection of handcrafted snow globes. Tonya thinks of them sometimes. She wonders if it is worse when the snow is falling, when the world is shaking, or when it stops. When you can shriek until you lose your voice, without making any sound.

* * *

The fire has died, but the grate still shivers. Anastasia lies flat beneath her blankets. Even the pillows no longer elevate her head. She is humming off-key. She has had too much morphine. The body thrums with too much morphine. The brain slows. Tonya remembers how Papa often was, after Mama died, the way his eyes glided over everything, caught on nothing.

Tonya takes a seat on the divan, as if it were any other visit. She feels weak, tremulous.

Anastasia's good eye rotates her way.

"If I may beseech you, Anastasia Sergeyevna," Tonya begins, "to speak to Dmitry on my behalf, to ask if I may be allowed out of my room—"

"Oh, child," says Anastasia. "You are a hand-fed lapdog who dreams of hunting elk in the wild, who has no notion of how lucky it is! My son takes wondrous care of you. Better than you deserve."

Tonya blows out a strand of hair, sucks it back in.

"Especially right now. You would not last ten minutes, without him." Anastasia gives a reedy laugh.

"I would rather be dead than live like this."

The mirth flees the old woman's face. "You're an ungrateful

little whore," she says, "and if you weren't carrying my grand-child, I'd see to it that you got your wish."

Tonya is the one to laugh now. Even if the events of these few months—the founding of the new government, the Tsar being run out of the city, the masses rising up—are amusing to people like Anastasia Sergeyevna, it's clearly not amusing to them when it happens in their households. A revolution on the streets, that's as may be. But a revolution in *here*, that is an entirely different thing.

"It's not your grandchild." She is still laughing. She has been feeling all pretense fall away lately, like she is shedding skin. "It's not *his* baby."

There is a long silence in which she thinks her mother-in-law may have already died.

"Dmitry left Petrograd in December, and was gone well past a month," Tonya continues, savagely now. "I last bled around Christmas."

"That's not what Olenka said." The old woman's voice is full of holes. "You must be mistaken. What does a girl like you know about babies?"

"I know the ones my mother lost. I know what they look like when they are born too soon. When the only breath they take is blood! When they must be wrapped up and buried in the or-chards! When—"

"Stop it. Stop it at once!" says Anastasia, but then her head droops once more. "Once you are a mother," she says, in a differ-ent voice, "you will understand me, Tonya. You'll see how helpless we all are in loving our children. Whoever your child is, you will forgive him anything."

"No," says Tonya hazily, "I won't."

"I promise you, you will." One tear falls, out of the good eye.

"We will speak no more. It cannot be borne. Read something to me, as you used to, before you go."

Tonya has not brought along a book. She no longer has any. There are no books in here, and in any case the light is so limited. But if she says nothing, she will be sent back to her room.

Make it up.

What? You can't just make it up.

Of course, you're right. I forgot. Where do stories come from again . . . ?

"In a faraway kingdom," she says, as Anastasia begins to hum once more, low and light, "in a long-ago land . . ."

The humming stops. Tonya looks to see if Anastasia is still awake. Anastasia's eyes are open.

The bad one is clearer than the good one.

It's not such a bad way to die, listening to a fairy tale, and Tonya keeps going, in case her mother-in-law's spirit is still in the room and wants to hear more. The old woman was not evil, after all. She once gave Tonya a handkerchief. A pretty handkerchief for a pretty little girl, even if it is gone forever, by now, and so is the little girl.

* * *

Dmitry motions for her to make space in the bed. The cloying stench of liquor seems to form a cloud around him. He says he wants to tell her about Anastasia's funeral, which Tonya was not permitted to attend. They had a small *litia* in church. Anastasia will be buried by the dacha at Tenevoe.

"It is beautiful up there," he says.

Tonya does not answer. Beautiful and remote. There will be no witnesses if Dmitry imprisons her there. Buries her too.

Tonya was sixteen years old the day she met Dmitry. It was spring and the orchards of Otrada were beginning to bloom. She was coming in from the creek with Nelly, the two of them holding up their skirts and bast shoes, giggling madly. She was carrying a posy of wildflowers in her free hand. They turned toward the house, and a man was standing there, on the veranda—

"Mother died happy. She spoke of nothing but the baby, in the final weeks." Dmitry removes his cravat. His breath is strong and tart. "Should I have Olenka run you a bath? Fix you something to eat? Whatever you want, Tonyechka. You're the lady of the house now."

After Nelly ran off, still giggling, the newcomer introduced himself. He was from the capital. He was visiting the area, had heard of her family, had come to pay his respects. He offered Tonya his arm—

"I want"—she grinds the words out—"to leave my room."

"It's not safe."

"You don't care about my safety. You don't want me to go to *him*."

Dmitry slaps her, cleanly, across the face.

The blow is hard, but Tonya feels nothing. They have never spoken of the affair, of the real reason he keeps her here, but why shouldn't they? Why shouldn't he admit that he would sooner see Tonya stuffed and hung above the mantelpiece, rolled out like a rug in one of his display rooms, than let her go? Why shouldn't she beg him to do it, so that she does not have to go on like this?

"Do you know who *he* is?" she spits.

Dmitry hesitates, long enough that she can see he doesn't. It seems that Natalya kept some of Tonya's secrets, at least. The servants, too—the whole household, from top to bottom.

Maybe they knew what he would do, if he found out.

She is going too far. But she feels so light, so loose-limbed, that she no longer cares. "You *know* him, Mitya. His name is Valentin Andreyev. He is the leader of the Vyborg Committee. He is their speaker in the union. He is head of the workers' militia—"

He hits her hard again, and then again, this time drawing blood from her nose.

"The baby is his. It is *mine!*" Her screams explode between them. "No matter how long you keep me in here, it will never be yours! *I* will never be yours!"

The alcohol in his system has dulled. She can tell by the way Dmitry climbs astride her, the way he might move a chess piece. With painstaking care. He straddles her and she begins to spread her legs, wanting it to be over, but he holds her in place. Tonya opens her mouth but nothing emerges, so she clamps down on her tongue until it's bleeding too and the pain bursts out of her eyes instead but still she doesn't make a sound, even as the blows are different, deeper, intended to lay waste.

"I hope you're happy now, Tonyechka," Dmitry says, from somewhere, "because you have just signed his death warrant."

In taking his arm, Tonya dropped her wildflowers.

She has often thought how they must have looked later, abandoned in the soft earth, the stems broken, the color lost, the petals crushed into nothing.

* * *

"Please drink, Antonina Nikolayevna." It is Olenka. "You have gone a day without."

Tonya sits up, somewhat, with a moan. She accepts the cup

and spills water down her nightgown, but there is already wetness in the bedsheets. She submerges her hands in it, this plummy
liquid, and then she holds her fingers up. They are webbed with
blood.

"It is less now," says Olenka mournfully.

"Why am I . . . ?"

Olenka hangs her head. "The doctor thinks you have lost your
pregnancy."

Tonya gazes at her hands. She is not sure what she hopes
to see.

The baby couldn't have had a good hold in there to begin
with, and Dmitry jarred it loose. He cracked Tonya open at last
and something fell out—but she was the one who waited too long.
She should have run away from him before any of this. Instead
she let herself and her unborn child ripen, mold, split like summer
fruit gone to spoil.

She feels oddly dry. Perhaps she has already bled out. She
looks back at Olenka, who appears terrified and has begun to
cough.

"Olenka," Tonya says, "you must help me."

The maid only coughs harder.

"I can't stay here any longer. You must unlock the door for me
tonight."

"Oh." Olenka's eyes are wide and pained. "I can't—"

"Was there never in your life," says Tonya raggedly, "a time
when you needed somebody to take pity on you, when no one
else would? Has one person's kindness never made all the difference? I know there is such kindness in you, Olenka. I know it!"

"I can't, Antonina Nikolayevna," is the meager reply.

"You *must*!"

The maid begins to weep, over her coughing. It makes a wretched cacophony. Tonya thinks for one wild moment that she can simply overpower Olenka, that she must look like a madwoman anyhow, a murderer, in these stained sheets, with these stained hands, and it does happen, that women come apart after they lose a baby. It happened, at times, to Mama. She feels it, even without saying it, the swell of insanity.

"Anastasia is dead," says Tonya, keeping her voice a hush. "There's nothing to keep you here either. You should take everything you can carry that's of any value, and leave this house. Don't you know that they are building a new Russia out there, while we languish in this one? We must all take sides in the end, Olenka. Or they will be taken for us."

* * *

It must be near midnight, but the sky looks only a deep maroon, marred by fog. The season will tip soon into summer, just as Dmitry said. How long has she been in here? Weeks? Months? She should have kept track. Should have marked the walls with her nails, instead of breaking them off trying to scratch through the door.

Tonya tries the door handle. She dares for a second to hope—
Unlocked.

Olenka has left it unlocked, and Dmitry appears to have made no other provisions to prevent an escape attempt. The doll does not even keep watch over her boudoir, anymore. There are no trapdoors in the floors, no barricades in the corridors. Tonya's legs are unsteady, her body off-balance, and as she descends the stairs one ankle lands badly. She makes it through to the front foyer and looks behind her. There is a slinky stream of blood leading up to her heels.

She plods on like an injured animal. Outside, the moon shines through the fog. It is crisp but not cold. She will keep to the Fontanka embankment until she reaches the Neva, will stay close to the water all the way into the Vyborg.

There is little sound on the streets except for the cry of birds, the lapping of the water.

"Tonya!"

Keep going, keep going—

"Tonya, stop!"

How can it be? How could he know? How could he have heard? But she has bled all the way from the house. She has led him directly to her.

"Tonya." Dmitry has her by the arm. His grip is iron. She tries to go limp, hopes he will loosen his hand. He doesn't. "Come home," he says. "Look at you! Thank goodness I found you before someone else did."

Her reserve of strength, her resolve, is gone. She is about to reply, to ask him to kill her, because she would rather be sent to the bottom of the river than return to that house, and the baby's dead anyway, it's finished, it's all finished. But before she can speak, she sees movement in the mist. A flash of red. Bright, blazing, as a bonfire. There is somebody coming.

Now she hears a new voice. It is her own.

"Help," she shouts.

"Be quiet," says Dmitry. "Let's go home—"

"Help me! Please, help me!"

She doesn't know if they will. She doesn't know who they are. But she sees them approaching. Roving, as if they are on the lookout for prey. Young men, rail thin and flat eyed beneath their wayward mops of hair. She sees the red again: the bands of the Bolsheviks, tied around their upper arms. One of them carries, extended in his hand, a hunting knife with a birch handle, the kind that a peasant might use to gut a goat. He is clearly their leader.

"What goes on here?" he asks.

"A private matter," says Dmitry, tersely. "She is my wife."

Tonya sees the youths stiffen. They don't believe in *private*, or possibly even in wives. Dmitry may not understand them, but she does.

She has seen one of them up very close.

In a faraway kingdom, in a long-ago land . . .

"He's lying," she cries. "He's not my husband. He is a bourgeois! I am one of you! Please, Comrade!" She pulls furiously on her sleeve, reveals the red ribbon that still clings to her wrist. *"All power to the Soviet!"*

It is enough. Maybe it's what they've been looking for. The young men encircle her and Dmitry and two of them grab Dmitry by both arms and Tonya wrests away from him. She watches as the one with the knife plunges it into Dmitry's side. Once, hard. Deep.

Her mouth tastes coppery. Dmitry sways like a pocket watch on a chain before he falls. Stillness for a moment, and then the others drag her husband to the side of the rail, preparing to throw him into the water. Tonya asks if they can pull the coat off the body. She puts it on over her sullied nightgown. The youth with the blade is wiping it off on his armband, red against red. *When the true socialist revolution comes, blood will run through this city like any other river,* Valentin said to her once. A warning. Or perhaps a vow.

* * *

She will sleep when she gets there. She only has to make it there. She tells herself on every corner to go one block farther. She has no idea what time it is, only that it's darker now, that the moon has slipped behind shards of gray clouds. Rain begins to fall as Tonya turns into Valentin's courtyard. The stairs leading down are the most difficult. The streets have torn holes into her slippers.

She knocks on his door. No answer.

"Valentin?" she calls out, faintly.

The rain shows no sign of slowing. Thunder rolls overhead. She can feel another rivulet of blood on her inner thigh. He will understand, of course. No matter how long it takes her to explain.

The door opens, only an inch.

"It's me, Valya, it's just me!" The rain pounds the steps behind her, punctuates her words. She is soaked. Nearly wilted. She doesn't want to talk anymore, only wants to be near him. "Please, let me in—"

The door opens wider. Standing there is a young woman with sweaty-damp, light brown hair, her arms and shoulders bare, a sheet pulled around the rest of her body. Her large doe-eyes blink rapidly at Tonya.

"I thought I recognized the voice," the woman exclaims. "We've met before. You remember me? Viktoria Pavlovna?"

"Oh," says Tonya dumbly. "I don't—"

"If you're looking for Valentin, he won't be back for a few hours. Shall I tell him you stopped by? Just remind me of your name. Was it Anna? Anya?"

"Tonya." It is all she can manage.

"Could *this* be yours?" asks Viktoria, extending an arm. Her smile seems to drip down her face. "I've been doing some cleaning, since moving in, and I found it by the bed. I've been wondering whose it might be. You know our Valya, it's hard to narrow down the options. . . ." A syrupy laugh.

It is Anastasia Sergeyevna's handkerchief.

The gold thread glints obscenely against the drab background of everything around. Tonya nods, takes it wordlessly, keeps nodding so that her wet hair falls in her face, until she can't see well enough to tell if anyone is still there. She backs away, up the cellar steps, turns, and compels herself to keep going. The same way she came, one foot in front of the other.

The rain falls hard as bullets. There is water in her eyes, on her lips, no matter how much of it she wipes away.

* * *

Tonya pays the servants advance wages, tells them to pack their bags. She sells or barters away everything of value. She likes the house much better now that there is nobody and nothing in it, but she has no choice but to return to Otrada. To Papa. She cannot stay here. The larder is empty. The breadlines are impossibly long. Petrograd is in complete disarray; people are leaving in droves. As a result, she has not had to explain Dmitry's absence to anyone.

Until the Countess Burtsinova and her daughter, Akulina, come to call.

Natalya's presence is abrupt and yet predictable. The Countess never fails to turn up when Tonya is least prepared to receive her. A day or two later, and Tonya would already be gone, but as it is, she has nothing to offer her guests, not even tea. This morning she ate her last slices of rye, soaked in sunflower oil, thickened with water. She may not eat again until she is back in her village.

"Where is Dmitry?" asks Natalya sharply, with a glance to both ends of the Blue Salon as if he might be hiding in a corner.

"He left," says Tonya.

"Left where?"

"I'm . . . not certain," she says, focusing steadfastly on the waves painted into the wallpaper. It is meant to look like the sea. People are supposed to be able to submerge themselves in it. She does feel a little like she is underwater.

Make it up—make something up—

"You do not *know*?" Natalya's voice is like a horsewhip. "This beggars belief. Dmitry wouldn't leave without telling me. Let me talk to the servants myself, then, and see if I can't scare it out of them. Where are they? Or have they all run off too?"

"I had to dismiss them."

"*Dismiss* them!"

"There has been a lot of trouble at the factory," says Tonya, absently, as if it is only now occurring to her. "The strikes, the violence . . ."

Natalya's fingers knead her silver cross like dough. "And so?"

"They say the union is up in arms. That many have joined the Red Guards. It's happening everywhere, but it is worst in the Vyborg." Tonya shifts her gaze from the wallpaper, back to Natalya. "My sense, Natalya Fyodorovna, is that something may have happened to Dmitry. Because you are right. He would not just leave. He is meticulous in his methods."

"You mean that the workers might have hurt him?" is the lash of a reply.

"The whole world has been turned upside down. Who can say what has happened? What is happening?"

Natalya's eyes have narrowed into pinpoints. "Or perhaps just one worker, with his own reasons."

Tonya attempts a scoff. "Valentin Andreyev has better things to do."

"If it *was* your Bolshevik, if he's dared to lay a finger on Dmitry," says the Countess, "he will suffer for it. If anyone has hurt Dmitry, I will repay. You know I will. Fair is fair."

This fixation with *fairness.* Natalya should have become a Bolshevik herself.

"In any case, leave it to me, darling," Natalya says, breezily now. "What's to become of *you*? You would be safest up at Tenevoe. You remember, from last summer? I visit my own dacha at least once a month, and I am thinking of stashing the children there—if Akulina would only agree to go," she adds, with a glance in the direction of her silent daughter.

Tonya has entirely forgotten Akulina's presence. For somebody with such fiery hair, she fades very easily into the wallpaper.

"I'm leaving for Otrada," says Tonya.

Natalya makes a moue of distaste. "What on earth is that?"

"My family's home. In Tula."

"Gracious. How would I reach you there? If need ever be?"

There are no telegraph machines in any of the nearby villages. The post is inconsistent at best. Tonya retrieves one of the atlases from the study and tears out a map of Tula province.

Under Natalya's watchful eye, she draws a rough symbol for a house next to her village. *Otrada*. It doesn't seem likely that she and Natalya will ever see each other again. Tonya may never see anyone from Petrograd, ever again. In time, the only reminders she will have of these years will be the shadow-kicks she sometimes feels low in her belly, as if her body cannot comprehend that the baby is gone.

Natalya offers her some money and Tonya accepts even though money is useless now, with inflation, and she escorts her guests out to the foyer. The Countess stops to stare into the towering cabinets where Dmitry's precious trinkets used to stand. Sold, Tonya explains, briskly. Everything has been sold. It is all in the grubby hands of pawnbrokers and street sellers.

But better that, than behind glass.

13

Rosie

MOSCOW, JULY 1991

Cyrillic cursive is nothing like the block letters of published Russian books or street signs.

I sit cross-legged on the living room floor, trying to make sense of the wrinkled handwritten pages I pulled out of Otrada-doll's head last night. The penmanship is coiled as a spring, and tiny. Each paragraph is taking me twenty minutes to decipher. It's turning into an unpleasantly warm morning, and I feel limp with fatigue. I almost wish Alexey would hurry back from his fake trip to Leningrad and give me proper work to do.

Lev comes in, sits on the sofa, chugs half a bottle of water. He looks as if he has never been more bored in his life.

"Can you keep the water away from these pages?" I ask wearily.

He half-smiles at me and begins to pull his hoodie over his head. The gray T-shirt underneath rides up his bare torso. Bloody *hell*. I try very hard to avert my eyes, and only end up looking harder. He shrugs off the hoodie, lowers his arms, catches me red-handed.

"Need some water, *devushka*?" he says.

My cheeks ignite. "If you're looking for something to do, I could use some help."

"With what?"

"Can you read this?" I hold up the first page, and Lev squints at it.

I would never have believed Mum capable of writing so closely, so carefully. Moreover, the pages are written in pencil. Mum never used pencils. She had a vicious allergy to them, or to erasers; she was always complaining that Papa left his pencils everywhere.

Could she have started using pencils anyway? Her eyes were so bloodshot at the end, it's not as if I would have been able to tell.

But the pages are fairy-tale stories. Her type of stories.

"I'm pretty sure my mother wrote all this," I say, mostly to persuade myself. "They're in her trademark style. . . ."

"This is Russian," Lev replies, in his own trademark style.

"I know that. I—"

"You can't *read* Russian?"

"I find cursive tricky. I haven't lived here in fourteen years. Remember?"

He frowns, rubs at his jawline.

"I know you don't think I should be here." Maybe I've inherited a touch of Mum's allergy, because my whole face feels hot and stretched. "And clearly you resent me for the fact that you're here. But I didn't hire you. I've tried to tell you to go, but you're staying. So, fine. If you don't want to help me, you don't have to, but stop sulking. Stop stomping around. And stop, stop calling me *devushka*."

His expression is as indecipherable as the cursive.

"You know what, I'm going to do this later," I say, standing up. "I'm going into the city center. I have to pick up some books. You are not coming. I do not wish to spend the day with you."

"I'll meet you at Red Square at five," he says, unperturbed. "I can drive you home."

"I'd really prefer to take the bus."

"I'll help you," he says. "With the reading."

"*Kozyol,*" I say, under my breath, and to my shock, he laughs.

As soon as I'm alone again, I make a pile of the pages. They have that aggravating, nerve-racking quality of old paper, like they might fall apart in my hands. I'll go through them later, I'll try to find clues, I'll probably see clues that aren't even there, but in the end, they're just story-scribbles. They're pure fantasy. They're Mum.

* * *

On a sunny Saturday, the open-air Vernissage market at Izmaylovo is overpopulated with tourists. Their cameras swing from their necks and their maps flap in the wind. They peer at the Cheburashka plush toys and birch-bark baskets and milky bottles of Stolichnaya while the more experienced shoppers, the native Muscovites, haggle with the vendors. The scent of coffee and tobacco fills in any gaps in the narrow lanes.

Mum often brought me and Zoya here as kids.

She seemed to know everyone. She'd make her rounds, chatting, laughing with vendors and customers alike, as if *she* were selling something, rather than the other way round. But Mum was always curtseying low as her fandom showered her with praise. Always holding her breath, seeing if their applause could outlast her.

I pass an array of baggy shawls and move on to a gleaming collection of samovars, followed by trays of diamond earrings; bracelets and necklaces in robin's-egg blue enamel; wooden Khokhloma handicrafts; miniatures and matryoshkas.

On the next table over is a display of porcelain dolls.

A broad-featured woman with dark chin whiskers spreads her arms wide across her wares. "Such a lovely girl," she says, picking up one of the dolls. I'm not sure whether she means me or the doll. It looks more alive than any in Mum's collection, the glass-blown brown eyes holding my gaze as the woman hands it over for my inspection. I wince at the false curve of the elbow, the sandy feel of the hair. I turn it over, trying not to be too obvious, looking for the line where the scalp can be split.

At the nape of the neck, there is a signature.

E. S. Rayevsky

It's the same artist who made Mum's dolls. At least the ones I have at the dacha.

The vendor is hovering, the way they all do, like sand flies. "You like it?" she asks. "Handmade, down to the heel. It is a craft that has been passed down in his family, generation to generation! Like lacquer painting in Fedoskino! His grandmother taught his father. . . ."

I widen my eyes, as if I'm impressed, just to keep from rolling them.

E. S. Rayevsky. The name means nothing to me. Mum might have bought her own porcelain dolls right here, at Izmaylovo, right while Zoya and I dashed between the stalls, right behind our backs. But Mum wasn't merely a hobbyist. She was utterly devoted to her collection. She and my father used to have such impassioned fights over supper about spending hard-earned money on *toddler-toys that you really should have outgrown by now, Katya* that she would end up heaving dishware at his head. It would shatter into a hundred pieces right behind his ear, and he wouldn't even blink. *More fish soup?* he would say to me and Zoya, while that soup slid down our walls.

Oh, how much I wanted to be like Papa in those moments. The one who never blinked. The one who could act like nothing happened.

Turns out Mum could do it too.

"I think the doll maker may have created some pieces for my mother, when she was alive," I say. "Would it be possible for me to speak with him?"

"Speak?" she echoes, a bit unhappily.

"I'll buy this one. But I'd like to"—I cast about for the right word in Russian—"commission another."

The woman frowns, the liver spots around her mouth quivering. "I can ask. You come back next week? What is your name?"

"Raisa Simonova," I say, handing her a wad of rubles, which she pockets eagerly, her sun-beaten mouth arranging itself into a smile. I fall back in line with the passing crowds, my new doll under my arm. Soon I'll have enough to open my own stall.

I reach the edge of the market and stop at the wooden bridge that leads away from the craft stalls. It's as busy as it ever was, in my childhood, and from here, it looks like nothing in Russia has changed. From here I can't watch the parliamentary debates on telly; can't hear the new liberal politicians taking on the hardline

Communists; can't read the covers of the independent newspapers on sale at the kiosks; can't see the long lines for the most basic goods wrapping around whole city blocks. From here, I can almost pretend that I am a child again. That I am going home to my whole family. That Papa and Zoya were never shattered on the walls, left in a hundred pieces on the floor, ruined beyond repair.

I cross the bridge anyway.

Watching a group of European tourists block the other end as they check their maps, I ache with homesickness for England. I could be using my bag as a pillow right now, seeing the blur of lights below as the airplane begins its descent into Heathrow. Richard would be at the gate to meet me.

Welcome back to your real life, Ro.

But I'm doing all this for Richard's sake too. For the sake of our future together.

They're the ones that died. I should be the one living.

* * *

A group of young men in grayish blue camouflage fatigues are gathered in front of the GUM department store in Red Square, leaning casually, gracefully, against its archways. They talk low, occasionally pausing to eyeball passersby. They have small metal badges pinned to their chest pockets and oval-shaped patches with a yellow insignia on their sleeves. Lev is the only one in civilian clothing, but he doesn't stand out. Whoever they are, he is too.

Military? Some kind of police?

One of them turns, just enough for me to see the lettering.

OMON.

The OMON are, among other things, crowd control. Riot police. Part of the repressive machinery of the Soviet state, designed to keep the people down and at arm's—or better yet, sniper's—length. I know them only by reputation: the "Black Berets." It's all anybody would want to know.

Lev separates from the pack. "You're late," he says, reaching me in a few strides.

"I missed the metro stop."

I feel off-center from staring too long at the colorful onion domes of St. Basil's Cathedral, and it doesn't get any better after we locate the car. He floors it, forces it into traffic, before I even have my door closed. The engine growls, the wheels catching, the gears grinding.

I lean against the door, trying to regain balance, at least in my head, but Lev is—for the first time—the first to speak.

"Who is Zoya?" he asks.

My entire body clamps down on the answer. I curl up, pull my legs into the seat.

"You were shouting the name last night," he says. "When I went into your room."

I don't remember saying it. "My older sister," I say almost inaudibly.

"Not too common a name. Like Raisa."

"Yeah. Well. My mother named us. She liked to stand out."

"You don't?"

"They're just names. Labels."

"But they can have a lot of power."

I glance at him in surprise, but he's still facing the road. He doesn't say anything further, and the noise of traffic quickly replaces conversation. He seems more restless than normal, even trying the radio, managing to snag onto a recording of *Swan Lake*. The music swells in crescendo, approaching a climax, and as the notes spill over, I want to spill over too. I want to tell somebody, anybody, everything, but all I know how to do is let it out in bursts. In screams. In names.

"Those soldiers, back in Red Square," I say neutrally. "You're OMON?"

"Until a month ago." His tone matches mine.

"You quit?"

"I was—temporarily reassigned. To this."

To *me*, is what he means. It's obviously a punishment, if a light one. People don't just drop in and out of the Black Berets. They don't join either, unless they have their own demons. Lev is looking over at me like he can hear my thoughts, and I rally a smile. When I think of the OMON, I think of them as one being, one entity. They are always faceless and featureless, behind their shields and balaclavas. It's strange to imagine them as individuals. As people.

* * *

Now that Alexey's back, he plans to stay only for dinner. Later tonight, he'll be headed to a formal function; he explains that there has been an unceasing flow of invitations and engagements since his return. Alexey Ivanov made it possible to talk about the gulag in Russia, and now people expect him never to stop.

"Have you managed any reading, Rosie?" he asks, sitting down with me in the living room.

"Three so far." I show him my spread of books and paper. "Do you want anything more specific?"

"I have something else in mind."

I put down my pen. This must be where the real work begins.

"I spotted this yesterday in a shop." To my dismay, Alexey pulls out yet *another* book. Its dust jacket is garishly new. "It's a memoir of the Russian Civil War, by an aristocrat called Natalya Burtsinova. She was famous—infamous—at the time. You know the years of the Civil War?"

Now I do. "1918 to 1922?"

"Burtsinova was arrested for smuggling and speculation by the Petrograd Cheka in 1920. She wrote this memoir in jail." Alexey sounds rueful, almost regretful. Maybe he knew her. Blimey, maybe he visited her in prison. "There are so many interesting people forgotten to history."

But *he* rose above the fray, didn't he? Alexey Ivanov will never be forgotten.

"This memoir—the original copy—was discovered in someone's basement a few years ago." Alexey turns his attention back to me. "I want you to find out whose basement it was."

"Oh," I say, unable to conceal my surprise. "Absolutely. I'll contact the publishers."

"I already did. It was given to them by Natalya's daughter. Her name is Akulina Burtsinova. She lives here in Moscow. I want you to go in person and talk to her."

Is it just me, or is he fobbing me off? Again? Is this a way of keeping me away from the *real* project, whatever it is? Just like I have to be kept away from his *real* residence?

"About Lev," I say, a bit guiltily.

"What about Lev?"

"Is he necessary? He's very nice...." To look at, if nothing else. "But I don't know if..."

Alexey's smile is as burnished as the book's cover. "I am a researcher, Rosie," he says. "I did my due diligence, before I hired you. Your sister and father were murdered here in Moscow when you were a child. The killer was not caught, not even identified. You and your mother used underground—anti-Soviet, if I understand correctly—connections to defect. She must have thought he would come back for the two of you. Kill you too."

That man could have killed me. He chose not to. I want to explain, but this is what Alexey does in all his talks, his lectures, his restaurant-serenades. He steals your ability to speak.

"I appreciate that you may have an ulterior motive in returning to Russia," he goes on. "You wish to—come to terms with your loss. But it's only been what, fourteen, fifteen years, Rosie? Has it never occurred to you that just as you have been waiting for your chance, that man has also been waiting for his?"

* * *

After dinner on the terrace, Alexey promptly leaves. Lev sits, smokes, reads over a story while I align the pages we've already gone through. There aren't too many, but I'm going to staple them together, make a small book of them.

Mum must have meant them to be a collection, the way she addresses the reader in the beginning.

I didn't know she needed readers. I didn't know Mum ever thought of anyone but herself.

You must close your eyes to see what I am about to show you....

I do close my eyes, for half a second. Nothing changes. When

I open them again, Lev is regarding me, appearing bemused. I break eye contact and return to sifting through the stories. Just look at this one: "The Silver Queen" is about a queen whose magical silver necklace enables her to live forever. If she removes it, she will die.

The story literally ends on a question mark. I feel myself flushing with something close to anger. Why didn't Mum believe in endings? In answers?

"Why are you reading these," asks Lev, "if you don't enjoy them?"

I close the makeshift book. "It's not that. I just don't see the point."

"The point of what?"

"Stories like these. My mother, she was always reading, daydreaming. She preferred to spend all her time in this world that was fake." I never realized how much I begrudged her that, until now. "It's probably why she didn't like *The Last Bolshevik*. Because it was true."

"Are these stories meant to be allegorical?" he asks, after a moment.

"I doubt it. She wasn't a subtle person. She just wanted entertainment. Escape."

"But she chose her words with care," he points out. "I see places where she erased the original word she used and wrote another."

That could be why it had to be pencil. It *still* bothers me; I never saw her with a pencil. But who knows what she got up to when I wasn't around? It's like Mum was another one of her porcelain dolls, only I never had the chance to pop *her* head open. See what was hidden inside. Well, I lost my chance. She's been cremated.

Dark thoughts, Ro.

"All this reading has to do with your family," he notes. "With you, trying to—understand the crime. Why you've come back to Russia."

"Yup."

Lev leans over, stabs out his cigarette. "I don't know what it's like to care about something so much," he says, in a plain, pensive tone I didn't even know he had. "What is it like?"

"It's . . ." I can feel my smile fading. I don't know why I was smiling in the first place. Just to be polite, I suppose, because he was looking over at me. It's like taking off a mask. Now I can breathe. "It's unbearable."

"But you are bearing it."

Just about.

"I heard what Alexey Alexeyevich was saying to you earlier," he says. "Nothing will happen to you here."

My throat itches. "Nobody can make a promise like that."

"I'll do my job."

Darkness is falling, and only the glow of the cigarette stub illuminates his face. There is universal male conscription here in Russia, but most people get it over with as quickly as possible and then repress the memory. And that's just the normal military, which is brutal enough. What drew him to the OMON? And what *was* his job? What did he do all day? Climb through the windows of burning buildings? Tear down barricades with his bare hands?

I already know the answer. He did whatever he was told.

Years ago, here in Moscow, my family had an elderly neighbor who collected *samizdat*, illegal dissident material circulated by the anti-Soviet underground. Sometimes, when Zoya and I were home from school, he would share it with us. Poetry, novels, even diaries. And though I was too young to understand most of it, I gleaned the message that emanated from his every pore: There is *them*, and there is *us*.

Lev is one of *them*.

* * *

Since I have to keep the lights on, I might as well read.

The memoir begins in the year 1895. Natalya, the future Countess Burtsinova, is an awkward, socially stunted six-year-old with carrot-red hair and a breathy lisp. Her father has just remarried; her stepmother is an opium-addled woman who hosts raucous salon parties and desperately wishes to get into the good graces of the Imperial Family.

Natalya comes into her own over the years. In adolescence, she starts to fancy a childhood friend whom she calls *dearest Mitya*. She romanticizes their summertime encounters by the lake where their families keep dachas. Her stepmother, getting wind of this, responds by arranging Natalya's union with a wealthy aristocrat.

> *It was not out of weakness that I gave in to my stepmother's wishes. It was out of fear....*
> *I could not confess my feelings to the man I loved.*

Natalya's most cherished possession is her mother's silver Orthodox cross, which she wears on a necklace. I can understand why she would cling to this small piece of her birth mother. To the idea of a parent she lost, and a life of which she must have felt robbed.

I'm no countess, but I feel a sudden camaraderie with her.

The next few chapters of the memoir deal with her family life. The Count is a dreary man. They rapidly have two children. Natalya is bored and unfulfilled by motherhood. She throws herself into the whirlwind of St. Petersburg society, and finds herself empathizing with her stepmother, of all people.

It is when everyone else's attention is upon us, that we can forget the one person whose head we fail to turn—

The Count's health declines. Natalya struggles to connect with her children, in particular her daughter. She takes lovers, but she never stops longing for her friend. He has no romantic interest in her, and I suspect that this is why she focuses her intense feelings on him. She doesn't know how to be loved back.

In the summer of 1915, there is a foreseeable turn of events: *Dearest Mitya* gets married.

His new bride was the most ornamental-looking creature you will have ever seen.

But there was something in her eyes I did not trust.

I was reminded that rare diamonds are kept behind glass not only to preserve them, not only to prevent thievery.

Also because they are cursed.

I read on until I reach 1918, the start of the Civil War. A self-proclaimed monarchist, Natalya joins the effort to aid the White

Army, which lands her in prison. Here the memoir reaches her present moment: It is 1920, and the Countess is writing out of a jail cell in Bolshevik-controlled Petrograd. She has negotiated with the guards for various favors, including paper. They don't treat her badly, but she has just been told she faces execution.

They have taken my belongings, my children, my home, my freedom.
I have nothing but the silver cross around my neck.
When they take that, they will have killed me.

A silver necklace that she will wear until death.

Just like in "The Silver Queen." Mum's little story. The one that has no ending.

I slap the memoir shut. I'm about to shove it away, under other books, when there's a slight, scraping noise at my door.

"Lev?" I call out.

There it is again.

I go to the door. "Alexey?" I say, peering out.

Nothing. The hallway is dark, empty. The floor is bitterly cold as I take a few furtive steps. The farther I go, the more I hear it.

It's somebody coming up the stairs.

I see just the top of a head. A woman's head. Long hair, like mine, wavery in the darkness. And I already know, the moment she—it, whatever this is—reaches the landing, she will lift her face. She will look through the hair.

She will look like me.

I turn, run back to my room, and slam the door so hard the rolltop desk closes itself, in one rippling motion.

In a way, I prefer when things are obviously wrong, when

there's blood seeping into the woodwork and your mother is sobbing hysterically in the kitchen as the police are hauling all the neighbors out of their apartments, and there is no question that the underlying bedrock of your entire life has been obliterated.

This is what I can't stand. When you can't tell what's wrong. All you know is that it's there.

* * *

I go downstairs hours before I usually wake, to get a head start on deconstructing Mum's fairy tales. There's coffee at last. I make it over the stove, sit down with a cup that's much too hot to drink, but at this point I'm content just to inhale it. The silver necklace, the fact that it turns up both in Mum's story and in Natalya Burtsinova's memoir, bothers me less this morning than it did last night.

Maybe I've been wrong about coincidences. Maybe events that appear improbable, impossible, just happen. Mum might have even heard of the Countess, if she was so famous, and felt inspired to write her own story.

Maybe.

I'm reading through "The Silver Queen" one more time as Lev comes in. He is freshly showered, from the looks of it, and shirtless. He rubs off his hair with his hand like it's a towel.

I can feel a small, funny space between my lips; I've formed an *oh* without meaning to.

"Your hair," he says.

My throat feels scalded, and I haven't even tried the coffee. "Sorry? My hair?"

"Your hair is down. Usually it is ..." He makes a vague gesture.

171

What? "At least I'm dressed."

He shrugs. "No one is around."

I suppose I don't count.

"Back at work," he comments, nodding toward the stapled pages. "After dinner. Before breakfast. You never take a break."

I don't know what to say to that. I lower my gaze to my cup, see shapes in the coffee, like an inkblot test. Mum used to say similar things, when I was a schoolgirl. She would complain to Papa that he was turning me into a workaholic.

I hope he did. I hope I was always this way.

"I did not say it was bad, Raisa."

I look up again, quickly. Lev treats me to one of his slight smiles. I feel a frisson down my spine, the undoing of a knot in my stomach that I wasn't even aware of.

Oh, *no*. No no no no.

I let out my breath. It's mostly steam. "I have to make a phone call. The Countess's daughter."

And Richard. I need to ring Richard.

The dacha's telephone sits on a three-legged stool in the entry hall. I cradle the receiver as Lev heads upstairs. The frisson tapers off as soon as he's out of range, but I need to step more carefully. I'm doing so much digging into the past; I don't want to overturn anything else. I tell myself, more than once to reinforce it, that it was nothing, that whispery feeling, just the way he said my former name. *Raisa*. Like I have never been Rosie at all.

My heart beats so hard, it makes my ears ache.

Without Rosie, there's nowhere to go from here.

The Silver Queen

The Queen sits at her silver-gilt vanity table, combing her silver-gilt hair, as her daughter watches.

The daughter asks, "Mama, why do the common people say our family is cursed?"

The Queen says, "There is no such thing as a curse."

The daughter asks, "Mama, why do they say you use dark magic?"

The Queen says, "They are jealous, and all they have is their pitchforks."

The daughter says, "Mama, people say that you made a pact with an evil *bes*. That he gave you the silver necklace that you always wear around your neck. That as long as you wear it, you will live forever, but the moment you remove it, you will die. Your head will roll off your neck, all the way out of our world, and into his."

The Queen begins to pull the silver-gilt strands of hair out of the comb, one after another. She puts down the comb. She weaves the strands around, one after another. She smiles at her daughter in the mirror, or the reverse of a smile. She holds up a new silver necklace, beckons her daughter closer, closer, closer, until the girl is right in front of the mirror herself.

The Queen says, "That is nonsense. Nobody lives forever."

The daughter says, "Mama, how can we make the people stop telling one another such stories?"

The Queen ties the necklace of hair around her daughter's neck. "Do they tell one another," she says, "or do I tell them?"

14

Antonina

It has been two years since Tonya was last in Tula.

She feels twitches in her stomach on the train, stronger than ever before, and then again on the coach to Popovka. Below her ribs, past her belly button, toward her hip—an unraveling. She feels them even stronger when she arrives at Kirill and Nelly's home, leaning against their masonry stove, holding herself still.

The oil lamp gives off a moony light, by which Nelly spins hemp at her wheel, round and round and round. Everything goes round and round and round in the countryside. The never-ending cycle of seasons, of births, deaths, festivals, rituals. Very little changes.

Kirill keeps saying that Tonya's father is dead.

Tonya does not believe him. She's had no word from Papa since she married Dmitry, but Papa just about stopped speaking altogether after Mama's death, and there was no proper good-bye when Tonya left with Dmitry for the last time. Only a hand lifted briefly as he looked up from his hothouse roses. It could have been to reach for his pruners.

A new scent is in the air, overcooked and overdone. Nelly has stopped spinning. Kirill says that since spring, attacks have been happening all over the provinces. At Otrada, mobs armed with nothing more than farm tools came at night and hanged all the servants in the birch forest. They ransacked the house, but they did not destroy it. Otrada still stands. Other estates have not been as fortunate.

There it is again, at the base of her belly, that slippery sensation.

"Tonya," says Nelly, "are you alright?"

The scent of coal, here in Nelly and Kirill's small thatched home, is spicy, comforting. The lowing of the animals outside is surreal, sleepy. Round and round and round it goes—but then, there are *small* changes. Just twitches, like the ones in Tonya's belly. The willowy, winsome Nelly is Kirill's *wife* and is wearing a *panyova*, a long checkered skirt, ungainly, unbecoming, the costume of grown women. Kirill has a beard now, broader shoulders.

"Let's talk more tomorrow," offers Kirill.

Tonya does not answer.

Much later, she lies in the crawl space above the stove, imagines herself walking toward the veranda behind Otrada, through the orchards. It is such a vivid picture in her mind that she can hear the barking of Papa's borzois. The French doors are open. Something slinks between her legs, the family cat, Sery. Mama is in the doorway, smiling, summoning her.

Everything and everyone is gone.

But there it is again. That unearthly twinge, like someone is painting her on the inside. She presses up and down along her body. She's felt a hard ridge like this before. It was as big as Mama ever got. Mama once said pregnancy makes you smell things stronger than normal, and the burned-leaf scent of Nelly's candles did make Tonya want to retch. Somehow, right now, she can even smell the unharvested orchards of Otrada, fervent and filthy, like the stink from the estate is hanging over the village. It reminds her of Dmitry's cologne. As if he has followed her here.

She still huddles alone in the crawl space, but her eyes are dry.

Not everyone is gone.

* * *

Nelly, who confides that she is hoping to fall pregnant herself, fetches the midwife the very next day. The midwife says she has seen it before: bursting, blood, in the early weeks, but the baby unharmed. The Lulikov family doctor was wrong. Whatever Tonya lost in all that blood, clotty as kasha, it was not her child.

Tonya begins to write to Valentin, painstakingly, a letter a week. She is careful to get the spelling right: *a baby—due in autumn—if you would like to meet.* But all Kirill ever brings home from the city is the latest newssheets. It is incredible that Valentin would not answer. No matter how many Viktorias he is sleeping with, no matter what he might think of her for never meeting him in February, he would answer. He *must.*

She writes and writes, as if she is in a trance.

On a stale evening in September, the trance breaks at last. Tonya stands from the rocking chair. Nelly is spinning, making the whole house spin too. Maybe Tonya worked too long today. But peasant women all work until they give birth. Some even try to work through labor. Mama never worked, barely even left the bedroom, sometimes not even the bed, and that did not save any of Mama's babies.

The pain again, sharpened now by fear.

Nelly's eyes turn to beads. "Is it coming?"

"I don't know," Tonya gasps.

"I'll go for the midwife," says Nelly. "Lie down on our bed, dearest. I'll be back right away."

It cannot be the baby, but of course it is. It's time, even if Valentin isn't here, even if she hasn't chosen a name, even if she's only a child herself, not quite nineteen. But these doubts are soon blasted away. She groans, grips her sides.

A moment's relief, and then it is worse.

Tonya has no idea how to have a baby, at least not a live one. She saw all those dead ones come out of Mama, too many, and they are all she can see right now, the way they were bluish, furry, with their cords thick and gray and hung round their necks. The midwife would tie off these flaccid ropes with flax and blow on the tiny faces, on the hands, the feet, while Mama would flop over like a fish, like she was the one who could not get any air—

"Let me help," says a voice. A male voice.

Tonya flares one eye open.

"I was passing by outside, and heard your cries." It's a stranger, someone she has never seen in her life, but she has no presence of mind, no strength to protest. "It's easier if you sit up and brace yourself against me."

She lets out a sob, leans against him. She is ripping open, and she screams, loudly enough to unseal the windows.

"Breathe," the voice continues. "*Tishe edesh', dal'she budesh'.* No?"

The slower you ride, the farther you go—

"Here's the head," he says. "It won't be long."

Something breaks, surges. Tonya falls back against the bed, feels her tongue roll out of her mouth. *Is it alive?* she tries to ask, but he's already saying something about the afterbirth, and then he has wrapped the baby in cloth. *Baby girl,* somebody exclaims; Nelly has returned. Kirill too. The little house is full of people. Tonya reaches out. She feels clumsy, careless, as she looks down at her own child for the first time. Who knew that newborns could be like this, red-faced and furious, milky and warm, with breaths like a small bird?

"Oh, Tonya!" says Nelly, brushing a finger over the baby's head. "Oh, I must have one too. I must."

"I wish to thank the man who helped me," says Tonya, hoarsely. "I was alone, and he— Is he still here?"

"No, he left." Nelly's smile tightens. "Must have been just a Good Samaritan."

* * *

The baby has a tuft of dark hair on her head, mossy, soft as cloud. Tonya writes of their daughter in every free moment she has, to Valentin. She no longer bothers with politeness or proper spelling. *Our child is born. I call her Lena, for my mother. Please come.*

But one day new papers make their way into Popovka, and Kirill reads aloud to Tonya and Nelly in a strangled voice: There is no more Provisional Government. No more Imperial ministers; no more links to the reign of the Tsar. There has been another coup, another revolution.

The *true* revolution.

The Winter Palace itself has been taken.

Petrograd belongs to the Bolsheviks.

Soon after, Kirill brings home smaller, no less stunning news, in a letter so stiff it could be parchment.

My husband has gone away to the front. I am afraid this address will no longer be in use. I will pass on all prior messages to Valentin when he returns.

Yours sincerely, Viktoria.

The girl with the milk-saucer eyes, standing in Valentin's doorway.

The longer Tonya looks at the letter, the more it blurs. Lena wails in her arms, writhes with fury, so Tonya lowers her blouse and lets the baby feed until it is the only thing she feels.

Around the time of the spring thaws, a brigade of Bolshevik Chekists arrives in the village and sets up camp. There is a washed-out quality to their faces, like a piece of laundry gone over one time too many. Within days they begin to barrel into peoples' homes, their leather greatcoats making them look like flayed animals, demanding the surplus grain they claim is hidden in the kulaks' floors, clothing, bellies. They overturn the farm tools, the horses' harnesses, the kettles, the pots, the churn. They pilfer barley liquor until they are so drunk, they wouldn't see surplus grain if it fell on their faces like snow.

Every time, Nelly shouts at them, curses at them, and they only laugh at her, while Tonya tries to soothe Lena.

"We are at war," Kirill says one evening, over supper.

"Of course," says Nelly testily, "with the Kaiser—"

"The Bolsheviks have signed a peace with Germany. The new war is with the White Army, the forces who fight for the Tsar. Vladimir Lenin has called upon the Russian people to help weed out all enemies of the revolution."

At night, Tonya remains slack atop the stove, as the baby rustles angrily on her belly, roots for a nipple. She feels her bowels burning, her breasts leaking, maybe her heart breaking, whatever is left of it. She will not write again. Valentin will never answer her letters. He may not even read them before feeding them to the flames. They will burn down to nothing, like the rest of Russia.

Valentin Andreyev has reached the future, *his* future, and she is in the past, and the space between them is infinite.

* * *

With the utmost caution, Tonya removes the sleeping baby from her breast. Having fed for hours, Lena has sniffled and snuffled herself out at last. The room is quiet. Nelly is at her wheel, eyes large and unfocused. Kirill stands, head lowered, in front of the small shrine to St. Nicholas. He says the same prayer again and again, one of the Psalms: *De profundis clamavi ad te, Domine.*

From the depths, I have cried out to you, O Lord.

It could be because the spring plowing has been tricky, with the Chekists breathing down their necks. It could be because Nelly started her monthly bleeding; it was a week late, giving rise to such high hopes. Nelly has been doing everything people say you need to do to conceive, a rigmarole that Tonya witnessed for years with Mama. The village ladies are full of old, witchy wisdom: which herbs to consume, which side of the road to walk along, which surfaces to sit on, how many times to spin your wheel before you stop.

That piece of advice Nelly doesn't heed, for all she does is spin nowadays.

Round and round and round it goes.

"Let us alone for a moment, Tonya," says Kirill, without glancing her way.

Lena appears settled in her blankets, so Tonya throws her shawl around her shoulders and slips outside. Her blouse is pickled in baby spit, and she shivers.

The moon is slung low in the sky, but gives no light. There are no streetlamps in Popovka. There is nothing to guide her way. Tonya finds herself leaving the road behind, seeking out the serpentine pathway that curves around the trees, onward to the creek. It is a quiet night for spring. The birds of the canopy do not sing.

The way to Otrada is overgrown, overwhelmed by weeds and thickets, invisible to anyone who doesn't know it's there. The villagers have not gone near the house since the massacre last year. With the bodies buried in the birch forest, they will not venture there either. The fields by Otrada may lie fallow forever. The orchards are rotting. The house will too, in time.

In a way, it started after Mama died, as Papa turned inward.

Tonya used to believe Papa wanted her to marry Dmitry for the money. Otrada was on the verge of bankruptcy, after all, had been in decline since the end of serfdom. It was no secret. But she thinks now that anyone could have asked to marry her, and he would have given her away. She was a reminder of Mama, and Papa was too weak to stand it.

One day Lena will be a reminder of Valentin.

Tonya will stand it.

She carries on in the direction of the creek. There is a small clearing, right where the path dips toward the lake, and a man is leading a horse by the nose, a mare in full winter coat. He is a soldier, in the telltale greatcoat of the Chekists. He doffs his cap at Tonya, showing a glimpse of light, startling hair.

"It's you," she says, surprised. He is younger than she thought, perhaps her own age. "You are a deputy?"

He smiles generously, as if he has no idea who she is.

"You helped me the day my daughter was born. I am grateful to you."

The Chekist pats his horse on the barrel as it drinks from the stream. "I was only passing through," he says. "I helped deliver my siblings, so . . ."

She goes closer, curious. "Are you not one of the local brigade? In the village?"

"No. In Tula city."

"And why have you come back?"

He turns to face her. His eyes are luminous, and he moves with an uncanny grace. Like Mama and Papa, whose family lines could be traced all the way to ancient Muscovy, whose blood was so blue they could nearly glow in starlight. "My unit is looking for a place to requisition, for our own purposes, Comrade. The estate they call Otrada may suit us."

"What use would you have for Otrada? What's your name?" she asks, almost a demand.

"Ozhereliev. Sasha."

That cannot be his real name. He is an aristocrat, Tonya is sure of it, an aristocrat turned soldier, actively hiding his background. Though she can hardly blame him for that.

"And you are the one they call *Kukolka*?" he asks. "I heard about you, in the village, when I stayed at the inn for a night. I heard all manner of local lore—they spoke of nothing but immortal tigers and pagan sacrifices and water spirits. The *muzhiki* are such imaginative folk."

"It is like that out here," she says succinctly. "It doesn't matter how many revolutions, how many mobs, or how many people like you overrun the country, we will always prefer the stories whose endings we already know."

"You should be careful, in our new Russia," he says in measured tones, "your parents being who they were."

"How do you even know who I am?"

Ozhereliev leans forward, comforts the horse with a whisper she can't hear. "*Kukolka,*" he says, "who else would it be?"

"What do you mean by that?"

"They call you that because of how you look, surely."

She has lingered here far too long. Every breath she takes now is chilly. "Do they?" she says, meeting his eye. They are in such proximity now that she can see herself in his irises, bizarrely detailed: the stitches of her shawl, the sweep of her lashes, the tint of her mouth, the black sheet of sky behind her. "Or do they call me that because I was not born, but *made*?"

He stares at her.

"Do you want to know what they really say about me, Comrade Ozhereliev, when no outsiders are listening? They say my mother made a deal with a demon to get pregnant. She was desperate for a child, and I am what the demon gave her. Beautiful on the outside, but on the inside . . ." She passes a hand over her own face, as if parting a curtain, and he flinches. "I look human, I feel human, but I have no human soul. I am empty."

Ozhereliev's face is as pale as his hair.

"I wish you luck finding your way home. They say these woods are haunted," Tonya adds, primly.

The mare nickers, presses its snout against him. Sasha looks away from Tonya, coughs.

She buries a laugh in her shawl. But as she is holding in her laughter, she thinks suddenly of Otrada itself: the untended vegetable plots, the unharvested fruit, the larders so long you can get lost in them, if you don't know your way. If you were not born to the land; if it does not run in your veins.

*　*　*

He's a Chekist," says Nelly, in snipped tones, as she sews. "He's a killer. You shouldn't have anything to do with him."

Tonya eases Lena off her lap. If Nelly were her usual self, Tonya would confide right now that *she* is a killer. That Dmitry died because of her. But Sasha Ozhereliev is right that there are already too many whispers about her in Popovka.

"I'll befriend him if it means saving Otrada," is all she says.

Nelly bites off a piece of thread alongside her words: "Some people just don't belong here."

Every day, as spring turns to summer, Tonya works the fields with the others. The soil is shuddery, like fresh clay. She binds, threshes, weeds until the skin comes off her hands. Lena stays at Tonya's heels like a sheepdog, crawling, clinging, soon walking. Refusing to be left behind with anyone. The peasants are rankled, rubbed wrong by the demands of the Chekists. Tonya can feel their anger as she works, and now that the hours are long and the fields are long too and the people are tired, the murmurs become raised voices: Is *Tonya* the cause of their bad luck? Didn't it all start when she came home from the capital? And where in the world is Nelly?

Tonya asks herself that question too when she sees Nelly at home, sewing a scarf that never seems to end. Nelly will look at Lena and then at Tonya and the look says, *Some people just don't belong here.*

* * *

Sasha Ozhereliev seats himself at the table and accepts the offer of bread and tea. Lena is eating a baked potato, shoving it in with both fists. The Chekist reaches into his coat, produces a miniature wooden rocking horse for which the baby lunges. He catches her and sets her on the ground with the tenderness he showed his mare, and Lena wobbles away, prize in hand.

Tonya resists the temptation to glance over at Nelly, who is pricking away at the scarf that nobody needs. "I didn't know if you would come," she says.

He stiffens. "Well, you wrote to me, and I am here."

"Where is home for you, Comrade Ozhereliev?"

"Saratov."

Saratov. Saratov is on the Volga, that mighty river that divides this country into east and west. Valentin spoke often of the city, birthplace of many famous radical writers and revolutionaries. *Valentin.* The name feels like a pinch. "I know of Saratov," Tonya says, too vehemently. "There is a rich black soil unique to that region, isn't there? I have heard that in such fertile earth, anything can grow, even a cause as unlikely as—ours. All it takes is a single seed."

"You?" he responds, incredulously. "You are one of the *Bol-sheviki*?"

Tonya shows him her right wrist. She has fortified the ribbon with yarn, for the original material is only a wisp. The redness remains. "Since I lived in Petrograd."

"What do you want, Comrade?" he asks, sitting back, folding his arms.

"As I said in my letter, to talk about your plans for Otrada. I think that perhaps—"

"We have already decided on what was formerly the Dashkov place." There is a twitch in his cheek. "Otrada was in too sorry a shape."

From across the room, Nelly makes the closest thing to a laugh anyone has heard from her in weeks.

"You could have just written me back to say so," says Tonya.

"I don't like writing," says Ozhereliev.

"You came all this way for nothing."

"We will live, we will see," he says obliquely. He seems to like proverbs. Well-worn answers.

When Sasha has gone, Nelly begins to reel in the shawl. She finally breaks her monkish silence: "There's something not right about him."

"He is Bolshevik secret police, Nelly."

"All the Chekists are cold-blooded, of course. But not like this one."

"He helped bring Lena into the world—"

"Oh, isn't this just like you!" Nelly breaks into a shout. The windows rattle. "That man is from Lord only knows where, and he's come to take from us, to plunder us. But you'll cozy up to him, won't you, if there's any chance it'll get you out of a peasant's life! Lulikov was exactly the same. I told you, didn't I, that he was bad news? I *told* you!"

Tonya stands from the table slowly. "Don't speak to me of Dmitry—"

"You agreed with me, or pretended to agree with me, and then you went and married him anyway! And off you went, whisked away to Petrograd like the princess you are! God forbid the *princess* should have to live like the rest of us! Hay and harvests and working with her hands! You know what I thought, Tonya, when you told me that you believed Dmitry made you lose the baby? I thought—well, if he had, you would have got what you deserved!" Tears stream down Nelly's face. "But you'll never learn your lesson. The very next man to look your way—"

"I will leave here tomorrow morning."

Silence.

"You don't have anywhere to go," says Nelly.

"This is your home, not mine."

"Tonya." Nelly rises too, from her wheel. "Tonya—"

Lena drops her new toy and begins to wail. Tonya scoops Lena into her arms, hears nothing over the sound of the baby's chesty sobs. She feels exhausted, bruised. Tonight her sleep will be fraught and fleeting, and tomorrow she will be out on those fields again, feeling the gaze of the village on her back, hotter than the low-lying sun.

* * *

Nelly has fallen asleep, and Tonya is fixing a hole in Nelly's *panyova*. She tugs on the thread, pulls it through. Every so often the thread breaks. Once, just after their betrothal, Dmitry took her to the fields to watch the village folk at work. Instead of sunflower nubs to snack on, he said, she would have Antonovka apples and plums. Instead of the stink of her own sweat, she would have perfume water from Paris. Instead of country dress, she would have ball gowns to rival the Tsaritsa Alexandra.

Yet here she is, fixing a hole in a *panyova* because it is the only thing she can fix.

Kirill comes in and sits by the shrine. Tonya can tell how troubled he's become. It's not only his beard that is now crested with white. Also his hair, the look in his eye. He doesn't say anything as he lights a candle to the saints.

De profundis clamavi ad te, Domine.

"Nelly is hurting. It has nothing to do with you," says Kirill. "She loves you."

"I would have gone anyway."

"But where?"

"Otrada."

"You can't go back to Otrada," he protests. "There's nobody there. Write again to Andreyev, and wait just a bit longer."

Tonya looks up at her oldest friend; his face appears shrouded in the candlelight. "All the things that ever held up my world have come crashing down, Kiryusha. Mama and Papa—the Tsar—Imperial Russia—my marriage. None of these were ever laws of nature. They were always destructible and man-made. And maybe it is the same, with Valentin. Maybe our love was never meant to be like the ones in Mama's storybooks. In poetry. In Pushkin. Maybe I was a princess once," she says, pricking her finger slightly as she pulls, "but there are no fairy tales."

15

Valentin

SOUTHERN RUSSIA, 1919

They are leaving behind the plain, parched grasslands of the steppe. Here the land has not yet been ravaged by occupation and conflict, and here it has a shape, hills and furrows and shallow valleys that distinguish it from the flat, unbroken sky.

In the late afternoon they make an encampment atop a small hill, and Valentin stops to survey a Russia he has never known: the white chapel roofs, the blue lines of rivers, the sprinkling of wooden houses. He stands still, lets the wind blow against him. A horsefly buzzes by his ear. He looks back to where his fellow prisoners are huddled, their faces chalky with dust. A jug of water is being passed from hand to hand.

Valentin is always thirsty now. He could drink all the rivers beyond and not quench that thirst.

"Something you're trying to see out there, brother?" someone yells at him, the emphasis on *brother* a mockery of the way the Don Cossacks address one another.

A sound begins to rise, above the scuffling of the horses' hooves, the agitated swarming of insects. The White officers are *singing* again, around their campfire. How many times can they sing the same folksy ballads, the same sailors' chanteys? How many times can Valentin hear them before his ears start bleeding? But the singing is over quickly tonight, and they have begun to make elaborate, impassioned toasts. The greatness of the Tsar! The glory of the empire! That prima ballerina onstage three years ago, her pale, slender neck!

The smell of honey from the bird-cherry trees; the sight of home in the corner of one's eye from around the curve in the road . . .

Valentin wipes something wet from his lips. He is *crying*. What little hydration he still has, he is wasting on them, the enemy, but he can't help himself. He can envision it too, that world in all its decadence, its obscene beauty, with the ugly, steaming, seething masses below, and in the middle of it all, himself and—

Tonya.

The toasts are turning to curses, the drunken cheers to indignant anger. Home is no longer there, not as it was, because the peasants have looted the estate; the bird-cherry trees are a smoking ruin. The Tsar has fallen.

"Let's go into the village," comes the furious cry.

The mood of the prisoners shifts. They know what this means, what will happen. They will be gathered up, too many to a wagon. Human cargo. Down in the village they will be locked in barns and left to suffocate in the miasma of horse manure while the Whites storm somebody's home. Whatever they find, whomever they find, they will take.

The sound of one child screaming will be louder than all the warring armies of Russia put together.

Valentin shuts his eyes. He gropes for a thought, a line, a philosophy that will comfort him, but all that comes to mind tonight is that countryside and the light wind that swept through, brushing up against him, out of nowhere, carrying her touch with it.

* * *

Valentin no longer participates in conversation with the other prisoners, whose number includes farmers, soldiers, stragglers, deserters. They are all tired of war. Many recall seeing their home villages burned by the Whites, their Jews and Tatars beaten to bone. Others claim the Red Army does all these same things.

Valentin wants to defend his side. The Reds act out of principle. In the annals of history, centuries from now, the rightness of his Party's cause will be obvious to all. *The past cannot be allowed to defeat the future!*

But he is too thirsty to speak.

The prisoners sleep most nights out in the open now, because of an outbreak of what locals call the *flu*. The longer Valentin spends out here, living like the nomadic hordes of the steppe, looking up at that canopy of stars, the more he loses his bearings. The more he wonders how he came to be here in the first place. The more his throat hurts.

The local flu is typhus.

He is transferred to a special barracks, where he fights a high and hungry fever for weeks, in the care of a nurse with a foreign accent. *You are east of the Volga,* she explains. He doesn't remember crossing the Volga. He suffers delirium, visions, convulsions. The nurse's voice sounds like someone playing on the frets of a balalaika. Sometimes he thinks he hears the men to either side of him plotting over his head their escape from these barracks, from Russia altogether: *past the bridge, into the village, onto a stolen horse...*

He is trapped in the space between night and day. *Between.* Valentin did not even believe in the existence of *between,* before. Only in the one and the other. In opposites. In opposition.

Valentin...

He feels a cool hand on his hot forehead. He sees Tonya in front of him, her white shawl over her head, longer even than her hair. The moon seems to rise behind her, and when she smiles, he cannot tell if she is standing in the light, or if she is the one to give light.

"Take a bite. It's kefir." The nurse is waving a spoon in his face. "I'll write to your sweetheart, lad, if you tell me her full name...."

Valentin coughs, gags on the syllables. The image is fading. You cannot chase light, anyway. You cannot even hold it.

It is too late.

"Tonya," prompts the nurse. "You've been asking for her."

No, he tries to respond. *My wife is called Viktoria. My wife is the woman I love.* But even as he thinks it, shapes it with his lips, he knows that it isn't true. Maybe it didn't matter before, that he doesn't love her. It didn't matter the day they married, when they went down to the registry office and Viktoria was on his arm saying how perfect they were for each other, how much sense this made, and there was no arguing with that, or with her happiness on the way home. He cares for Viktoria. He wants her to be happy.

But if it didn't matter then, it matters now, now that Valentin is going to die.

I've made a terrible mistake, he tells the nurse, but he hears only a murmur of sympathy in reply, a whispered promise, in Russian, or in her native tongue: *It'll be over soon, lovely lad.*

16

Rosie

This is my first real task as Alexey's assistant: contacting the Countess's daughter to ask her about her mother's memoir. I desperately want to prove that I'm reliable, hardworking, everything I claimed to be when I applied. Not just the sole survivor of a massacre.

I can't imagine that the daughter of a countess could actually be living somewhere in this city, but when I call Moscow information, the operator gives me the number for Akulina Burtsinova. With a name like that, it's unsurprising that there's only one.

She picks up quickly. She has a crackly voice, a log on a fire. I tell her that I'm a historian's assistant researching her mother's era. Would she be willing to answer some questions?

"If you can come to me," Akulina says, with a harsh cough. "I don't travel."

I'm about to take down her details when I hear it: a labored rendition of a classical piano concerto. Tchaikovsky's First. Not coming from any room in the dacha, not from outside, not down the telephone wire. Just *around* me, like I'm sitting in the orchestral pit of Moscow's Symphony Hall.

"Ms. Simonova?" she barks.

This was my father's favorite piece. He used to play it on the wine-stained keys of our upright piano while Zoya would put her hands over her ears, moaning that the music was too depressing, too old, too wordless. Mum would be in the kitchen, smiling as she cooked, because classical music was the one place where my parents' interests touched, like the meeting of two electrical wires. Papa would ruin the mood over supper by launching into his monologue about how music was only mathematics, and Mum would get upset: *How can you say that, Antosha! Music is art, it's beauty, it's nature, it's life!* And Papa would say that all those things were only mathematics too.

Zoya tried to jump in once: *If that's true, Papa, why don't you write music?*

One day I'll try, he said. *I like to try new things. New mediums.*

You could even put a code in it, Zoya pointed out.

Yes, he said, looking straight at me. *I could.*

My father could encode *anything.*

Stories?

Fairy tales?

My father, who wrote *only* in pencil—

"Hello? Hello!"

The soar of the climax, and then, as discreetly as the chords began, they dwindle to nothing. I feel the weight of the present moment settling back onto my shoulders, the way it does after I've watched a long film.

"Hello! Is anyone there? Do you want to come over or not?"

"I'm so sorry," I say, scrambling for the pen. "Yes, of course. Could you repeat the address?"

* * *

Through the slits of alleyways, I glimpse a few playgrounds and open spaces, but nothing that tells me where to go. If Lev is as lost as I feel, he isn't showing it. He stays in the background, blending too well into the silent high-rises, the dark tower blocks, that dominate this neighborhood. I step into a puddle, less than two inches of water. It feels like more.

"There must be somebody to ask for directions," I say uselessly, looking down the street, but there are only kids kicking at some discarded tires. Too young to know. Too young to be playing alone. The breeze picks up a chill somewhere and nicks at my thin coat. I feel small, straitjacketed into the passages between the monolithic buildings.

I button up my jacket as high as it goes.

We are an hour late by the time we find Akulina Burtsinova's door, steel and spray-painted with obscenities. There are several doorbells, none of them marked. The door opens, revealing a gray-haired woman whose face is a road map of grooves and ridges. She is chewing on something, a repetitive, maniacal chewing, a cow with a cud.

"I saw you coming from my—" She stops. She is staring at me with deep-set green eyes. "You," she says. "*You're* the girl who called me?"

"I apologize for how late we are—"

"Not too late," she says. "Come in."

The lobby of her building is stuffy and dingy. Akulina shakes her head at the rows of postboxes as if she finds the whole lot unseemly. We ascend the stairs, with Akulina coughing every few seconds, moving like she's in pain. A calico cat is keeping watch at her open door, and its tail loops around my ankles as I go by.

"In here is best," she says, leading us into her living room. "I breathe better."

The cat follows us. I peek out her window to see the streets below, those deflated tires, the heaps of rubbish, looking better from above, sparkling in the sun. Lev is right behind me, taking a look for himself. He steps close enough that I'm reminded of that heady moment at the dacha, the way he smiled. The way my stomach plummeted.

I duck quickly beneath his arm, presenting our hostess with a box of chocolates. She accepts without a word, her jaws still working. Maybe I should have brought chewing gum.

Akulina's prepared more than the usual smattering of Russian hospitality fare, breads and rolls and cookies with jelly. She invites us to sit down on the sofa, and disappears to fetch drinks. The cat rolls over by my feet. My back is ramrod straight.

This is her. The Countess's daughter. We are about to take tea with Imperial nobility.

Akulina is absent for a noticeably long time, and by the time she returns, I'm feeling jittery. She takes the armchair. Her cough is a brassy rattle. "You said this was about my mother," she says. "You should have told me the truth."

What does *that* mean?

I can feel Lev tense up beside me. Overhearing Alexey has clearly turned him paranoid, because he has been far more on guard the past few days. No longer just slouchy and stony. I resist the temptation to reach over and pat his hand, calm him down. My family's killer is not going to pop up from behind Akulina's armchair.

Akulina coughs more. I await further explanation, but she only goes back to chewing. Her whole face is coming unhinged.

"As I said on the phone," I say, "I'm a research assistant to a historian. He's interested in your mother's memoir. The original was found in somebody's basement?"

"It was mailed to me," she says crisply. "Years ago."

"Mailed? You mean in the—"

"In the post."

"By whom?"

"The person who found it, I presume." Akulina spits something into her hand. A piece of toffee. "I thought maybe after the book was published, I'd hear again from this anonymous donor, but I never did."

"Forgive me for asking this, but if you received the manuscript in the post, anonymously, how could you be sure it was genuine? Not a forgery? Your mother being a well-known figure of the Civil War—"

"Because," she replies loftily, "they sent my mother's necklace along with it."

I hesitate. "The silver one?"

"Exactly. The cross. It was a locket. Inside there was an inscription. My mother showed me once. Perhaps one could fake a memoir, though I don't see why anyone would, but there would be no faking that necklace. And the part about someone's basement . . . Well! That was just the publisher's idea. Books are always being found in basements these days. It is a selling point.

Makes it seem like the material was hidden on purpose. Illegal or illicit." Akulina clears her throat. "So you've read the memoir, then."

"Um. Yes." I'm still taking in everything she's said. "She was a beautiful writer—"

"She was a terrible mother," Akulina interjects, matter-of-factly. "After the revolutions, when my younger brother and I were only children, she began to conspire against the Bolsheviks. I begged her to stop, for our sake. It was so dangerous. But she did not stop. She was arrested, and my brother and I were sent to an orphanage. I hated her for her selfishness. I vowed never to forgive her."

The cat leaps into my lap, pinioning me in place.

"But . . . now you have?" I prompt.

"The memoir helped me to understand her. My mother had a great, impossible love. I myself have experienced the same. And some women are just not meant to be mothers. Again, I am among them. So the two of us, we did have some things in common, in the end." Akulina speaks without reservation. "I saw, for the first time, how it must have been for her, belonging to a world that ended in a heartbeat."

"How did your mother die?" I ask, and then wince. I already know. It's in the editor's foreword to the memoir. I'm not thinking straight.

"Natalya Burtsinova was executed," Akulina says, scornfully. "By the Cheka, in 1920. Your historian doesn't know that?"

"Right. Of course."

"There *is* no historian, is there?"

"Excuse me?" My Russian comprehension isn't *that* poor. She didn't just say—

"You're lying about why you're here. You want to talk about Tonya."

"Who?"

Akulina reaches into the pocket of her mousy jumper. "I've just dug this out for you. I hope you appreciate it."

I lean over her cat, feeling like I'm reaching into a museum display, and Akulina drops an object into my hand. A wooden frame, not much larger than an icon, brittle and blemished. The photograph within is black-and-white, behind glass that looks new. It shows four people: two young kids; a frizzy-haired teenager who bears a whimper of a resemblance to Akulina; and a woman in a whitish frock.

The woman is me.

"What . . ." I start to say. The picture gives off vibes, electricity. It can't be me. I don't own any ankle-length dresses. I've never worn my hair cropped just below the chin. I've never even laid eyes on these children. Whoever this is, she smiles into the camera in a way that tells me she doesn't mean it. I wouldn't mean that smile either.

Lev takes the picture from me. He lets out a low whistle, not an admiring one.

"You can have it," says Akulina, indulgently. "And I'll tell you as much as I know. Tonya and my mother knew each other socially, before the October Revolution. Years later, after my brother and I ran away from the orphanage, Tonya adopted us. Took us in. See, he's that young boy there."

"Wait. Just wait. Who is Tonya?" I stammer.

Akulina dissolves into coughing. When she looks at me again, her eyes are red rimmed. "Obviously a relation of yours. Just look at the two of you! Was Lena your mother?"

"Lena?"

Her nostrils flare at us. "Tonya's daughter. She's there in the picture too."

"My mother's name was Katya. You're mistaken. This is some kind of mistake." My voice is rising. I didn't come here to be confronted with something like this. To be blindsided. The cat's velvety fur suddenly feels like needles. "I don't know any Tonya. I don't know why she—I'm—"

"Can I pour you more tea, Akulina Stepanovna?" asks Lev, with more manners than he's ever shown toward me, and Akulina responds, smiling, displaying a row of coffee-browned teeth, but I see it as glee, like something's lit up behind her features, like the glint of gold leaf beneath lacquer.

*   *   *

Alexey instructed us not to take the Mercedes on this visit, so as not to draw too much attention to ourselves in this area of town, but now I'm wishing we had. I need to close my eyes, clear my head. Instead, Lev and I have to board a minibus, to endure the return journey through the jungle of apartment complexes. Akulina's photo frame is in my bag, the strap singeing my shoulder.

I don't know what's going on, between the silver necklace, Alexey's increasing elusiveness, and this Tonya person, but I can't let it scupper me.

I'm in Moscow to find *that man*. To understand why he killed Papa and Zoya.

Nothing matters except getting my answer, and leaving forever.

"You're thinking too hard," says Lev, all of a sudden. "Let's get off here. I have friends who live just around the corner. We can stop in and say hello."

"People do that?" I ask, swallowing.

"Have friends? Yes," he says, with a straight face. "And social gatherings. And even food."

He's right that I'm thinking too hard. I can almost feel steam coming out my ears.

His friends turn out to live in an apartment that once belonged to a renowned dancer. It does look like the kind of place Mum would have liked: high ceilings, a lot of windows, plenty of space. Enough to put on a show. The couple show us every room, with modest pride, and then they lay out food and more spirits than even Mum could comfortably imbibe.

Lev takes a seat next to me on their sofa. He has obviously known these people for years. The three of them chat as I sip raspberry kvass and nibble on snacks that sear my tongue, gherkins and salty fish.

If not for *that man*, that one night, I might be chatty and cheerful too. I might not mind living in a place that once belonged to a dancer.

Their laughter seems to hum in my veins; their Russian is rapid-fire; the apartment is warm. I begin to feel sleepy. Lev moves his arm, gestures that I can lean against his shoulder, and I do. I feel bizarrely calm, even though I can hear everything going on outside the apartment: tram bells clanging, car horns honking, pedestrians shouting, dogs barking. I hear it, and yet I do not hear it. It is like being in the eye of the storm.

"Raisa, wake up."

"What?" I say groggily.

"Time to go."

The night air stings as we emerge from their building. The hours seem just to leach away here in Moscow. We catch a taxi because I don't think I could stand up well enough to take the metro; I'm still mostly asleep when we arrive at the dacha. Lev has stayed faced away from me this entire time.

I can't look at him either.

But at the back door of the dacha he stops, turns to me at last. He plays with the key, like he's weighing it in his hand. Weighing something else. The moment feels so removed from the rest of our day that I might be able to frame it later.

Better not to think of frames.

"Having funny thoughts?" he says.

I attempt a smile. "You can tell?"

"Your face, it's . . . How do you say it?" In a tone I might almost call shy, he speaks in English: "The open book." Seeing whatever my face is showing now, he adds in Russian once more: "*You* are very open too. I have never known anyone so . . . who just says what she is thinking. Very strange things, of course. But true things."

That's not possible. That's the *opposite* of me. I am closed.

At least I was. In England.

Lev bends his head, so that his forehead nearly touches mine. He closes his eyes briefly, as if he needs to remind himself of where he is. In darkness like this, we could be anywhere. We could be anyone. I look up at him, without entirely meaning to, and his mouth is so close to mine, I can feel his smile between my own lips.

If this is desire, it is alive inside of me. It's breathing right under my skin.

It's the opposite of how I feel with Richard—

Richard.

I don't need to stop Lev. I need to stop myself. I cannot throw over my life, my future, for a complete stranger, no matter how tempted I might feel in the moment, no matter, nothing matters—

Nothing matters except getting my answer, and leaving forever.

I have to put some space between us.

There is only one way I know, to put space between myself and the things I cannot face.

"I think my father wrote those fairy tales I found in the doll, and not my mother," I whisper.

"Tell me." He sounds amused. Like he knows what I'm doing.

"My father was an amateur cryptographer. It was his dream to study it, the way I do. He also thought my mother's stories were nonsense. The way I do." Come to think of it, I do a lot of things just because Papa did them. "But what if he wrote his own stories, in code? In ciphertext? He always talked about encrypting music. Why not literature? And maybe . . ."

"Maybe . . . ?"

"I wonder," I say, slower now, "if he *knew* that someone was going to kill him, but he was scared to put me in danger by telling me. So he encrypted these stories, wrote them down, hid them for safekeeping in one of Mum's dolls—I mean, she probably boasted what a great hiding place they were—knowing that one day I, of all people, would be able to break the code."

"Is that why you're chasing porcelain dolls around Moscow?"

"I know. I've gone a bit mad." I hear my own voice like it's behind a wall, mumbled, faraway. "All these theories. All this mental energy. I just can't help it. I wish every day that they hadn't died." It's all boiling over now. "But at the same time, it's almost like—I wish they would. I wish they would just die."

The second I say it, my shame—my deepest, darkest shame— evaporates.

Gone.

I should have said all this out loud years ago.

"I think that is normal," says Lev.

"Normal? To feel two opposing things at once?" To *be* two things? To be two people?

"*Konechno*. It's normal." His expression is grave. He means it. When I don't move away, he tucks a strand of my hair behind my ear.

He doesn't have to remain a complete stranger; right now I could ask him anything, and he would answer.

In about a second he will be impenetrable once more.

"I'm engaged," I say.

"You're . . ." Lev stops.

I show him my left hand. It's a family ring, smart, but not flashy. It has never felt heavier on my finger than it does at this moment. "I'm getting married in September."

"You're wearing it on the wrong hand," he observes levelly.

"In England we wear it on the left."

I can't imagine that he's hurt, beyond his pride, but I can sense the sudden emptiness between us. The real darkness. He nods, doesn't reply. We go inside. He goes upstairs but I stop to make myself something to eat. It's just an excuse. The fizzy sensation in my skin isn't going away. I sit and stew at the kitchen table, mired in self-loathing as I recall how I slept against his shoulder.

As I do, I realize that I didn't feel haunted this evening.

I felt free.

I could have been more sympathetic toward Mum, who always gave in to her own temptations, her own vices. They must have been a way of forgetting things, expunging them, at least for a little while. Much as I have done, tonight. Only she forgot to stop at a little while, and couldn't get anything back.

* * *

I crack an eye open. My skin feels sandpapered and there's a furriness in my mouth. I forgot to brush my teeth last night. I also forgot to go to bed. I'm on the sofa, all my books and notes fanned out across the coffee table.

I'm about to turn over when I see Alexey enter the living room. Quietly he begins to stack the sofa cushions, the ones I jettisoned to the floor. And then, just as quietly, he halts.

He pulls something out from under one of the cushions.

It takes me a moment to realize what it is: the framed photograph of the woman named Tonya, the one that Akulina gave me yesterday. I do not quite recall taking it out of my handbag, much less stashing it under a cushion.

Yet here it is. In Alexey's hands.

His expression drains like someone's pulled out a bath plug. His mouth forms a single word, but he does not utter it.

Tonya.

It takes every ounce of willpower I've amassed, years of not wrenching vodka bottles out of Mum's grasp, to keep from jumping to my feet.

He *knows* Tonya.

If he knew Tonya, he must have anticipated that Akulina Burtsinova would recognize me as her doppelgänger. He knew

Akulina would say, *Hey, you look like someone I used to*—or even: *I know where Tonya is, right now. Wanna meet her?*

Alexey is using me to find this woman.

I didn't choose this job. I was *chosen*. That's why he's got me set up in this dacha. He's letting me while away the days, keeping tabs on me via Lev, buying time. I'm not a research assistant. If anything, I'm *bait*, and he's going to dangle me in just the right spots until somebody bites. And they will, they're already biting, because of how alike we look.

Why do we look so alike?

Maybe the real question is: *Do I actually want to know?*

Mum sent me to a psychologist in England exactly once. He said I was locked in a cycle of *intellectualization*, in response to my childhood trauma. It's a common defense mechanism. It's probably what got me into Oxford. People who use *intellectualization* are ready to plan, plot, and pen their way out of everything. They claim not to like questions, but what they really dislike are solutions.

I always thought that was complete rubbish.

Alexey plants the frame back beneath the cushion. He dusts off his hands, straightens, but it's too late. Now I'm sure. There's something *behind* that smooth surface of his, that public persona. Something with serrated edges. It's shifting around, like Nessie in the depths of Loch Ness, never so much as making a ripple up above.

* * *

We've stopped just far away enough to turn back without being seen. Lev holds up a hand to block out the sun that blazes over the Vernissage.

"It's hot today. We could go get ice cream instead," he says, in a tone that suggests he'd rather do just about anything than visit a doll vendor's stall. It seems that nine years in the Russian military do not prepare you to face a miniature army of the undead.

"I left Moscow when I was ten," I say with a short laugh. "I'm not ten anymore."

The figure standing by the stall is silhouetted against the sun, so I can't make out any features clearly, and by the time we get there, that person has disappeared. There's nobody here. Nobody guarding the dolls. They're keeping their own watch, rows and rows of them, layered, leaned against one another. It's like a mass grave.

"Raisa Simonova?" someone says, from behind me. "Is that you? I am the doll maker."

E. S. Rayevsky, the artist himself. The man who made all the head-holes in Mum's dolls. The man behind the collection. I peel my gaze off one particularly forbidding doll who looks like her eyes were gouged out with spoons. As I turn, Lev steps in front of me, as if he senses that something has gone wrong.

This is all wrong.

The man who made all the head-holes.

I want to speak, but my mind is untethering. I *am* ten. I'm still ten years old, after all these years; I'm still standing in my family's living room. I'm still looking at a man dressed in dark clothing, his gloved hands holding a pistol, himself an island in the middle of all that blood, his gaze resting on me as if he wanted me to see him. As if he wanted to get caught.

He must still want to get caught.

"You may not remember my face," he says. "It has been fourteen years."

PART

II

The New King

In a faraway kingdom, in a long-ago land, rain began to fall. The new king stayed dry in his castle, and he gave special coats to his soldiers so that they could protect themselves. But the townspeople were not given coats. The townspeople learned not to look into one another's eyes, in case they should get rain in their own.

One day a soldier stopped to talk to one of the townspeople.

"I'm sure the rain will be over soon," the soldier reassured her.

"I have heard," she said, "that even soldiers are not safe now. That our new king will take your coat when he has a fit of temper."

"That is true," said the soldier.

"I have heard," she said, "that the only way for someone like me to gain a coat is to betray someone else to the king."

"That is also true," said the soldier.

"Why is our rain so red?" she asked. "Is all rain, in every country, as red as this?"

The soldier only smiled at her. He was already telling her too many things, and it would not help her to know the truth. The rain was red because the new king made the rain. He made it from the people.

17

Antonina

Mama! Mamochka!" Lena appears on the veranda, rushes down the steps to the garden. "Mama, somebody's here to see you and I think she might be a *princess*!"

Tonya stands up from the plots, sets down her spade. There is enough dirt beneath her fingernails that she may never dig it out. "Is she wearing a crown?"

"No," Lena replies sagely, "that's only in stories. But she asked for Antonina Nikolayevna. That *is* you, isn't it, Mama?"

"The same way you are Yelena Valentinovna," says Tonya somberly, and Lena gives a blissful sigh.

Lena has already deposited their visitor in the front parlor. The formal rooms of Otrada are furnished simply, nothing like the Blue Salon in the house on the Fontanka, with its portraits and chandeliers and Savonnerie carpeting.

That might be why the visitor stands out like a skin rash.

She is the same height as Tonya, but she wears shoes with heels like ice picks, to go with an ankle-length flax-trim dress that hangs off her arms and waist. She turns, and her mane of red hair turns with her. From her fingers is draped a slender, yellow-tipped cigarette in a holder. She could have stepped out of a dinner party from ten years ago.

"Oh, darling," says Natalya, "it's only me." Her green eyes flicker over to Lena, who is clearly awed. "I see that my presence here is a shock. You might have heard that I died in Petrograd. Rumors do take on lives of their own."

Will Tonya *never* be rid of this woman?

The Countess Burtsinova sits without being asked. She makes the wood-backed chair look even more sparse. Tonya hurriedly dispatches Lena to the kitchen. She did not hear just that Natalya died; she heard that the Cheka executed the Countess over a ravine, sprayed her with bullets, abandoned her to the pits. Only they didn't do it, apparently, with enough bodies piled on top to keep her from climbing back out.

"Have you come for your children, Natalya Fyodorovna?" she asks, as soon she's sure that Lena is out of earshot.

Natalya's smile pulls thin. "My children?"

"Akulina and—"

"I think I know what their names are."

Tonya feels a wretched flutter of pity, watching as Natalya finds that old silver necklace, closes a hand around the cross. She relays the tale as quickly, as quietly, as she can: Akulina and Little Fedya were placed in a state residence home for children after Natalya's arrest in 1920. The conditions were appalling. After hearing of their mother's death, they escaped, returning to the Burtsinovs' former mansion on the Zakharevskaya, only to discover it had been converted into housing for some twenty-odd families. Akulina found the map of Tula, hidden at the back of a drawer in one of the bedrooms. They did not know where else to go.

"They believed you'd been shot by the Cheka," Tonya says. "They said people were singing about your death in the streets."

"The Cheka let me go," says Natalya. "We struck a deal. I thought it would make things easier, if people believed me dead. I looked for my children. I looked everywhere. But how could I have thought to look *here*?"

"Akulina's traveling now, near Krasnoyarsk, but we get occasional letters from her. I'll give you the address we have." She doesn't say it, but an address won't be any use. The Countess might locate Akulina in the vastness of the east, but the night Little Fedya died, something went missing from Akulina too. Something that would be buried the next day alongside her brother, in a coffin that was already much too small.

Akulina cannot be found. Not by Tonya, not by Natalya. Not by anyone.

"What about Fedya?" asks Natalya.

"Fedya never fully recovered from his time at the orphanage."

"Never recovered?"

"He died two years ago." That day, Lena, then not quite five years old, vowed that she would never let anybody else die, ever. She'd grow up and find a way to end death. *Nobody, never, and don't you believe me?* And Tonya said yes, because people will say anything when someone is dying, like how after Mama died the servants said that she was finally going to be with all her unformed babies.

Natalya makes a soft sound, maybe just a breath.

"It was painless," says Tonya.

"You're good to have taken in my children." The Countess looks up again, from her lap. "I'll return the favor one day, Tonya. Fair is fair."

The door to the parlor opens, and Lena comes in, moving as she does, like a gust of wind, her long dark hair swinging. She places the tray on the table, rearranges the cups. She is starry-eyed when she smiles. Just like Valentin.

"My name is Lena," she says, sounding thrilled. "Are you a princess? Do you want tea?"

Natalya lifts a teacup, and Lena pours. "I'm not the princess," says Natalya. "What stunning hair you have, Lena."

"I got it from my father," chirps Lena.

"Lucky girl. And where is your father?"

"Far away. But I have never met him either, so don't feel sad," she says, in a tone that suggests that fathers are as make-believe as princesses, and as Tonya motions for her to leave, she flies back out of the room, dashing down the hallway, footsteps quickening, disappearing.

"She's got his eyes, too," says Natalya. "Andreyev doesn't know?"

Tonya pours her own tea. "It's not a secret. He went away to the war. I have had no word since."

"I see my opportunity to return your kindness. I've had a recent and unexpected encounter with Valentin Andreyev, in fact. In Moscow." Natalya points the cigarette holder in Tonya's direction. "Your Bolshevik had a bad bout of typhus at the front, it seems, which weakened him. And now, well, after such a harsh winter . . . you may not remember, living down here . . ."

All Tonya remembers of harsh winters now is *him*. That she could stand in his crowds for hours, losing all feeling in her fingers, losing herself. The memory of it still warms her. Still burns. "Is he not well?" she asks, the words stilted.

"I advise that you go straightaway, if you have anything to say to him," says Natalya archly. "You will not have another chance."

But have they not already run out of chances, Tonya and Valentin?

Why would he want to see her now? Has it not long been too late?

"Thank you for telling me, Natalya Fyodorovna," says Tonya. She cannot keep the sharpness from her voice.

"Call me Natasha," is the airy reply. "We are all comrades now, aren't we?"

It is only hours later, when the Countess is long gone and Lena is helping to set the table for dinner, that Tonya realizes she failed to ask why Natalya had come all the way to Otrada in the first place.

*　*　*

In the evening the lake between the birch and pine forests is draped in fog. Tonya sits at the edge of the water, which laps icily against her bare feet. She presses her face into her hands, hard enough that they turn as numb as her toes. Mama used to say that if you sit here long enough, in the white woods, you turn into a birch tree yourself. That is why their bark is like human skin, to the touch.

Why does it feel like this? Will it always feel like this?

Tonya hears an exclamation of surprise from behind her, but she doesn't raise her head to see its source. It's Nelly, who crouches now at the water, waving a hand to get her attention. "Tonya," she says, "what are you doing out here? I was on my way to Otrada to see you."

Overhead, the moon shines faintly, a gas lamp in the sky. Nelly will be able to see her tears.

"Oh, Tonya! What's wrong?"

"I had a visit from an old acquaintance today. She told me that Valentin Andreyev is very ill. I must go to Moscow if I wish to say good-bye." Tonya sinks her feet deeper into the water, which breaks gently. There are no waves, no tides, in such lakes as this.

"Then you must go," declares Nelly.

"But—"

"Kirill and I will look after Lena. Go."

"Why have you come looking for me?" Tonya asks, unsteadily.

Nelly produces a plain peddler's bag. It looks like Grandfather Frost's sack of toys. "Somebody left this at our house. Your name is on it."

Tonya unties the string, reaches in with both hands. She lets out a cut-glass cry.

A doll.

A porcelain doll, just like the first one. In fact, it is identical to the first one, except for its clothing. Gone are the gem-studded headdress and the silken swanlike gown. In their place, a shawl over the head, tied not in the front, at the chin, but at the back of the neck; and a one-piece sack-dress with broad pockets. A worker's costume. Both the shawl and the sack are red, a sumptuous shade, like garnet. Like blood. Like fire.

Around the wrist is a thin red ribbon.

"Oh, my," says Nelly, with a shudder, "why would anyone leave you such a thing? And why do I find it so unsettling?"

"Because it was made to look like me," Tonya says, or maybe she only thinks it. Maybe she has been rendered speechless. Mute. Just like the doll. "It was a gift. A gift from my husband."

18

Rosie

Eduard Rayevsky has chosen a hole-in-the-wall, a place where the seats are red and plasticky and a tape player on the counter is chewing up a cassette. There are piles of dirty dishes on every table. I am suffocating in secondhand smoke.

In a way I wish Lev were in here with us, but I'm also glad I insisted he go home. I need to do this alone.

Rayevsky pushes a plate of *pelmeni*, dumplings, across the sticky tabletop. "I'm sorry if I waylaid you at the Vernissage, Raisa." He rolls up his sleeves, revealing a landscape of tattoos. "I couldn't believe it either. That it was you."

Sweat slides down both sides of my face. Every night for the past fourteen years I've gone to bed with hatred for the man sitting in front of me stewing in my stomach. Determined not to become Mum, determined not to fall into her self-medicating, self-immolating haze, I've held on to that hatred. It's spread to every part of my body by now, disseminated through my bloodstream, and I feel a rush of it as we look at each other. He wants this to be civil? Does he think the passing of time has rinsed away any of the blood he spilled?

"Why did you kill them?" I ask bluntly.

He leans over and saws through one of the *pelmeni* with his knife, as if he thinks the reason I haven't started eating is that I can't use the cutlery. In my mind, *that man* has always been fixed in time. Like the people he killed, he never ages. But now that he's closer than ever before, I can see that he has an age. Sixty-five, maybe. Threadlike lines sprout from the corners of his eyes. His hair runs gray at the crown.

"It's time," he says, putting down the knife.

"Time?"

"Your mother and I were having an affair."

I hear myself laugh. Mum was a flirt, sure, but only because she liked to teeter on her tiptoes. My parents fought constantly; she had twice the emotional charge of most people and Papa had none. But they would never have been unfaithful. They loved each other.

Didn't they?

I blot my face with my serviette. I can feel a terrifying migraine looming at the edges of my consciousness.

"I didn't intend to kill anyone," he says. "I was in town and only wanted to talk to Katya in person. I'd misunderstood. I thought your father would be away that night. Obviously, he wasn't. She was."

"But you're . . . You make porcelain dolls. She has a collection of your . . . She had . . ." *This* is why Mum collected dolls like postage stamps? As souvenirs of a fling? Can the explanation for the worst night of my life really be this meaningless?

I see sudden sparks of light going off like cherry bombs. This is the man who murdered my sister and my beloved father. Two innocent people. He murdered Mum too; it just took longer. There's got to be more. "Tell me what happened," I say.

"When I arrived, there was a confrontation with your father, and . . . it got out of hand."

Out of hand, he calls it.

"It was a tragedy, I don't deny that. . . ."

A *tragedy.*

He's making it sound like something that happened on the news. To other people. Something that we could both walk away from. I can't walk away from it. But I can't go on sitting here at this moment, either. I stand up, and then I'm grabbing my bag, I'm shoving my way outside, pushing through the humidity and the smoke and the other patrons.

Out on the pavement, against the door of the restaurant, in full view of several horrified onlookers, I begin to vomit.

I heave and gasp, buckle over from the strength of it, until I'm on my knees.

"Raisa, poor girl." Eduard Rayevsky is behind me, grasping my shoulder. "Come on, let's find somewhere else to sit down—"

"Get your hands off her," somebody snarls. A voice that is very familiar, but I also don't know it in the least. *Lev.* I don't feel the hand on my shoulder anymore. I can't see anything clearly. I hear the sound of glass shattering. In my head, it's all of Mum's dolls, exploding together.

I stand, sway on my feet. People are shouting.

I run.

I don't know this area very well, but I run like I'm being

chased, and people give me flummoxed glances as I go past. They must think from my clothes and my panic that I'm a foreigner. That this is my first summer in Russia. But it's not.

I lived eleven summers of my life here. I'm still living that last one.

Into the metro. Down the escalators. Underground. I can't stop, or I might start *thinking*, and if I start to think, it might start to make sense. What he's said might start to feel true.

When I'm out in the open again, the migraine turns vindictive, pinching me at the temples as I board the minibus. I hold my head with both hands on the ride to the dacha. I cut myself on the house key trying to get inside. Thankfully the dacha is empty. I won't have to explain why my clothes are covered in vomit and blood, why I can't even take a breath.

In the front entry, I grope for the telephone, smear it as I start to dial. The operator puts me through.

Richard picks up. "Hello?"

"It's me. It's me."

"Hi, Ro," he says affectionately. "Wasn't expecting to hear from you today."

"Richard, I—"

"Sorry, Dad's just got here," he says. "We're off to London. I have to dash. Could we do tomorrow rather? I'll—"

The line is dead. The connection from here to Oxford has always been uneven. It hardly matters, because it's not comfort or conversation that I need. What I'm after is a reminder that I can reach out and touch something of Rosie's anytime I want. That I haven't been sucked into the vortex of my former life so fully I may never get out again.

But the dacha is not empty. I am not alone.

I hear it behind me, a skewed sound. I whirl around.

It's not real. It's not real. I'm dreaming.

Wake up, Ro, wake up wake up!

She does not quite fill the doorway, the girl in the nightgown. Her hair falls over her face, but she reaches a hand to try to pull it back.

I pick up the telephone, cradle and all, rip it from the wall, throw it at the thing in front of me. *Go away go away go away go away....* The telephone smashes against whatever it lands on, in the living room. The foyer is empty again. Everything is quiet.

I'm quaking all over. I retrieve the pieces of the phone. *Great thinking, Ro; damage the only literal lifeline you have in here.* My headache is screaming. I go to the kitchen and try to make myself a cup of tea, but my hands won't cooperate. I have to lie down.

I pull out the bin and I'm about to dump out the tea leaves when I notice something in the rubbish.

A crumpled photograph.

The picture of Tonya.

I'd forgotten all about Tonya. *That man* has always had that effect. Taking over my world. Wiping out everything in it. I grab the bin and shake it out. Bits of glass fall like beads. Has someone wrecked Akulina's frame? Taken a hammer to it?

There's another photograph, in the debris.

I sink to the floor. This picture is made of a weaker material— cut out of newspaper, it looks like—and it shows a young man addressing a huge crowd from a high, street-side balcony. This photograph must have been hidden behind the one of Tonya and the children.

Valentin Andreyev, Moscow, 1922, reads the caption.

There's *definitely* something familiar about this fellow. Not in the astonishing way that Tonya is familiar—in a subtler, subliminal way. The line of the jaw? The ridge of the brow? How he looks in a dark suit and tie? The quality of the photograph isn't high, but that's how imagination can take over. I can almost make out one voice above the crowd, a voice trying to change history, cutting through all other sound. . . .

Just like Alexey's.

Alexey, the only person besides me and Lev who knew about this frame—and who has been alone in the dacha since.

My thoughts are as scattered as the glass: Did *Alexey* destroy the photo frame? Or even Lev? But why would they? Why would anyone? The creature, the ghost—the girl—whatever it is, in this house, that I've been mistaking for me, because it looks like me— what if it's actually Tonya? What if *she* did this? Can she touch physical objects? Break them?

How long can I live like this?

I need to sweep all the glass back into the bin. I need to clean up the tea leaves. I still need to lie down, but I can't even move. I feel something on my cheek and hear a sound and then realize that it's me. Crying, even though I never, ever cry. I'm like Papa. I'm not a crier. I pride myself on it. But I am crying. I'm crying all the tears I didn't cry for Papa and Zoya, the tears I didn't cry when Mum and I arrived in England, the tears I didn't cry when I heard she was dead.

The tears of the past fourteen years.

They've become backlogged, like orders at a restaurant, and now they're all coming at once. They might never stop.

* * *

I lie on my side in bed. Lev and Alexey have returned. I can hear them talking in the hallway outside my door, Lev saying he thinks I'm not feeling well, Alexey expressing concern.

Tomorrow Alexey leaves on a four-day trip to Novosibirsk. More lectures, more talks, more pages in the literal book of his life.

It's only one chapter, though, isn't it?

Nothing is known about Alexey's life before his arrest. Nobody knows where he came from or who he was. He's never said. In *The Last Bolshevik*, he doesn't even describe how he felt, being sent to the White Sea Canal. He gives the visceral details of his existence in exile, the day-to-day, and his writing is lyrical. It carries you along.

But this evocative picture serves only to distract from what's not there: he, himself, the person.

Alexey Ivanov's façade is charismatic and compelling. No doubt it's one he nurtured over time, and no doubt it represents some part of him, maybe the part he most wants to be, but it's a façade nonetheless. Whoever he really is, it's still lurking.

Or else he destroyed it. Violently. Like the photo frame.

It would be ironic if Tonya were the one haunting this house, while he's scouring all of Russia looking for her. Unless it's not ironic. Unless it makes perfect sense.

What if his whole quest to find her is a façade?

What if he already knows she's dead? What if he killed her? What if—

"You're awake."

I sit up, slowly. My face feels brittle from too much crying. Lev sits on the bed and hands me a glass of water, and I have to force myself to take a sip. It's flat and sour as lime, Moscow tap water, but it washes down the remnants of my nausea.

"You didn't kill Rayevsky, did you?" I croak.

"When he wakes up tomorrow, he'll wish he was dead."

"Thanks for fulfilling my revenge fantasies, but I need him alive."

Lev doesn't smile. "Why?"

It's coming back to me in patches: the dumplings, the revelations, the reasons. Maybe Eduard Rayevsky killed my father in a jealous rage during a heated confrontation. A crime of passion. I might believe that. But why *Zoya*? It doesn't feel right. It's not like he was afraid of leaving witnesses. He let me go, after all. And why was he armed? *How* was he armed? Nobody I knew owned a gun.

"He explained what happened. He said it was an accident." A *tragedy*. "But it was like—disinformation. Like he's headed me off at the pass. I want the truth."

A long moment goes by.

"You want what is true," says Lev, "or what feels true?"

I thought I couldn't possibly cry more, but I may have busted a pipe behind my eyes yesterday.

"Perhaps it is easier for you," Lev says, softly, "to stay stuck. Easier to keep looking to the past, to something that already happened, because it is known. The outcome is unavoidable. What is scary is the unknown. Your own future, your own life, without your family—"

"There is no *my own life*!" *Stop, Rosie, stop!* "My father dreamt all this up for me! I don't even like Oxford! I don't even enjoy studying encryption!" What if I never stop? What if I can cry forever? "Of course I'm scared. I don't sleep at night, I see things, things you can't even imagine, and I don't even remember what it was like to be—"

I stop.

I press a hand against my face. It feels too warm. "Sorry for shouting."

"That's not shouting," he says.

"It is in England."

He laughs. He looks more like himself.

I blink sweat and tears out of my eyes. "I have to look at my mother's stories again. I want to investigate my theory that they were my father's. I just have to break down the letters. . . ."

"Get some rest, Raisa." To my surprise, he leans over, kisses me on the forehead. "The truth isn't going anywhere."

* * *

I am hot with fever, but at the same time, I feel a sensation of cold that penetrates to the bone.

Something—someone—is standing over me.

This ghost isn't haunting the dacha. She's haunting *me*. In England, she was only a presence, a chill, a strange smell, a memory. Now that I've brought her with me to Russia, she's much stronger. Growing stronger still, every day. Our worlds no longer overlap only occasionally. They're melding.

I hold my eyes shut for a moment, and then open them.

At first I see nothing. It is night, and the door to the balcony is wide open. By morning my room will be flush with mosquitoes. I look blankly into the darkness, searching the whole room, and then, right in front of me, I see her.

Sitting on the bed, right where Lev was, only hours ago.

Her hair covers most of her face like carpet. The dress looked like lace from a distance, but I can tell now that it's just cotton, bulky, oversized for such a thin frame. Her hands are so pale they disappear in places.

Is she a vision of the future? Of me? Or is she a ghost of the past? Tonya?

A smell fills the room, and this one is unmistakable.

It is the smell of that two-in-one Ivushka shampoo from when I was kid, which came in a squat glass bottle and foamed like it was rabid. Zoya had long, glossy halo-hair, and if she was close by, you wouldn't be able to smell anything else.

One, two ...

Those hands reach up to her face, to part the cobwebs of hair at last. There, in the center of her forehead, right above the eyes, is the hole.

It has been fourteen years and she is still bleeding.

How can *this* be Zoya? Zoya, who was strong, impervious, imperious, always bossing me around, acting like she knew what was best for me? Zoya, who was in many ways the mother Mum should have been? I always desperately wanted my sister to come down from her high horse. To lower herself to my level.

Now I have what I want.

"Help me," I say, choking on the words. "Help me, Zoya. Please. I'm so, so lost. Tell me where to go from here."

But she's already gone.

19

Valentin

There's a hush over the city tonight that Valentin finds disconcerting. Moscow has been livelier than Piter by far, especially since they moved the capital here. Even in the middle of the night, he can usually hear the clamor from the nearby hotels, neighbors arguing, shutters opening and closing, someone singing "The Internationale."

It should not be this quiet.

His neck aches from poring over paperwork. There is so much of it he can't see out his own windows.

The quiet is interrupted by the sound of rapping at the door. Viktoria, most likely. If she's been in the neighborhood, she'll sleep here. Every time she does, he misses her, misses the company, the lovemaking, the laughter, of their marriage. Before he left for the front, he enjoyed working while she practiced piano. The notes had a way of smoothing out his thoughts.

But it was not enough.

They are still married in name. Viktoria doesn't want to upset Pavel. It's immaterial to Valentin. Everything else about his life is a sham, anyway.

Valentin rolls up a cigarette, knocks over the filter paper. He should start looking for his own place, one that doesn't echo with old melodies. Old memories. One that's closer to the ground, because nobody should live this high up. Whenever he looks outside, he feels like he's living on the podium. Giving a speech that never ends.

"Is that you, Vika?" he says, opening the door. "My neighbors won't appreciate your . . ."

It is not Viktoria.

It is her.

Antonina Nikolayevna.

He can't find enough voice to say her name.

In his memory, her image has softened over time; it has been seven years. Now he will have to start forgetting her all over again.

She still wears that dastardly shawl, and he still feels like shredding it with his bare hands. He brings the cigarette to his mouth, leans against the doorframe as if he expected this, expected her, just another pretty face from the past come to beg for favors, now that he's a commissar. It does happen. There's only one kind of favor he's willing to give.

Tonya appears confused, the rosiness high in her cheeks. She pulls off her gloves. Her hands were always pure, polished, to the point of looking fake. Now they are coarse peasant-hands. He catches himself staring.

"Can I come in?" she asks.

"Yes," he says. "Of course."

Valentin shows her into the main room. There's hardly any furniture. Viktoria wanted the chairs with the long French names, the porcelain pieces that used to line the shelves, the decorative wall hangings. At the time, just after his return from the war, he wanted her to take everything. It was symbolic. A cleansing. Valentin had been living a lie too long, even before he went south to join the Ninth Army. He already knew that the hierarchy of Russian society had not been overturned, only inverted; that he was part of this new elite. The new ruling class; the new aristocracy of the new Russia.

Things can be very new, and not different at all.

It never crossed his mind, as he gutted his own home, that he might be trying to re-create that dank, empty cellar room in Piter, and the possibility that Tonya might be coming by at any moment.

Well, here she is.

Valentin tries once more to converse normally. It is like pulling words through a loom: "What are you doing here?" He regularly speaks to hundreds of people. It should not be this hard to speak to one person.

"Somebody told me you were dying," she says, with a probing look, like perhaps he's only hiding it.

Dying? Is that why she's come? Guilt? Penance? Or curiosity? What would kill a young man in his prime, after all, with his whole life ahead of him?

This, perhaps.

"Sorry to disappoint," he says coldly. He must be careful. Even now there are unbidden moments when he replays in his mind the last time he ever saw her, the last time they ever spoke. The gunpowder, the smoke, the promises they made. They were children, believing in their own games a little too hard.

But he was twenty-one years old then. He is almost twenty-eight now. He's not the innocent boy Bolshevik that he was. And she, judging by her hands, is no longer the princess.

"I saw a photograph of you once," she says, in a tone he can't interpret. "A few years ago, in *Krasnaya Gazeta*. You were a hero of the war, it said."

He knows the one. Revolution Square, right here in Moscow. He hates that picture. He hates that person. "A lot has happened."

"You must be doing well for yourself. This apartment is beautiful."

"It belongs to Pavel Katenin."

"Your father-in-law?"

How does she know *that*? Did they say so, in *Krasnaya Gazeta*? What else did they say? That he married Viktoria in 1918, that it was a sensible union? That he'd have sawed off his left arm to fall in love with his own wife? That there was once, after he returned from the front, his marriage finished, his career floundering, when he met a girl at a party—whose party? Impossible to remember now—with just enough gray in her eyes that he invited her home, had her against the wall, whispered Tonya's name?

"Your wife wrote to me," she says. "During the war."

"My ex-wife."

"Oh. I am sorry." Tonya hesitates. That peculiar, probing look again. "You never received my letters?"

"What letters?" Did she have something to say to him? Was that poem not enough? *I loved you, and perhaps that love* . . . Valentin's jaw aches from holding back too many words, all the replies that he made up in his own head in the months following her rejection. He wrote letters too. He never sent them. *Lyubov' moya, prosti menya . . .*

What was he asking her forgiveness for? He still doesn't know.

"To tell you about our—" She breaks off.

"Our what?" She seems to be thinking over her answer, but whatever she's about to say, Valentin needs her to stay back— He needs her to stay— He needs her—

"That night, in February 1917," says Tonya, "I was going to go to you."

"I don't want to talk about that night."

"I'll talk about it. I must explain—"

"No," he says. "I never think of it anymore."

He can feel himself slipping into his podium-voice. It's like being on Revolution Square again, that day in 1922, rallying the crowds to a cause he no longer believed in. The real Valentin was still dying somewhere far away, of typhus, of Tonya, while the podium-Valentin fed off the masses. Off of lies.

"I am part of an organization here in Moscow, made up of people who believe that Comrade Stalin must be removed from power," he says, stronger now. "The Party has been corrupted, has betrayed the Revolution. Where is the free speech that Lenin promised? Where is the true socialism? But a phoenix will rise from the ashes—the human ashes—of revolution and war. We will do it again, and better this time. This is all that matters to me, Tonya. The plight of the people."

"Always the people," she says, as soft as his voice is hard.

Valentin never wanted anything the way he wanted her. He refuses to go back to that. To live like that again. To hunger. To hope. "If I believed in any gods," he says, "I would thank them every day that you did not come that night. You saved me from myself."

This has an effect. Her eyes nearly change color.

He has won.

It does not feel like victory.

"Since you have come all this way, you can stay the night," he says, and she nods, but she is already turning away.

20

Antonina

The fireplace purrs, the flames throwing shadows upon the walls. This room has little in it except for the bed-stead and several large, glass-fronted mahogany cabi-nets. Tonya cannot sleep, so she touches the glass, peers at the spines. These are not books Valentin would read, at least the Valentin she knew. These are books she would read to him, stories he would pretend to enjoy. Perhaps they are Vikto-ria's. Perhaps they are Pavel's.

If Tonya *had* gone that night, Valentin Andreyev would still be living in a basement.

Or would they have moved elsewhere for the baby's sake? Scraped together enough for an apartment at ground level? But when you let yourself wonder, as Mama used to say, a thousand more wonderings unfold and unfurl, like flowers in the sun. They will be unstoppable.

Suddenly she sees him there, reflected in the glass, behind her. She turns halfway.

Just shout it out, she tells herself. *Tell him what happened, tell him everything*, but some other part of her only answers, *To what end?* He doesn't wish to hear it. He said so himself. He has everything he needs. He might look the part of that young factory worker—his collar askew, the first button undone, the sleeves rolled up—but he is no longer hers.

Be silent. Sleep.

Or speak.

I tried to come to you—my husband discovered me—I was locked in my room—kept there—I would have gone to you. I chose you—

I would still choose you—

Is she speaking? Does he hear?

If he leaves now, it is finished forever—

His hand grips the doorframe, and then he lets go. Valentin comes up to her; she turns the rest of the way. Her heart beats hard, like bird wings. He takes her by the hand, touches her wrist, stops.

"What is this?" he asks.

It is the red ribbon.

He curses, softly. She pulls down her sleeve, strangely humiliated, but neither of them turn away. He held her like this once before, years ago, on a tram that was so full of people it seeped at the corners like a jam candy. Money and tickets were making their way over the passengers' heads and the tram thudded hard, propelled her forward, tipped her into his arms.

How do you always find me in a crowd? she asked him then.

What do you mean, he said. *You are the only one I see.*

* * *

Valentin is already asleep. His breath is quiet in her hair. Why can't she sleep too? What is this furry feeling up and down her arms, like something has just brushed her by? Is it Natalya's trick, now gone astray, telling Tonya that Valentin was unwell? The Countess must be bored. That's what happens when everyone thinks you're dead.

Is it Tonya's conscience, because she has not yet told Valentin about Lena?

Is it that he is a *counterrevolutionary*?

Lenin's Red Terror is supposed to be over; the grain brigades no longer swarm the countryside; the lists of traitors no longer appear in the newspapers. But the Chekists, or whatever they call themselves now, are no less dangerous. Maybe they let Natalya Burtsinova live, but Natalya was willing to cut a deal. In his heart, Valentin is a martyr. And martyrs do not cut deals.

"Tonya . . . ?"

"I want you to come home with me tomorrow," she says, turning her face to his. "To Otrada."

He pulls away, to look at her. "You know I can't. My meeting can't be rearranged. There is too much risk. But I will come as soon as it's over."

"You once said we would live two lives," she says, "and I thought you meant one life, then another. But what if it means there are two possible lives that lie ahead of us, right now? What if it means—"

"I will come," he says patiently. "Nothing will keep me away from you. You have given me such detailed instructions for Otrada, I wouldn't be able to forget them if I tried." Dipping his head to her neck, he murmurs: "Of course, there are ways to forget everything. . . ."

"Again?" she says, smiling, but her doubts loom.

"I have been living like an Orthodox monk, Tonya."

"I would have thought monks do not lie."

He grins. "I have missed you," he says, suddenly. "I have missed you so much that even now you are here, I still feel it. Perhaps I do not believe it yet."

Tonya believes in it more than she ever has. *Love should not be a frenzy,* Mama used to say. *You will know it by how quiet it is. How it grows over time, every day a little bit more, a little bit stronger, without anyone noticing, until it's all you can see, like the White Nights of St. Petersburg. Until it is just a fact of life.*

* * *

They are outside the station. The rushing, the clamoring, the clattering, make it impossible for her to think.

Now that they're here, about to part, the trains arriving, leaving, wheels grating on tracks, whistles blowing, someone shouting political slogans above all the noise—*Comrades! Workers and peasants of Russia, hear ye, hear ye!*—now it has returned.

The feeling from last night, almost spicy, trilling in her veins.

Tonya agreed to this plan, and it's better for her to go on to Otrada alone, so she can prepare Lena for Valentin's arrival. So what is this resistance? Why does she want to beg him to come with her?

"I just— I don't think you can have both," she says, uselessly.

"Can't live two lives?" he asks.

"Be serious, Valya!"

"I'm more serious than I've ever been. I'm coming to you. I'll be there by tomorrow night. We will be together. Now, and always. There will never be anyone for me but you, Antonina."

She feels something wet, filthy, on her eyelashes. "Promise me."

"I promise."

The sky is white. A few gulls circle the clouds. He kisses her lightly at first, then harder. Another promise. As he walks away, he looks over his shoulder. *Wait for me,* he mouths, and she musters a smile. The sun has come out at last. The light reaches her, staining everything it lands on, even her hands as she holds them over her mouth. She does not cry out. She does not let the tears fall.

* * *

Tonya waits for a day, two days, three. Nobody comes. In the old days, she was the unreliable one, not Valentin. The day a courier finally drags his sorry wagon cart into the relay station, she is already there waiting. She has grown accustomed to waiting.

There is a letter for her. Could it truly be that Valentin has changed his mind? That he doesn't want her?

But it is not from Valentin.

And now you will know how I felt.
Fair is fair, darling.
Until the day we meet again—
     Natasha

21

Rosie

I wake up feeling much better, alone in my room, with sunlight bleaching my bedsheets. My temperature seems normal, my tear ducts intact. I dress quickly and pull my hair into a high ponytail. It's noon—I slept until *noon*.

Eduard Rayevsky's explanation of the murders has now marinated long enough for me to be sure it's skewed; at the very least, it's a version of the truth, but I've always had one of those at hand. My own.

First, there are other strands for me to follow. Alexey wasn't holding open auditions for young women who happened to look like his long-lost *Kukolka*. He *targeted* me. His advert was on the notice board of my favorite café in Oxford. I was hired before I even learned about the job.

There is a connection between Tonya and my family. People don't look that similar by chance.

The whole dacha smells sweet, but especially downstairs.

Wildflowers have bloomed gaudily outside in the garden. I've become so used to smells in my head that I forgot what it's like, to smell something real. I stand on the veranda for ages, saturating in it, until Lev comes around the porch, and for a second, reality wavers.

Is this *our* house? Are we just going about our lives in the Moscow suburbs?

Would every single day smell like this, if we were?

In the kitchen, I make a stack of every book Alexey owns about the Bolshevik Revolution and the Civil War. I prop up the newspaper photograph of the young man that I found in the garbage. *Valentin Andreyev. Moscow. 1922.* Total nobodies do not give speeches in city squares. They do not appear in newspapers.

He was someone. He's got to be in here somewhere.

Many of the older books have no indexes. But in several of the bog-standard, cut-and-dried texts, Valentin Andreyev is given a few lines. One book even includes the picture itself, with a longer caption beneath.

Noted Party orator Valentin Andreyev addresses a crowd in Revolution Square.

He was known for his oration. Just like Alexey.

I jot down some notes. Valentin Mikhailovich Andreyev, born in St. Petersburg in 1896. Orphaned at age nine, after which he encountered the radical writer Pavel Katenin. Under Katenin's tutelage, the young Andreyev became prominent in the revolutionary underground in his own right. Following the Bolshevik victory in 1917, Andreyev married Katenin's daughter, the pianist Viktoria

Katenina; in 1919, he was handpicked by Stalin to join a regiment of the Ninth Army as commissar, to boost morale; in 1922, he returned from the Civil War to a hero's welcome; in 1924, he was stripped of Party membership and found guilty of counterrevolutionary activity. He was exiled to a new kind of penal colony in the Solovetsky Islands, in the north. In the White Sea.

The first stirrings of the Soviet Gulag.

Valentin Andreyev was never seen or heard from again.

* * *

In the central knoll of Dzerzhinsky Square is a tall, imposing statue of Felix Dzerzhinsky, original head of the Bolshevik Cheka. Behind Iron Felix, above the traffic going around in circles, looms the infamous, if relatively benign-looking, Lubyanka. The home of the KGB, Soviet secret police, it is made of pretty, soft-yellow sandstone.

"Miss Simonova?"

A man with an impressive mustache waves to me as he approaches. This must be David Antonovich, from the human rights organization Memorial. Unmarried, childless, and highly educated, David has dedicated his life to the memory and recovery of victims of political repression, particularly under the Stalinist regime.

His own parents were processed in the Lubyanka.

Across the street, David shows me the Solovetsky Stone, a rock that made an arduous journey from the islands all the way here to central Moscow. Its placement last year was organized by Memorial, in honor of the lives lost in the camps. It is small, unremarkable, sitting atop granite.

Yet it stands out against the Lubyanka.

We head down Teatralny. David tells me about the research he does, the material he goes through. Most prisoner files are nothing more than manila folders with photos and a few inter-rogation records. Name card, prisoner number, stamp in the corner. The full archives of the Lubyanka are not yet public, but Memorial hopes they will continue to open up.

"It's hard to cross the line, between the Soviet Union and the camps," says David. "Every time we do, each of us, we fear to van-ish into the ether. I've stood where you are now. On the line."

I do feel a bit wobbly. "No one's ever found anything on Val-entin Andreyev?"

"Not much," says David. "Historians know he was arrested here in Moscow. He's believed to have died in the Solovetsky Is-lands. But who can say? So many records were destroyed in the decades to follow. So many people fell off the map."

Alexey's said something similar to me, about people disap-pearing. Lost to history.

But what about people *reappearing*?

What if Valentin Andreyev was sent into exile, and Alexey Ivanov came back?

I still have trouble reconciling Alexey's placid, room-temperature personality with the act of smashing through a framed photograph, but maybe seeing Tonya in such an unex-pected place, in such an unexpected way, set him off somehow. When I took this job, I assumed *Kukolka* was a family member, friend, or lover, and that any reunion would be joyful. But it could equally be that he wants to confront her. Or harm her.

David gives me a kindly pat on the shoulder. "Some people

say that the north is white because it's made of human bone, Raisa. You're not the first to wish those bones could speak."

* * *

For supper, I've decided to make *pelmeni* the way Mum used to make them for me and Zoya, when we were little. The slablike ones I had in the restaurant with Rayevsky made me nostalgic for them, funnily enough, for the way Mum would add her flourishes— sprigs of parsley, garlic, sour cream—and arrange them on a plate like bird eggs.

When did she start making nothing but sandwiches? Was it because I stopped asking for anything else?

Lev appears in the doorway, watches me. He has been out the whole afternoon. The brief separation makes it feel even more like this is our normal life, like he's come home from work and so have I, and now we're having a meal together. But this is nothing like my normal life. I never sleep in, read for hours, cook for pleasure. I'm always exhausted, existing on fumes, working, overworking. It's like I never stopped defecting from Russia. Never stopped running.

"You met with the researcher today, from Memorial," he says.

I glance up from the dough. "I think he really wants to help, but there's not much they can do. He hopes that eventually there'll be full public access to the Lubyanka records."

"Not everyone will want to know what's down in those tunnels."

"Wouldn't you?"

"People did bad things. But it's done. We can't absolve anyone now."

"Huh," I say, rifling in a drawer for the rolling pin. "Like your family, maybe?"

"Why do you say that?"

"I just mean— You're in trouble with the Ministry of the Interior, aren't you? That's why you're stuck with me all summer. But it's such an easy assignment, a nothing punishment. We all know how things work over here," I say, with a shrug. "Someone's got your back. A parent? Family friend? You don't have to tell me. I'm just saying, most people, in relation to the Lubyanka records, would think of the victims. You are thinking of the perpetrators."

He doesn't answer. I may have offended him.

I put down the rolling pin. "Can you help me put the filling in the dough?"

Lev pulls out a chair, without a word, and gets to work. His fingers are quicker at it than I expected. He's obviously done this before.

"Where were *you* today?" I ask.

"To see my mother. Speaking of family."

"Yeah? Just for fun?"

"I wanted her advice."

"Advice on what?"

Again, he doesn't reply right away. The kitchen is beginning to feel musty with spices. I wipe my hands on a tea towel. I'm used to the silences by now.

"My father is a general," he says, like that's what I asked.

"Whoa."

"He's a security advisor to the Kremlin."

"*That* kind of military family."

"He's also an old-school Communist who can't stand Gorbachev. He wants things to go back to the way they were under—"

"Stalin?"

Lev laughs. "I was going to say Brezhnev. But yes, my father is unhappy about how much control the Party has lost. How much power. That's what he blames for a lot of the hardships the past few years. He doesn't like change. He was the one who secured this—what you call a punishment—for me," he says, after a pause. "He hates Alexey Ivanov even more than he does Gorbachev. I think he hoped I might do some spying."

I prod the dumpling into shape. Lev is confiding in me. Trusting me. "What did you do?"

"I was involved for a while with this woman. I didn't know who she really was. I didn't care. Turned out she was a journalist, looking for dirt on some of my superiors. Maybe even my father. They found out, so here I am."

"I'm sorry." I try to wipe my cheek on my shoulder. "Spying would have been much more exciting than dumplings."

Another laugh, but this one is a bit different. "It's not that bad." Something in his voice makes me look up again. He's reaching into his jacket. "I brought you something. From my mother's garden."

It's a small, single pink rose.

People are well versed in the language of flowers here in Russia, but I've been away too long. I have no idea what this means. All I recall is that red roses signify deep feelings and that a bouquet should always, always, *vsegda*, contain an odd number of flowers. But for all I know, this is the only thing his mother grows.

He is looking at me intently.

"It's gorgeous." I reach for the rose, cough a little. "Thank you."

"Raisa, I want to—"

"I'll find a vase for this." The spices are making my eyes water. I can't do this. I just can't. "I've got to get to cooking."

* * *

David shares a number of interviews that Valentin Andreyev's wife, Viktoria Katenina, gave to journalists and historians in the last decades of her life. He also gives me the contact information of Viktoria's daughter-in-law, who is a professor in the faculty of physics at Lomonosov Moscow State University. I milk my affiliation with Oxford and manage to get on the line with her. Marina agrees to meet with me at a café off Pushkinskaya Square.

She's already ordering at the counter when I go in. She's in her fifties or sixties, with a frosty smile and short hair. She shakes my hand, a gesture I've never seen a Russian woman use.

We find a table by the window, and wait as the waitress puts out the tea.

"My husband wouldn't like that I'm talking to you," says Marina Katenina briskly. "Journalists and historians hounded his mother for decades. I'm here to tell you to leave our family alone. I'll give you some quotes, you go home happy, you never bother us again."

My stress levels are rising with the steam off my tea. "Why did they hound Viktoria?"

"Her father, of course! The downfall of the great Pavel Katenin!" Marina rolls her eyes. "And everything else too. Daily life in the purges. Her early career as a pianist. Whatever it is. She died so old—only ten years ago now?—that she became fashionable. Look at *you*, thinking you can understand what somebody like Viktoria experienced. I assure you, young lady, you can't. You're barely alive by comparison."

This is not going well.

"Viktoria was a good person," she says, calmly unwrapping the foil of a chocolate. "I'll go on record with that."

"I ... um ..." My mouth has filled with saliva, and not because of the chocolate. "I'm not interested in your mother-in-law. I mean, I am, but it's because I'm trying to find out what happened to Valentin Andreyev. Her husband."

A sleety silence.

I plow on: "I've read all of Viktoria's interviews. She never talks about Valentin. And your husband, Mikhail, he took her surname. Katenin. Was Valentin his father?"

"Your Russian sounds strange to me," says Marina.

"I've been away a long time."

"Shall we speak in English?"

"That's not—"

"You're barking up a bad tree," declares Marina in English. She has a precise, posh accent, one that makes me feel like we might be just around the corner from Oxford. She draws back from the table, as if to reassess me. "Valentin Andreyev was the Bolshevik, wasn't he? The one who died in a labor camp, sometime in the 1920s? My husband was born in the thirties."

There goes that idea.

"What is your interest in Valentin Andreyev?" Marina asks, begrudgingly.

How can I say that I'm increasingly convinced that Valentin became the historian Alexey Ivanov? How can I explain that he might have penned one of the most famous memoirs of the past century, or that he shares his life story—part of it—with hundreds of strangers at least once a week?

"I think I know him." The English words seem to stick to my teeth as I say them. I'm out of practice.

"You think you *know* him," she repeats.

I feel myself blush. "I'm gathering evidence."

"What does that mean?"

"If I'm right, Valentin is living under a different name. I believe he's looking for someone who may be in my family. He's away right now, but he's due back in Moscow soon. . . ."

Now would be a great moment for Zoya to intervene. To show me something the way she showed me the remains of Otrada. To help me prevent Marina from leaving, because she's already reaching for her handbag. But there's nothing: no smells, no visions, no Tchaikovsky. In classic sibling fashion, Zoya shows up when I haven't invited her, and ditches me as soon as I need her.

The thought almost brings a smile to my face.

Marina is sticking out her hand to shake mine once more. Her wrist jangles as she does, with a slim charm bracelet.

"Ballet slippers." I've switched back to Russian without meaning to.

Marina lifts an eyebrow, withdraws her hand.

"Your bracelet. You're a fan of the ballet?"

"More my husband."

"My mother was a ballerina. At the Bolshoi. Katerina Simonova. She's, um, she died, but . . ."

"Katerina," Marina repeats.

"You've heard of her?" I ask, eagerly.

"No. I'm afraid I haven't." She sits back again, lets go of her bag. "I just—had a very strange thought, that's all." She scans the café, as if she thinks someone may be listening. A short breath, and then: "Alright. Let's say I help you, Raisa. A little, because we do not know each other, so the trust is fragile. Everything I say must stay between us."

I don't know what's changed, but I will myself to keep drinking tea.

"Valentin Andreyev survived exile," says Marina. "He came back in 1933, in secret, through Pavel Katenin's connections. They didn't tell anyone."

"What?" It comes out as a yelp. "Why not?"

"Viktoria's father was popular with the regime. Trotskyite ex-convicts didn't fit Pavel's image, I would imagine. But it was also the 1930s. People tried not to talk too much in general. Everyone was hiding one thing or another."

"Couldn't Viktoria divorce him? Why go to the trouble of hiding him?"

"I told you, my mother-in-law had a good heart." Marina shrugs. "Valentin returned traumatized. He needed help. He couldn't be taken out in public anyway, so they just pretended that he never came home. Something like this."

"Viktoria said all this?"

"Not directly. I put it together on my own, over time. My generation, we know how to listen."

"Why didn't Viktoria reveal any of this in her interviews? Historians still believe Valentin died in the camps—"

"Viktoria tried her best to give people the glimpse they wanted, into such terrible times. But she had her own heartbreak, her own sorrows." Marina looks meaningfully at me. "She was not a living archive."

I drop my gaze to my lap.

"Valentin left the family years later. Abandoned them," Marina continues, "and Mikhail never saw his father again. But as I said, Valentin was sick in the head, after so many years in the camps. It's possible in theory that you are right, therefore, that he took a new name and just—became someone else."

"Do you know when he left them? What year?"

"In the late forties, early fifties, I would think. I don't have all the facts. My husband finds the subject very difficult." She clearly knows more than she's saying, but from the way she's straightened in her seat, our discussion is over.

1940s or 1950s. Alexey's memoir of the White Sea Canal wouldn't be published for decades yet. No one knows what he was doing then. Or living as.

"If his father were alive now," she adds, "Mikhail would want to know. Of that, I am sure."

Reuniting Marina's husband with his father is not my primary motive. But it could be that it's a way to crack Alexey. It's been too easy for him to avoid hard questions all these years, because every time he speaks, he renders everyone else speechless.

If he is in fact Valentin Andreyev, I doubt he could keep denying the truth while looking his own *son* straight in the eye.

"I must give all this some more thought," Marina says, decisively. "Tell me how to contact you."

* * *

Upon his return from Novosibirsk, Alexey is his usual sanded-smooth self. His first question is whether I made any headway with Akulina Burtsinova. I tell him that I went to see her and learned that the manuscript of the Countess's memoir was mailed to her.

"There was never any basement," I clarify.

He nods. He seems neither surprised nor disappointed.

"I'm going back to see her."

He zeroes in on me now. "Why is that?"

"Just to ask a few more questions." When that doesn't seem to satisfy him, I try another answer: "Maybe she can show me the original of the manuscript."

"Great idea," he says, relaxing again. "It's a valuable primary source."

It dawns on me: I'm still catching up to him. He's already done all this legwork. He knows all the surface stuff. But for someone who's well into his nineties, who's trying to complete this impossible, epic quest before he shuffles off this mortal coil, he just seems so *casual*. Where is the urgency? The desperation? Why isn't he parading me up and down Tverskaya, seeing if he can smoke *Kukolka* out? What crucial element am I still missing?

"Is there anything else you'd like me to do?" I ask.

"For the moment, just keep taking notes," he replies. His eyes flash in my direction, but they stay unfocused, like he's looking at somebody behind me. Alexey Ivanov is haunted too, only his ghost won't say his name, and he won't say hers.

* * *

So now you want to speak with me," says Akulina Burtsinova. The Countess's daughter sits in her armchair like it's a throne, half swallowed by a blanket. "Last time you couldn't get away fast enough."

Her cat maneuvers between my crossed ankles. "I'm so sorry,"

I begin, "but the frame you gave me has been destroyed. Just the frame. The photograph is fine."

"And how did that happen?" she asks, stroppily.

"The historian I'm working for used to know Tonya. I think he did it." I hesitate. "I have a picture of him, if you'd like to see."

"What's his name?"

"Alexey Ivanov."

"Never heard of him. What does he look like?"

"He's old," I say, and she chuckles, more like a goat's bleat than a laugh. I retrieve *The Last Bolshevik* from my bag and show her the back cover. "Here. That's him."

Akulina shakes her head. "I don't recognize him."

"Tell me about Tonya. What happened to her?"

"I don't know that either," she says. "I told you how she took us in, my brother and me, but we lost touch after I went east. She was still living at Otrada. By the time I made my way back, she was gone. That was it."

"Otrada." I've been using the English *r* all this time. No wonder Marina thought my Russian sounded strange. It's less scary to use English-language sounds; in Russian you have to let it go, or the rolling doesn't happen. *Otrrrada. Rrraisa.*

"Tonya's home in Tula province."

"I've been there. My mother left me a map." I can't believe how normal I sound. There's the connection between me and Tonya, right there. "The person Alexey is looking for, he calls her *Kukolka.* Was that Tonya's nickname?"

"Not that I knew." Akulina sounds unimpressed. "Well, good luck to him. Tonya had many admirers." She pauses, and then realization dawns. Our eyes meet, hers glassy with age. "But—wait. You look just like her. Is that why he hired you?"

"I think so." I've gone a bit blank.

"Did he say so?" she exclaims.

"No."

"You should quit," she says, with a wet-sounding cough. "What if he tries to hurt *you*, and not just photo frames?"

"Alexey isn't dangerous," I say. "He's too slow-moving, for one."

Akulina harrumphs noisily. "I would still quit, if I were you."

I can't. But it's hard to explain.

"The original manuscript of your mother's memoir," I add. "I'm curious whether you still have it. Could I see it?"

"I'm not going to live forever." Akulina's tone tells me that she knows how much time she has. "It's yours if you want it. Just take care, Raisa. Don't let the historian anywhere near."

* * *

Night seems to fall faster at the dacha than it does in the rest of Moscow. Neither Lev nor Alexey is anywhere to be seen. I seize the opportunity to take inventory. Turning on all the lamps, I place everything on my bed, where it all looks especially dramatic, against the tapestry of lace.

One key, to Mum's drawer in the *stenka*.

One map of Tula province, with Otrada marked.

Two porcelain dolls, courtesy of Mum: one from my family's apartment; the other found at Otrada. A third porcelain doll, purchased in Izmaylovo, from the vendor. All are marked on the back of the neck with the same signature: *E. S. Rayevsky*. Their hair curls in the same places, in at the temples, out at the cheeks. Their eyes are all the same color.

All three have upturned smiles, as if held up by string.

Stapled sheets of paper, the fairy-tale-style stories. All hand-written in pencil. Mum's stories? Papa's? I still don't know. I haven't reread them.

I might be avoiding them.

Two black-and-white photographs: one of Tonya and the children, provided by Akulina; one of the orator Valentin Andreyev. All badly crumpled, presumably in someone's fist, and retrieved from the bin.

And now this, my latest addition: a shoebox containing the original manuscript of Natalya Burtsinova's memoir, which I have not yet inspected, but which—one assumes—is fairly close to the published version I have already read.

I turn the chair away from the rolltop desk, take a seat, and stare at it all.

There's a noise from downstairs; somebody is home. I'll put this away under the bed. The upside of having such drippy covers, such an explosion of embroidery, is that nobody can begin to see under the bed from the door. I grab the first doll and lift the corners of my duvet.

Zoya is there. Under the bed.

If I speak, if I let out any sound, I'll scream.

She reaches a hand forward.

What does Zoya's ghost want with me, if that's what she is? If I take her hand, will she come out? Or will she pull me under?

She is waiting. I reach out too. Our hands touch. Her palm feels smooth, flat as slate. She does not grip me, does not try to hold on.

Raisochka, she says.

She can speak.

Can we speak to each other?

But her eyes flick upward.

"Raisa?"

I drop the duvet in an instant, get to my feet. Lev looks at me, at the smorgasbord of oddities, but he's used to such things by now. He smells a bit soapy, seems to be a bit dressed up. I suppose he was out with friends.

"What's all this?" he asks.

I sink onto my bed. "It's my . . . collection."

A collection. I'm officially turning into Mum.

"I haven't seen that before." He indicates the shoebox.

"I went to see Akulina Burtsinova again. It's the original of her mother's memoir." I open the box, suddenly weary, rifle through the sheets. "It's not really . . ." I pick up a page. Handwritten. I expected typewritten.

Handwritten in *pencil* . . .

I put down the box, snatch up the stapled stories, the fairy tales. "The Silver Queen." "The Wedding Veil." "The House on a Wide River."

It's the same penmanship.

The same person wrote these. The stories, and the memoir.

"Are you okay?" asks Lev.

"Yeah, yeah. Why?"

"You're crying."

"Am I? It's just that—" I swipe at my face, but it doesn't help. "I've been staying away from these stories lately, and now I understand why. I had this hope, this idea, that my papa might have written them. That I was going to crack this cipher of his, and somehow—hear his voice again—" Now I can barely speak through my hiccupping. "But he didn't write them. Now I *know*. Papa couldn't have and he didn't, and it was stupid to begin with, because he hated fairy tales, because this isn't what encrypted messages could possibly look like, and now it's like I've lost him all over again. He's dead. My father's really dead. He didn't leave me any secret message from beyond the grave. He's dead."

I sit on the bed and cry, but after a moment, the tears stop coming. I never realized there was a middle ground between never crying at all, and spending the whole day in bed squeezing yourself out like a sponge. But I don't think I can blame my parents. I had to find this place for myself.

"I think you were right. About the stories." My breath shudders in my chest.

"How so?" he asks.

"My father used to tell me that snowfall is only a cover." I feel for the words. "These fairy tales are another kind of cover. They're hiding something, but there's still a way to go beneath. Didn't you say that you could see the original words, ones that were erased?"

"Yes," says Lev, "why?"

"Because," I say, "I'm going to exhume them."

PART

III

The Boy
and the Waves

In a faraway kingdom, in a long-ago land, a boy was swept out to sea. The waves carried him farther and farther away, until he was so far from the shoreline that he could not see it anymore. He did not know if it was still there. He did not know if he had already drowned. He began to weep. *Hush,* said the waves, *and we will help you, since you have made us stronger with your tears.*

Hush, and we will carry you home.

The waves kept their promise, but when the boy stepped onto land again, he was already an old man. He did not recognize anyone, even his own family, and they did not recognize him. He went back to the waves and he shouted at them: *You've brought me to the wrong place. This isn't home.* And the waves replied: *Home is not a place.*

22

Valentin

My name is Valentin Mikhailovich Andreyev. I was born in St. Petersburg in 1896. My name is Valentin Mikhailovich Andreyev. I was born in St. Petersburg in 1896. . . .

His thoughts spiral, spiral, spiral, until they go to darker and darker places.

To the White Sea.

A log floats on the surface of the river in his mind, only it is not a log. It is a person. That person might be him. He holds his breath but he still smells the bilge, the salt water, the wet wood. The mold. He gasps for air.

We need to take him to a hospital, Papa, somebody is saying, out there in the haze.

Vika, I don't know how many times I can explain this to you. Nobody must know he is here. He is a traitor. Do you know how many strings I had to pull, to bring him home? We'll find a doctor I can trust. Just keep him quiet for now.

Papa, he's sick. Papa . . .

"Tonya?" says Valentin, turning, reaching for the space beside him. But of course Tonya isn't there. Everything is in his head: The blinding storm. Blood being spit through his teeth. The lighting of a paraffin lamp to reveal the shivering body of a bunkmate. Someone clipping off the dead tips of his fingers. Heavy bandages. More blood, trickling down the side of his neck, hot and fetid.

Tonya isn't here, says the voice from above.

He opens his eyes. "Where am I going?" he asks, huskily.

"Nowhere." A face appears overhead. "It's me. Viktoria."

"Where is Tonya?"

"She's not here, Valya. I'm sorry."

"How long . . . how late . . . ?"

"You've been away for eight years. Six in Solovetsky, two on the Canal—"

"Tonya is waiting for me at Otrada," he says. "In Popovka. First you take the train to Tula city. You . . . you . . ." He feels himself drifting away, on those white-tipped waves.

"Keep talking," says the voice. "Stay awake, speak to me. Tell me where Tonya is. How do I find her? I'll bring her here, to you. . . ."

But Valentin is already elsewhere. In a cargo hold, maybe, where the darkness is complete, with the others around him claiming they are not headed for home, but for the White Sea Canal, except that there is no such thing as the White Sea Canal.

There will be.

Valentin still sees and hears nothing. The only thing he knows is that he is dividing into parts: One part is filling wheelbarrows, stumbling through ice floes, subsisting on gruel and foul water. The other part is pulling away. Try as he might, he cannot reunite these two halves of himself. It is such a complete separation of mind and body that he is losing hold of both.

23

Antonina

The Interrogator does not believe her. His job is not to believe anyone. He leans back, long enough that Tonya wants to squirm in her chair, but she only lowers her eyes. The Interrogator's office is cozy, intimate. They have been meeting like this for half a year, and every detail of the meetings still feels staged. A radio broadcast plays in the background, describing the latest machinations of Hitler, leader of the Third Reich. The hallway outside thrums with life.

They are in the Lubyanka building, headquarters of the NKVD, Soviet state security, the most recent incarnation of the Cheka.

The Lubyanka sits on busy Dzerzhinsky Square. *Stop a moment,* people often say, *to have a drink at the corner tavern, or to admire the bowl of Vitaly's central fountain. Take one last look around, before you go inside.*

* * *

The season has not yet turned. People hurry home from work dressed in their warmest wools, with their earflaps pulled low. Darkness trickles down from the sky, settles in over the city, and the cobblestones are quickly glazed with frost, though there may not be any cobbles much longer. Many streets have already been asphalted to accommodate automobiles, like the Black Crows of the NKVD, though *they* come out only at night. Nocturnal hunters.

Tonya, heavily pregnant, walks as fast as she can. She does not want to be stopped.

For a long time, living like this seemed sustainable. They have been in Moscow for five years: Valentin in recovery, Tonya working at the orphanage, Lena going to school, now away at university. But the atmosphere has changed over the past year, now that Stalin has begun arresting, persecuting, executing members of the Old Bolshevik Guard, for conspiracy and treason against the state. He is purging the Party and the country.

Thanks to Pavel Katenin, Valentin has new identity papers, a new name, but the danger is palpable, if still unseen. Like the baby that Tonya carries.

Valentin rarely gets nightmares anymore. He has joined the quietly burgeoning anti-Stalin resistance in the capital; he edits their newssheets, and when he speaks of it, often at length, he almost sounds like he could be back on the overturned carriages of a wintry Petrograd. What he never speaks of at length is his own exile, at least not the two years he spent on the White Sea Canal. If Tonya asks, he will get a certain look upon his face, and make a quip about using garden shovels to dig through solid granite.

That is what the expression is, too. Solid granite.

She knows, every time she enters the Lubyanka, every time she leaves, that if the state security arrest Valentin Andreyev a second time, it will be for good. He will not make it back again.

* * *

Tonya does up the locks from the inside. "Hello?" she calls out, and her voice bounces back. It's in the echo that she hears her own fear. She never hears it at the Lubyanka. "Valya? Are you home?"

The door to the kitchen opens.

"Back at last," he says. Valentin drops a kiss to her forehead, soft as cricket legs, his hands coming to rest on her distended belly. Tonya will have to visit the Maternity House soon enough, that ugly brick building with a sign like a foghorn: INPATIENTS. Fathers are not allowed to attend births.

She will give birth to their child without him, like last time.

"I wonder what he wants from you," murmurs Valentin. "Why any interrogator would do this, bring you in week after week, for months and months."

"You're safe as long as it keeps going."

Valentin sighs, deeply enough that he has to clear his throat. He's had that baby's rattle of a sound in his chest since the day he came home. *That's what blasting through one hundred and forty-one miles of solid granite will do to you*, he's said, like it's a joke. *All of it has to go* somewhere. "It's not necessary, Tonya. The NKVD don't have anything on me. If they did, I'd already be in the Lubyanka. As before."

"It's different now. They don't need evidence."

"You can't do this forever."

"If you would agree to leave Moscow, I wouldn't have to."

"I just said you don't have to."

"Let's not fight," she says, placing a hand on her stomach. If she says more, all her fears will fall out of her: that he'll leave the apartment one day when she's at the orphanage and he'll go to the Lubyanka himself, he'll go right up to an NKVD officer and he'll say, *Yes, I am an Old Bolshevik, yes, I am an anti-Soviet enemy of the people who is working to overthrow this regime and everything it stands for, yes, I will continue to do so until the day I die.*

That *will* be the day he dies.

She'd never speak it aloud, but that's probably how Valentin *wants* to die. On the grand stage, making one last stand. He has probably already written the speech he plans to make, and when he is alone, he mouths it to himself, the way he did when they were young, before the October Revolution, before the demise of the Romanovs. Before he and his Party got everything they ever wanted.

* * *

The Interrogator has a name, but Tonya refuses to use it. She prefers to think of him as a character, because she's determined to turn this into a story when it's all over, maybe another one she can tell the younger children at the residence home.

The Interrogator plucks people off the streets, like insects off a picnic blanket. They are shepherded into his personal vehicle, a black Emka with a red stripe down the side. At the start he tries to make it sound exciting, meaningful: *How much we depend on such brave, valiant citizens like yourself to aid our great nation in identifying wreckers and traitors!*

Only sign this sheet of paper.

Sign.

Sign.

Sign.

He never says that to be an informant is to be half a prisoner and half a guard. To live the worst of both. He never explains that the state is consuming itself, turning the people against the people. Everyone in Moscow now knows the dangers of opening one's mouth by accident. To tell the wrong joke. To speak the wrong name. Better not to use names at all; to make everyone a character in a fairy tale.

* * *

Your daughter, Lena," says the Interrogator. He cocks his head, examines Tonya off angle. Today the radio is off, but the small gramophone in the corner plays a folk song, something a *muzhik* might tap a felt-booted foot along to. "I've learned that she studies at the State University in Leningrad. Biology? Medicine? You've said nothing about your Lenochka."

Lenochka is drawn out, so that it billows.

"She doesn't know anything about her father," says Tonya. "He was sent to the Solovetsky Islands before they had a chance to meet."

The folk tune is still playing. It goes on and on, this kind of music. Designed to last a feast, a wedding, a celebration in the fields. How can he stand it? Does it remind him of a faraway childhood, his father smoking a goat's-leg pipe, his mother embroidering the pillow slips?

"I can't give you more leeway," he says, "when you haven't given me anything." The Interrogator pulls his hands out from behind his desk for the first time. He is holding a bundle of letters, tied with string. He undoes the string and pretends to look for something, but he knows what he's looking for. Just as he did that day on the street, six months ago, when he first plucked *her* off of it.

"These arrived from the Investigative Section in Solovetsky," he says. "I imagine there's much more we don't have." He slides one across the desk to her. "See for yourself."

March 1925

Tonya, lyubov' moya

They say that [indecipherable] *will come to visit us here, so perhaps I can appeal to him. The lighting is poor, they keep it dark, so I keep this short* [indecipherable] *the only light is my memory of you—*

Valentin

The Interrogator takes the letter back, tweezes another one from the bundle.

July 1926

*Hands are hurting from today's work but I will write to you
as long as they stay on. There are other former Party
members here, like me. They ask me if Koba knows what is
happening to us. I am going to find out. I am going to
survive, I am going to come home, I am going to tell the world
the truth about this place. Please take care of yourself—
I believe you will read this, I send all my love with it—
wait for me—*

    Your Valentin

Tonya's throat constricts. *Koba.* Stalin. It's treason enough just to say the name, and it's only one line from one letter.

"I've enjoyed our sessions," says the Interrogator. "You have a gift for telling stories. From the very first, I've wanted to see how many you had. If you would ever run out."

The first story had been an accident. He'd asked for information on anyone she knew. She hadn't known what to say, so she'd made it up, the way she does for the orphans. She'd seen something unexpected cross his face at the end, as if through her words he had perceived a different, uneventful existence for himself—one in which he'd stayed in the countryside, married for love, never left home at all.

"But I am trying to build a career, you know," he says. "And the pressure is increasing."

The song is over. The record has finished. The Interrogator has planned this, timed it perhaps. He pulls out a new sheet of paper. He writes her name at the top. The mention of her daughter was strategic. He will say Lena's name again if Tonya does not sign. Say it in that gluey way he did, like he was moving it around with his tongue. *Lenochka.*

"Save yourself, Tonya," he says. "Valentin Andreyev is past your help. He belongs to the state. But you, your circumstances..." He makes a small gesture, up and down. "Sign against him, and when he is arrested, you will be spared. You have my word."

He speaks of her pregnancy as if he's seen *into* her. Same as he has the letters. There is no violation too obscene, because there is no such thing as a private life.

He opens his palm, reveals a pen.

"Wait. Just a moment, wait." There is a droplet in Tonya's eye. Sweat, maybe. It must not fall, or he will think he has made her cry. "What if I can give you somebody even better? Someone who can make your career?"

The Interrogator laughs aloud. He doesn't believe this either. "Find somebody better quickly," he says. "Make my career."

* * *

Pregnancy tea is thin and tastes dirty, like plant roots. Tonya sips slowly as she reads through Valentin's typewritten pages. The more she does, the more bitter the tea tastes in her mouth. It is all powerfully expressed, but none of the things he hopes for will come to pass, at least not in their lifetimes. He witnessed two revolutions, his side triumphed over two regimes, and now he must think revolutions come easy.

"What do you think?" he asks, sitting down beside her.

The liquid burns in her mouth. "I think we will all die on the altar of your ideals, Valentin."

"I lived through the camps." His expression darkens. "I have a duty to the people, to speak, and to fight. I have to take the moral path."

"Then you leave *me* to take the immoral one! To lie, to tell stories, to stave off the Interrogator—"

"If the NKVD come, then they come, Tonya."

If. He is like a young Lena, trying to end death. You almost do not want to wake people up, from such dreams. "They are coming," she says ferociously. "They could come tonight. You act as if you're not afraid, as if you don't care! We should have left Moscow months ago, years ago, only you had to carry on with all *this!*"

"You always knew it would be like this." His tone is tranquil, but he pushes away from the table. "You know who I am. This is the choice you made."

"It isn't just about you and me anymore, Valya. There's Lena. There's the baby! If the choice is between your family and your politics, what will *you* choose?"

Valentin gives her a slanted smile before he leaves the kitchen, slams the door behind him.

Tonya holds her nose, lets a gulp of tea sit in her mouth. They have fought over all manner of things, these five years. For a long time he wanted her to sleep in another room, for fear of lashing out at her during one of his episodes; she refused. He used to beg her to leave him. She refused. He hates when she asks about the White Sea Canal. She still asks.

The baby took them both by surprise, but it is the one thing they seem to agree on.

These quarrels never last long. If she calls him back now, it can be like it never happened. But this time she needs him to stay away, so that he doesn't see her take several of his pages, press them flat with her hands, and tuck them into her bag.

* * *

Tonya curls up on her side like an inchworm, eyes open, ogling the darkness. She lets out puffs of breath. What is she awake and listening for? A car engine? Boot steps in the hallway? The shouting, the shuffling, the series of knocks?

She already has a bag packed at the foot of the bed.

Listening like this, she doesn't even hear the sound of Valentin coming into the room, or the rustle of bedcovers. He often works late into the night. He sleeps as little as possible, on purpose. They have not spoken since their heated exchange earlier, and she turns awkwardly, as best she can, burrows into his shoulder.

"Let's go to Leningrad," he says, kissing her hair.

"To visit Lena?"

"To live."

"What? How?"

"I know someone who can arrange a *propiska* for settling there." A wry laugh. "We don't have to. It's up to you."

"But you've always said you're too involved with things here." Tonya half believes him. She half thinks this is wild-eyed nonsense. Another of his castles in the sky.

"You were right to accuse me. I've put other things above our safety." Valentin shifts, rests his arm lightly on her belly. The baby rolls in response. "I'm sorry," he says, thickly now. "I am afraid, Tonya. Not of the state, but of myself. Afraid that if I look around me too closely, if I examine it all, I'll start to see cracks in this life, flaws, inconsistencies. Little things that will tell me that you are not actually here, that I have conjured all this in my mind. That I never came home."

"Do you feel the baby?" Tonya presses his hand harder against her. "Do you think you could imagine this?"

"I'm afraid," he continues, and she can feel the wetness on his face as he kisses her, "that one day I will wake up next to you and I won't know you anymore, won't remember. That I'll be trapped there, in the camps. That there isn't any escape, no matter where I go."

If there are cracks, flaws, inconsistencies, they are all inside of him. But at least, at last, he has stopped pretending to have healed. At least he is showing her his wounds. She lets him cry, like a little boy, while her own tears flow silently.

Valentin is soon asleep, but she lies awake. Perhaps a drink of water will help. She moves to get off the bed, achy, woozy. A gamey smell moves with her.

The sheets are covered in a pink, bloody, stretchy fluid.

It's early. Much too early. There are two months yet to go. The spring thaws have only recently come.

Tonya pictures the rivers of Russia all running at once, a great, gushing torrent of water, and then she feels it on her thighs, streaming down her legs. She sees it on the floor between her feet as she tries to stand. It is the last thing she sees.

* * *

People speak over her head. It's an emergency. It's not just one baby. They didn't know until now. They begin to cut, to turn Tonya into shreds of flesh. Somebody shows her a glimpse of a tiny, dusty face, two faces. Her twins will be taken to a special hospital for premature babies and will stay there until they are strong enough to go home.

She's lucky, declare the midwives. If she'd arrived at the Maternity House any later than she did, the babies would already have gone. And if she weren't in Moscow, with the help of professionals, she'd likely have joined them. And if there were no special hospital with special tubes for feeding babies as immature as these, they'd last only a day or two. Someone asks if they should send for Tonya's husband and she says that she killed her husband and they laugh. *All the women feel that way but he's very much alive. He brought you in, but we don't permit visitors obviously*, and the first person says, *Rest now, my dear*, as if anyone can *rest* when there are a dozen other women in the ward shrieking, screaming, begging for relief.

If anything is lucky, it's that the Interrogator was not here this time, because Tonya is sure that she would have confessed to anything. That there is no torture like childbirth.

* * *

Tonya?" A hand on her shoulder. "It's me. Viktoria."

Tonya opens her eyes. Valentin's ex-wife is smiling uncertainly down at her. Now in her early forties, Viktoria has a face that is round as a coin, and quiet features that come to life only at the piano bench. According to Valentin, all Viktoria does is play piano. She composes too, though she doesn't seem to care for fame in the way her father does.

They have barely seen her since she left Moscow.

"The twins are doing well." Viktoria's voice is soothing. "Come on. I've had them ready your bag."

"Valentin?" Tonya says, more a wince than a word.

"He's at our dacha. The NKVD have been at your apartment, Tonya. They're looking for him. If you both could leave right now—but of course, the twins need to stay in the hospital. So I am taking you to my father's apartment—Papa has agreed—and there you will just have to wait."

"Valentin hasn't seen the babies? Yekaterina and Mikhail?"

Viktoria shakes her head. "Beautiful names."

Outside the Maternity House, Pavel Katenin's chauffeur is waiting. The car's engine is running. The leather interior is slippery sleek, like Tonya's insides. Viktoria speaks to the driver and he throws the car into gear and jolts them down the road. With every turn there's a fierce ripple down Tonya's torso, through her womb. She has never been to the Moscow residence of Viktoria's father. She can't imagine him doing something so mundane as *living* somewhere, because nowadays Pavel Katenin is everywhere all at once.

He is so famous. Nearly as famous as Comrade Stalin.

* * *

When Tonya met Pavel Katenin for the first time, in 1933, he was alert and cautious, and walked with his cane out in front of him, as if feeling his way forward. But five years in the spotlight, and now it's all Pavel sees. *This* Pavel has dined with Stalin, has written plays for Stalin. Stalin would greet him personally on the street. This Pavel thinks he is invulnerable.

He is wrong. Tonya has learned a few things from the Interrogator: The better Stalin knows you, the more vulnerable you are.

Pavel announces at breakfast that the traitors in the Politburo deserved their fate, as does everyone imprisoned in the Lubyanka. He waves his cane in the air to make his point. Was it always gold tipped? Did it always resemble a scepter? He calls them *the enemy within*, and there is something furtive in his face as he says this. He must have signed somebody away himself. A friend. One of his actors from the theatre. His own soul.

"So many are being arrested," says Tonya. "How can they all be the enemy?"

"Any innocents caught in the net are a necessary sacrifice." He makes a dismissive gesture toward his maid, who is shredding a gummy candy into his tea. "When the forest is cut, the chips will fly."

Viktoria, seated at the end of the table, says nothing. Her eyes, already too large, often seem to go too long without blinking. She seems small, even shriveled, compared to her father, who is robust, red-faced, booming. The maid, Annushka, shares Viktoria's browbeaten aura. Does Pavel Katenin simply have this effect on people? Or does he cow them into this silence? Coerce them? Force them?

"On the whole," Pavel is saying now, "the system is designed to be discerning."

Tonya lacerates her pancake with her fork. "And if Valentin is a chip again?"

"Aha!" says Pavel grandly. "You make my point for me. Valentin was *guilty*, was he not, at the time of his arrest! But he learned his lesson. Also, Comrade Stalin has become my good friend. No harm will come to any of us in the end."

It's like Pavel sees all this as one of his stage plays. *None of it is real! Silly girl!*

Pavel saved Valentin's life. He loves Valentin deeply. But there is something about a certain kind of man in power, a certain kind of man who likes to go around *saving*, who embellishes everything he owns with gold, who treats the women around him like furniture, that Tonya simply cannot abide.

Furniture does not have eyes and ears. He's wrong about that too.

"So you see, there is nothing to fear," Pavel says, setting aside his cane. "Any interest in our Valya will pass. I'm sure he's enjoying himself at my dacha in the meantime. When the babies are strong, your family can summer there, you can all get fat on the native strawberries!"

The most dangerous stories are the ones people don't realize they are telling. Tonya smiles along with him, as if she can already taste the succulent sweetness of wild strawberries, can imagine the juice running down their faces like blood.

* * *

The Interrogator does not say a word as he reads. When he looks up, his face appears anemic by lamplight, or perhaps it's because his usually reliable bulb is weak today, beneath its silk-scarf lampshade. "I've heard you gave birth to twins," he says. "Congratulations. Do they run in your family?"

She shakes her head. This already feels like a lie. Mama had twins once. Almost-twins.

"More village folklore, then." He smiles, bares his fangs. "This is excellent material, what you've brought me today. You did keep me on tenterhooks, but it seems it was all worth it." He swivels in his chair. "You've made the right decision. We will arrest Andreyev immediately."

"You misunderstand. These papers I've brought you have nothing to do with Valentin Andreyev." The words flow like water. "I'm living with Pavel Katenin. They are his. If you raid his home, you will find even more."

His smile dims like the bulb. "You're lying."

"It will help the both of us."

"I ask you not to do this for *your* sake, Tonya. Why risk it? For Andreyev?" The Interrogator's composure is slipping. "There are a thousand more *zeki* out there, come home from the camps, out of their own minds, for you to play nursemaid to, if that is your calling!"

"I already know my calling." Tonya sweeps a hand across the table that sits between them like a cinder block. "Like you know yours."

"This is a mistake," he insists. "I can help you with your expenses for the babies. I can protect you!"

"I love him, Sasha," she says. "I will make any mistake."

Sasha Ozhereliev lifts his eyes to hers. The lamp has died. She almost cannot tell where he ends and the darkness begins.

"As you would say," she whispers, *"chemu byt', togo ne minovat'."*

What will be, cannot be escaped.

He says something about believing her for half a minute, that she is a decent liar. But she is not a liar. She is a storyteller. One day, she will turn it all into a story.

* * *

As Tonya walks to the hospital to stop in on the twins, it starts to rain, but there isn't enough water in the world to wash away what she has just done. After all these years she has learned to live with fear, to stay laced into it like it's a bone corset; she can learn to live with other things too. Even this. She will always re-member the night Dmitry lay bleeding at her feet, the way that young Bolshevik's carving knife went in, and whenever she does, she remembers that the choice in this country is not between right and wrong. It is between life and death.

24

Rosie

The breeze is as light as the evening sky overhead. I walk until I find myself standing in front of the Bolshoi Theatre. This building is neoclassical, impressive, iconic, but not exactly beautiful, marked by the hammer and sickle that sit at the apex. *You* sink *into everything,* Mum once said of this theatre. *The floors, the champagne, your seat. There's a gravitational pull to the stage. And the people on that stage, they are otherworldly.*

I've never been inside. My mother was a dancer here, in the most famous ballet in the world, yet I've never attended a performance.

There's a faint hum in my ears, a splash of champagne in the air.

Zoya is back. And this time, I am not afraid. I *sink* into the image she shows me, just as Mum said to do, and the famous white foyer of the Bolshoi appears in my mind's eye, a double staircase, a cascade of red carpeting. People everywhere, dressed for the occasion. There is the main stage, and the audience is quiet and the orchestra strains and the lights are turned low and I know I have been drawn into the past. I nearly expect to see Mum step out of the wings.

But she's seated in the audience.

She looks young. My age. Maybe if she turned, she would somehow see *me*, our parallel universes might intersect, but I can tell that she won't turn. Nothing exists to her at this moment but the ballet.

There's something odd about the rapture in her expression. It's not the look of someone who is already a dancer, because *that* person would know that all this is a fantasy. Everyone up there is human. Their toes are taped. Their bones are being ground to powder. It is a profession. Not a dreamworld.

My mother is in a dreamworld. She looks up at that stage as if she was never there. As if Katerina Ballerina was just another fairy tale.

The image is gone. I am standing alone in front of the Bolshoi, staring up at the façade.

I understand my mother's fairy tales at last.

The real story is in the white spaces on the page. The real story is unwritten.

*   *   *

*B*ozhe moy, you're hard to get rid of," Akulina says over the phone, but I think she sounds pleased. "What is it this time? Has someone lit my mother's memoir on fire? Would you like to take my cat home?"

I smile at this, but I stop when I hear her cough. She's not coughing out; she's coughing *up*. "Tell me," I say. "Did Tonya tell stories, folktales, that sort of thing?"

A drier cough. "All the time. To Lena. To my brother, before he died. But I wouldn't call them stories. That's too weighty. More like she sprinkled them around like sugar, and if you listened, you might catch a speck of it."

"I have a collection of stories that belonged to her. They're handwritten."

Akulina guffaws. "She never wrote anything down."

"I took a sort of—forensic look at it. It's in pencil—"

"I'm not even sure she *could* write."

"Pencil," I repeat, "I think because she had to correct so often for spelling and grammar. But I found something else, at the top of the first page. The words *For Lena, beloved daughter* have been erased. It's unmistakable."

I had intended to tell Akulina that her mother's memoir is in the same penmanship as the fairy tales, but suddenly I don't think she's supposed to know that. I think the memoir answered questions about Natalya—and Natalya's choices—that Akulina spent her whole life asking, and I can only imagine how that feels.

I can't take it away.

"For Lena," Akulina says, digesting this.

"My mother left these stories to me," I say, "and I wonder if her own mother might have given them to her. If Tonya is my grandmother."

It's frightening to say. Family members don't just pop up like that. It's not like Mum's died and now the factory is sending a replacement.

"That was my first thought, when I saw you," says Akulina.

"But then I realized you couldn't be Lena's child. Lena was born the year of the October Revolution. You're too young."

My insides are as tangled as the telephone cord. "My mother never spoke about her family, not siblings, nothing. Do you have any idea where Lena is now? How I might find her?"

"Unfortunately, no." Akulina sounds wistful. "Lena was lovely. A very determined child." Her tone shifts, loses the sadness. "She'd go around saying she was going to be a doctor and live in a house on a wide river. Though I think the last part was put into her head by Tonya." A gravelly laugh. "Tonya loved to tell stories about her former house in Leningrad, on the Fontanka. Her husband's house. She was downright obsessed with that place."

A house on a wide river.

That's one of the fairy tales.

"I didn't know Tonya was married. Was her husband Lena's father?" I ask.

"If I recall right, Lena's father was a Bolshevik." Akulina sounds fully herself again. "I still remember the room where they served tea, in that old house. You cannot know the grandeur of that world, Raisa! The chandelier. The paintings. This strange blue wallpaper. It all feels so impossible now."

"I'd like to see it," I say. "Do you remember the address?"

"If I look at a map. I'm good with maps." She's chewing and chomping again. Those jaws might keep working even after she dies, whittling her teeth down to the studs, reducing her gums to pulp. Then she adds, in a whistle of a breath: "Be forewarned. Those old houses, they are like mazes."

"But I'm going to tie every thread together," I say. "That's how I'll find my way out."

288

* * *

It is a long, sleepless night on the Red Arrow train from Moscow to Leningrad. I lie flat on one of the bottom bunks. Lev sits on the one opposite, playing idly with his lighter. If he flicks it open just so, the red velvet curtain tassels on the windows could catch fire. This whole compartment, to my eye, looks eminently flammable. I must trust him, because I could ask him to stop, and I don't.

It's not just that I trust him.

Right here, in this moment, I feel—

Safe.

The thought alone gives me palpitations. Safe is something that I never, ever feel. I don't *let* myself feel it. My belief is that everything can end, abruptly, without warning, in one second, whether it's this train compartment burning to cinders or my family being murdered. And after all, weren't the golden wreaths of the Romanovs ripped off the gates of the Winter Palace practically overnight? Wasn't this whole country wiped clean, all at once?

That's just how life works.

We all know what happens to people who feel safe.

"Lev," I say hesitantly, and he looks over. "You wanted to tell me something the other day. I stopped you—"

"*Ne vazhno.* Forget it."

I turn onto my side. I don't know why I mentioned anything in the first place. Maybe I'm still bothered by the idea that Mum might not have danced in the Bolshoi Ballet. The *Bolshoi Ballet.* It doesn't even *sound* real.

I could telephone them and say that I'm the daughter of Katerina Simonova, ask if she ever danced for them, but I don't think I've ever admitted that readily to being Mum's child. At least not since moving to England. Yes, I'm *Kate's* daughter, folks! Kate, who sometimes wanders outside in her dressing gown and falls asleep by the postbox. Kate, with her lemony complexion and cheesy breath and her stories, those awful, drunken stories, that she starts telling—*shouting*—to anyone within earshot: *In a faraway KINGDOM! In a long-ago LAND!*

But if she was never a ballerina, I think I would resent her less. I'd feel a bit sorry that someone would be insecure enough to lie to her own family about who she was. Maybe Mum couldn't bear who she was. Maybe that's why I never figured her out either.

So much for Mum hoarding all the answers. She didn't have them. She was literally making it all up.

Before I know it, I'm laughing. That's the flip side of never crying; I rarely laugh. It dies out quickly. I want to be someone who laughs like that every day. All the time. But you can't laugh if you don't feel safe, because it *is* just like crying. When you do it, you're naked. You're defenseless.

Lev meets my eye, smiles, just a little.

I wonder if it is the walls of this rickety train, hurtling through unfamiliar terrain, headed nowhere I have ever been, that make me feel safe, or if it is that the walls are coming down.

* * *

The taxi driver takes us along a sinuous route, as meandering as any of Leningrad's rivers, until we reach the Fontanka embankment. He deposits us in front of a three-story mansion of dull-pink granite. Several of the first-floor windows are boarded up with plywood, and the stucco is coming off the façade, revealing the stone underneath.

The house calls little attention to itself—if I glanced this way from down this street, I might not even see it—yet it taunts anyone who looks closer. *I survived everything,* it's saying. *I'll outlive you too.*

I rattle the brass knob of the front door. Unlocked. Lev and I step over the threshold, into an empty foyer. I am reminded of the day Mum and I moved into our first flat in England, how she ran her hand just above all the surfaces, never quite touching all the walls and windows. Communing with the house, was how she explained herself. Because what people won't say, houses often do.

But the silence in here is steadfast.

Above our heads are the skeletal remains of a chandelier and a high molded ceiling of what looks like marble. In front of us is a staircase that leads to a dark upstairs landing. I almost want to call out to Zoya for reassurance that there aren't other ghosts in here, but I also don't want to awaken the house.

A door just past the stairs groans open. A woman toting a netted bag emerges, and when she sees us, she squeals. "I'm the superintendent," she says, putting a hand over her heart. "Who are you?"

"Are these apartments occupied?" I ask.

"More or less," she says. "The top floor is full. Many families. The floor above me belongs to someone who is never here. Why? You need housing?"

"Yes. Housing."

"You two are married?"

"Sure. Newlyweds," I say, and Lev snickers. "My grandmother

used to live in this house, decades ago, and I think there's something romantic about it. . . ." My voice falters. There *is* something romantic about it. There is something here that I find beautiful. I could stay here, live here. I could wake up every day in this house, look out those windows, take in the view of the river. "I hoped," I say, regrouping, "that we could take a look around. Right? Lyova?"

I don't think I've ever used his diminutive name before. The smirk leaves his face.

"Could we see the one you said was empty?" I continue. "If the owner is never here."

The superintendent purses her mouth. "I'm not sure. It belongs to the writer Alexey Ivanov. You've heard of him? He is an important man."

What?

Lev steps in. "Please," he says to her, "my wife is an orphan. She knows so little about her family. I don't know Ivanov, but maybe he would understand wanting to discover the past."

"He might," she says suspiciously.

Lev is already reaching around for his wallet. If I learned to do it like that, I would get the best tables in all my favorite restaurants. Soon the superintendent is handing him a key and saying she's going out to the shops so don't take any longer than that. Lev begins to head up the stairs, but I stop on the bottom step.

"Thank you," I say. "I'll pay you back. For everything."

"Don't," he says, without looking back.

* * *

Sunlight steals through the plywood, creating hints of color here and there. The kitchen has several stoves, gone to gray, a reminder of what must have been, before there were spiderwebs strung like banners across the ceilings. I swing open the door to a bedroom. This place hasn't been used in years.

"I don't get it," I say, as we step inside the room. "Why keep an empty apartment in Tonya's old house? Does he think she might come back here to live?"

"He can afford to keep apartments wherever he wants."

I go to the far wall and touch the bare, powdery spaces where the wallpaper is coming away. It was sloppily glued. But that's not what's bothering me. I touch it a bit more, rub my fingertips, and pull at the paper.

There's something underneath.

Writing.

I pull harder. More writing. More and more, in tiny, spidery Cyrillic script that is nearly invisible.

"What are you doing?" asks Lev warily.

"There's dates here." I start to peel another panel of paper off the wall. "Someone used this room like a diary. Look! January 15, 1942. January 18, 1942. It's everywhere, all the way to the window. It's . . ."

1942.

The Leningrad blockade. This is a siege diary. Someone lived in this room during the Second World War, when Leningrad was surrounded by the German army and cut off from the world. When a third of the city's population starved to death.

I wonder where the writing ends—and when.

"My cursive literacy isn't up to this," I say, lowering my voice. "Can you read it?"

Lev begins to read, also quietly. It takes me a full minute to realize that I already know what it is that he's going to say next.

This isn't a diary. Maybe the dates refer to when the writing took place, but the text itself has nothing to do with the blockade. This isn't an account of a devastating winter in wartime.

This is Alexey's memoir.

The Last Bolshevik.

Word for word.

Alexey must have spent the war in this house. He must have written his memoir of the White Sea Canal *in here* while the blockade was happening out there. It almost makes sense. *The Last Bolshevik* has the look, the feel, of something composed with restraint, with self-censorship even. Lev was right when he said not everything could be included. That not everything could fit.

Literally.

"Raisa," says Lev.

"Yes?"

"I think this is the handwriting in your mother's stories." He sounds like he doesn't want to say it. "And in the memoir."

I'm still in a daze. "That's not possible."

"With the same mistakes," he says. "Only here they're uncorrected."

My mind spins. I'm used to my mind spinning, of course, when I'm working. Juggling all the little bits and pieces at once, nonstop, until I get where I want to be. Right now the spinning goes something like: Either Alexey Ivanov didn't write *The Last Bolshevik*—or else he wrote everything. His own memoir, Natalya's memoir, and the fairy tales. *For Lena, beloved daughter.* I assumed Tonya, Lena's mother, was the one to write that dedication, but it could have been her father.

Lena's father was a Bolshevik, is what Akulina said to me.

Valentin Andreyev.

Alexey Ivanov used to be Valentin Andreyev.

Normally I might be telling myself: *I was right. I knew it. I knew it all along, and I still might not know what Alexey really wants, but I'm going to find out, and I'm going to get there first.*

But staring at these walls—at 1942, appearing over and over again—I don't tell myself anything. I don't say anything else to Lev either. I let my brain stop whirring, calculating. I'm done.

Now I know there are ghosts in this house. They should be the ones speaking.

* * *

Bombastic music blasts over the loudspeakers as we step back onto the Red Arrow. Lev looks mildly annoyed, but it doesn't bother me. The overnight train makes me feel as if we are leaving Russia in 1991 and entering some other era, and I don't know what the way back would be.

I take one of the top bunks this time. Predictably, I can't sleep, but it's something new keeping me awake. I just can't tell what it is yet.

I break out the first few pages of Natalya Burtsinova's handwritten memoir, which I've brought along for exactly this purpose. The details are much more specific than in the published version—names and addresses, for one. *Dearest Mitya's* full name is given: Dmitry Lulikov. The family's neighborhood in St. Petersburg: the Zakharevskaya. The dacha where they spent their summers: Shadow Lake; there's even an address.

These details prove the writer's intimate knowledge of the subject matter. Who could have written this, if not Natalya herself?

An expert storyteller, adept at weaving whole stories out of single threads?

Around nine, the attendant brings by some tea, waking me up. I shimmy down and peek out the window, brushing aside the curtains that give our compartment a whiff of grand decay. The northern sky is the color of a seashell. We're leaving the land of the White Nights. No wonder I'm feeling carried away by the romance of it, by the idea that there's some poetry, some symmetry, behind all of this.

"You can sit, if you want." Lev swings his legs off his bunk.

I gesture to the window. "The light is beautiful."

"Yes, when you notice it."

I let go of the curtain and sit down on his bunk.

"I feel . . . I feel different," I say. "When I was in that room, with the writing, something happened. I can't explain."

"You don't have to."

There's no sound except for the rhythmic creaking of the train. *Chug-uh-chug-uh-chug.*

We are sitting so close that I can see flecks of gold in his eyes. Before he can say anything else, I turn back to the window.

Richard. Think of Richard.

Richard didn't impress me when we first met, in Michaelmas term of my first year at Oxford. He seemed like every other stuck-up toff in the place, with an accent that could shear a sheep, and he was *always* talking, in hall, in the library, in the café where he first really looked my way. It was only after a few reluctant dates—I used him, admittedly, for nice meals out at first; who wouldn't, with my own suppers consisting of canned beans?— that I understood it wasn't that Richard just liked the sound of his own voice. He'd been taught to fill silences. I'd been soaking in them for years. It felt like we were made for each other.

But what about *my* own voice?

The sky over Russia does not reply.

This sojourn to my homeland was never about *that man*.

It was about closing the chapter of my life that included my family, Papa and Mum and Zoya, forever. I would finish it off and be able to embark on my proper English life, beginning with marrying Richard, a proper English bloke. I'd finally be proper English Rosie. But instead of putting the Russian part of myself to rest, instead of expelling it, I've become more aware of its presence.

I haven't buried anything by coming here. I've brought something back to life.

Chug-uh-chug-uh-chug.

The silence between me and Lev is stretching to its breaking point, as it often does. But this time, unlike most other times, I don't feel stretched out along with it. I don't want to talk any more on this journey, just in case we are traveling back in time. Maybe I want to be carried away a bit more. Just a little longer.

A House
on a Wide River

In a faraway kingdom, in a long-ago land, a princess returned to visit the palace by the sea where she had lived as a young woman with her former husband, the prince. She had once been her husband's prisoner within its walls, and she liked that the palace had been humbled. She liked that her dead husband's books had all been burned, his belongings stolen, his carpets cleaved from the floors. She liked that it belonged now to the common people. And when it happened, by chance, that one of the rooms in the palace was empty at a time when she needed a place to live, she decided to move back into it. Her new husband understood, because he had been a prisoner himself, but in a different place, by a different sea. He understood that you have truly escaped only when you can freely return.

And so the princess lived once more in the palace by the sea, but it was no longer a palace by the sea. Those days were over. It was only a house on a wide river.

25

Antonina

Tonya is in hell. A white, frozen hell that reeks of turpentine. Or an antechamber of hell, because they are suspended in time, waiting for the Nazis to march into Leningrad, or else to grow restless and leave. To pass the time, Tonya has begun to tell the twins the longest story she has ever told, padded with frivolous details, unnecessary characters. Katya and Misha hang on her words. Valentin acts like he might be listening, but he isn't.

Lena is the impatient one. *For goodness' sake, Mama,* she'll say, *just tell us how it* ends, *would you?* And Tonya wants to reply: *That's why I can't tell you, Lenochka. As soon as you know the end, you won't have anything to wait for.*

* * *

Whatever Valentin has heard in his head since he came home from the White Sea Canal, eight years ago, he is hearing it louder and louder as this blockade goes on. Maybe it's the cold. It is a *malicious* winter, as Mama would say. The kind that comes around once every few decades. Or maybe it's that Leningrad has been severed from the rest of Russia.

Like the camps.

"Drink something warm." Tonya pushes a glass toward him, across the kitchen table. She uses the same tea leaves every morning, but the ritual is a remnant of life before the war. She will do it until the leaves are brewed into air.

Valentin smiles distantly at her. She wants to throw the glass at that smile.

Throughout the autumn there were air-raid sirens day and night, German airplanes humming, antiaircraft guns whirring, children howling higher than the sirens. Lena would hurry the twins down to the basement, where they could huddle against the walls with their hands on their ears. Tonya would look back and Valentin would still be there, at the top of the stairs. He would look at her without any fear in his face.

Without anything in his face.

Granite.

Valentin raises the tea to his mouth at last. He likes to use the glass with the crack along its rim. As he drinks, there is a button of blood on his lips. He does not seem to notice.

* * *

The luckiest of their neighbors were evacuated out of the city in summer, just after war with Nazi Germany was declared. The only neighbor Tonya has seen for weeks is Comrade Kemenova, who lives upstairs and has grandchildren the same age as the twins. In Tonya's small communal apartment, the other residents are missing or dead. The bedrooms are empty again, the furniture unused, the beds untouched, the curtains closed.

Just the way Dmitry liked to keep them.

Sometimes Tonya will go into the apartments downstairs and peek into what used to be the Blue Salon, or Dmitry's libraries and galleries, now partitioned into single-family rooms. She can wander as much as she likes. As if it's hers now, this house on the Fontanka, when once it was the other way around.

"This was where you used to entertain?" says Lena, when they go down together one day. "Why was it called the Blue Salon?"

"It had blue wallpaper." Tonya runs her fingers along the wall. Now the wallpaper is yellow and floral and chintzy. Cheap and dry. "See, Lenochka, parts of the original paper remain."

Lena scrapes a bit off with a nail. "It's like a secret room under there. A secret world."

It was Lena who dropped by one Sunday afternoon in June with the message: *Kiev and Sevastopol have been bombed by the Germans!* A week later Lena went to work digging slit trenches at the city limits. Every day she telephoned to tell Tonya that they should have Katya and Misha evacuated to an estate in the country. Most other young children had gone, by order of the Leningrad soviet, including the occupants of the children's home where Tonya worked. *You're much too sentimental, Mama!*

One day Lena called with something new to say: *The circle has closed around Leningrad. They've cut off the last railway—*

The line was cut off too.

Not long afterward, Lena took a bad fall in those deep, dirty trenches, and broke her arm. She was sent to the hospital, and then home, but her apartment had been shelled, so she came to live with Tonya and Valentin. She still keeps the arm tucked into her side, still wears her sling.

Nothing can heal in hell.

"Let's go back up," says Tonya, but Lena is in the grip of the blue wallpaper, entranced by that old sea-surface pattern. Tonya never liked the blue, never cared that it was custom mixed or hand-painted. But she does think it would be better for there not to be secret worlds where nobody can go. Where Valentin now lives.

*　*　*

You should have become a writer for children's magazines, Mama," says Lena assertively, after the twins have fallen asleep to another installment of Tonya's bedtime story. "Like *Murzilka*. Better yet, you should publish your own story collection! One of those beautiful ones with the illustrated covers. I love those. Really, your talent's been going to waste at the orphanage."

"I prefer telling to writing," says Tonya, glancing at Valentin. He doesn't seem to have heard. His face looks dull, blue around the eyes. Tonya blinks, and the blueness is gone.

She must have spent too long the other day staring at the wallpaper.

Before the shelling started, Valentin was full of opinions. He would often try to engage Tonya in political debate, but all she knows is that whether it is aristocrats and peasants, politicians and citizens, or German bombers and Russian civilians, those above do not care for those below. Those below are always on their own.

"I prefer reading to hearing." Lena laughs, a small sound. "But would you tell a different one now, Mama? One of your older ones, from when I was little . . ."

"Why?" Tonya asks, dubious. They're only silly, short, baby's-breath folktales. It's folly—lunacy in fact—to think that any of them could be published. They don't adhere to the Communist worldview, in which royalty is evil and the peasants and workers always vanquish their enemies and talking animals say only the right things.

"Please," says Lena. "Please, Mamochka."

Valentin brings a hand to his mouth, like he thinks he might be smoking. He touches the place where his lip was cut, bloodied by the glass. Every day they do this; Tonya and Lena pretend that everything is normal, while every day, Valentin looks more and more like the tea leaves, being strained into dust.

"In a faraway kingdom, in a long-ago land . . ." Tonya has not told this one in twenty-five years. She no longer remembers how it ends. She begins it anyway. "A princess lived in a palace by the sea. . . ."

* * *

In the middle of Leningrad, trolleybuses stand frozen in their tracks. The streets are lined with bodies half buried in snow; other corpses are hauled around in sleds, covered in sheets. Tonya always pulls her facecloth higher and resolves to keep moving. *Look ahead. Only look ahead.*

She can't do that at home.

They are running out of food. Today she's had nothing from the shops. The breadline closed just a few people ahead of her:

Come back Saturday, the sign on the door read. There may be fewer people in the queue on Saturday, but only because more will have died.

When Tonya enters the kitchen, she finds Lena alone, napping in the corner by the tiny handmade stove. They have run out of kerosene, too. They'll have to burn paper and books. Next will be the furniture. The parquet floors. Eventually the whole house may be fed into that stove.

Upstairs, Comrade Kemenova does not have any kerosene to spare. Tonya asks if her young grandchildren have visited lately and Comrade Kemenova says yes. Comrade Kemenova inquires after the family and Tonya replies that Katya sucks her thumb for hours on end and Misha keeps to his play-world of trains and tin soldiers and Valentin barely speaks and Lena's calm company is the one thing she can depend on, only she *isn't* saying any of it. She's just standing there, blank, frozen as the trolleybuses. She doesn't know where to go.

Comrade Kemenova's expression sharpens and she leaves Tonya by the door and then comes back with a tin of milk powder and says it should go to the twins.

"But what about your grandchildren?" asks Tonya unwillingly.

"I was being polite," says Comrade Kemenova. Her tone sounds a bit like Valentin's, Tonya is only noticing now. "They are dead."

* * *

Tonya sits down on their bed, presses on the lumps in the pillows. So this is where Valentin goes, while the rest of them sleep in the kitchen, the only tolerable room of the apartment. He stands by the window with a hand on the curtains, looking into the darkness. Is he restless? Has he woken from a nightmare? Does he see something out there? Or has he simply decided never to sleep again?

"I can feel all my fingertips, Tonya," he says.

Valentin is missing the barest ends of two fingers on his right hand, too bare for most people to see. He feels what isn't there. Just like he hears, senses, dreams what isn't there. But what about the ones who *are* here? When will he see *them*?

Tonya's hands are not too cold to curl into fists. "I want to help you," she says. "But you must let me."

He turns away from the window. "Help me how?"

"My mother used to say that a memory is a foreign object in a body," she says, fervently. "You think it's part of you. Inherent to you. But as soon as you remove it, you see it for what it is. If you get it out of you, it can't destroy you from within! But you have to pull it out!"

"That is only another of your mother's stories."

Valentin speaks so quietly it hurts to try to hear. How can this be the same person who once shouted across city squares? Over hundreds of heads? No wonder he comes in here alone. He is turning into this room. He is freezing solid right in front of her.

Tonya stands, joins him at the curtains. She will reach him. She has to. "If you can't do it for your own sake," she says, adjusting her voice to his, "then you must do it for the people. No one has ever written an account of the White Sea Canal." She feels almost delirious with the idea. "Maxim Gorky visited the camps at Solovetsky, even if the report he published was nonsense. But no one has ever written about the Canal. And now the Canal is finished! The people may never know how it was."

"Nobody would want to know."

"Stop it," she says, "I don't know who's speaking, but it's not you."

"What if it's the memory speaking?" His smile is stark. He is beautiful, breathtaking, like this; it is almost frightening, and yet she can't look away. Maybe that is how *he* feels, when he stares out into the endless night. "What if I have become my memories? If you pull them out, there won't be anything left. They're all that I am."

A single tear falls hotly down her cheek. It is the warmest thing she has felt in months.

Love does not save people from that endless night. It is just not enough. That is something Tonya learned decades ago, as a child, seated at Mama's bedside, Mama with her black-opal eyes, her bloodless lips, speaking of love as if there were no greater protection, no greater power. *Do not cry, Tonya; I will always look after you,* solnyshko; *I will always be watching.* But Mama is not watching. Nobody is. They have all been left to suffer, to starve, to die.

But Tonya will make her last breath her longest.

"I don't care," she says. "We must try. Maybe it will be easier than you think. If you can wax so poetic about memory, then you can speak. If you can feel all your fingertips, then you can pretend that you are whole."

*   *   *

One morning after the New Year, there is a dark mass splayed out at the top of the staircase, just past the corridor. A dead cat, one of those lanky, short-haired, self-sufficient breeds.

Tonya gathers the pitiful creature in her arms and smooths

down its eyelids. She swallows her doubts, forces them down. It's only meat, and she would skin every animal in the city to get her family through this winter.

Inside, in the kitchen, Lena is alone and awake, wrapped in blankets by the stove.

"You can't make me eat that," she declares.

"How are you feeling?" asks Tonya. She sets the cat down on the table, rolls up her sleeves. Last night she saw Lena retching silently over the sink, but nothing came up. Lena did not seem distressed afterward, only climbed back beneath her blankets. Tonya plunges her hands into the cleaning bucket, begins to rub them raw. That horrid heap of blankets. They're making Lena look bigger than she is.

"Well enough, Mama." Lena's face is contorted into an odd smile.

There is an order of decline in families, people say. Babies die first, then the elderly, then men and women. Young, healthy women last of all.

So why does a shiver of fear go through Tonya, as cold as the water?

At supper, Valentin and the twins eat the cat-stew. No matter how Tonya insists, begs, Lena will not be convinced. She says it in the same high-handed manner she once used to announce she was going to become a doctor, to save lives: *I refuse to eat a cat. I'm not hungry anyway.* Lena is lying. Wants it all to go to everyone else.

If she throws up tonight, even less will come up.

Once the others are asleep, Tonya leaves the apartment and goes downstairs to the Blue Salon. She carries with her a cobalt-blue caviar dish, a piece of a set left behind by neighbors. She starts by the window. The wallpaper glue comes off in scraps, collects slowly in the dish. She moves from one strip to the next, and when she has gathered all the glue she can, she peels the paper from the walls. It comes off like clothing.

She has revealed the Blue Salon, but the telltale silver-blue wallpaper is no longer proud. It is tired, missing in places. Torn in others. It does, in the end, look a bit like the sea, a bit like where the Baltic bleeds into the Neva Bay, where the gulf is full of rocky islands that hug the coastline, and around those islands are schools of fish and herds of gray seal.

Now Tonya finally sees it.

Now she will destroy it.

Another layer of paper means another layer of glue. Tonya sits in the dark, scratching, pulling, until her fingernails split. She will cook the glue in broth. She will burn the paper for fuel. She will do this in every room of the house; if only there were some use for bare walls—

But perhaps there is.

* * *

I was transferred out of Solovetsky in autumn 1931. My prisoner transport arrived in September at Soroka, a village on the southern edge of the White Sea, on the mainland. From here, they told us, the Canal would connect all the way to Lake Onega. Soroka is now called Belomorsk, but first I should explain." Valentin's breath catches. "The White Sea is an inlet high in the north. It stems from the Barents Sea, even farther north. . . ."

Solovetsky, Soroka, Onega, Belomorsk, Barents.

The north is only a curtain of white to most people. They will already feel lost among these places.

"Should I continue?" he asks.

Tonya breathes into her hands. She's brought along a dozen indelible pencils, the kind that you have to wet with your mouth, and a handful of fountain pens, courtesy of all the other apartments in the house. But their bedroom is so chilly that everything is covered in a web of frost. It will take downward pressure to prompt the pens to roll ink onto any surface. There also seems to be glaringly little space for error. Once they write on these walls, they will be written on forever. You can hardly get the purplish ink of an ink-pencil off of anything.

"I should be the one to write," she says.

"Why?"

"You're thinking too much about the reader, Valya, about the audience. This is not like . . ." She has to stop herself remembering it, as she says it—"It is not like when you were a Bolshevik. You must not think outward, or look outward. In fact, it would be better if you close your eyes. I believe it will help you return."

"Am I trying to return?"

"If you don't go back, you can't leave. Trust me." Tonya doesn't quite trust herself. She's done little writing in her life. Only letters and lessons for the orphans. Nothing like this.

"If that's what you prefer," he says.

Once upon a time, Valentin could make people believe in anything. Once upon a time, they were *both* storytellers. Her stories began far away and long ago; his began here and now. Her stories had already happened, and his had yet to happen. He wanted to be heard by everyone in the world, while she needed to hear only herself.

He helped her. And now she will help him.

The walls of their bedroom appear naked, stripped of wallpaper. The layer beneath is faded into white. Much like Valentin. Tonya's hope all these years has been futile; she knows that by now. He is never going to be the person he used to be. He will remain like this forever, and every month, every year, he will become a little bit *more* like this, until the day she screams his name and there is nobody to answer.

But even on that day, she will still be here.

Tonya grips the pen hard.

"Close your eyes," she says. "Tell me what you remember."

* * *

Valentin sits at the table with Katya on his lap. Katya is sucking on her thumb. *Tsh. Tsh. Tsh.* Misha plays alone in the corner. Lena lies on the floor by the stove. Her face has gone dark red, the color of currants. She keeps her hands locked over her chest.

I'm going to be a doctor, Mama. I'm going to save people!

Lena's few, feathery eyelashes settle like she's falling asleep. Tonya drops to her knees beside her daughter, takes Lena's hand. It is hotter than the stove.

Just save yourself, Lena. Save yourself, save yourself, save yourself first.

But Lena has always been more like Valentin.

"Something's not right," says Tonya, lifting her face. But there's no way to take Lena to any hospital. There are no more hospitals, at least none that she knows of, that weren't laid to waste by the Germans and that have enough staff to function. And it's coming on night. They would die of exposure, traipsing through the snow for hours, toward the hospital that does not exist. There are no trams, no cars, nothing.

It doesn't matter. Tonya and Valentin will carry her. Lena is leaf light, since they are all starving. Tonya will find something, somebody who knows what to do. She will ask Comrade Kemenova to look after the twins. They'll—they'll—

"Mama."

"Lena," she says, "we have to find help."

"My arm."

"You've come down with something—"

"My arm," Lena says again.

Tonya yanks the blankets away, one after another. Beneath all those blankets is Lena, trapped in still more layers, coats, sweaters, nightshirts, and Tonya unbuttons and grabs and forces while Lena shivers, shivers even though she is piping hot, until they have reached a layer that Tonya can rip open and there it is. A lump that was once an elbow, wrapped poorly in dressings.

"I'm sorry, Mama." Lena weeps, or maybe Tonya is weeping. It's hard to tell, with the tears falling like the bombs that used to rain down on Leningrad, explosions rocking the streets and fires combing through the buildings. Tonya was caught in it once, had to stop beneath an archway by the canals. The water was as black as pitch. The Germans had just shelled the Badayev warehouses, which contained the city's food stores, releasing a mushroom cloud of smoke, gritty with burned sugar. The sky in every direction was red, streaky, splattered with searchlights.

That is what Lena's arm looks like.

With tangible dread Tonya begins to undo the dressings. The smell is worse than the sight. She knows, even as she is unwrapping, round and round, that there is something dead below. Her heart ceases to beat in rhythm. Her pulse is in her mouth. Her lungs contract with the breaths she cannot take. The final piece of dressing is adhered to Lena's skin, and when Tonya tries to ease it off, the skin breaks too, in strings.

The elbow is black. Slick as scales in some places, rough in others. But black.

"Tell me what to do, Lena. Tell me what to do!" Tonya is shaking her. "Lena!"

But Lena's eyes are closing again. Tonya shakes harder. *Wake up*, she screams, *wake up. I'll tell you the end of the story just like you wanted, only wake up*, and this is all Valentin's fault that Lena is like this—Valentin, who always thought only of the *people*—because Tonya can hear Lena's voice as if Lena *has* woken up, as if Lena is talking, saying, *It's nothing, Mama, I just didn't want to worry you, you should focus on the twins, it's other people that need you, not me—*

But she sees Valentin staring at her, and then he cracks too, like his favorite glass. He is racked with silent sobs, sitting there with Katya still on his lap, Katya's mouth still clamped around the thumb. *Tsh. Tsh. Tsh.* It is the only sound.

"Please, Lena, please don't leave me—Lenochka—"

Tsh. Tsh. Tsh.

"*Lena!*"

Lena's expression is knowing. Secretive. There is a hidden, hollow place inside of everyone, and that is where they go right before they die. You cannot see it from the outside. But you can hear the echo. The time lapse. Tonya has witnessed it a few times. By the time the echo reaches your ears, its source is already gone.

Lena is gone.

* * *

It is the longest February of Tonya's life.

There are a few hours of weak sunlight every morning, before the dark arms of winter fold over Leningrad. There is nothing left to burn. There is no food in the larder. Tonya forces Katya and Misha to eat the old tea leaves, the ones from which she has brewed the last sliver of life. She eats one herself and it tastes like tar. She boils down her old shoes, the straps of her purse. Her remaining strength boils down with them. Misha no longer looks at his trains. Katya does nothing but work on her thumb.

Lena's body is kept in a different room. It may never break down.

The cold air of a *malicious winter* can preserve anything.

* * *

With Lena gone, Tonya writes on the walls more than ever. Valentin tries to stop her sometimes, says they've done enough for the day, touches her shoulder. She feels his fingers by her clavicle. She is a sailor lost at sea, bones showing where she'd not known people to have bones.

"I believe that one day people will find this," she says, numbly. "Will read it. But we won't be there to see it."

He brings her into an embrace that feels new, it has been so long.

"I must tell the world my own crimes," he says.

Tonya runs her tongue over her lips, chafed, bleeding. Only Valentin would think it still matters. Maybe he stole food. Cheated someone, shirked his work, failed to help a fellow prisoner, let them drown to save himself. If there was any crime, it was that Valentin Andreyev proved human. Just like the rest of them.

"People should know the truth about the things I did on the Canal to survive," he says, suddenly fierce, and now, briefly, finally, he sounds like the old Valentin. "This story should be about that too—"

"No," she says, "the story's over, it's over now," and he buries his face in her hair and he speaks into it, says something that sounds like *Antonina*, the way he often did when they were young. She is astounded, because she has long believed that the Valentin who liked to do that, to say her full name, never came home. That he was still out there on the Canal, in the water, looking out to the horizon as he always had.

* * *

Tonya blinks fast. Her brain hungers, strains for a point of reference. She looks around the kitchen, wallows in the silence. Nobody else has stirred. She pushes aside the blankets and gasps at the cold. It comes down like a set of jaws.

Her body moves of its own accord. She finds the sharpest knife she owns, tests the weight of it in her hand. She goes out of the kitchen, down the hall, until she reaches the bedroom where Lena's body is being stored. She has not looked in on it since. She has not been able to bear it.

Tonya uses a final shudder of strength to push open the door. The walls, the floors, are sticky with ice. Most of the furniture is gone, burned to embers.

The body on the bed, under a sheet, looks like a stowaway on a ship. But the body is not her daughter. In fact, it is as far from

Lena as anything on earth can be. It is the opposite. Tonya pulls on the frozen sheet. It cracks as it comes away. Her thoughts crack along with it, become jumbled.

She'll never be able to use this knife again afterward. She'll never be able to tell anyone. But there's hardly anybody left to tell, and it's only the murder of people for food that is considered a crime. Not the consumption of a corpse.

Go on, Mama, Lena would say. *I would do it, in your place. For Katya and Misha.*

Go on.

You're too sentimental, Mama!

But she can't. She can't do it. She sags against the bed.

What *can* she do?

With her free hand, Tonya pinches her own thigh, through her stockings, and holds it. Waits for it to hurt. It doesn't. She moves her fingers along, down to her calves. Pinches more. It's not much, but there's something. It is a funny thing that happens to some, people have noted in the breadlines: Most *of us grow skinnier and skinnier, until our heads begin to bobble on the sticks of our bodies, but* some *of us blow up like balloons!*

The twins and Valentin have grown as skeletal as Lena. *Tonya*, on the other hand, is thicker, rounder, than ever before.

She will gouge out her own flesh and feed it to her children.

Straightening, filled with renewed purpose, Tonya pulls back the sheet to reveal Lena's face, blanched as birchwood. She lowers the sheet, to adjust Lena's clothing. She will not come in here again until they have the strength to bury the body.

She feels the hair before she sees it.

It is unthinkable. It is unimaginable. And so she cannot think. Cannot imagine. She pulls the sheet farther down, farther, farther.

It is a porcelain doll. Tucked into the crook of Lena's arm.

With macabre curiosity Tonya withdraws the doll in its entirety. She already knows what it will look like. The color of the eyes. The slackness of the lids. The shine to the skin. But this doll is not the peasant-princess, nor is it the factory worker, drenched in Party colors, or just in blood.

This one wears a Red Army uniform, from the cap down to the woolly winter *valenki*, much better dressed, and likely better equipped, than most Soviet soldiers Tonya has ever seen. The khaki dress is flat fitting and starchy, the collars folded down, the sleeves lit up with red piping. An imitation canvas belt loops around the waist, embroidered in pale silver. It is all too dazzling to be a real uniform, a real design; the same way the princess's *kokoshnik* stood just slightly too high.

It is not meant to reflect, but to represent.

It is the first time it has occurred to her: These dolls are not just gifts.

They are *messages*.

The doll is smiling one of those vacuous doll-smiles. It looks a bit like Lena's.

26

Valentin

The evening is lush as Valentin and Tonya walk through the Summer Garden with the twins, picturesque enough that he feels there *must* be young lovers and old friends just around the corner, eating ice cream, laughing hard. There *must* be many more children than Katya and Misha, running and playing leapfrog by Krylov's statue as their parents smoke and read the papers. There *must* be plenty of people beyond the wrought-iron gates of the Garden, headed to museums and cafés and university lectures.

One day there will be. The war is over. Piter is in recovery.

They have buried Lena. They no longer write on the walls. Tonya has asked if he wishes her to render the story on paper. Should it be recorded for posterity? Should they try to find an editor, a publisher, a public? There is a bleak sort of beauty in the words: *The prisoners slip beneath the water, and they find no reason to come up for air. . . .* Sometimes Valentin stands in their bedroom and simply reads, rereads, rereads, in a rhythm, like the sea itself.

He feels it all wash over him, yet he does not drown.

Tonya stands close by as they watch the twins, who are tumbling over each other, yelping with glee. He is not touching her, but there is nothing between them.

"Tonya," he says, "will you marry me?"

She laughs, a pretty but jarring sound, like wind chimes. "Marriage," she says. "A rather bourgeois convention, don't you think?"

"A sacrifice I'm willing to make."

"A sacrifice! What a proposal, Valya."

"Marry me," he says, and she turns to him, her smile sweetly astonished.

"You're serious," she says.

"Marry me, and repaper the walls. Or paint over the words. Or get it all published. *Mne vsyo ravno*; none of it matters to me anymore, so long as you are here," he says. "Do you know, I used to have a dream in which I saw the moon rise behind you, Antonina? I saw the light all around you—but you were not in it. The light came from you, and it found me even when I was turned away. Even when my eyes were closed. Even when I was alone in the inhuman dark."

*   *   *

One day, when Valentin returns to the house with Katya, they find something awaiting them on the doorstep. Katya gives a cry of delight, falls hard upon it: a doll. The painted, porcelain kind. It is tightly swaddled in white cloth, like a newborn.

Like the dead bodies that people carted around this city in wagons, in the winter of 1941.

Valentin couldn't say where or how, but he's seen a similar doll.

Long ago, in yet another memory swept away by the White Sea . . .

He wants to leave the doll or better yet, throw it away, but Katya gazes at it so hungrily he cannot deny her.

"Keep it if you want, but be careful. It's porcelain. It is more delicate than it looks. Sometimes you cannot see all the breaks," he says, and Katya nods solemnly. *Yes, Papa.* She hugs the doll tighter to her, and he has a brief, scalding flash of doubt. Like he has just made an irrevocable mistake.

27

Rosie

MOSCOW, AUGUST 1991

The radio gives off a grating hum, and the announcer on *Ekho Moskvy* speaks too fast for me to keep up: *Emergency Committee . . . to save the Great Motherland . . . mortal danger . . .*

"It's a coup," says Alexey. "A coup by the old Party elite, to oust Mikhail Gorbachev."

I glance at Lev, who only draws on his cigarette.

"They're saying that Gorbachev has taken ill in the Crimea," Alexey continues. "And that Yanayev, the vice president, will act in his stead."

"What's this about an . . . Emergency Committee?" I ask.

"It's made up of Gorbachev's political enemies. As I said, it's a coup." He sighs. "I have to make some calls. They might switch off the phone lines."

Alexey utters this so casually that I don't startle until he's left the kitchen.

Switch off the phone lines?

The radio plays a quick jingle, and then stops. I fiddle with the dials. Only two stations broadcast in Moscow. It's not hard to jam everything.

Again, Lev only takes a drag. A deliberately long one, I would say.

"Will your family support this coup?" I ask.

"My father's involved."

"You know that?"

"He and his friends have never come around to *perestroika* and *glasnost*. It's all been brewing for a while."

But is this all it takes to undo those reforms? A reported case of the sniffles in the Crimea, and a bunch of Party and military officials can just steamroll their way to victory?

Lev still isn't meeting my gaze.

If he were in the OMON now, he would be working for the same people who might switch off Alexey Ivanov's phone lines.

Alexey strides back in from the foyer, exclaiming that Boris Yeltsin will not allow this to happen. The president has asked all concerned citizens to gather at Manezh Square, and calls for popular resistance! Alexey is clearly about to tell us to throw on our shoes when the phone rings, and he disappears to answer it.

"I'm not my family, Raisa." Lev stabs out his cigarette.

"I know that."

"Do you?"

"It's for you, Rosie," says Alexey, reappearing. "Marina Petrovna?"

"I know her," I say quickly. "Thank you."

On the phone, Marina speaks in English. I get the feeling that there's someone listening in on her end. And there's always someone listening in on *my* end, isn't there?

Though Zoya's been quiet lately.

If I didn't know better, I'd worry something had happened to her.

"My husband and I discussed it over the weekend," Marina says. "Mikhail would like to know more about this man you suspect to be his father. If we could—"

"Meet me at Manezh Square," I say. "I'm on my way there now."

* * *

By the time we get to Manezh Square, there are plenty of people already milling around, most of them looking bewildered. Some cheeky chap with a loudspeaker is helpfully informing everyone that it was all a ruse, that Yeltsin never intended or planned to have anyone meet up here. *Go home, my friends, go home!* I, for one, am tempted to take this advice. The sky has split open overhead, and it's starting to rain. Just the right amount to dampen enthusiasm for a protest movement that doesn't look promising.

"Hurry up, Rosie," Alexey yells at me, from somewhere in the growing mass of people. "We have to lie down to stop the tanks! Let's go!"

Stop the *tanks*?

I can't see Lev anywhere. People press in on all sides, and the rain falls harder.

"That's—We can't stop *tanks*! We can't just lie down!" I protest.

"Exactly," he says, "we can't."

It's the last I hear from Alexey before he too disappears into the crowd. An awful sound begins to blare from across the square; it's the tanks that he knew would come, because he's endured a lifetime of this. Alexey is used to the people and the rain and the loudspeakers and the way the ground seems to ripple beneath our feet, like an earthquake, because nothing is certain anymore. There is no foundation to this world. I might wake up tomorrow in a different one.

People begin to shout as the tanks burrow deeper into the square. Their noise is like thunder. *Please don't shoot! Don't shoot us!*

I can't imagine what possessed me to tell Marina to meet me here—they'll never find me—but I wish she would. I want to see a familiar face, because I've never been more surrounded and yet I've never felt so alone.

This.

This is why I want to be Rosie and not Raisa. Because *this* is what being Raisa feels like: small, confused, exhausted. Raisa always chooses the worst possible moment to be anywhere. The worst moment to open the door to the living room, to find her family dead, to *see*. But that's the thing, because she doesn't really. She doesn't understand any of it. She doesn't know who *that man* is; she doesn't know why Zoya and Papa are lying without moving like that; all she does know—and she just *knows*—is that she is alone.

Completely alone.

It's time. . . .

A tragedy . . .

A woman grabs my arm. "OMON!" she exclaims. "Over here!"

"I'm sorry," I say in English, pulling away from her. "I have to—I have to go."

"Oh, excuse," she says in dismay. "Yes. Not yours."

She means that it's not my problem, what's happening, and

she's right. I have a British passport. I could squeeze all the way back across Manezh Square, because by now they've cordoned off the parts that are usually only for vehicles. I could go back to the dacha and pack my things and hail a taxi and grab one of the last flights out before they shut down air travel and lock down the country, if that's where all this is headed, and why should I care if it is? So what if things go back to the way they were, if Gorbachev is pushed out and Yeltsin is defeated and all the reforms are peeled back? They can keep the whole country under martial law forever if they want!

What's it to me? Why should I care?

Why can't I leave Russia right now? Why does it matter who *that man* really is, or what he really did? What does it matter what Alexey really wants? Or who I really am? What more, what deeper, truth do I need?

Whatever we are looking for will not be there, was what Alexey said.

I don't even know what I'm looking for anymore.

Maybe I never have.

OMON buses and tanks have already stopped in the square, but the surrounding protestors don't look angry or scared. In fact, they're handing out food and candy to the troops, who are just standing by, accepting these goody bags.

No shots are being fired.

The OMON have come over to the side of the people.

Lev is suddenly there, right in front of me, taking me by the hand. I can't hear a thing above the tanks and the crowds and the pounding in my ears. He seems to be glancing back, wondering why I'm taking so long to follow, why I'm resisting.

I'm no longer resisting.

Lev turns around and begins to say something, but he doesn't finish. He must see it on me. Something flashes in his eyes and then he's got my face cupped in his hands and I'm on my tiptoes and we're kissing, hard, with force. Without any hesitation. The wait has been too long. People push by, shoving and shouting, but somehow I hear him, feel him, speak. *Since that first day we spent together,* he says, against my mouth, *it seems to me that I have been waking up from the longest night. . . .*

The tumult around us continues. We do not stop. It is almost painful, but we do not stop. I am bruised with it, nearly bleeding, the rain keeps coming, flooding, but I never want to stop.

The more time I spend in Russia, the closer I get to the truth, the more I know, the less I understand.

All I can do is *bask in it, bathe in it, drown in it.*

* * *

Something is bubbling on a stove top. Coffee. I rub my eyes, peek over the blanket. *Where am I?* Various items of clothing are strewn over the floor: my sundress, looking shoddy from yesterday's rain; my ballet pumps, layered in mud; my bra and underwear in a shy, shameful heap by the far corner.

I got a full night's sleep.

I'd forgotten what that feels like.

"It's eleven." Lev is in the doorway.

There's no hint of anything that happened between us in his expression. If not for the branding-ironed memory of it in my brain, I might think I had imagined the way we came in here yesterday, saying nothing at all, like words would only ruin things; the way Lev tossed his keys on the kitchen counter and lifted me by the waist, against the wall, like I weighed the same as the keys; the way my hands slipped beneath his shirt, feeling many more scars than I ever knew he had, in rivers all along his side and up and down his back, his years in the Russian military written all over him.

The way he never took his eyes off me, like he thought I might disappear into thin air if he did.

"Is this . . . your place?" I'm in a bit of a stupor. I guess I wasn't paying close enough attention, yesterday.

"It was closer than the dacha," he says, dryly.

I feel the tickle of a blush.

"I spoke with Alexey Alexeyevich. He said he'll be speaking at the White House rally today at noon. He wants you to attend." Lev looks back in the direction of the kitchen, listening for the coffee. "He also said your friend Marina called again. We should pick her up on the way."

I have to telephone Richard.

Richard with his soft, unruly hair and slightly hooked nose; Richard, who walks with just a touch of a shuffle. He looks comfortable in any context, against any background. He fits in so well, he is nearly invisible.

It's what I always thought I wanted.

"Could I . . . use your phone?" I ask. "And take a shower . . ."

"I'll pick up Marina and her husband and come back to get you," he says.

I wait until Lev is out the door before getting to my feet. The flat is dusky and dark. It seems chilly for high summer.

Or could that be Zoya?

Where has she *been*?

"Are you there?" I ask aloud, as if that's ever worked.

On the telephone, the operator puts me through to London. Richard's father picks up. "Hello, darling," he says. "Richie! Rosemary on the line."

"Hi," says Richard, coming on. He already sounds unhappy. "We're seeing everything in the news, and I think you should come home. What are you still doing?"

"I—"

"Are you hurt? Is something wrong?"

"I'm fine." Where will I go, when I get back to England? My flight leaves in two weeks. Term doesn't start until the end of September. I haven't made close enough friends in my life to be able to ring someone up and ask to stay on their sofa.

Could I really go back to Mum's apartment?

"Then what is it?" Richard asks. "Are you coming home?"

"This is home, Richard." I cradle the phone against my shoulder. "I belong here. And once I've finished my degree, I'm going to move back here. Things are changing, and I want to be part of everything that's happening."

"What are you talking about?" He sounds much farther away than London. "You know how unstable things are over there. It's sodding *Russia*! You shouldn't have gone in the first place. You shouldn't have—"

I suddenly understand that I tried—I *really* tried—to make myself feel safe, over the years, when Mum couldn't. I did everything right. The right marks. The right boyfriend. The financial security. The future. I thought safety was an external thing, that the feeling could be achieved by putting in enough locks, closing all the doors and windows, closing myself. Of course it didn't work.

The feeling is internal.

I have to open myself.

"My soul is Russian. My soul is here." Mum would be proud of me. Talking about the soul like I believe in it. "I'm so sorry, Richard. I've been living so long as two disconnected halves. I thought I could become whole by erasing everything and starting over, but it turns out I only needed to look harder."

* * *

I pull the door shut behind me and pop on my sunglasses. Today the sun is out, and the sky is a bright liquid blue. No sign of yesterday's clouds. Lev is around front, standing by the driver's door of the Mercedes. Mikhail and Marina are in the backseat.

The effort to build barricades in the city center has left it looking like a lawn dug up by dogs. We park quite far off and pick our way through the streets on foot. The flotsam and jetsam of mass protest are everywhere: abandoned umbrellas, boxes, discarded clothing, pieces of wire mesh, even fragments of concrete. The closer we get to the White House, the seat of the Russian parliament and the symbol of a burgeoning democracy, the more the mood of anticipation is heightened.

Today the people know what they want. Today they're going to get it.

Mikhail is sporting thick bifocals, and each time I look at him and Marina, I see him look back at me, his dark eyebrows wrangled together right above the rims, like the two of us just don't know what to make of each other.

We reach the White House, where an enormous rally is taking place. Different speakers are appearing on the balcony, taking turns decrying the Emergency Committee. All around us, people are climbing onto abandoned tanks for a better view; tricolor flags are flying. Every few minutes, a chant rises from the crowd: *Russia is alive! Yeltsin, we support you!*

"Is he in good health, the man you think is my father?" asks Mikhail, addressing me at last.

"I'd call him sprightly. That's him!" I point to the balcony. "He's there!"

Alexey Ivanov has appeared at the rail. He's holding a megaphone, though part of me doubts he even needs it. This attempted coup has aged him backward, if anything. He looks younger now, beneath unforgiving sunshine, than he did in that café in Oxford.

"Is it him?" Marina asks her husband. "Can you tell?"

We are all staring at the white-haired figure. A pall of silence settles over the crowd as he begins to speak.

Alexey's voice is so intense, so rich, that it feels almost like he's never stopped speaking, not since the last time he took the stage here in his homeland. He was a Bolshevik then; he is the *last Bolshevik* now. He's here to fight for his final cause. He's come all the way around, through a century of bloodshed and violence and dashed dreams, to arrive at this spot, to speak to these people.

He is hypnotic. As he raises his hand, closes it into a fist, the crowd cheers. The skin on the back of my neck prickles. He lifts his arms upward, toward the sky, as if he derives his conviction from the heavens themselves. I can feel myself being lifted up too, higher, lighter, than I've ever been.

"We have lived in the shadows long enough!" Alexey shouts. "We will have our freedom!"

In the shadows.

Too many shadows . . .

The wind blows hard.

I whip my head around. "My mum," I babble. "She said something to me—before she died—"

Lev gives me a sharp look.

"It's not him," says Mikhail.

We all turn to him. His eyebrows have fallen back into place. He shakes his head.

"I don't know who that man up there is," says Mikhail, "but that's not my father. That's not Valentin Andreyev."

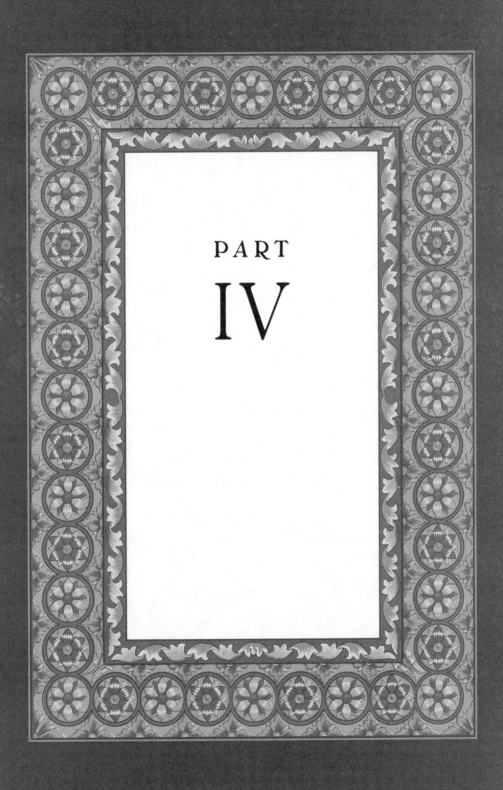

PART

IV

28

Katya

Katya is ten years old, and she already knows what she's going to be when she grows up: a ballerina. She tells this to anyone who will listen. Mama says that people are always listening, that she should be quiet sometimes, but Katya doesn't like staying quiet. And there *is* that story that Mama tells, about the heir to the throne of the old Russian empire, the Tsarevich, who grows bored with the ladies of the court and is drawn to the peasant girl who has slipped into the palace by chance, because she stands out from the rest.

Katya wants to be the one who stands out from the rest. She hopes her own Tsarevich is watching.

Katya has an older sister who died. It happened during the war. Mama and Papa have never explained how, so maybe Lena charged headfirst into enemy lines. Misha says that Lena probably died because she tripped on the street and hit her head on a rock. It makes Katya want to hit him on *his* head. They fight a lot.

Mama always says to *Stop squabbling, kids*, which is unfair, because Katya is not allowed to say *Stop squabbling, Mama and Papa* when *they* do it.

If Mama and Papa are arguing and somebody mentions Lena by accident, then everybody goes quiet. She has a lot of power for someone who is dead.

* * *

One day Katya is snooping and she finds something interesting beneath some of Mama's things: a small notebook. It might be an old diary and she gets excited because all she knows about her parents is from eavesdropping. They don't tell her anything. Like the time Papa said that Mama's eyes reminded him of Lake Syamozero by night, and Katya asked him whether the family could visit. He said he would never go north again.

When did he go the first time?

The notebook is not a diary. Just stories. They're short and there are not many. It's strange because Mama writes magical stories for children's magazines, but on her typewriter, not by hand.

On the first page there is one line above all the others.

For Lena, beloved daughter.

No mention of Katya. Just Lena.

Lena, who is not even here to read it.

Katya feels so betrayed she almost can't believe it. But it's right there. In ink.

No, she thinks savagely, *no, it's not written in ink, it's written in pencil. And pencil can be erased.* And before she knows it she's found an eraser and she's starting to erase it. Katya doesn't like using erasers because they make her skin itch and her eyes hurt but it's worth it, because now at least nobody will ever know, even if this notebook is published too, that Mama loves only one of her daughters.

Lena, the dead one.

* * *

Misha often makes fun of her dolls, says the dolls are her only friends, but Katya has caught him playing with them before. Having a tea party. She doesn't tease him. She's been blessed with a tremendous talent for dance, while Misha doesn't have much talent for anything, and it would be cruel. When he teases *her*, she simply looks past him and pretends that she is staring down an auditorium of people—not just any auditorium, but the big one, in Moscow—and holding her pose for however long it takes before the curtain falls.

Of Katya's many dolls, two are made of porcelain. The porcelain ones are special and thrilling and *secret*, because they came from an unknown, mysterious doll-giver. They were left on the doorstep and contain small gifts; inside the heads are spaces large enough to store pieces of candy and toy rings and silver spoons.

The gift in the most recent doll was a miniature ballerina figurine. A *ballerina*.

Katya has her first fan.

It is a little embarrassing and she would never, ever admit it to Misha or to the girls at school or to anyone else who is alive, ever, but she daydreams sometimes about whoever it is that left the dolls. She daydreams that it's a youngish sort of *he*, and that he made them himself. Maybe he even made the ballerina. Katya's not sure how such things are made, actually.

She asks Mama casually if she can visit the famous Lomonosov Porcelain Factory and Mama laughs.

I'll take you if you explain why, says Mama.

This leads to Katya showing her the ballerina, stupidly, which Mama shows to Papa and Papa says he has no idea where it came from, but Papa *does* know the porcelain dolls were left at the front door, and Mama didn't know, and soon Katya is confessing to everything, tearfully and tragically, even to the daydreaming.

But Mama does not confiscate the porcelain dolls. Instead, Mama and Papa get into the biggest fight of their lives. Katya and Misha cower in the living room while they shout at each other in the kitchen and Misha doesn't have to say it, because she's already beating herself bloody with it.

This is all your fault, Katya. This is all your fault.

* * *

Mama and Papa seem to speak only in whispers now. Dasha at school says it means they're likely to divorce and they don't want anyone to know yet. Misha says that if that's true, then it's Katya's doing. Her and her dolls. Dolls are for *babies*, Misha says, and Katya yells that she's seen him having the odd tea party and that if they're making rules about dolls, then dolls are for *girls* or isn't that right? And he turns red around the ears and he says, *I wish you weren't my sister.*

He says things like this all the time but this time it feels like he means it because she hates herself too. Mama and Papa are divorcing because of her.

* * *

Katya isn't sure how she came up with the plan, but it's taken her long enough. She is going to run away. The family will be happier without her. Mama and Papa won't have to divorce. She is going to go live with the doll maker. Somebody who can create beautiful treasures, who treasures *her*. Maybe he can do other things, too. Draw. Paint. Sculpt. Anything with his hands. He'll have enough talent of his own that he won't mind when she has to do busy-ballerina things, like perform on the Big Stage. Like tie up her ballet shoes.

She doesn't know much of what ballerinas do, besides that.

She adds *A Ballet School* to her list of places the doll maker should take her to visit, right underneath *The Lomonosov Porcelain Factory* and *Lake Syamozero*.

The only problem is that her plan requires money, and she has none. Nobody she knows has much money except maybe Vitya at school, who brags a lot, but she's not about to ask *him*. He's a scrawny schoolboy. Nothing like the doll maker.

Katya thinks and thinks, makes lists, doodles in her schoolbooks. She can't sell the dolls; the doll maker might never forgive her. She watches Mama working one day on the Underwood, typing hard, oblivious to her presence—See? They might not even notice when she's gone—and then inspiration strikes. It hits her right as she's standing there.

Maybe this is how the doll maker feels when he adds just the right glob of paint to the right spot on one of his masterpieces. It *must* be. After all, they were both born to be artists.

* * *

Mama's editor is called Vladimir Stolypin. Katya's family have been to their home for dinner many times. Vladimir and his wife, Anna, weren't able to have kids. Katya knows this because she once heard Mama and Papa talking, saying that Anna Stolypina was told she will never have a baby, and for some reason this made Mama sad, which seemed silly because Mama and Papa have had three children, including Lena. *Three.* That's nearly enough that they could have given one away to the Stolypins.

Katya walks there after school with Mama's notebook of stories in her hands.

The Stolypins are at home. They seem distracted. Katya shouldn't delay. She says she's brought a notebook with stories she's written and she'd like to sell them to the magazine, please. Anna Stolypina looks stiff at this, like she might need to use the toilet. Vladimir Stolypin asks to see the notebook and Katya congratulates herself on how he won't realize it's Mama's because it's handwritten. He reads only a page or two, which she finds disappointing, and then he says: *Are you sure you wrote these?* And she confirms that she did.

Katya, says Vladimir, *please be honest.*

Her lower lip wobbles.

Anna Stolypina takes a look at the stories. She asks, *Did your mother write these, Katya?* and Katya bursts into tears. She does break easily, she's noticed. Anna comes over and puts an arm around her and says that everything's fine; it's just that these particular stories aren't meant for kids.

Katya thought *all* stories were meant for kids.

Vladimir Stolypin clears his throat and says he's going to hold on to the notebook for the time being. He says maybe there's something to them after all. His wife looks surprised. He asks if Katya can come back next week, a different afternoon, to talk with some friends of his. Katya nods happily now. Her tears have dried. She'd love to talk. She loves talking.

* * *

There are three men sitting in the Stolypins' living room when Katya visits the next time. Vladimir Stolypin must have many friends. Katya doesn't have even *one* real friend at school. Misha is the opposite. Well-liked. Funny. He says *she* will never make friends until she stops telling everyone she is going to be a prima ballerina and she feels chilled on the inside when he says this.

One day, Katya, she promises herself, *they're all going to adore you. They're going to hang on your every word like ornaments on a tree.*

Like how Vladimir Stolypin's friends are doing right now.

They don't resemble Mama and Papa's friends. They are dressed like they want to match. There was a time when Mama dressed Katya and Misha to match. In fact, these men do seem to act like twins or in their case triplets. Katya notices how they steal glances at one another, speaking in their own silent language. She and Misha have their own language, or they used to.

"So, Yekaterina," says Triplet #1. He has a face that is young, almost pretty. "If we may ask a few questions . . ."

"Please, call me Katya," she says regally. They see her as equal to an adult; she can already perceive this. A lot of people call her *Katenka* without even asking and she *hates* that.

"Your mother is Antonina Radakova. Is that right?"

"Nobody calls her that. She goes by Tonya."

"And your father is a man called . . . Anatoly Radakov."

"That is my papa," Katya says proudly.

"Of course it is." Triplet #1 smiles and she beams in return. "Now this notebook, Katya, I want you to take it and put it right back where you found it. Alright? But it *is* interesting to us, and you deserve a reward. We can come by your home and—"

"No! You can't." Katya flushes. "I just need— I want to sell it."

"Oh, yes. I see. It's a secret." He holds a finger up to his lips. "In that case, don't tell your parents about this meeting between all of us, eh? We'll contact you again through Comrade Stolypin right here and arrange something. But just be sure to put the notebook back."

Something in her stomach turns at this. She doesn't like how he said *Comrade Stolypin*. Mama does not call her editor Comrade Stolypin. But on the other hand, Triplet #1 probably does not know that Anna Stolypina cannot have kids, and Mama does.

Where *is* Anna Stolypina?

"Thank you so much, Katya," says Triplet #2, speaking for the first time. He is an older, horsey version of Triplet #1. She feels annoyed. She didn't say *he* could call her Katya.

* * *

Tonight Mama comes in to tell a bedtime story. Mama is radiant when she tells stories, like starlight. But Katya wonders why, whenever Mama is like this, she has a terrible urge to say her older sister's name, just breathe it out. *Lena.* It must be because she wants to hurt Mama, deep down. Because she is a bad person. Because she's never been as amazing a daughter as Lena was, and Mama and Papa will never love her the way they did Lena.

But that is all about to change.

After Katya runs away, *hers* will be the unspoken name. *She* will take Lena's place in the family. The perfect one. The immortal one.

* * *

When Katya gets up for a drink of water, she sees light beneath the door of the kitchen. Mama and Papa are still awake. They are finally speaking in normal-volume voices.

Mama says: *The notebook was missing for almost two weeks. And now it's back.*

Katya goes closer. She stands behind the door.

Papa says: *You think Katya took it?*

Mama says: *I know she did.*

But why?

Curiosity?

Yes, probably.

I'll keep it in my pillowcase from now on. But have you been reading the papers, Valya? There've been more arrests lately. Another wave. And the dolls—somebody has been watching us. I think it's time to leave Leningrad.

Then we'll go. As long as we are together, Antonina . . .

Katya pauses with her hand on the knob.

Nobody calls Mama *Antonina*.

And who on earth is *Valya*?

Who *are* these people?

* * *

Deep in the night Katya is awoken by a *thump*. Misha, in the other bed, sits up straight. *Thump*. Neither of them speak. *Thump*. Mama bursts into the room. She gets everyone out of bed. There are people in the apartment. They are standing in the hallway. They're in uniform, with dark blue caps, red stripes. Papa is there too. Misha whimpers that he has to pee.

The uniformed men have their shoulders pulled back and their chests stuck out. They say to go to the living room, to sit down on the sofa.

Katya sees Misha's expression and she knows it mirrors her own. That's what twinship is good for.

"What are they looking for?" asks Misha fearfully. The men are overturning everything on Mama's work desk, in Papa's bookshelves. They flip through the books. They shake out a drawer. They pull up the rug. They look bored. Mama doesn't answer.

Katya isn't sure how she knows, but she knows.

They are looking for the notebook.

They have been sent here by the Triplets.

Katya put it back where she found it, like the Triplets asked her to do, but now it's in Mama's pillowcase. Should she reveal where it is? Then they'll take it and go away, and all this will be over. Mama can just re-create the stories from memory later—

Mama's gaze is on her. Katya wonders if Lake Syamozero ever looks like *this*. Maybe the very bottom. Mama shakes her head in a small way. Her hair, down around her shoulders, looks like satin. Now Katya doesn't want to say Lena's name, or dim Mama's radiance. She doesn't even want to run away to the doll maker.

She just wants to climb onto her mother's lap like a baby and hold on.

The apartment is a mess. The intruders leave the same way they came. *Thump, thump, thump.*

Katya hears Mama exhale like she's been holding her breath for years.

* * *

The next day Aunty Vika is in town. Aunty Vika visits only a few times a year, but each visit is a treat. Once she even invited them to her home in Kalinin, where she has a piano that takes up half a room. Katya was so disappointed that Aunty Vika no longer plays. It is something to do with weakness in her wrists. Sometimes Mama and Papa talk behind closed doors about how the war changed her. Changed everyone.

Whenever Katya tells her she's going to be a ballerina but nobody else believes, Aunty Vika looks deep into her eyes and says very seriously: *You're already a ballerina, Katya, and don't let anyone say otherwise.*

Katya loves Aunty Vika.

"Aunty Vika!" Katya cries out and Misha comes running too and Aunty Vika squeezes both of them hard. Then she shoos them away and says that she's here to talk to Mama but as soon as *that's* over she'll come find them and hear how everyone is doing. *Boring Adult Stuff first,* she says.

Katya hovers as Aunty Vika sits in the kitchen with a cup of tea while Mama hangs laundry on the line. Aunty Vika looks over and winks and Katya slinks out of the room. She sits outside against the wall. Should she tell Aunty Vika about her plan to run away? Though the plan has lost some luster the past few days. Ever since those stompy men came through. Katya felt oddly protective of Mama and Papa while sitting on that sofa with them.

It really is Boring Adult Stuff. Katya is considering getting up to play or going outside until Aunty Vika is done, but then Mama says—

"We're leaving the city tomorrow."

Katya didn't think Mama and Papa were serious, the other night, speaking of leaving Leningrad. Where is there to go? Dasha at school has family in Siberia and says it is a wasteland. Dasha says her cousins have farm animals sleeping inside their house with them. She swears that they still think there is a Tsar, one who's not human, but a *god*. There is no way that people in such places have heard of something as sophisticated and high-minded as the ballet.

How will she ever attend a ballet school or perform on the Big Stage?

How will the doll maker find her again?

"There's something I must confess, before it's too late." Mama's voice sounds funny. "It's been on my mind so often. Every time I learn of another arrest."

Katya feels dizzy. She isn't sure she wants to hear this, either.

"Tonya," says Aunty Vika, a warning.

"I was the one who denounced Pavel."

Pavel. Another name Katya has never heard. Another name, no doubt, with a secret history, like *Lena*.

Like *Valya*.

"I knew," says Aunty Vika. "But I forgave you."

"Some things are unforgivable, Viktoria. Sometimes I think that if anything happens to my family, it's only a punishment for everything I've done."

Unforgivable.

"And what of the many things I've done?" asks Aunty Vika, in a perfectly steady voice. She does not sound funny at all, not like Mama.

"That's different," says Mama. "I understood you, about the letters—"

"And I understood my father," says Aunty Vika. "Papa had plenty of blood on his own hands. I stood by as he denounced our friends, even family members. How many more would have died because of him? How many people did you save, by denouncing him? But then, Papa did save Valentin, didn't he, at great risk to his own life? These things are never as simple as they seem. Oh, they will try to make it look black-and-white later; but you and I know better."

They are still talking, but somehow that word of Mama's, spoken like that, *unforgivable*, still rings in Katya's ears. It goes on so long, she begins to worry she will never stop hearing it.

* * *

In the night there is another *thump*. Katya closes her eyes and hopes it's only Misha falling out of bed. It is not. It's the men in uniform again. This time they find what they are looking for: Mama. Mama's hair still looks like satin, even when someone else's fist is in it. Katya and Misha watch from the doorway and

Katya feels that this is a nightmare. This must be a nightmare. Misha is crying so hard he cannot stay standing; he has to bend. It all happens so fast it's hard to believe these are the same people who made such a mess, last time. The door clicks behind them.

The look on Papa's face is unlike anything Katya has ever seen before.

29

Rosie

Having spent my whole life trying to hide from shadows, I am now headed directly into one.

Shadow Lake looks misplaced on the map. Sitting northeast of Leningrad, it is only a droplet compared to nearby Lake Onega, and it is much harder to get to. As the taxi driver tells me how stunning Finland is, this time of year, like he thinks he can convince me to go that far, I quickly double-check the pages I've brought along from Natalya Burtsinova's memoir. *Tenevoe.*

I don't know what I'm going to do when I reach this address, or how I'm going to explain my presence.

Too many shadows.

The taxi driver is a forty-something fellow with a jolly, jaunty look about him, a bit like a baby animal. "This motorway goes straight up to Murmansk," he affirms. "Have you ever crossed the line between the tundra and the taiga?"

"You can tell where that happens?" I ask, staring out the window.

"Oh, yes. I used to live in the Arctic Circle. In Vorkuta," he says. "The railway there was built by gulag prisoners, you know. It was a hellscape."

Jolly and jaunty indeed. "Why were you in Vorkuta?"

He scratches his sideburns. "I was born there. My mother was a prisoner in the Rechlag special camp before she got married. She worked in the coal mines."

My mother was a prisoner. It seems so incredible that people here could have survived what they did. But in a way these experiences were ordinary, weren't they? Millions lived through the same things. They just don't say.

"The Rechlag, the river camp," he goes on. "Maximum security, for political prisoners and terrorists. Established in 1948. Short-lived. The whole gulag system was dissolved within a few years of Stalin's death in 'fifty-three, of course. My mother never left Vorkuta. Still lives up there."

We have passed the route he'd prefer we take, into Karelia. We turn onto a new highway; *this* road can take you all the way into the White Sea, if you're not careful.

The land is mostly flat, dotted with rustic-looking houses and dry shrubbery set against a patchwork of trees. But I don't think I have ever seen such a distance, through such a small window.

This is not quite the Arctic. This is not the taxi driver's idea of hell. But it is the high Russian north, higher than I've ever gone, ever experienced. There is no real summer here, not even when the wildflowers are in full bloom. The freshwater lakes are always cold.

From today onward, the days will grow shorter until they disappear, and this desolate land will freeze over and freeze its secrets with it, as it does, year in and year out.

* * *

The taxi driver pulls up along the road to a large house made of stacked logs, shaded darkly by pine. The trees give off an unnerving butterscotch smell, maybe of sap. I can't see the lake from here, but I can hear it, at least what sound like waterfowl. The taxi driver will wait for me in the village by the chapel, he says, but if I'm not done by four, he's got to get back to Leningrad. Soon enough he's driven off on the only road in sight.

Nothing to do but knock.

A woman answers the door. She wears a red bandanna over her streaky gray hair, an embroidered blouse, and a friendly smile. She holds needles and a piece of knitting. "Are you lost?" she says, agreeably.

Of course she'd think so. Who would come out here on purpose?

I must look even more lost than the others, because her expression shifts from sympathy to pity. She has started to knit the thing in her hands.

"It's . . . A family called Burtsinov may have lived here a long time ago," I say. "Would you know . . . Does that ring any bells? Natalya Burtsinova?"

She lowers her knitting, considers me. "Well, my mother was called Natalya. But the surname is not known to me."

Could this woman be Akulina's *sister*?

Is that why the memoir-writer included the address? As the slightest enticement, or even invitation, to Akulina, to return to the dacha of her childhood, where she might encounter the family she doesn't even know she has?

Mum used to tell me and Zoya a grim little tale that began in a cemetery in the far north. *It was summertime,* she'd say. *All the coffins had bobbed to the surface. They'd been buried above the permafrost, and when the active soil layer thawed and washed out each year, they reappeared. Every grave was marked by a wooden cross, and every cross had a plaque with a name spelled out in copper letters. . . .*

"My mother died decades ago. Decades," the woman emphasizes, presumably so that I don't say something inane like *I'm sorry.* "I wish I could be more help to you. But if you go into the village and ask around, someone might know. . . ."

Over the lake, the mist seems to be lessening. In a moment I will be able to see to the other side. "What about the name Tonya?" I ask.

"Tonya." Her hands go still. "Yes. In a manner of speaking. I've known one Tonya."

While listening to Mum's story I would whimper, imagining a decomposed grave with the lid coming off. Mum only chuckled at me.

You didn't know, Raisa? In the north, everything rises. Everything emerges.

"Tonya was here, here in this house. For a night," she says.

"One *night,*" I say, in case I've misunderstood.

She cracks her knuckles, continues knitting. "It is a vivid memory, sadly, because that was the day before my mother died. But yes, I remember Tonya. She was an old friend of my mother's, come to say good-bye. Mama was in very poor health by then; I was here taking care of her full-time. Tonya and I cooked together, and she told me a lot about her daughter. Something with a *K*..."

"Katya." It burns my tongue. "*My* mother."

"Katya, that sounds right. So you're her ... ?"

Tonya is my grandmother. Mum never mentioned her parents, and Zoya and I didn't ask. We assumed they were long dead, because so many people are long dead. Papa *did* ask once, and Mum described a dumpy woman who smelled of walnut cookies and herbal tea before dovetailing into an anecdote that was clearly made-up.

That's all she ever gave us. Fairy tales.

The woman looks at me keenly. "I liked Tonya a lot. She gave me her address, and I wrote to her a while later, to tell her about Mama, but a friend wrote back to say that Tonya too had died."

Zoya may not be here, but I can conjure it on my own this time: that smell, that sweet volcanic charcoal-smell.

Did Tonya die in the fire that destroyed Otrada?

The mist over Tenevoe has lifted, leaving only the light. I had a grandmother and then I didn't. I found Tonya and then I lost her again. I wanted to know, and now I do. Alexey will never get his *Kukolka* back. The casket has slammed shut. This place is the end of the earth; I can't go any farther. There's nothing beyond.

* * *

By the time I'm back in Moscow, it's well past sunset. Every window is dark at the dacha, except for the kitchen's. The Mercedes is in the drive.

I find Alexey at the kitchen table, bent over paperwork. He does everything with a younger man's ease, but his legs are apart, his trousers rising up, and I can see the white hair and marbled skin of his ankles. When he smiles, his face crinkles like tissue.

He pops his pen into his mouth. "There you are."

"Where's Lev?"

"I've given him the night off." Alexey pulls the pen from his mouth. "I thought it would be best for you and me to speak, just the two of us, at last."

"I know who *Kukolka is,* Alexey."

He doesn't appear surprised.

"She's dead," I say.

"So they say," he replies, laid-back as ever.

The walls of the kitchen seem to constrict, pull inward, like a pair of lungs. The weirdest thing is that he doesn't seem any different. Even now that I know everything between us has been built on lies, he still looks the part of Alexey Ivanov, scholar and historian and writer and speaker. Gentlemanly and distinguished.

"Who *are* you?" I ask.

"You have chosen the right time to ask," he says calmly, "because I have finished."

"Finished?" My voice is only an echo. "Finished what?"

"I have made a doll of *you,* Rosie," he says. "It is the last one I will ever make. I have put everything I have left into it. But it is the most beautiful thing I have ever done."

30

Katya

The nightmare refuses to end. Mama is gone. Katya and Misha stay home from school. Papa spends all day locked in the living room. Aunty Vika comes to help. One afternoon she makes honey cake and sits with Katya and Misha in the kitchen.

"As you know, your mother has been arrested," she says.

"But *why*?" Misha demands. "Papa won't tell us anything!"

"I'll tell you everything I can," Aunty Vika says. "Your mama's editor gave her name to the secret police. He claimed she wrote a notebook of stories filled with anti-Soviet content. Maybe he made it all up, maybe he wanted to divert attention from his own family, but—"

"It's *your* fault!" Misha whirls on Katya. "Stupid Katya! I know you stole Mama's notebook! I saw you with it! You *showed* it to someone, didn't you!"

"Stop it, Misha," says Aunty Vika.

"She showed it to someone!" he shouts. "Is it the one you scribble about and drool over in your schoolbooks, you pathetic idiot? That one! Didn't you!"

Katya feels herself breaking again, just like she did at the Stolypins'.

"Schoolbooks?" asks Aunty Vika, like that is the point of all this.

"The one who sends her *dolls*," Misha sneers. "Katya's in *love*!"

"Mikhail, enough! Katya, what is he talking about?"

Katya shakes her head and sniffles.

"Forget it then. Now, listen to me, both of you. You're ten, soon to be eleven years old. I'm being honest with you, and I need you both to be honest with me."

Katya pulls her legs up and rocks herself. *It's okay, feeling like this, it's okay. This is how it'll feel onstage one day, too. Pure nerves. Pure fear. Pure terror. You just have to keep ahold of yourself until the curtain falls, Katya. That's all.*

Aunty Vika takes a deep breath. "We don't know what's going to happen. But in the meantime, don't say your mother's name. Ever. In any conversation, with children or adults. We can't know who's listening or what anyone wants. We don't know whom to trust. Your best chance to have your mama back home is never to speak of her. Is that clear?"

Katya and Misha are both crying now. Katya tries to take his hand. They used to hold hands a lot. It used to feel like they were one person. But he crosses his arms, stuffing his hands beneath his armpits. Like he'd rather cut them off than touch her.

Unforgivable.

* * *

Aunty Vika has to return to Kalinin and she forces Katya and Misha to go to school again. At least the other kids give Katya a wide berth. Misha goes off with his friends afterward and Katya goes home and there is nobody there. The door to the living room is open. The room still smells of Papa. She walks around anxiously for a few minutes and then makes a snack and then falls asleep in bed and then Misha is hollering her awake and says, *Aunty Vika is back now. Where's Papa? Where is Papa?* Misha is sweaty. He looks sick.

"I don't know," Katya says uncertainly, "he wasn't here when I got home from school."

"Then where *is* he?" says Misha, and she worries that he'll shout again, but he doesn't. His eyes are so wide they may pop from his face.

Aunty Vika calms everyone down. Aunty Vika says that Papa has been through a lot in his life. *He spent almost a decade in the camps, before you two were born,* she explains. This is the word she uses, camp. *Lager.* Katya and Misha are both confused.

"The way our neighbors go camping in Novgorod?" Misha asks.

"No," says Aunty Vika. "Labor camps for political prisoners. Your mama's arrest may have reminded him of this, and he isn't himself right now. But he loves you. He'll come back."

"When?" says Misha.

"I don't know."

When Katya gets back into bed she can't fall asleep, of course, because she spent the whole afternoon sleeping. She has the feeling—stronger than a feeling—that Papa left because of her. Because he too knows the truth. *She* caused this. She brought this upon the family. Just like she brings it upon herself, what the other girls do to her at school. *Your face is too pretty, let's help,* they say as they yank her hair and spit in her eyes and hold her down to kick her, and Misha sees this, sometimes, but he doesn't come to her defense. He acts like it's not happening. He acts like he doesn't know her.

Nobody knows her. She is alone.

* * *

Papa does come home. He has the eyes of a wild animal. Katya watches as he goes straight to Mama's pillowcase, shakes out the notebook, and begins ripping out all the pages. He doesn't clean them up. He goes to the kitchen and Katya hears him breaking things in there too.

Katya slowly, carefully, picks up every page.

She folds them into her own pillow.

She's just keeping it for when Mama returns, even if Misha says Mama isn't ever coming back. It's been weeks now. Maybe more than a month. Misha is getting tougher. Mouthier. Katya is turning softer and weaker. But it's always this way with twins, people have said. They'll *always* be opposites! One will be quiet and the other loud. One will be serious and the other silly.

One twin will be good, and the other will be bad.

* * *

Today a pair of ballet shoes has been left at the front door. Katya is relieved that nobody else found them first. Nobody else would believe they were for her.

They fit perfectly.

There is a message fitted inside one of the shoes.

KATYA, meet me today in front of the Kirov State Academic Theatre. You will know me by what I am holding—I can wait there until 6.

The doll maker has never used her name before.

He knows who she is.

He wants to meet her.

He wants this to be real.

It is more than real. It is *fate*.

Katya packs the shoes and her dolls into one of Papa's old suitcases, with her clothes wrapped around them. She's just about to leave the apartment when she remembers Mama's stories. She doesn't *want* to take anything else. The dolls are heavy enough. But somehow she cannot leave the pages behind. It's okay. She'll toss them out one day. She'll toss everything out, this whole ugly horrible pointless *unforgivable* life of hers *unforgivable unforgivable* and she will never, ever look back.

31

Antonina

Tonya closes the door behind her hard. There isn't time to waste. "Hello!" she calls out. "Is anyone here?"

Valentin appears in the doorway of the kitchen.

"I'm back," she says. "I'm back, and we need to go. We'll get the children from school. We're leaving. I can explain everything later."

He doesn't move.

The apartment has not been this quiet since the first winter of the blockade.

"Valya?" Tonya goes up to him. When she tries to touch his face, he turns to avoid it. "They've released me. The charges were dropped—"

"Then why," says Valentin, eerily calm, "are we going away?" His eyes glitter down at her. "I've seen you before," he says. "Pretend-

Tonya. Dream-Tonya." He puts his mouth by her ear. "Prove to me that you're real, or I won't do anything you ask."

He's drunk. But worse than being drunk in the middle of the day is that he doesn't sound it. The granite that lodged itself in his chest on the White Sea Canal, which refuses to erode no matter how many years it's been, is in his voice. Tonya has not heard that voice since the blockade. He has been so well, so incredibly well, these past few years—

She forgot what this was like.

"Valentin," she says harshly, "it's me. Antonina. I am home. I have been at the Bolshoi Dom. Right now we need to—"

"Katya is gone."

"What?"

"Katya is gone." He repeats it in a way that lets Tonya know the words have lost all meaning to him. "Katya. Gone."

"I don't understand." Tonya's own voice sounds too high-pitched. "Gone where?"

"She's run away," he says. "She took the dolls."

* * *

Viktoria's hands twist and turn in her lap. They never stop moving, despite the pain that prevents her from playing her beloved instrument. Valentin smokes at the other end of the table. Every so often, Tonya hears him mutter to himself: *My name is Valentin Mikhailovich Andreyev. I was born in St. Petersburg in 1896. My name is Valentin Mikhailovich . . .*

Tonya has to ignore him. *Hold on, Valya, please; just hold on.*

"I think my husband is alive," she says to Viktoria. "Dmitry

Lulikov. He was the one who gave me the very first porcelain doll. He was partial toward . . . collections. He liked to buy the same item in different styles and forms. I received dolls myself, over the years, before he started sending them to Katya."

Viktoria twists her hands harder. "You think he's kidnapped her?"

"Stop it," says Valentin, and they both look up. "Who is this person?" He aims his cigarette in Viktoria's direction. "Why have you let her into our apartment, Tonya?"

Tonya presses one hand flat against her temple. "It's our good friend. It's only Viktoria—"

"I don't know any Viktoria!" he shouts. "Who is this?" After a moment of silence, the look of indignation passes, and he slumps back into his chair.

Tonya turns back to Viktoria, whose whole face is puckered with worry. "I know someone who might be able to help me," Tonya continues, lowering her voice. "I will have to go on my own, to speak to her. It will be a journey of several days. Will you look after Mikhail for me?"

"Of course I will." Viktoria looks at Tonya mournfully. "Do not be long, Tonya. Your family needs you."

In the middle of the night, the curtains are closed. The White Nights are over, but it isn't as dark as Tonya would like. She is packing a bag, and Valentin is watching her. At least he is no longer muttering. When it is time to say good-bye, he dashes out his cigarette and he says, sounding lucid, "I'll miss you." But then the focus of his gaze narrows.

"I will miss you," he says again, less certainly.

Tears burn behind her eyes. "I already miss you."

* * *

Tonya does not remember Natalya's family dacha looking so downtrodden and dreary, but it is obviously still inhabited. She knocks as loudly as she can. There are no neighbors to disturb out here, only the geese and the swans on the lake. She pounds now, until a young woman peers out, round-eyed beneath her spectacles.

"Are you here to see my mother?" The young woman peers farther, toward the empty road. "Do you have a way back?"

"I'll walk to the village. Does Natalya Fyodorovna still live here?" If not, Tonya has come all this way, lost all this time, for nothing, and meanwhile Katya could be anywhere and Misha is left with only one parent. Half of one parent. "I am a friend. A very old friend."

The girl looks exhausted, even for late evening. "You've come just in time," she says, letting Tonya by. The house's interior is over-insulated and humid. "Mama is resting, but she'll wake up for dinner."

A throaty laugh from the opposite end of the entryway startles them both.

"That couldn't possibly be *you*, could it, Tonya darling?" comes the drawl. "Or has my mind gone the way of all my other organs?"

Darling. The word itself is ghostly.

Natalya Burtsinova steps forward. She is holding a candle, close enough to her body that Tonya knows she cannot hold it any higher. Her hair, her face, are as white as the wax. Another spurt of laughter escapes her. "It *is* you! Of all the people to knock at my door, at this late hour. Later than you could know."

"So you do know this person, Mama," says the girl, sounding relieved.

"Please. I knew her before she knew herself."

"I need to speak with you, Natalya Fyodorovna," says Tonya, formally, as if this were not the very same person who ruined her life—one of her lives, at least, the one in which she and Valentin and Lena lived happily at Otrada for the rest of time. But perhaps it would not have been happy. Perhaps Valentin would never have learned to live without his politics, without the people. It was the White Sea that taught him how to survive without all the parts of himself.

There is no way to know.

If you let yourself wonder, as Mama used to say.

"Honestly, darling, if *you* can't call me Natasha by now, nobody can," says the Countess. "Let us take tea together one last time, and you can tell me everything."

* * *

They sit out on the back porch. The small silver cross, nestled in the fleshy folds of Natalya's neck, catches what little light is cast from her single candle. A few fireflies and mosquitoes dance around the table edges, but other than that, the evening is peaceful.

"I've come about Dmitry," says Tonya.

"What about him?" says Natalya, blandly inquisitive.

"I didn't kill him." Tonya stares into the fickle light. "I witnessed his death, or believed I did. But you must know the whole truth. You punished me for it. *Did* he die? Did those young revolutionaries dispose of the body? Throw it in the river? Feed it to dogs? What happened, that night?"

Natalya pulls her thin lips into a line.

"Is there any chance—that Dmitry might still be alive?"

"Are you sure you haven't told so many stories over the years," says Natalya, "that your storytelling instinct is taking over everything? I've read your children's tales, you know, in the magazines! I enjoy them. I like to remember the poor little rich girl you were in Petrograd, hiding behind your shawl, on Dmitry's arm like some kind of handheld marionette, how you always did have a look on your face like you were somewhere else. And in your stories, I suppose, I see where you really were."

Tonya has no time for this. "I suspect that Dmitry has been following me for years," she says, bitterly. "And now my daughter is missing. Katya is only ten years old—"

"Dmitry, following someone for years!" Natalya moves uncomfortably in her chair. "Your husband was showy, Tonya, and proud. He would never be content to remain out of view, to follow, to fade into his surroundings."

"Natalya—*Natasha*—"

"His body washed up by the Moyka," Natalya interjects, softer now. "He did not survive the stabbing. Dmitry is gone. As for your daughter . . ." A breath or a sigh. "I know how it feels. I am also missing one."

Tonya draws back from the flame. "You never found Akulina?"

"I did find her, after you and I met at Otrada, so many years ago. But she wouldn't listen to anything I had to say. She said I killed Little Fedya, and that as far as she was concerned, I died during the Civil War as everyone said I had, and she had had no mother since." Natalya laughs weakly. "Now I *am* dying, and my deepest regret is that Akulina thinks I never loved her."

Tonya never believed that Natalya loved Akulina, either. Or

that Natalya could love anyone except for Dmitry. And maybe herself. "Well," she says, "you could always choose another of your regrets to be the deepest."

"Such a sharp tongue! And on someone who writes for children. I almost think we might have been friends, you know. If things had been different." A familiar glint appears in the Countess's eye. "I'm sure your daughter has only run away, and once she's had a taste of life on her own, she'll be back. That age, they are flighty. In the meantime, if you think you have a stalker, it is not difficult to disappear, darling, not in a country like ours. Use a pen name for your stories. Tell no one but your most trusted friends where you are. I know that when you are being followed, your instinct tells you to run, but you must slip behind instead. You must seek out the shadows."

"You mean live *in* the shadow? Like you?"

"If anyone ever comes by here, asking for you, I'll have Galina tell them that you drowned in the lake." Natalya's laugh turns hoarse. She reaches around her neck, begins to unclasp her silver necklace. "I never repaid you for taking in my children, Tonya. This is for you. As a gesture of my gratitude."

The cross looks small, shrunken, in Natalya's palm, no longer where it belongs. Tonya shakes her head. "It should stay in your family."

"It has taken me all my life to understand that this necklace is not my family." Natalya is clearly using up her final vestiges of strength to hold it up. "Take it, please. Let me die without any debt."

It is very much like the Countess to think a scrap of jewelry, decades later, can make up for anything, but Tonya has no energy left for despising Natalya. She would rather take it and sell it, or just throw it into the lake.

With a short sigh, she takes it.

She had not realized it was a locket. It opens to reveal an inscription, two scratched-out lines.

For my Natasha, from your loving mother

You are beautiful, we are bound.

"I think of the old days often, you know. The parties, the music, the dancing! The fun we had, the lives we led!" Natalya's eyes have lost their gleam. "If only I could return, just for a moment. I would give anything to see it all again."

The candle dies. It was a stub to begin with.

Natalya Burtsinova is all that is left of the world into which Tonya was born: Otrada, Mama and Papa, princes and princesses and counts and countesses. The Bolsheviks might have stormed the Winter Palace, but they did not witness the true end of that era. It is ending only now, in the form of a diminished figure in a quiet house.

Nobody will witness it. Nobody will even know when it occurs.

"I can help you return," says Tonya. "Close your eyes." She doesn't know what she's about to say. She hears herself talking as if she is another listener, as if she could fall asleep now, forever, and the story would simply carry on without her. "In a faraway kingdom, in some long-ago land . . ."

32

Valentin

All Valentin knows is that he is not where he is supposed to be.

He is alone in a bed that is otherwise cold. The apartment is otherwise empty.

He stumbles through the rooms, searching for signs. He finds a lighter and some cigarettes on the kitchen table, so he lights one, lets the smoke fill his lungs, lets it blunt the feeling of everything else. He can smell drink on his own breath, so perhaps that's the cause of his headache. The ache is mixing things up in his mind, churning them. Memories. Images. Words. Lena lying by the stove; Pavel with a hood over his head, the cane cracked in two; Katya clutching a doll so hard its hair is knotted with hers; Tonya . . .

He is supposed to *meet* Tonya somewhere, isn't he?

Valentin is often missing his bus, his *marshrutka*, appointments, lunch dates, anything that can be missed. He's always late, by an hour or two here, a day there. But he's never missed this badly before. She must be waiting for him right now. At Otrada, yes, at Otrada! He told her he would be there. He made her a promise, though he should have just gone with her when she asked him to. He should have boarded the train in Moscow.

But he's going now. They're going to be together.

He leaves a note on the kitchen table, in case anybody comes home:

It has all been my fault. I am sorry for everything. I should have done this a long time ago.

If you are reading this, I am gone.

If people ask where I am, tell them: in the darkness of Lake Syamozero.

We will all live two lives—

This one is over.

* * *

His head. His *head*. He tastes mud. His face and hair seemed to be caked with it. He rubs his eyes but it doesn't help. He manages to stand, to locate what looks like a vegetable stall on the other side of the road, set up on somebody's front porch. The word *Grocer's* appears in big letters on a placard propped up against a tree stump. A bearded man sits in a rocking chair, whittling away at something.

"Where am I?" rasps Valentin.

The man must be the grocer himself, because he puts down his whittling, selects a vegetable stalk from the table, and bites down into it. His hair is cut slackly around the ears. As he eats, pieces vanish into his beard.

"You've been in that puddle all night," the man says. "Ever since the coach dropped you. You were dead-drunk, but I've the thing."

The grocer reaches behind the tree stump, produces a bottle of spumy liquid. Valentin doesn't know if it's water or worse. He staggers over and holds it to his lips. He coughs, looks around. This village is not one he knows. The sun is rising over the trees, turning everything golden. Valentin takes another drink, and then, in a stroke of clarity, he remembers how he got here.

Tonya told him the way to Otrada.

Made him memorize it.

"I need to find Otrada," he says.

The man's bushy eyebrows are furrowed. "What you need is rest, my friend."

"I've come to meet her." Valentin laughs, a beefy bellow. There is a pair of *babushki* staring at him now from across the lane. They frown, their faces shaded by age. He wipes the laugh off his mouth. "I made it. I'm here." *Wait for me.*

* * *

Valentin brushes away a branch, ducks his head to avoid another. The sunlight has receded, caught like a fly in the web of foliage overhead. There's the creek at last, high and pounding, the banks being sloughed off by the current. The path continues from the other side of the water. Valentin takes off his shoes and socks. On the wet stones he slips and nearly falls. He can't feel his toes, the few he still has.

Tonya, I'm coming. . . .

The path leads down to a hand-mirror lake. Past the lake lies a birch forest, just as she described. Valentin goes around and into the trees.

Tonya, I'm here—

Day has bled to evening by the time he comes upon black gates. Valentin's headache has returned, digs in its fingers. He goes through the gates, past the enormous stone lynxes, onto a wide walkway surrounded by open fields. The walkway ends at a large house of indistinct color, the exterior marred by dry, cracked plates. The front entrance is a modest set of wooden doors. Tonya once said Otrada was made mostly from birch, which is not a good material for making houses. Too fine. Too dainty. That is why, in the local folklore, the house is hungry, seeking substance.

Valentin presses against the doors. Just inside, the floor feels like moss. His feet sink low with every step. He hears a voice at last. She is here. They have found each other. He moves forward blindly, testing everything with his hands, into the cavity of the house.

Antonina—

He fumbles for his lighter. The flame is unspeakably bright as he holds it aloft. Something will give way. Something will open up and he will fall back into his everyday life, his normal life, and he will wake up next to Tonya.

* * *

The pain in his head is sharp as a needle. In every gulp of air is the smell of char, rotting teeth, the exotic sweetness of jasmine. He raises his eyes, sees the floaty face of the village grocer, sees walls covered in vines behind him. Smoldering ruins, still smoking.

What has he done?

Did *he* set this fire? Did he destroy everything, because he has always been the one to destroy everything?

Where is Tonya?

How can he have *missed* Tonya the way he misses his appointments, his buses, not only by a minute, an hour, or a day, but by an entire lifetime?

I just don't think you can have both—

Can't live two lives?

Be serious, Valya!

I'm more serious than I have ever been. I am coming to you—

Valentin wants to put his hands over his ears, to block everything out, but he knows he can't block out what isn't there. It's happening again, after all these years. He is falling into the abyss. He thinks he sees a face bending over him again, pale as the moonlight, but he too is on fire. He feels nothing. He is there again, in exile. Or else he has never left.

33

Rosie

Alexey says he'd rather explain everything out on the veranda, as evenings are his favorite time of day here at the dacha. Until now I'd not seen him smoke, not once. He does it with a small tremor, like he might have been addicted in his youth, and his shoulders relax. He's going to speak, but it's going to be without his usual rhetorical flourish.

He leans back, looks up at the sky. "I still believe your grandmother is out there," he says. "I don't believe she died. No matter what anyone says. I genuinely hoped you might find her, somehow."

Is he in denial? Is that *his* defense mechanism?

"*My* story begins," he says, "on a day I was at home, in Saratov, in 1915. My family was wealthy; my father was a renowned doll maker. One day a man showed up at our door. He had brought along a photograph of a young woman. He referred to her only as

Kukolka. She had a very unusual appearance, and he wanted a doll made to look just like her."

My heart thuds in my chest.

"As I was my father's apprentice, the task fell to me," he says. "I created that doll so intricately, so indelibly. I loved it; you could say I became obsessed. I didn't want to sell it, when the man returned. My father forced me to. Our relationship was never the same after that."

Alexey pauses, but I don't speak, so he goes on.

"I was drafted into the war with Germany, soon after," he says. "I deserted, joined the socialists. And then, one day in 1917, by luck, I was in Tula, making our rounds. In one village or another, people were saying that *Kukolka* had come home. She was well-known in the area. Once I met her, everything changed."

I have too many questions to formulate even one. "Changed," I repeat.

"Having seen the real thing, not just a photo," he says, "I decided I needed to turn *Kukolka* into a series. The most special dolls are always in a series, you see. So I made Tonya in various iterations, over the years; and then her female line, all different versions of herself, of course. Lena, your mother, Zoya, and now . . . you. Each doll captures an extraordinary moment in time, in history, and each one shows how fragile, how fleeting, yet how perfect, that moment is—"

"I don't—I don't understand. Do you mean you made all of Mum's dolls, the ones she kept in London?"

"No, no," he says, waving away some of the smoke, or the suggestion. "I am not nearly as prolific as that. Eduard made those. My youngest brother, who inherited my father's workshop."

Eduard.

Rayevsky.

I may throw up. Like I did outside that restaurant.

"Ah, Katya really never told you anything, did she?" Alexey sighs, pinches off the end of his cigarette with his bare fingers. "When your mother was ten years old, I made a doll of her. I always planned to give it to her as a gift, and I thought I would show my face to her, so she'd know she had a friend in the world. She was such an unhappy child. But when we met in person, she insisted that she could never go home, as her mother had been taken away by the secret police—because of her!—and it turned out to be true. She promised to go back if Tonya went free, so I used all my connections in the state security, and I was successful. Tonya was released. And what then? Tonya disappeared *again*! And Katya's father apparently committed suicide. Well, you can imagine the impact this had on your mother. I think she went two whole years without speaking. I tried to find Tonya, in the meantime. I traced her to Tenevoe, where I was told she was dead. And so there we were, myself, my brother, and this very strange orphan child we had no idea what to do with. So we raised her ourselves." He sounds exhausted. "It was not easy. You know how Katya could be. She was convinced her dolls were some kind of replacement for her family. She was so attached to them, and Eduard indulged it. . . ."

I don't think I know how she could be at all. Or could have been.

"Alexey," I say, and it feels strange now, because I'm sure that's not his name, "why did *Eduard* kill Papa and Zoya?"

"Oh, Rosie. You should let this be the end of all that."

It would make a good ending, wouldn't it? An old man, a young woman, an inky sky, a milky moon. Just another summer night in Moscow.

If only all the summer nights had been like this.

"I don't know precisely what happened, I'm afraid. I haven't had contact with my brother for decades, not since Katya stopped living with us. Now then." Alexey clears his throat. "I do always give the doll to the person who inspired it," he says. "I do not make them for me. And so, Rosie, I will now give your doll to you."

Alexey pulls back one of the other chairs, to reveal that we have not been alone all this time.

The doll *is* beautiful. It surpasses all the ones I have here at the dacha. The face, especially, is so bright, so wide-eyed, so innocent, it's like looking at myself through a warped lens: Here she is, an ideal of me, the one whose family never died, the one whose mother never drank, the one whose gaze looks up and around and forward, rather than behind and under. She is that other me, still perfect. Still unbroken.

The doll wears a dark crop top, a short, splashy skirt over tight leggings, and flat shoes. The very clothes I often wear.

Western-style clothing on a Russian doll.

Western-style everything on a Russian country.

Each doll captures an extraordinary moment in time. . . .

"You had no right to make this of me," I hear myself say, "or to lie, to keep me here just so you could—could *work* on this."

"No *right*?" Alexey laughs, deeper than usual. "I've paid for everything—I took care of everything—I even hired Lev, just in case Katya's fears of Eduard were justified—and that's not all. I helped you and Katya get out of Russia, didn't I, because she was so terrified? After that night? I paid your Oxford fees—there was no scholarship!—and I bought that apartment for your mother. I have been in the background all your life, Rosie, helping, protecting, observing. I just needed you to stay a bit more *still*, so that I could get the finishing touches just right, but I plan to leave you everything I have: my fortune, this house, absolutely everything. And you speak of *rights*."

You go, you look—

"This doll," he insists, "is the very last of my *Kukolka*-series. It represents this, what is happening right now! Don't you see we are on the precipice of something monumental, something historic? This doll represents the choice that the people of Russia, of the entire Soviet Union, must make, between the safety of the known and the freedom of the unknown! This doll represents *all that*! You must see how glorious it is!"

You choose.

No easy visa, no rent-free housing, no live-in bodyguard, no amount of *safety* is worth this.

Alexey Ivanov, or whatever his real name is, won't be watching me, watching over me, any longer. He is an old, old man clinging to an illusion of himself, and the closer he gets to his own death, the harder he clings. Just like the Soviet government; just like the Communist Party. It's only fear that gives them power anymore.

I rise. I pick up the porcelain doll.

Alexey exhales, a plume of smoke.

I smash the doll against the table with all the strength I have.

The sound it makes is almost a scream. It is so loud I know I will never hear those gunshots go off again. Alexey, too, is screaming. I step on the shattered pieces of myself as I leave the veranda behind, and they are sharp, but they do not slow me down.

* * *

Lev opens the door. He is mussed-looking, like he has just emerged from a pub fight. He's grown significant stubble, and he rubs at it as he looks me up and down. "Alexey told me you'd gone home," he says. "Have you changed your mind?" If his tone were any drier, it would snap. "Or do you need a ride to the airport?"

"Can I come in?"

"If you want." He lets the door swing open.

I'm able to get a better look at Lev's apartment this time. It's minimalist, barely furnished, one of those depressing *khrushchyovka*-style apartments. It's a bit like him, actually, at first glance. The home of somebody who just can't be bothered. Who will risk his life on a daily basis because it means nothing to him.

At first glance.

"What's going on?" he says, looking at me more closely.

"Lev . . ." I raise my sore eyes to his. "I kind of need a place to stay until my flight. My real flight, I mean."

He runs a hand over the stubble again, doesn't speak.

"I can't really . . . explain it well, but . . ." This is the worst I've ever explained anything. "Alexey, he made . . . dolls. He . . . he copied down the writing on the walls, you know . . . to help get me and Mum out of Russia. . . ."

Lev doesn't look doubtful. Or disbelieving. Maybe it's all anyone needs, in the end. To tell their story and to be believed.

"I think Mum tried to tell me what happened that night, with *that man*," I continue, "through her fairy tales. There was one she told all the time, about a young girl, about a blood-red house, her own blood-red hands . . . her siblings . . . but I don't know who is who in that story. I don't know what it means. And I'm starting to think all I'm ever going to have is the fairy tale—"

Or is that all the past is, in any form? Fairy tales?

Just the stories we tell ourselves?

It wasn't just that Mum didn't want to talk; it was also that I refused to hear. I couldn't stand being in the same room with her, because she hadn't been in *that room* with me. I shut her out in every way I knew how. I stopped looking her in the eye whenever we spoke; she started looking into her dolls' eyes. I pretended she wasn't really there; she pretended her dolls really were. I spent fourteen years thinking about, obsessing over, the wrong person—while my mother was standing right in front of me the whole time.

Fourteen years of asking, *Who was he,* that man, *and why?*

Fourteen years of failing to ask, *Who were you, Mum, and why?*

Maybe one day I will have all the answers.

But first I need to learn to ask the right questions.

"You can stay here," says Lev, in his completely understated way.

"I'm not a doll," I say, "and I don't think she was either," and I don't know if I'm talking about Mum, or Tonya, or even Zoya, but if we are dolls, then we are the ones that always fit together, each one kept safe inside of another, even when they are apart.

* * *

The apartment turns cold at night. I hear the pitter-patter of feet, soft as rain. Lev is asleep beside me. The pillows are damp with tears. I pull a blanket over my shoulders, follow the sound into the hallway. There, just by the front door, is my sister.

Raisochka . . .

Something new occurs to me: Zoya's not my older sister anymore. She's my *younger* sister. I grew up. She'll always be a child. She was never given the chance to be anything else.

You're not real, I say, and I hear how sad I sound.

She does not reply.

She is not my sister.

She is my pain, and I have been holding on too long.

I thought that I needed you, I say. *I thought that you would lead me to all the answers. That you would help set me free.*

Her hand falls away from her face. She is already fading.

But it turns out, I say, *that I am the one who will free you.*

* * *

Lev is at the wheel of his own car this time, a rickety Lada. The radio is squawky and the window rollers are stuck in place. In the aftermath of the failed coup, the city feels sluggish and drowsy. Many Muscovites have decamped to their summer getaways, to sun-soaked beaches. And yet the traffic moves no faster through the city center. I rest my head against the seat belt.

It's on the radio again, as it's been every hour today, that Alexey Ivanov died overnight, in his home, or one of them. His heart gave out. Or else it broke. The commentators have a lot to say about his death, of course. As peaceful and silent as his life was turbulent and momentous. An ending worthy of a national hero.

I find myself remembering that old line that Mum loved, from *War and Peace.*

Patience and time; they will do everything. . . .

I can still picture her in that nightgown, hear it swishing by her ankles as she sits at my bedside. I can hear her reciting: *It is possible to love a person dear to you with human love, but only an enemy can be loved with divine love. . . .*

I remember I stopped Mum at some point. I couldn't keep up. I'd heard enough.

She shut the book. Seeing how irritated I was, she said that we would start a new book the next day, but of course we didn't. Mum wasn't someone who moved on easily. The next night we picked up right where she left off.

It's time, now. It's time for me to start something new.

The car slows as we approach a turn.

"I'm not engaged anymore," I say.

The words are as slight, as insignificant, as the way Lev reaches for my hand and laces his fingers through mine, just for a second, before he has to change gears again. But this may be the first time in fourteen years that I find myself in the present moment without anything else hanging on, and right now, I could be weightless.

34

The Man in the Rocking Chair

He sits in the rocking chair and rocks. Nelly is moving around, keeping busy. She says, *Are you hungry*, and he rocks. They have buried Kirill this morning, and Nelly will not sit down. She flits back and forth like a bird. She asks, *Do you remember when you moved in with us all those years ago*, like she wants to reminisce. He doesn't remember. He knows he was in and out of consciousness for weeks after Kirill Vladimirovich, the grocer, dragged him out of the fire at Otrada.

He has never even recovered his name.

Nelly is hard to pin down today. Still moving. He doesn't try to intrude. He has never fully understood their kindness, Kirill and Nelly, taking in a troubled stranger. *Life's funny*, Nelly is saying. She never had children. Couldn't get pregnant. But now her husband's gone and there's still somebody here for company. Life is funny.

He rocks, rocks, rocks.

He never had children either. Or if he did, he hopes, assumes, that they can't even remember him. It's for the best. Look what a burden he'd be, like this. Unable to do any work but simple physical labor, chopping wood or rigging a fishing line. Only able to speak in incoherent bursts. Sometimes he laughs and laughs and laughs and can't stop.

Because life is funny.

And so he rocks.

35

Raisa

A painted sign for a bookshop is a beacon in this heavy snowfall, and I duck inside, shaking the flurries off my jacket. The shopkeeper looks up hopefully from her novel. The foreign currency in my bag is probably worth more than this entire shop, with the collapse of the Soviet regime in December 1991, and subsequently the economy.

"I'm looking for a book," I say, "called *The Snow Was Porcelain and the Rain Was Glass*. It's a collection of fairy tales . . . published not too long ago?"

She joins me by the shelves. This might be enough books even for the likes of Mum. I feel a low pang, because I gave away all of hers. Now that I'm moving to Moscow, I've finally had to sell her apartment.

The shopkeeper sweeps her fingers along the spines. "Here," she says. "This is the one, *da*?"

This is the one.

I've been trying to get Mum's fairy tale collection published, or Tonya's, rather. I thought that might be what Mum wanted. Readers. But when I sent the pages to Russian publishers, ahead of this trip, I got a jaw-dropping response from one of them.

These stories are already published here in Moscow.

They thought it was a bad joke.

They certainly weren't joking.

It's a hardbound book with a hand-drawn cover of a bird taking flight, bursting with red and purple plumage. I flip it open, and blink for a moment just in case, but it's exactly what it seems to be: a printed, *published* version of the fairy tales.

Published in 1989. How? How can there be another copy? Not just another copy, but this eye-catching volume, rebound and reworked and reimagined, replete with *pictures*? I have to get in touch with the author. I'm sure I'll have to pay a hefty bribe to the publisher, but luckily bribes work magic these days.

I check the dedication page. *To my children*, it reads. I can see the snow falling ever harder outside. The shopkeeper has returned to her novel, making satisfied noises as she turns the pages.

I start to read.

All the stories have been lengthened and polished, and several new ones appear. The final story in this copy is entitled "The One and the Other." It's set at a gulag camp in which a political prisoner called the One is struggling to survive the harsh winter. The One worries for her young daughter, whom she has left behind.

In the hospital, she encounters, to her amazement, an enemy she hasn't seen in decades. This former nemesis is called the Other.

The Other is serving a life sentence for multiple murders and is only in transit between prisons. She's due to be transferred to another facility in the south, but she knows she will die before any transfer. The two women make a pact. The One will tell stories about their lives before the Socialist Revolution, before the fall of the Tsar. About the luxury, the magnificence, the way Imperial St. Petersburg glittered like the gems around the throat of the Empress Alexandra.

Stories that help the Other forget her pain.

In exchange, the Other will enable the One to take her place when she dies. *Fair is fair.* And that is what happens: The Other dies. The One is transferred to a different prison. In warmer temperatures, without hard labor, her lungs recover and her body heals and her strength returns.

But—the twist!

Joseph Stalin dies soon after, and the dismantling of the entire gulag system follows. The vast majority of the political prisoners of the USSR are quickly released—except for our main character. The One is now destined to pay for crimes she did not commit. To serve the full sentence of her oldest enemy.

She will never see her daughter again.

* * *

Lev drops his sports bag on the kitchen floor and meets my gaze. Even if we've been writing regularly, it's been almost a year and a half since we last laid eyes on each other, and in that time, the end of the USSR has left behind untold wreckage.

But we are not part of the wreckage, he and I.

As if I've said it aloud, his expression grows quiet. *I will be the "open book" this time,* he wrote to me not long after Christmas 1991. I was in Oxford, anxiously watching replays on television of Mikhail Gorbachev's final address to the nation as general secretary. Watching the whole world collapse in real time. *I am leaving the OMON. I may not find new work so soon.*

But when you return to Russia, we will be on the same side of the barricades.

"You've come," is his greeting.

"Of course I came."

His apartment is even smaller than I remember. The heat seems to be broken; from what I recall from childhood, frozen pipes are usually to blame. They burst in these temperatures. I'll have to corner the landlord tomorrow.

Life is harder in Russia, right now, than it was when I was a child. Lev might lose his new job anytime, and we don't have his parents to fall back on anymore. His father was angry about Lev's departure from the OMON, and I don't blame him. If I were him, I'd want Lev back in the OMON too. I'd want as much as possible to be the way it used to be.

I don't have a job. Only savings. And I know that there are university professors driving taxicabs now. I know that people are moving to their dachas, to live off the land. I know that I will not be as comfortable as I once was, in Oxford, as Richard's fiancée, for a long time. If ever again.

But there is hope for the future. Of this country. Of its people, all the way down to me.

Lev approaches. My heart begins to hammer. I can see those golden specks in his eyes. He kisses me, and for a few minutes we're only kissing, but something is holding him back. He isn't letting himself fall into it.

"You may miss England, *devushka*," he murmurs, "once it's really behind you."

"I will miss it," I say, smiling against his kiss. "But there are always a hundred lives not lived. There will always be a hundred paths I did not choose. And this is the one I do."

* * *

With every blast of wind, my teeth clink together like coins. The snow on the streets has turned to sludge, but there's enough of it to bury a person alive. At the corner, an old woman is hawking homemade potato cakes. I've seen other such women at the mouths of the underground walkways, outside the metro stations. Their pensions are gone. Their money is worthless.

Opening the door to the café is like opening a portal to another dimension. The fragrance of coffee and pastry; enough electric heaters running that I might melt.

Bribing the publisher worked. The author of *The Snow Was Porcelain* deigned to speak to me on the telephone. I said I would pay if we could meet in person, and to my surprise, she directed me here. I anticipated it would be somewhere with a snide waiting staff. I anticipated feeling out of place.

But I don't feel out of place at all.

There is an old woman there, sitting quietly at the only occupied table, dipping a spoon in and out of a cup.

By now I am used to ghosts. I have heard them here in the capital, in the laughter of the children playing with their wooden sticks on the frozen Moskva. I have glimpsed them in the teenage girls outside the shops, with their all-knowing smiles and unmistakable airs. These ghosts live on in everyone; I can see them everywhere. They don't scare me.

But I did not expect to see the ghost of myself.

Not here, not like this.

This woman is what Mum would have been. What I will one day be.

She is silver haired and tiny; her smile is open-mouthed. Friendly. She wears round tortoiseshell glasses, and I can feel her eyes on me. The past is beginning to slip in through every crack, through every crevice, coiling around us. Now that we have found each other, it will never let us go.

"It is you I'm waiting for?" she says.

Somehow I am able to move toward her. Her smile changes. She is seeing what I see. Now I notice that there is something flowy, something faraway, about her. It is the same quality I often observed in Mum, and I thought it was simply *foreignness*, a person living in an adopted country, but it's not. It has no name.

"Who are you?" she asks.

I know I've ambushed her.

"Who are you?" Again, harder this time.

"I'm Katya's daughter," I say. "I'm your granddaughter."

* * *

Tonya burns bright, somehow, with hope. She looks like the kind of person reporters might interview on *Vremya* about the future of Russia. "Raisa," she says. "Now I understand. You're the one who met Misha during the August Coup. He said that there was an English girl who reminded him of Katya, but he never got a good look because she was in sunglasses. I did not think more of it. When you lose people, you see them everywhere."

"You mean—Mikhail Katenin?"

"My son."

I swallow. "Mum never said she had a brother."

"Misha said that this girl had a peculiar theory," Tonya says. "That the famous dissident Alexey Ivanov was, in fact, his father."

"I now know that Alexey Ivanov was *not—*"

"Ivanov was known as a decent public speaker." Her expression cools. "But that's not hard. A voice is only another kind of costume. And people are easily distracted by costumes. By uniforms."

I recoil a bit from her gaze. "You know who Alexey Ivanov was?"

"As much as anyone can," is her reply. "But I wasn't so surprised to see him become famous. He was always ambitious. The Chekist," she says. "Or the Interrogator."

The *doll maker.*

Should I tell her that Mum lived with him? Everything that happened? How much time do she and I have?

Not nearly enough.

I grope helplessly in my bag for what I want to give her: the handwritten stories. I can't find the pages, so I start to pull everything out, place it on the table. Keys, wallet, ticket stubs.

"What is *that*?" Tonya says, in an entirely different voice, one that suggests her other one was only a *costume* too. She's sliding something out from under my wallet.

It's the rag that I received from the old man in Popovka a full year and a half ago. It's so sheer I didn't even realize it was still in there.

"Oh, right," I say. "That was a gift."

"A gift? A gift from whom?"

"An old villager. I was in Popovka—"

"A villager! Who?" she says, not even questioning why I was in her tiny two-horse hometown, of all places, to begin with.

"Um, Kirill, I think?"

"*Kirill!* Kiryusha, and Nelly, sweet Nelly! Oh, I lost touch with them so long ago. They were my best friends; they were— How does that happen? How did I let it happen?" Tonya turns the rag over. "I must go see them. I will go right away. Oh, look at all that you've brought with you, Raisa," she says, suddenly. "I can't believe that you're here. I can't believe that we are sitting here together. Come. Come closer."

I am shocked to see that Tonya's eyes have blurred with tears. She lets go of the handkerchief at last, reaches out for my hand, and puts it on her face. I see a glimmer of a different smile, my mother's smile, through her tears, through mine, as if Mum is still here. Right between us. Right where she has always been.

* * *

Tonya tells me where the stories came from, what Mum did with them. My grandmother is not interested in having the pages back and tells me to keep them. Today she and I are perusing a few tables in a makeshift marketplace where people have put their whole lives for sale. We pass a table of porcelain figurines, and she stops to admire them. Some stand adorned with enamel, soaked with glaze, while others are a raw and naked white. One is a ballerina in a tutu with a pink bodice, her arms raised high above her head, hands not quite touching around the top. Her pink ballet shoes are laced around the ankle.

Katerina Ballerina, preserved in time.

I think of the burden Mum must have carried from girlhood, when she was too young to understand. I always thought she was glory seeking and attention addicted. Self-absorbed and selfish.

Maybe she was, but that's not how I'll remember her.

Before I sold Mum's apartment in London, I opened up each of her porcelain dolls. It solved the mystery of why their eyes never blinked: The pendulum inside the head needs to be able to swing, and every head was full of paper. Handfuls and handfuls of paper.

The same message was written on each page. They felt like letters.

Forgive me

Maybe, by the end, she was writing them only to herself.

To the one person who could never forgive her.

With the paper removed, the pendulums could swing once more, and the dolls could blink.

See, Mum, fixed it for you.

I put the dolls' heads back together as best I could and I put the wigs back on too and I laid the dolls flat on their shelf, so their eyes could finally close. *There you go,* I said, talking out loud. *There you go. It's okay. You can rest now.*

36

Antonina

Tonya touches a small spot on the car window, rubs away the condensation. It is raining, a fresh-smelling rain that happens only this time of year. Raisa, who is at the wheel, has said little on the way. Her friend Lev appears cramped and unused to the backseat of the car. At least he doesn't wear the maroon jacket of the new Moscow gangs. At least he does not call Tonya *baba*. In fact, she likes the way he smiles at her granddaughter, even if he does not smile much in general.

"Sorry, I'm still learning to drive. This was where we met the old man who gave me the handkerchief," says Raisa, stalling the engine, and Tonya peers through the slashing rain.

Nelly and Kirill's home, indeed.

She remembers once standing in this very spot, looking into this place. Nelly in the rocking chair on the porch, still working on that scarf, longer by then than the creek. Kirill saying that they would visit soon, help her fix up Otrada. Lena, wriggling in Tonya's arms.

"Do you want us to come in with you?" asks Raisa.

"No," says Tonya, "even if there's nobody around, I'd like a few hours here on my own."

"Hours?" says Raisa dubiously. "It's raining quite hard."

It's why they've made this trip, so Tonya can feel this rain, can breathe this air, can touch this earth. She will walk all the way to Otrada; she will never be coming this way again. She's begun to think this is what she always needed, to go home one more time, before she dies.

She hasn't told her granddaughter this, of course.

"I've seen worse in February," she says, already opening the door.

Raisa shouts something from behind, but Tonya doesn't turn around. The weather this time of year can be strange. Change-able. There was unusually good weather *one* February, long ago; it was warm enough to draw people from their homes and out onto the streets. Warm enough that she can still feel it on her skin, seventy-six years later.

Tonya approaches the porch. There is a rocking chair, as Raisa said, but there is nobody in it.

"Is anyone home?" she calls out, glad for the shelter from the rain. "Is anyone there?"

No answer.

"Hello," she tries once more, "please." She reaches into her coat pocket for Anastasia's handkerchief. Once lighter than air, it's gummy now. It's lived her lifetime too.

The door opens.

"It's raining," says the man in front of her.

Tonya claps a hand over her mouth, smothers her own cry. She's seeing things. Everyone sees things in places like this. Immortal tigers. Water spirits. Doll-girls. How wrong she's been! Maybe the appearance of Raisa in her life made her think she could dare to face the past once more, but she can't, she *can't*!

He is squinting at her.

He can't *see* her. He is blind, or as good as blind.

"Let me inside," says Tonya, shaking, "I'm so cold." And he opens the door wide enough for her to come through.

The house is much as it always was. The stove, the crawl space where she used to lie, the shrine to St. Nicholas, now an icon corner, the jars by the window right where Nelly used to keep them. This *is* the past. Tonya has entered it, and this is where Valentin has been waiting for her, all this time.

Perhaps he first came here looking for her.

"Valentin," she says, and the name has a taste, a texture. "It's me. Tonya."

"Have you lost your way?" he asks, like he doesn't understand.

So this is how he is.

Tonya used to read, over and over, the note Valentin left, and in the depths of mourning him, missing him, she had nothing to cling to but the bitter relief that at least he would not become *this*. She always knew this was going to happen. The White Sea stole too much from him, and people do not regenerate like that. She knew that one day they would be looking right at each other, and he would not remember her, not recognize her, not smile at her, not tease her, not hold her, not even touch her.

In a way, she has long been ready.

"No," says Tonya. It seems like the rain is still falling, even indoors. She brushes the water from her cheeks. "I've found my way."

"You know where to go?"

"I'm already there."

Her answers seem to dissatisfy him. His clouded eyes look through her and he says, "I don't know you, Comrade."

"It doesn't matter if you know me." Tonya squeezes the handkerchief. "I have some time. Why don't I tell a story?" He's shaking his head, but she wants to keep talking because otherwise she won't be able to start again. Her eyes are too full; her mouth is too salty. "Far away," she says, "and long ago, a princess lived in a palace by the sea, far from the city, far from the people. One day she escaped the palace walls, but she didn't know which way to go. She walked all the way into the kingdom—"

"Stop," he says.

"When she overheard a voice that captivated her—"

"Stop."

"Alright," she says ruefully. "You never did like my stories that much."

"No," says Valentin, "that's not why."

"Why, then?"

"I've heard it," he says. "I've heard it before." He looks at her again, and whatever he sees, it's enough. "I've heard you."

Tonya lets go of the handkerchief, lets it flutter to the floor. She goes to him, embraces him, puts her head against his chest. His breathing is harsh and uneven. His arms close around her but it could be for support, to be able to stand. *I have loved you longer than anyone,* she wants to say, *and I will love you longer than everything that has just ended, longer than any of this around us will last,* but she can't speak anymore. She made the mistake of stopping. Valentin says something into her hair, maybe her name, or maybe nothing; maybe it is only in her mind. But of all the things that have been in her mind, of all the endings she has ever imagined, she could not have imagined this one.

But wait. It is not the ending.

The final story is only the beginning.

She will close her eyes to see it: They are young again, in a city called St. Petersburg again, on the embankment of a frozen river. The old Russia is no more; the new Russia lives. *Run away with me, Antonina,* he is saying, and she runs, runs until it feels like she is flying.

Author's Note

In December 2011, Vladimir Putin's United Russia Party achieved victory in the State Duma elections, a result that prompted widespread allegations of electoral fraud. What followed were mass political protests across Russia, an unprecedented wave of opposition to Putin, the emergence of key figures such as Alexey Navalny, and a frenzy of international media attention. At the time, I was a PhD student in the department of Slavonic Studies at the University of Cambridge. In early 2012, an anti-Putin activist who worked on the ground in Moscow alongside the opposition leadership, such as it was, came to speak to my department.

He believed their time had finally come. Everyone in the audience believed it, too.

It was what I'd call, looking back at it, *a moment.* Everything was all happening so quickly, and in a way that hadn't been seen since the fall of the USSR; furthermore, in the wake of the Arab Spring, the idea that pro-democracy movements organized in large part via social media could topple seemingly invulnerable regimes was a compelling one.

Not long before, I'd breathlessly written my master's dissertation on the burgeoning online civil society sphere in Russia and the new ways in which anti-Putin resistance could take hold. In the course of my research I'd become swept up in the incredible optimism of the people in that sphere, and maybe as a result, the whole process became emotional. It became personal.

That thesis is as starry-eyed a piece of writing about Russian politics as you will ever find.

Most of it was wrong.

Fast-forward a decade, and not only is Putin still in power, not only is the White Revolution barely a blip on the radar of post-Soviet politics, but recent events have shown what that power can mean. What that power can do.

The Last Russian Doll is many things: a love letter to Leo Tolstoy's *Anna Karenina* and other epic novels by the great Russian writers I grew up reading and adoring; a product of my fascination with untold stories, stemming from my own family history and its many blank spaces. But most of all, *The Last Russian Doll* is a tribute to several hugely important aspects of twentieth-century Russian history. It is an exploration of the brutal excesses of Stalinism; the Soviet labor camp system; the political repression and persecution undertaken by the state security that characterized nearly all of the Soviet period. It aims to show how these structures and strictures first emerged, in 1917, and ultimately, how they collapsed, in the early 1990s; but also the personal impact they had on the citizens of Russia. On one family. On their everyday lives. On the victims. On the survivors. The continued reexamination of this history is absolutely necessary, not only as a way to grapple with and learn from the past, but also as a lens through which to critically view and fully understand the present. I would argue that the future of Russian civil society and democracy hang in the balance.

Under the Putin regime, that history is being whitewashed.

Unlike horrific, large-scale military actions, this revisionist process is insidious, and often invisible outside of Russia. It is the manipulation of popular memory; it is the creation and dissemination of new stories while systematically deconstructing the old. It is the erection of "Stalin centers," to honor Stalin and rehabilitate his image in the public eye. It is the rewriting of his legacy to highlight the Soviet victory in the Great Patriotic War (WWII) while enacting a government-enforced shutdown of organizations such as Memorial. Founded in 1989 to support victims of political repression, and to study and expose the crimes of the state against the people, Memorial was officially dissolved in early 2022.

It is the same Memorial that Rosie in *The Last Russian Doll* contacts in her quest to discover what might have happened to Valentin in the camps.

I have been fascinated by Russian history for most of my life, starting with my own family's favorite story, of how my grandfather, who hailed from northern China, was part Russian. As a child, I invented a fantastical story-on-top-of-a-story involving the long-lost Princess Anastasia escaping captivity in Yekaterinburg, fleeing on foot across Siberia, ending up in China, looking to start a new life, and falling in love with my great-grandfather. In a way, it's the first fairy tale I ever wrote!

The fairy tales that appear in *The Last Russian Doll* were written by me and are not based on preexisting stories. Each one has up to three readings. The first reading is the story itself, as it appears on the page: a monster crawling out of the sewers, for example. The second reading is to do with Tonya's life: She is the woman killing her husband without anyone noticing. The third reading is to do with an event in Russian history: The monster is the Bolshevik Revolution; the dead husband is the Romanovs. I may not have accomplished what I set out to do with each story, but the process has given me a new appreciation of the depth of fairy tales and folktales, of the way many of them say so much while saying so little, and often in such simple language.

Likewise, *The Last Russian Doll* is about Rosie and Tonya and their lives; it is also about the historical periods and events that it covers; and taken as a whole, it is also an allegory. I will leave you, the reader, to determine what you think the final interpretation of this novel should be. (There's not really a wrong answer!)

I drew inspiration from many sources in the writing of this novel. The character of Tonya and the doll motif were first inspired by Aleksandr Afanasyev's *Russian Fairy Tales*, specifically the tale of Vasilisa the Beautiful. There are a few nods in *The Last Russian Doll* to other famous Slavic folk tales, including that of Koschei the Deathless. I also drew inspiration from people and places in real life: Popovka, Tonya's village, is the name of the hometown (also in Tula) of Prince Georgy Lvov, first head of the Provisional Government in 1917; the name Otrada was taken from an abandoned, and eerie, Russian estate with its own fascinating history. In many places, I took a degree of creative license; for example, Tonya easily moves into a communal apartment in the house on the Fontanka with Valentin, years after leaving Leningrad. From a logistical standpoint, although this would have been possible, it is unlikely. The difficulty of moving around from city to city in Soviet Russia is generally understated in *The Last Russian Doll*. (As an additional note, Valentin returned home in secret, but typically ex-prisoners were not permitted to settle in big cities.)

In the Siege chapter, Tonya is driven to such extremes as considering cannibalism. There is a distinction in the Russian language between murdering someone in order to eat them (*lyudoyedstvo*) and eating the flesh of someone who is already dead (*trupoyedstvo*), and while cannibalism did take place (with women being the most likely to engage in the practice), I want to emphasize that it was not a defining feature of the Leningrad blockade. For the vast majority of people, it was not part of their experience at all.

For anyone looking to know more about the history of the Soviet labor camp system, I would recommend Alexander Solzhenitsyn's *One Day in the Life of Ivan Denisovich* and *The Gulag Archipelago*. (I want to point out that the character of Alexey Ivanov in *The Last Russian Doll* is not based on the real-life Solzhenitsyn. There are a few superficial similarities that were convenient for the plot, but that is all.) An interesting contrast to Solzhenitsyn's works is Varlam Shalamov, whose *Kolyma Tales* is another must-read on this subject. The epigraph of *The Last Russian Doll*—taken from Sergey Yesenin's poem "Mne Grustno na Tebya Smotret"—also appears in *Kolyma Tales*, translated into English by John Glad. I was also inspired by Yevgenia Ginzburg's memoir, *Journey into the Whirlwind*. *Gulag: A History* by Anne Applebaum is another invaluable source on this subject; her explanation of the importance of storytellers in the camps lent much to the character of Tonya, and the way in which Tonya uses her storytelling talent to her advantage, in *The Last Russian Doll*.

In this novel, I opted not for any official system of transliteration from Cyrillic to the Roman alphabet but for what I hope is sheer readability, turning what might have been Aleksei into Alexey. (I also kept popular English spellings, i.e. Yeltsin.)

In the chapters that take place prior to 1918, the dates are given according to the Julian (Old Style) calendar. It was my preference to keep the months as they would have been then, to the characters involved.

Acknowledgments

I am deeply grateful to everyone who has supported and believed in *The Last Russian Doll*. First of all, a huge thank-you to my agents on both sides of the pond, Sharon Galant in Brussels and Stéphanie Abou in New York, for tirelessly championing this book at every turn. Thank you also to Thomasin Chinnery for guiding me through everything that goes on behind the scenes.

Thank you to my brilliant editor, Jen Monroe, for her passion and enthusiasm from the outset, and for helping to elevate this story beyond what I ever imagined possible. Thanks sincerely to Candice Coote, Daniel Walsh, Jessica Plummer, Elisha Katz, and Tara O'Connor, as well as to the copy editors, designers, and everyone else at Berkley who has helped bring this book to life.

I am grateful to Michele Rubin, Helen Corner-Bryant, and Kathryn Price of Cornerstones Literary Consultancy; your feedback was invaluable in the early stages. Being short-listed for the Caledonia Novel Award was a major turning point for me; thank you, Wendy! I remain as grateful as ever to my publisher in the UK, Allison & Busby, and to Lesley Crooks, for the beautiful UK/ANZ version of this book, published in those countries as *The Porcelain Doll*.

To all past and present members of my writing group, Sue,

Charlotte, Felicity, Melissa, and Marcelle: I can't thank all of you enough for your unwavering support. Catherine, what are the odds that two PNW-based writers of Russian historical fiction would be on the same course? Whatever they are, we beat them, and I'm so happy we did. Eleonora, you were among the first and most ardent fans of what was then *Kukolka*, and that means so much to me. Thank you. I would also like to extend thanks to several writer friends who have been so generous with their time, with shout-outs to Rachel and Jodie, Nicola Ashbrook, Michelle Christophorou, and Fiona McKay. I am also so appreciative of the wider book community, and of the many readers who have reached out to me.

To everyone who has helped along the way, thank you: Mr. Anderson, for believing in my writing from the very start; Dr. Cohen, whose influence on my work, my studies, and my self-confidence is immeasurable; Dubravka, for the help and wisdom; Samna, for taking such lovely pictures; Valia, for being my point person in London and tracking down the music I needed to write certain scenes!; Sasha, for answering all my questions; Sabine, for being such an ardent reader and a source of support. Samangie, I think we're due for another epic reading session in Hyde Park. Thank you for everything.

Words are inadequate, but thank you to my parents for your boundless patience and generosity; to Collin, for the most fantastic song and letting me use its lyrics in this book; my children, for being the sweetest, most eager, and most amazing people; and thank you, Steffen, for so many things it would take a whole other book to list them, but especially for keeping me well caffeinated.